W9-BAC-858

Praise for Sophie Littlefield's
AFTERTIME

"Stephen King's *The Stand* in a bra and panties....
The illegitimate love child of McCarthy's *The Road* and Romero's
Dawn of the Dead...Aftertime is a highly palatable amalgam of
post-apocalyptic fiction, romance, and horror. Hard-core fans
of post-apocalyptic fiction will love *Aftertime*. Romance fans
will embrace it. Aficionados of zombie fiction will be stunned."
—Paul Goat Allen, *BarnesandNoble.com*

"Littlefield turns what could be just another zombie apocalypse
into a thoughtful and entertaining exploration of many themes....
Littlefield has a gift for pacing, her adroit and detailed
world-building going down easy amid page-turning action
and evocative, sensual, harrowing descriptions that bring
every paragraph of this thriller to life."
—*Publishers Weekly*, starred review

"The fresh, original world-building solidly supports the unfolding
narrative and Littlefield's compelling writing will keep readers
turning pages late into the night to find out what happens next.
Outstanding!"
—*RT Book Reviews*, Top Pick

"Wildly original... Sophie Littlefield's *Aftertime* is a
new generation of post-apocalyptic fiction: a unique journey
into a horrifying world of zombies, zealots and avarice that
examines the strength of one woman, the joy of acceptance
and the power of love. A must read."
—J.T. Ellison, author of *Where All the Dead Lie*

"I'm geeking out of my mind after reading *Aftertime* because I felt almost the same way reading it as I do watching *The Walking Dead:* Captivated. *Aftertime* is hands down the best zombie book I've read all year. Hide your wife, hide your kids, and hide your husbands 'cause they're eating everybody out here."
—*All Things Urban Fantasy*

"[A] gripping read; sympathetic characters operate in a detailed, realistically shattered echo of modern society, and the emotional journey is as harrowing and absorbing as the physical one."
—*Paperback Dolls*

"Alternately creeped me the hell out and broke my heart repeatedly."
—*The Discriminating Fangirl*

"Littlefield excels at keeping the momentum going and she knows how to inject a huge beating heart into any story, even one in which humanity is barely alive."
—*Pop Culture Nerd*

REBIRTH

SOPHIE LITTLEFIELD

LUNA™

www.LUNA-Books.com

If you purchased this book without a cover you should be aware
that this book is stolen property. It was reported as "unsold and
destroyed" to the publisher, and neither the author nor the
publisher has received any payment for this "stripped book."

LUNA™

Recycling programs
for this product may
not exist in your area.

REBIRTH

ISBN-13: 978-0-373-80339-2

Copyright © 2011 by Sophie Littlefield

All rights reserved. Except for use in any review, the reproduction
or utilization of this work in whole or in part in any form by any
electronic, mechanical or other means, now known or hereafter
invented, including xerography, photocopying and recording, or in
any information storage or retrieval system, is forbidden without
the written permission of the editorial office, Worldwide Library,
233 Broadway, New York, NY 10279 U.S.A.

This is a work of fiction. Names, characters, places and incidents are
either the product of the author's imagination or are used fictitiously, and
any resemblance to actual persons, living or dead, business establishments,
events or locales is entirely coincidental.

This edition published by arrangement with Harlequin Books S.A.

For questions and comments about the quality of this book
please contact us at Customer_eCare@Harlequin.ca.

® and TM are trademarks of Harlequin Books S.A., used under license.
Trademarks indicated with ® are registered in the United States Patent
and Trademark Office, the Canadian Trade Marks Office and in other
countries.

www.LUNA-Books.com

Printed in U.S.A.

For M,
searching for four-leaf clovers

THE FIRST SNOWFLAKE AFTERTIME WAS LIKE NO
snowflake that ever fell Before. Cass nearly missed it, kneeling
on the matted dead kaysev plants, their woody stalks poking
into her skin through the thick leggings she wore beneath
her dress. Her eyes had been closed, but Randall had gone
on too long, the way people do when they are trying to say
something meaningful about someone they didn't know well.
After a while Cass grew restless and began to look around, and
there, not two feet away, the snowflake drifted past in a lazy
swoop as though it had all the time in the world.

Cass licked her cracked lips, could almost feel how the flake
would melt on her tongue. Until that moment she didn't realize she had actually doubted whether snow would ever return,
much as she'd doubted whether rats or sparrows or acorns or
moths would return. She wished she could nudge Ruthie,
or even Smoke—she knelt between the two, in the place of

honor up front—but a funeral was still a funeral, and so she stayed as still as a stone.

Maybe by the time they were finished, there would be more snowflakes. A flurry, a drift: the gunmetal sky looked grudging to Cass; there would be no storm today. Besides, the temperature would rise well above freezing by noon. These early snows never lasted long.

Next to her, Ruthie sneezed. Cass wrapped an arm around her and pulled her closer. Ruthie had loved the snow when she was a baby. She was still a baby—three years and two months, according to the Box's calendar. The month and date were metal numerals hung from nails on a wooden pole, the kind people once nailed to houses and mailbox posts, back when people still lived in houses. Each morning, the first shift guard changed the numbers. Today, it read 11 ★ 17.

Smoke held Cass's hand, his strong fingers wrapped around hers, and she felt his blood running sure and strong under his skin, circulating through his body and making him strong and back to his heart again, and she said the silent prayer that was part of her breathing itself now, part of every exhale: *thank-you-thank-you-thank-you-for-making-him-mine.* His touch, his closeness, that was what made her whole; he more than made up for every wrong man that had come along before. She closed her eyes and exhaled the prayer and waited for Randall to finish his rambling eulogy as the five other people in attendance fidgeted and sighed.

"And now Cass will say a few words."

So her turn had come, at last. Cass stood, nervous and hesitant. She gulped air as she took the few steps to the humble altar next to the fresh grave. Sieved earth was piled neatly. Gloria was in the ground, her body covered with six feet of rich Sierra mountain soil—Dor's grave diggers charged a premium for the full six, what with most folks settling for half that these days. Cass breathed out, then in once more, a rhythm she learned back in her early days in A.A., when she'd been torn between the paralyzing certainty that if she spoke during the meeting she would cry—and that if she didn't, she would never come back.

Back then, it had sometimes been all she could manage to say her name. Today she would have to say more. Not for those gathered here: besides Smoke and Ruthie, there was only Randall, standing at a respectful distance and twisting his handkerchief in a tight knot around his knuckles, and Paul, who never missed a funeral, and Greg, who'd spent some evenings with Gloria even after she was banned from working the comfort tents.

And then also Rae, who managed the comfort tents, and probably felt guilty about firing Gloria, since, when Gloria couldn't work, she couldn't buy anything to drink. And that was what killed her, in a way—after only a few days of forced sobriety she had drunk a bottle of Liquid-Plumr from the garbage hill slowly accumulating on the far side of the stadium's parking lot.

Cass gazed out on the others and swallowed back tears. Smoke had put on a clean shirt, not that you could see it under his heavy work coat. Ruthie wore a little red coat and matching hat that a raiding party had brought back last week. Everyone else was dressed in the usual layers of clothes splodged with stains, the heavy boots. No one looked directly at her, save Smoke. No one gathered here would care if Cass cried for Gloria, but it was important to her that she not be misunderstood, not now, not today.

She trailed her fingers along the scratched wooden top of the small table enlisted as an altar. Someone had brought it back from a night raid, a humble thing whose most appealing feature was that it was light and easy to carry. Cass thought it might—half a century ago—have been a telephone table, back when phones had to be plugged into the wall. On Sundays, Randall put a cloth on the little table, rested his Bible on top of that. He didn't lack for an audience. Cass didn't begrudge him his followers—nor did she begrudge them their hour of peace or solace or whatever it was they found in his words.

Still, today: no cloth, no Bible. It had fallen to Cass to plan the service. No one else offered, and Randall had come to stand in the door to their tent, hat in his hand, and asked Cass what would be right. Gloria had never spoken of God and Cass felt it would be presumptuous to impose Him on her now.

Cass shut her eyes for a moment and exhaled slowly. When she opened her eyes again, Ruthie was watching her expectently, lips parted in anticipation. For a child who didn't talk, Ruthie listened to others with great care, none more than her mother.

Cass produced a tiny smile for her daughter. She reached for the string around her neck and pulled from under her blouse the pendant she had made yesterday, and Ruthie did the same. They wore clothespins, the old-fashioned wooden kind, knotted to nylon cord. Cass held the clothespin as though it were a precious thing and considered it, turning it slowly this way and that.

"Gloria and I talked about clothespins once," Cass began, her voice rusty. "She told me about hanging clothes on a line."

Greg, dry-eyed and somber, nodded as though what Cass was telling was a story he'd heard a dozen times. That couldn't have been. Gloria made little sense when she talked; she dredged memories and unfurled them carelessly, moving in and out of time and sense. You didn't have a conversation with Gloria so much as an occasional glimpse into the ill-tended recesses of her mind. There was nothing there to hold on to.

She wondered what memories Gloria had shared with Greg, if they had talked at all. The comfort tents were places of shame; men and the occasional woman slipped in and out of them like shadows, bartering whatever they had for a grope in the dark, an awkward coupling, a muffled cry. Anything to forget the gone world for a while.

Those who worked in the tents usually had no other way to earn. That was the case with Gloria, who was too far gone to raid, to cook, to harvest, to mend or make things, or even offer knowledge that helped. But she had meant more than nothing to Greg.

"She told me about hanging clothes on a line," Cass said again. She cleared her throat. "And she…had someone, once. His name was Matthew."

Gloria had long, thick silvery hair. That, and her faded blue eyes, were the only clues to her long-ago beauty. She was lean and leathery. She'd broken a tooth and on the rare occasions when she was sober she was suddenly self-conscious and tried to hide the gap, barely moving her lips to speak. Her nails were ragged and dirty. Her clothes grew filthy and torn in the days before her death. The last time they spoke, Gloria had answered all of Cass's questions with noncommittal grunts and never once met her eyes. Ruthie had been afraid of her.

"She loved him," Cass concluded. Once, Gloria had loved. That would have to be enough. Cass had said all she knew— all that was important, anyway. Gloria never told her anything but his name; if he'd been a lover, a husband, a childhood friend, it didn't matter.

She bent to the earth, the rectangle of dirt raked carefully one way and then the other, crosshatched from the tines. She dug her fingers in and took a handful, then stood up and slowly sifted the earth back over the length of the grave.

She stood back as the others filed around the perimeter of the grave. They knelt and scooped their own handfuls of dirt, even Ruthie. The knees of her tights were smudged with dirt—another stain Cass would not be able to get out. She sighed. Each person shook their dirt back down onto the grave, and Cass wondered what words they said in their minds. Hers was *goodbye*—maybe everyone said goodbye.

The dirt was sprinkled and still they ringed the grave, waiting. Randall dug in his pocket. "Cass, perhaps you'd like to..."

He held out a plastic bag, gapping open; inside were dried kaysev beans, dull and brown. Cass looked at him sharply, but for once Randall stared back with a hint of challenge in his expression. Smoke squeezed her hand, shook his head. Smoke stayed far clear of Randall's Sunday-morning services. He had little to do with believers. He even did his occasional drinking at Rocket's—not German's, where believers tended to congregate.

Cass didn't want to take the beans. The funeral practice of sprinkling the grave with kaysev seed—it was based in the Bible, the passage in Matthew about the sower. It was a common practice, almost secular by now; a whole new culture of loss, its habits and practices as ingrained as if generations of ancestors had practiced them. It had only been eight months since the Air Force had rained kaysev down from the skies on their last flights, but eight months had been long enough to create new rituals. The plant was meant to feed the population; it had begun to feed their imaginations, as well.

Smoke saw everything through the filter of ideology and

he was resolute, and Cass was inclined to agree with him, at least on this. Terrible memories of the Convent were too fresh, the mark its zealotry had left on Ruthie too deep.

God had not taken up residence across the street in the stadium—of that Cass was sure.

But unlike Smoke, she was not ready to declare Him absent. Still, He was an elusive, crafty cipher to Cass, and for now she meant to keep Him distant.

When Cass did not take the plastic bag from Randall's outstretched hand, the frowning man narrowed his eyes and upended it himself, the beans falling to the earth and rolling into the crevices and fissures in the earth. *"He that received seed into the good ground is he that heareth the word,"* he intoned, his gaze never leaving Cass's face.

Then he stepped back from the grave, jamming the empty bag back into his pocket and brushing his hands together fastidiously. Everyone else followed him, retreating to the cleared area where the service had begun, shuffling slowly.

"And now we conclude our service for Gloria," Randall murmured, the wind snatching at his words and carrying them away, so that everyone leaned in closer to hear. Everyone, that is, but Cass, who picked up Ruthie and edged to the back of the small gathering while Randall raised his hands for a final benediction.

"Man, you are dust," he said, closing his eyes. "And to dust you shall return."

Not for the first time Cass considered that Randall was a fraud, cobbling together bits and pieces of faiths to suit himself.

What did it matter, though? Dead was still dead, and the rest of them were still here.

CASS GLANCED BACK OVER HER SHOULDER AS THEY
trailed the others back to the Box. The streets looked clear;
there had been no Beater sightings for a couple of days. Randall moved among the graves, straightening the crosses and
pulling weeds.

It wasn't much of a graveyard—the plot of land had once
been a tiny park wedged between residential streets two
blocks from the Box, but the trees that shaded it had died
early enough in the Siege that someone had actually taken
the trouble to cut them down to stumps and haul them away.
Some of the graves were marked with crosses carved from
wood, nailed together, finished to varying degrees. One small
one was painted white, with tiny shells glued along the edges.
Most of the crosses were raw, hastily made, not even sanded.

Some graves, like Gloria's, had no marker at all. For now,
the dug and piled dirt marked its location, but it would not be

long before the dirt would sink and level and no one would
remember where she lay.

Had it been up to Cass, she would have left the few plants
that sprouted this time of year. To her mind the reappear-
ance of each plant Aftertime was a miracle in itself, and her
garden in the Box had a small square marked out with stakes
and twine for each native species she found on her walks.
Firethorn, pepperweed, crupina. Each of them once assumed
gone forever. Each—through what combination of God's will
and hardiness and luck she had no idea—returned, pushing
through the wasted crust of the forsaken earth.

Greg, Rae, Paul—once through the gates, they slipped off
in different directions, not bothering with a goodbye, not
even for Ruthie. Cass wasn't sure how much longer she could
stay here in the Box, where gloom had settled and quashed
her hopes that it was a place fit for raising her little girl. Before, people made an effort for a child, even one as silent and
strange as Ruthie was now. Under the hat, her hair was as
short as a boy's; in the Convent they had shaved all the children bald. But by spring Ruthie should have enough for a
little pixie cut, something more girlie. Cass was self-conscious
of her self-consciousness: surely survival was enough of a par-
lor trick; should children really have to do anything more?

There were no fat Gerber babies Aftertime. There were
few babies at all. Starvation and the fever had taken so many,
early on; the Beaters claimed many more. Cass knew firsthand
how hard it was to look upon a child when your own was
gone. But she had been given a second chance; she had gotten
Ruthie back, and now she meant to cherish her. She would
dress her in the prettiest things she could find. She would give
her everything that the battered world could provide.

Ruthie's red coat was a gift from a quiet boy named Sam,

who'd lost an eye in Yemen in the Rice Wars. He stopped by Cass and Smoke's tent after a raid and pulled it from his backpack, a soft, finely made woolen coat with carved shell buttons. He wouldn't trade for it, but he had accepted a cup of peppermint tea brewed from the last of Cass's herb garden before a hard freeze took all but the thyme and chervil. Sam wasn't a talker, but he loved Ruthie. He airplaned her squealing through the air, carried her around on his shoulders and let her crawl all over his long lanky legs. Cass suspected Sam had once had a little brother or sister, or perhaps a niece or nephew. Whoever the child was, they were long gone, leaving Sam with a few good moves and, perhaps, an empty place in his heart.

Underneath the coat, Ruthie wore a blue corduroy jumper and a pair of white tights. Her shoes were too small; she was growing fast these days. All the raiders knew to keep an eye out—size seven, twenty-four European—but you never knew what you'd find, and the only sure thing—the mall at the far edge of town—was still infested with Beaters.

It had been more than a month since Ruthie's things had been washed. Sometimes one of the Box merchants had detergent for trade, but it was expensive, and besides, Cass and Smoke had agreed they were going to try to switch to homegrown wherever possible. That meant using the oily kaysev soap made from the fat rendered from the beans. It wasn't terrible for washing one's body or hair, but it wasn't great for clothes. It didn't take stains all the way out and it didn't do much for the lingering odors of sweat and smoke.

It wasn't like anyone else cared. Smoke was always saying Cass should just let Ruthie wear sweatpants and T-shirts like Feo, the only other child in the Box. But Feo was practically feral, a sharp-toothed, long-haired boy of eight or nine who slipped quick-footed and cagey among the tents and merchant stands, stealing and boxing with his own shadow. Dor let Feo stay only because he'd become a sort of a mascot for the guards, who'd found him squatting with an unkempt, semi-conscious old woman in a farmhouse past the edge of town back in October.

Cass felt protective of Feo, especially after the woman, his grandmother, died during her first night in the Box. But she didn't want her Ruthie becoming like him.

"I'm going to the trailer," Smoke said, as they reached the intersection in the dirt path that led to their tent. It had become his habit not to explain his dealings with Dor anymore, as their private meetings grew more and more frequent. He had become Dor's right-hand man in the months since he and Cass came to the Box, and Cass supposed that their daily interactions were necessary as Smoke learned more of the business and took over more and more of the daily operations of the security force. But Smoke also knew she resented these meetings, resented his alliance with Dor. Another couple might have talked it out. But Cass did not ask and Smoke did not volunteer.

She took Ruthie back to the tent. Inside, there was order. Cass had not been neat Before; she was neat now. Smoke had lined one wall of the tent with bookshelves bolted together; these held tattered books and empty glass jars and smooth stones. A dresser contained their clothes. The floor was covered with a beautiful rug, an ancient hand-woven thing that Dor said had once been worth many thousands of dollars. It was the one thing of luxurious beauty that Cass could stand to have in their home. Otherwise the things in their tent were plain, utilitarian and all chosen by her, because Smoke had understood that their choosing was healing for Cass, even before she understood it herself.

She slowly unbuttoned her parka then took off the dress she'd worn for the funeral and tugged on a wool sweater. She had wanted Smoke to see her in this dress, gotten only yesterday from a woman who'd arrived dragging a rolling suitcase stuffed with designer clothes and fine jewelry. It had cost Cass an airline bottle of Absolut and three 750mg Vicodin tablets. Cass hadn't touched a drop of alcohol in almost ten months and had resisted trading in it, but eventually she had to accept that booze and drugs were the Box's principal currency, so she and Smoke kept a stash locked in a safe bolted to a pole sunk in concrete in the ground under the tent floor.

The dress was knit of some synthetic fabric, cut on the bias and gathered at the low scoop neckline. It was a shade of deep aquamarine that reminded Cass of the ocean—specifically, of the water off Point Reyes where she'd once spent a long weekend before she got pregnant with Ruthie. She'd been with a lover—which one, she couldn't remember now—and he'd distracted her with expensive dinners and wine and blow, but it was the water she remembered best.

This dress was the color of misty mornings and rain-threatened twilights, of flotsam bobbing on waves before they broke on the shore. She had wanted to watch Smoke watching her in the dress, wanted to see his eyes widen and his lips part, wanted to watch him wanting her. Her body quickened at the thought, even now, when the moment was lost.

She took off the earrings Smoke gave her the week before and put them in the metal box where she kept all her little things, earrings and safety pins and buttons and needles and tacks. The earrings had come from a raid on one of the enormous homes on Festival Hill in what had been the rich part of town, a pair of diamond drops that would have cost more than a car Before. Aftertime was funny that way; it turned the value of everything upside down. Smoke had traded a Kershaw hunting knife with a black tungsten blade for the earrings and their owner had gone away satisfied.

After she got Ruthie changed into soft, warm clothes and tucked under her quilt for a nap, Cass poured water from a plastic pitcher into her pewter cup—engraved with a curly monogram with the letters *TEC,* spoils from the same luxurious neighborhood—and unwrapped a kaysev cake that had been spread with peanut butter. She ate her lunch mechanically and tried to concentrate her thoughts on Gloria. But her thoughts would not stay focused—they skittered like pebbles on a slide. Ruthie made soft mewling sounds in her sleep, and Cass listened and wished she could record them to play back later, the only way she could hear her daughter's voice.

Cass sat still and quiet and waited for Smoke. She was barely aware of the path of the sun through the sheer curtains at the tent windows, the crumbs of her lunch hardening on the plate, the condensation slowly gathering on the pitcher's clear plastic lid until a single drop fell with a soundless splash. Ruthie slept, and whispered, and moaned, the only sounds she ever made, the soundtrack of her nightmares, the leavings of her time in the Convent just across the road from the Box. Listening night after night was the price Cass paid for her carelessness, for having let her daughter be taken. She would listen every night until she died if that was what was owed.

But when the afternoon chill had settled into an ache in Cass's hands and feet and still Smoke had not returned, Ruthie twisted in her cozy bed and threw off the quilt and sat up, never waking:

"Bird," she said, as clear as anything, fear in her sightless sleeping eyes, and when she lay back down, oblivious of her dream-talk, Cass turned in astonishment to see Smoke standing in the door of their tent wearing no expression at all, blood dripping from his fists.

SMOKE WOULD NOT STOP TREMBLING AND WOULD not speak.

Cass swallowed her dread and searched him for grievous wounds, for bite marks. Finding none, she held him and kissed his brow and murmured over him and at last there was nothing else to do but take him out to the fire. Ruthie, who had forgotten her cryptic dream-talk, went placidly, carrying a stuffed dragon she had recently taken a shine to. Cass had looked at Smoke's palms and seen that the cuts were superficial, clean slices to the skin as though he'd held out his palms to be flayed. Already the bleeding had stopped, the wounds' edges going white; they bled again when Smoke forgot and flexed his fingers, but Cass allowed him to hold her hand and tried to ignore the stickiness between their flesh.

The fire pit was ringed in neck-high fencing. One of Dor's recent conscripts sat at the opening in a folding chair, feet up on a stump, clipboard in hand. His name was Utah, and you got the feeling he wanted you to ask him why. Cass did not ask. Utah's eyes were too hungry and his hair was braided and held with bits of leather and Cass was too exhausted by everything that had happened in the last year of her life to have time for people who still needed to be admired.

"Hey," Utah said, making a note on his clipboard. "All three of you, then?"

A stupid question, Cass thought, but she just nodded and led Smoke and Ruthie inside, where the dirt had been swept just that morning and stumps were set up all around the fire pit, which was six feet across easy and burning mostly clean, split firewood mixed with green wood. She and Smoke had privileges not afforded other visitors to the Box; among them, water and the baths and the fire were free. But they were marked on the tally nonetheless; Dor insisted on rigorous bookkeeping.

Only a few people sat around the fire. Most would wait as long as they could, coming in to warm themselves before bedding down, hoping their bodies would retain the memory of heat long enough to fall asleep and maybe even stay that way long enough to get some rest. Here, it was easy to believe Dor's prediction that by late winter firewood would become his most lucrative business. If only Cass could convince Smoke to go down mountain, to find a new place to be a family. There had to be somewhere warmer, more hospitable, some-where that hope still lived.

Cass led Smoke to the far side of the fire ring, away from the others. She spread out a dish towel on a stump, pulled a set of nesting plastic dolls from her pocket, saved for occasions when she needed to keep Ruthie occupied. Ruthie smiled and carefully pried the largest doll's halves apart as Cass took both of Smoke's hands in hers.

"What," she begged, leaning close enough to breathe his breath, ready to hurt for him.

"I broke the railing," Smoke said, staring at his hands as though he was just noticing the cuts. "Outside of Dor's trailer. It was cheap shit, aluminum..."

Cass pictured it in her mind's eye, the trailer Dor used for his office and now, in the colder months, his home, as well. Construction steps led up to the door four feet above the ground, the trailer up on blocks. Its railing was flimsy, it was true, but to tear it apart would have taken strength—and rage.

"But why? What did he say to you?"

Only Dor, founder and leader of the Box, tight-lipped cold-eyed trader and enforcer of the peace, had the power to change events, to change the course of people's lives. Smoke looked at her bleakly, his sensuous mouth taut with dark emotion.

"The school burned," he said softly. "It was Rebuilders. They came to Silva and they burned it—gave the women and the children a choice. Join or die. The men, all of them... gone."

Cass's heart seized. The school, forty miles down mountain, had been the first shelter she'd come to after she was taken, after waking in a field in her own stink, crusted with healing sores, with no memory of how she got there. At the school she thought she would die; instead she met Smoke and she lived.

"Gone?" she echoed, the word thick on her lips.

"Throats slit to save the bullet, then burned inside the building. Cass...Nora stayed behind. She refused to go with them. And she died."

The hole in Cass's heart widened and cold seeped in.

Nora had been Smoke's lover, once. Before Cass came. Nora's dark hair brushed her shoulders, her gaunt cheeks were elegant. Nora had hated Cass on sight, had voted for her to be turned out to die because of the condition she was in when she'd arrived at the school. Now Nora was the dead one.

"They killed her…"

"She fought." There—finally, there was the anger, flashing in his eyes. "She took one down with her, Dor said."

Dor. *Sammi*—what about the girl? Dor's daughter, only fourteen, whom Cass had felt a bond with even though their time together was brief.

"They say Sammi survived," Smoke said, reading her thoughts. "At least, there's a girl her age, her description, who made it through. But not her mother. It happened two days ago—they've probably taken her down to Colima by now."

"The survivors—they're all prisoners?"

"That's what Dor said," Smoke said flatly. "That's what he told me. Rebuilders sent a message here. Their man came today. That's what…what we've been talking about."

The school was gone. The little community of shelterers crushed, splintered, burned, and the survivors led away like stolen cattle. The men… Cass shuddered to think of their bodies stacked and immolated.

She had only been at the school for one day, just long enough for them to judge, yet release her, long enough for Smoke to decide to throw in with her quest to reclaim Ruthie. He'd intended to go back, back to Nora, but that hadn't happened. Instead he'd come here, and somehow they'd become…what they were. Lovers. A couple, perhaps. More, certainly, than Cass had ever dared to hope for. She had slept in Smoke's arms nearly every night and been glad of it.

And on some of those nights Cass had thought of Nora and wished she didn't exist. Such a wish didn't feel like the same sort of sin as it might have been Before. Aftertime, the odds of living to the next day were stunted; you learned not to count on the future. You said goodbye knowing it might be the last time…and then, eventually, you simply stopped saying goodbye. Encounters meant both more and less when you knew you might not ever see someone again. The old world had ended, and new morals were needed to survive.

Deep in the night Cass would think of Nora and wish her to simply not be. She didn't want her to fall to the fever, didn't want the Beaters to find her, didn't want illness or infection or a burst appendix to take her. She just wished she could erase Nora from Smoke's past, rub her away so completely that not even a shadow remained, so she and Smoke could truly start anew together. Cass and Smoke and Ruthie, and that wish had been enough, and Cass had caught herself wondering a few times recently if a kind of happiness might actually be possible someday.

But the emotions on Smoke's face did not leave a place for her. There was fury in the hard set of his mouth, determination in the line between his eyebrows. In his chambray eyes, the flint-sparks of something Cass knew far too well: vengeance. She'd carried the thirst for vengeance with her long enough to know that it was consuming and heavy and left little room for any other burden. Sometimes it left no room for the breath in your chest, your dreams at night—it stole everything.

But still she waited. She had not spoken Nora's name aloud since they first came to the Box. If she didn't speak it now, maybe her memory would let him go. Maybe, in death, she'd release him. Cass didn't know if she believed in an afterlife, was still trying to decide if she believed in anything at all— but in this moment she begged a wish from Nora, dead Nora, ghost-or-angel Nora:

Let me have him. He's no good to you now...just let me have him.

Smoke brought his hands together, clasping hers tightly and raising them to his lips. He kissed them so softly it was like the brush of a feather, and his lips were as warm as his hands were cold.

And Cass knew she would not have her wish.

"I have to go."

LAST NIGHT, SHE HAD GONE TO SLEEP HOLDING a stone, but when she woke up it was gone.

The thing that had interrupted Sammi's dream was a sound, a wordless shout but not a voice she knew, and then something breaking. But when she woke it was quiet and she tried to hold on to her dream, which had been about Jed. Everything was about Jed now—even the things that really weren't.

The sky had been orangey-pale through the windows high on the wall. A few feet away her mother slept with her arms wrapped tight around her pillow. She'd been doing that ever since Dad left, holding her pillow tight to her chest as though it might protect her from something. Her mother never moved when she slept, she lay still and elegant with her dark hair fanning the bed. Her mom was still hot for forty, especially for Aftertime—'cause face it, take away the BOTOX and the thermal reconditioning hair treatments and the eyelash extensions, and a lot of the moms at her old school probably didn't look all that great anymore.

Getting away from that stupid school had been the one good thing to come out of the last year. Not that it made up for everything else, of course, but the Grosbeck Academy had been a forty-five-minute drive and it was a shitty little third-rate girls' school anyway, but it was the only one her mom could find where she could spend twenty thousand bucks a year for the privilege, which she only did to screw over Sammi's dad anyway. And so they were up at five-thirty every morning and half the time they blew a fuse running all their blow-dryers at the same time, and wasn't that fucked-up considering they lived in the most expensive "cabin" on their side of the Sierras, six bedrooms and five custom bathrooms, three of which nobody ever used.

At least she'd had lots of friends at Grosbeck, but looking back she didn't miss any of them. She hoped nothing bad had happened to them, of course, though she knew it probably had, but she couldn't spend her time thinking about all the ways they might have died or she'd go crazy. "Just think about today," Jed always said when she started to feel the bad stuff coming on. Jed was always saying stuff like that—maybe it was because he had two older brothers and parents who were both therapists. Maybe it was because he still had his whole family—he was one of the rare lucky ones who hadn't lost anyone close yet. They had a room down the hall that used to be a conference room, and his mom was always walking around the courtyard, talking with people, holding their hands. Probably telling them to feel their feelings or something like that. Jed made fun of her, but you could tell he loved her.

And he loved *Sammi*. He had told her so, when he gave her the stone. It fit just right in her hand, and buried in its smooth gray surface was a vein of quartz in the shape of a heart. He'd found it near the creek, and he'd given her other things—books, a necklace, a thing of peanut M&M's—but the stone was her favorite.

But where was it?

Sammi had sat up in the pale light of dawn and rooted through her covers, warm from sleep, keeping quiet so she wouldn't wake her mom. Maybe she'd dreamed the shout, the sound of breaking glass. She ought to go back to sleep, wake up when it was really morning, help her mom in the kitchen before she went over to the child care room. Braid her hair before she saw Jed.

There—the stone had rolled off her mattress onto the carpet. Sammi cupped it in her hand and was pulling her covers back up over her shoulders when she realized that the light coming through the windows wasn't dawn at all.

It was fire.

THERE WERE CLOCKS, THE OLD-FASHIONED KIND with triple-A batteries, if she had wanted to know the time. One of the self-appointed holy men passing through had nailed them to posts around the Box, for comfort he said, but Cass had trained herself not to notice them. Knowing the time seemed necessary to some people, but to Cass, such details seemed pointless, almost profane. The reality of their life was inescapable, just like the fine dust kicked up along the well-worn path around the perimeter of the Box, finding its way into the folds of their clothes and the creases at their knees and elbows and neck and, she imagined, coating their lungs with a fine red-brown grit. Pretending that the time mattered was like pretending you could escape the dust, that you could ever really be clean again. It was no good.

Smoke went for a walk and Cass knew by now that when he went for a walk she was not meant to follow, so instead she hitched Ruthie up in her arms and went looking for Dor.

The sky was purpling dark near the horizon and the sun had slipped down behind the stadium across the street, and the smells of cooking wafted from the food stands, and people milled along the paths toward the dining area, a fifty-foot square in the dirt where picnic tables were arranged with precision, like everything that was Dor's.

Dor was not in his trailer, which was unusual for this time of day. He routinely made himself available in the early evening, seeing anyone who came to meet with him. As often as not, he ate his dinner alone afterward. Sometimes you'd see two or three people lined up outside at the park bench that had been planted there for that purpose, like failing students come to beg their professor for a passing grade during office hours. Nine times out of ten it was folks wanting credit, even though Dor had never been known to grant it. One of the cheap cots up front—yeah, sure, if there was one free. And he generally turned a blind eye to the food merchants who set their leftovers out late at night for scavengers. But if you wanted anything else you had to trade something, and that was that.

Cass was curious about the conversations that took place in the trailer, but she and Dor were not close and she didn't ask. Smoke didn't tell her anything, either. Dor had become a no-man's-land between them in the two months that Smoke had worked directly for him. Cass had never suggested that Smoke find some other work—what else was there, after all?—and she had no quarrel with Dor over the guards patrolling the Box and keeping the roads into town clear of Beaters. If she'd been surprised that Dor had put Smoke in charge of the entire security team, she had to admit the decision had been inspired: everyone knew about the battle at the rock slide, and while Smoke played down his role, that almost gave the story more power. He'd killed a Rebuilder leader, and the Box was full of stories of the Rebuilders' methods, their violent occupations of shelters, their killing of those who resisted.

Smoke did nothing to spread the stories, and in fact grew stone-faced and irritable whenever he heard people telling them. He had drawn inward since Cass met him, and while he was most comfortable with her and Ruthie and rarely joined the gatherings around the fire late at night, he seemed to be happy enough with the company of the other guards. He insisted he was only their scheduler, a facilitator, but everyone knew otherwise.

Cass didn't object to the guns Smoke carried, though she made him lock all but one in their safe at night. She didn't object to the long hours he spent training with the guards, target shooting and lifting weights and practicing some strange sort of martial arts with a guard named Joe, who had been awaiting trial at the Santa Rita jail until one day late in the Siege when the warden apparently opened the doors and let the lowest-security prisoners go free. She didn't even mind the awkwardness between Smoke and Ruthie; she knew he was trying and that Ruthie would warm up to him in her own time.

The truth was that Cass didn't know when the discord had started between them, the uneasiness. Things had been so good and they were still good, most of the time. They had the rhythm of a couple, the way they prepared a meal together, handing each other things without needing to speak. Laughter came easy when they walked in the evenings, swinging Ruthie between them.

But still. They didn't discuss Dor or what the two men talked about in the long hours they spent together. Smoke stopped telling her what he saw when he went on the raiding parties and hunting down the Beaters, and their conversation usually centered on her gardens and Ruthie and gossip about the people in the Box, the customers who came and went and the other employees they counted as friends. He often seemed preoccupied, and she sometimes woke in the middle of the night to see him sitting outside their tent, tilted back in his camp chair, staring at the stars. They didn't make love as often, and Cass thought she might miss that most of all, the moments of release when her mind emptied of everything but him, when every horror and loss in her life faded for a moment, a gift she'd never found the words to thank him for.

Now, she forced herself to admit that Dor might know Smoke better than she did. If anyone knew what had happened, what was in Smoke's mind, it would be him. She tried the front gate next. Faye was there, and Charles, playing cards with one of the older guards who went by Three-High, except by his new girlfriend, who called him Dmitri. Feo sat on Three-High's lap, chewing on a kaysev stalk that had been soaked in syrup until it was nearly fermented, the closest thing to dessert besides the pricey canned pudding or candy canes.

"Hey, Cass," Faye said, giving her a slanted smile, more than she offered most people.

"Hey. You seen Dor?"

They shook their heads, Charles and Three-High not lifting their eyes from their cards. "He was meeting with some guy, came in from the west this morning. Jarhead type."

"Don't need no more of *that*," Three-High said with conviction.

Cass nodded. The guards were jealously protective of their jobs, which most agreed were the best to be had. A guard job came with room and board, access to the comfort tents, a free ticket to the raiding parties with the understanding they got a split of the spoils. Plenty for trade, whatever you wanted, and Dor didn't much care what you spent your off-hours doing, as long as you showed up sober for your shift and got the job done. Dor didn't hire addicts; there wasn't a single one in the crew that Cass could tell, and she had an eye for it. Hard drinkers, yes. But no pill-poppers, no meth cookers. Every one of them loved something more than a high; for most of them it was danger, adrenaline, shooting and fighting and killing Beaters. For some, it was a fierce devotion to the Box itself, a place Cass suspected was the closest thing to home, to family, that they had ever known.

Smoke hadn't hired anyone new since Dor turned the operation over to him. He was looking for one more, someone to start on nights, but he'd told her it was important to get this one right, to pick someone who'd fit the crew. He said he was waiting for someone who had never been in the service. He gave a variety of reasons, but Cass was still waiting for the one that sounded like the truth.

Charles laid down a card with some authority. "This guy, he was big. Built, you know? And carrying. We took a Heckler & Koch MP5 and a clean little Walther off him."

"They're not there now." Three-High jerked a thumb over his shoulder at the locker where everyone but the guards were required to check their weapons upon entering the Box. "I was in there half an hour ago, didn't see 'em."

Faye to set down her cards, eyebrow raised.

"You sure?"

"Sure I'm sure. Shit, Faye, I—"

"Okay, okay," Faye said. "Don't cry or nothing. I just meant I didn't see him come back out."

"Probably day shift checked him out," Charles suggested.

"Maybe." Faye seemed skeptical. "But still, that would have been a short visit."

So none of them knew the visitor had been a Rebuilder. Of course, if they had, word would have been all over the Box as soon as he'd come through the gates. The stranger must have saved that information for Dor, who'd either killed him or found a way for him to leave without drawing attention.

The former was unlikely, since the Rebuilders always had a plan—*plans*. If the man didn't make it safely back to his rendezvous point, they'd return in larger numbers, make a show of force, demand a meeting. Or maybe they'd escalate straight to armed conflict, and either attempt to take prisoners, or simply burn the place down.

The peace between the Rebuilders and the Box was uneasy. No one liked it, except possibly Dor, who, as far as Cass could tell, was without loyalties to anyone but himself and his meticulously tracked empire. But everyone realized that the balance was a delicate one, and any provocation would end up with a lot of dead on both sides. The Box was recognized as neutral, and while the Rebuilders no doubt intended to take it someday, for now they would have a hard time outgunning Dor's arsenal and security force.

Cass decided to keep the information to herself, at least until she knew what the hell was going on.

"Maybe we didn't have whatever he was shopping for," Three-High said, yawning. "Kinda thin stock these days."

Feo, finished with his snack, wriggled off his lap and darted away without a word. It was his way; he was a restless boy, frequently affectionate, but easily bored. No one tried to get him to sit still, especially not his self-appointed guardians, who saw nothing wrong with his prowling and occasional thieving and who had made him a bed in a staff bunkhouse, where they could hear him if he cried out in his sleep.

"What are you talking about, the shed's practically full. And we got a shitload of new stuff this morning from those guys from…where was it…Murphy's?" Faye ticked items off on her fingers: "Tampons and toilet paper. Tea bags, olive oil, a couple dozen of those South Beach bars, liquid soap and detergent, all that shampoo. And an unopened bottle of Kahlúa and a case of Diet Canfield's and twenty-two bottles of Coors Light."

"That stuff tastes like piss," Three-High said.

"You'd drink it, though—tell me you wouldn't."

"Hell, yes, I'd drink piss if it got me buzzed."

The raiders had recently cleared a house where Beaters had been nesting on the far east side of town, and they'd come back with a good haul, but they'd lost a man in the raid. They missed a Beater who'd been sleeping in a powder room. It was weak and injured, bones showing through its flesh in several places and one foot twisted at an odd angle, and the others had probably left it behind when they moved on. It had taken only one bullet to kill, but not until it had clamped its festering jaw on Don Carson's ankle.

It had cost a second bullet to take Don down.

The raiding was growing more dangerous. When Cass had first arrived in San Pedro in the summer, Dor's people had cleared the town of nearly all the Beaters. The Order in the Convent paid well enough for live Beaters to use in their rituals that it was more worth Dor's while to scour the streets for them. But trade with the Order had dried up, and as the weather turned cold, Beaters had begun stumbling their way south, apparently traveling by some instinct unknown to their human brethren. With their preference for more densely populated areas, Beaters were quick to nest once they reached San Pedro, and quick to hunt. Dor still kept the main roads clear, and the guards picked off any who came too close to the Box—but come in on any of the less-traveled paths and you were taking chances. The Beaters had learned to stay away from the stronghold, though they roamed just out of sight. You could sometimes hear their moans and nonsense jabber carried on the winds.

When they caught someone, you could hear the screaming, human and once-human.

Recently it seemed like they were getting bolder. Last week Cass had been trudging back from the bathroom shed at the first light of dawn, the Box still silent and asleep, when she heard a shout at the fence. For a second she hesitated, shivering at the chill snaking up under her nightgown, and then she'd loped silently along the fence toward the sound, the tongues of her undone boots flapping.

She reached the source of the commotion, across from the rental cots near the front of the Box, in time to see the worst of it. George, the guard on third shift, had been backed up against the wall of a two-story brick building that once housed a jewelry shop on the first floor and accountants' offices on the second. Cass put it together immediately—she knew the guards sometimes smoked in the space where the stone steps met the wall of the building, where an overhang provided protection from rain and the curving staircase blocked the wind. They'd even dragged a chair there, and everyone used it to take breaks between laps around the Box.

Which was fine, unless you fell asleep.

George usually didn't take the third shift. He was covering for Charles, who was laid up with food poisoning puking his guts out, and as the long uneventful night stretched toward dawn he'd taken a break. Maybe he'd just closed his eyes for a moment.

Long enough for the four Beaters to prowl down the streets and alleys from wherever they'd carved their nest and find their victim practically gift-wrapped, to seize upon their prize with shrieks of delight and hunger before George had time to reach for his gun or even the blade at his belt.

When Cass arrived, heart pounding in her throat, Faye and Three-High had left their posts at the front gate and run down the block, but it was too late. The first bite was enough to doom George, but the Beaters would not finish him here. After a few slobbering crowing nips they hoisted him between them, each holding an arm or a leg in their scabby festering fingers, to drag him back to their nest where they would feast undisturbed. First they would chew the skin off his back, his buttocks, his calves, kneeling on his arms and legs so he couldn't move. Then they'd turn him and eat the other side, and as he weakened and his screams grew hoarse, they'd nibble at the harder-to-reach skin of his face, fingers and feet.

George knew what his fate could be. You could hear it in his screams. As Cass watched—others running toward the commotion, those who were already awake, those who heard the screams through their sleep and bolted out of bed —Faye and Three-High shot at the Beaters. And when George's screaming abruptly stopped she knew they'd been aiming at him, too.

There were still entire neighborhoods waiting to be raided, but people were getting nervous. Beaters, disease, toxic waste, depression and anxiety—all these things stopped even the heartiest at times. Some of the raiders had begun refusing to go out at all, just one of the many things Cass knew Dor and Smoke discussed.

"Hey, any kid stuff in the haul?" Cass asked, thinking of Ruthie, her tight shoes.

"Yeah, but older," Faye said. "You know, like that tween stuff. All the sparkly shit on the jeans. Hold on to it for Ruthie. She'll love it in a few years."

There was a sudden, awkward silence; it was an unwritten rule that you never talked about the future. Especially because it wasn't clear how much longer Ruthie would be welcome in the Box. Dor had made an exception to his no-kids policy for her, and another for Feo, but his continued beneficence was a gamble. "Or, you know, get Gary to take in the seams for now," Faye added.

"It's the shoes, mostly," Cass clarified. "I'd just like to get her some sneakers. Boots, too. I don't care if they're boys', either. Keep your eye out?"

"You know we do, Cassie," Three-High said kindly. Some of them, mostly the men, had taken to calling her Cassie. Cass didn't like it, but she also didn't want to tell them to stop. They meant well. "We'll find her something in plenty of time. Gonna find her a sled, too, little snowsuit."

"Thanks," Cass said softly. "But Dor…so the last you saw him was…"

"Not since morning," Faye said. "We see him, though, we'll let him know you're lookin' for him, okay?"

It was the best she could do. Cass thanked them and wandered back toward her tent. Maybe Smoke would return before dinner; maybe he'd changed his mind. Maybe he was looking for her even now.

SHE TOOK THE LONG WAY, SUDDENLY IN NO MOOD to talk to anyone else, weaving along the back of the tents where people hung their washing. When a slender shadow flashed in front of her from between two tents, her heart skipped, startled.

"I seen you comin'."

Feo had slipped from a space so narrow that it could not possibly have sheltered him, so it was as though he appeared from thin air, but that was how he always moved through the compound. In one hand he held a sticky, damp candy wrapper; his mouth was ringed with blue powder. She'd barely noticed him earlier, so intent was she on finding Dor; now, she looked him over more carefully. He was dressed in a hoodie meant for a much larger child. The sleeves completely covered his free hand and the hem hung halfway to his knees. Across the front was a design of skulls and flowers, a sword piercing the skull's empty eye sockets. Feo's sweats were pink and his sneakers had been slit at the toes to make more room; Ruthie wasn't the only child who needed new shoes for winter.

But his hair had been cut with care, the front grazing his eye in a stylishly asymmetric slant, the back shaved up with a design of stripes. "You've been to see Vincent, haven't you?" Cass said, dredging up a smile for Feo, the best she could do.

"He done this for me. All I had to do was dust off his stuff," Feo said proudly, running blue-tinged fingers through his thick black bangs.

Cass nodded. "It looks great."

Feo pointed behind him, along the perimeter of the Box where the chain-link fence topped with razor wire stretched the length of two city blocks. "I seen Dor, too. He went out the back. He's smoking."

Cass caught her breath, careful not to let her anxiety show. She would bet Feo had been waiting for her, not wanting to share even this small confidence in front of the others. He did not often speak when people were gathered, though she'd managed to coax half a dozen conversations from him in private.

"Thanks," she said softly, feathering his hair lightly with her fingertips. Experience had taught her that Feo could only bear the smallest of intimacies yet. He allowed the men to rough-house with him, squirming and laughing in their arms, but she glimpsed him lurking where women gathered, the look of longing in his eyes painful to see. It would take time, that was all. At least, that was the story she told herself.

"Thanks, Feo," she repeated. "Smoking's bad."

She knew she wasn't the only one who told him that. Funny how protective they were of the boy, what with men even hiding their bottles and cigarettes when Feo was around.

He flashed her a quick smile before he dashed back between the tents and disappeared.

The path around the inside perimeter of the fence was well-worn, the earth hard packed and smooth. Newcomers often walked it deep in the night when they had trouble sleeping, and the strung-out and far-gone paced like fevered wraiths at all hours of the day. Mealtimes were the only times that the path emptied, and Cass encountered no one else as she hurried in the direction the boy had pointed.

The break in the fence, hidden behind a thicket of dead snowberry shrubs at the back of the Box, wasn't exactly a secret—but only the permanent residents of the Box knew about it, and only the most fit could use it. It was Beater-proof—the break was only in the razor wire, where two sections had come loose at a joint, leaving the ends to hang down, and it was only a couple feet wide. Climbing the chain-link was more trouble than it was worth, even for someone as strong as Dor, when you could walk to the front gate in a matter of minutes.

Unless you weren't in the mood to talk to anyone. She didn't know Dor well but she recognized in him, one loner to another, the need for silence enough to hear yourself think.

Cass reached the break and considered for a moment. Across the street, the storefronts facing the Box had long ago been stripped of anything useful, their windows shattered and the glass swept away. Dor insisted that the streets directly abutting the Box be kept clean; trash pickup was among the new recruits' jobs, and despite their grumbling there was a sense of pride among the maintenance staff.

She knew where Dor would go. Smoke had shared this confidence with her. In their long talks into the night, he told her about the men and women he worked with, their habits, small details of their lives. He admired Cass's ability to see through people to the emotions underneath. Cass didn't ever tell him that sometimes she wished she could stop; he relied on her to be his divining rod, his translator.

Smoke was bewildered by Dor's habit of wandering so far off-site unarmed, but Cass thought she understood. Solitude was as short in supply as medicine or fresh produce, but for some, just as desperately missed. Time to oneself—even when it came with great risk—somehow made it possible to sort through your tangled thoughts, to remember who you used to be, Before. And to understand who you had become After-time. In the din and commotion of the Box, Cass sometimes felt that she would slowly fade, edges first, until she was lost.

Two blocks in, where the stores gave way to apartments and small houses, a yellow brick building ringed a small courtyard with overturned benches and dead gardens. A studio apartment on the second floor looked west toward the mountains and the setting sun, and it was here that Dor came to sit occasionally, in a chair pulled up to the window. It wasn't safe—there was no exit if Beaters found their way up the stairs, save a drop out the window to the ground, one that Beaters wouldn't hesitate to follow.

Cass might have regretted disturbing his peace—if she had any choice, and if it were anyone else. Instead, she scrambled up and over the fence, the wire cutting painfully into her palms and the impact of jumping to the ground jarring her legs. She jogged down the street, scanning for flashes of movement as she went. She had her blade at hand—she never went anywhere without it—but it would do little good if she encountered more than one.

The sun had slipped behind the building, casting its courtyard in shadow. The earth was cracked and scabbed despite the recent rains; patches of kaysev, leaf-dead and spindly, caught debris in their rigid stems. A foam cup, a plastic bag, a diaper, dried and desiccated.

The building's door had disappeared months ago, and inside, the litter hinted at stories of desperation. A torn suitcase spilled matted clothing across the tiled entry, and a stroller was overturned in the corner, its colorful fabric fuzzed with mold.

Cass took the stone steps two at a time, hand over hand on the banister, moving as stealthily as she was able—Cass had the sensation that if she didn't catch Dor unawares he would simply disappear, would magic himself away to somewhere else entirely. He had that way about him, an elusiveness, and when she rounded the top of the stairs and found herself staring through the wide-flung door into the room Dor had made his own, the sight of him—broad back and hints of a dark, tanned neck, inky black hair reaching almost to his shoulders, motionless in a canvas director's chair, the rest of the room stark and empty—it only underscored the sense that he was illusory.

Dor heard her and leaped from his chair, going down on one knee with the blade in his hand like an extension of his body, eyes flashing black and bright, and the surreal notion of him grew stronger still.

But then he said her name, and his voice was flat, almost disappointed. He stood slowly, lowering his blade hand, and the mythological strangeness of him began to evaporate. The scar across his forehead was almost invisible in the gloom and his expression was unreadable. The loops of silver that pierced the cartilage of each ear weren't noticeable, and the coal-black kaysev tattoos running up both arms were covered by his canvas coat. He almost looked like an ordinary man. "What do you want?"

"I'm sorry about Sammi."

Dor barely acknowledged her words. A faint lift of his chin, that was all. She knew he had decided long ago that his daughter would be safer sheltering at the school than here in the Box with him. Few people knew about Sammi: her very existence was something that could be used against him. So long as his foes believed he cared for nothing and no one, he was invulnerable.

Dor never spoke of her, and neither, by tacit agreement, had Smoke or Cass. If the Rebuilders discovered that they had Dor's daughter, the entire balance of power shifted, and the Box could be theirs for the price of a single life. Getting her back was key to keeping all of them safe. But Cass knew that Dor wasn't thinking about strategy now, that his mind was filled only with Sammi, with his fears for her and his rage at her abductors.

Cass pressed on. "Smoke says he's going."

"I told him not to," Dor said, then added in a tone only fractionally less cold, "if that matters to you."

"And yet he's going anyway."

"You want him to stay."

Cass shrugged. Of course she did...what did he think? She was a woman with a child; Smoke was more than just a body in the night—he was also a layer of safety. It should have gone without saying.

"You think he should stay." The same question in different words, or something else entirely? Dor did not invite her farther into the room, and she was aware of the space between them, of the still air that was even colder, if that were possible, than outdoors.

"Of course he should stay," she snapped. She needed him. But what she said instead was: "What can he accomplish? Even if he finds them, if he tracks them down, they're not going to be alone. They're not going to be *unprepared*—"

"Don't underestimate him," Dor interrupted. "If I were a betting man, I'd bet on him."

It was the rock slide, of course. The legend. Three Rebuilders dead, and Smoke untouched, not a hair on his head lost, while the two who fought at his side were dead. It almost didn't matter that it was true. Cass had heard the story retold a dozen times over a dozen late-night fires and sometimes it was twice that number dead, and sometimes Smoke took a bullet and kept on fighting, and once he had sliced off their ears as trophies and wore them on a cord around his neck.

"He's just a man," Cass said bitterly. "Lucky once. No one's lucky twice, not Aftertime."

For a long moment neither of them spoke. Then Dor bent and folded his chair carefully and leaned it against the wall, where Cass noticed twin marks in the paint. So, he left the chair in the same place each time. Glancing around the room she saw something she'd missed at first—there was no dust, no dirt. Dor kept this place clean. She wasn't surprised—anyone could see from his office that he was a fastidious man. She wondered what that said about him, what flaws or virtues it bespoke, what history it maybe whitewashed, and then she put that out of her mind and followed him from the room, a place she suspected she had defiled for him merely by her presence there.

THEY WALKED, EACH OF THEM KEEPING WATCH
in the way every citizen had learned to keep watch. It was
like breathing after a while: you were only aware of your own
constant vigilance when you stopped. By now Cass doubted
whether there was anyone alive in California who hadn't seen
a Beater. And seeing one, even once, was enough to change
you forever.

"You know about Rolph," Dor said after a while.

Cass nodded. Everyone knew about Rolph, a quiet man
who'd arrived a few weeks back, traded everything in his
meager pack for a bottle of cheap rum, drank it fast and stumbled out of the Box at dusk to piss on a wall across the street.
For reasons no one would ever know, he wandered the wrong
way; even drunk, his screams carried far into the Box half an
hour later.

"There's going to be more like him. A lot more."

"Some people say it's going to be better now that the days are getting shorter. You know, because there's less daylight."

"Don't believe it."

Cass didn't, though she knew why people clung to that particular hope. In the early stages of the disease, right after the initial fever, the pupils began to shrink, and kept on shrinking until, by the time the thing that used to be human was chewing its own flesh off, those eyes let in only a tiny amount of light. Beaters were blind when the sun went down, clumsy at dawn and dusk. Even at high noon you'd sometimes see them staring up at the sky as though they were trying to absorb all the light they could, as though they couldn't get enough, as though they would swallow down the entirety of the sun if they could.

On a recent sleepless night, Cass's restive mind had spun a dream-image of the sun sinking down to the earth. The great golden globe came to rest in a field, and the Beaters stopped what they were doing and ran toward it, throwing themselves at it—at its trillions of watts of light—swarming with the same fevered passion that they attacked the living.

Their hunger was insatiable. A Beater feasting on its victim made sounds of such sensual release that they almost sounded sexual; a Beater denied would throw itself against walls and fences until it bled, unmindful of the pain in its longing and need. In Cass's dream, the Beaters—all the Beaters in the world—raced toward the light, plunging into the million degrees of the fire, flaming and dying in the ecstasy of their need. They were incinerated to nothing, their bones burned to powder that floated away on brilliant flames, the sun flickering only for a moment before it blazed down again as it had for all time.

If only.

But even then it would not be over. Because as long as the blueleaf strain of kaysev grew, as long as some citizen somewhere mistook the furled and tinted leaves for the ordinary kaysev and ate it, more would be infected, and more would die.

"Here's what you have to understand, Cass," Dor said. "People believe what they want to believe. They always have, and they always will. They want to believe the Beaters will go away. So the mind keeps coming up with ways. You've probably heard as many theories as I have."

She had: the Beaters would age out. They would turn on each other. The first hard freeze would kill them. They would go to the ocean, like lemmings, a plague of them following the summons of God.

Still, Dor's cynicism rankled. Cass had little hope, but she had the decency to pretend, for others' sakes. She couldn't help thinking that he, of all people—a leader, a benefactor even, if a reluctant one—ought to do the same. People listened to him. People cared what he thought.

"People say crazy things, yeah, but isn't it just as irrational to always expect the worst?" she challenged him.

"Come on," Dor muttered, "you don't really think that."

A moment later, though, he stopped, putting a hand on her arm, turning her so she had to look up at him. "Cass."

In the twilight Dor's eyes looked even darker. He was half a foot taller than she was, and her gaze fell to his throat, his collarbones, to the twisted fronds of the tattoo that wound around his arms and shoulders and almost met under the hollow of his throat. In this moment he seemed returned to that larger-than-life, invulnerable avatar. He was so close that she imagined she breathed the same air he did, and—trick of the moment—her lungs seemed to expand, to want to drink in more. From where the errant impulse came, she had no idea. Something visceral and instinctive, nothing more than a sensory trigger. She stepped back, trying to get away from the marked air.

She had come for *Smoke*. She had come to ask Dor to change Smoke's mind.

But Dor pulled her closer, his fingers closing tight around her arm. "There are things you need to know. Things are going to get worse before they get better—if they ever get better, which seems unlikely."

"I *know*," Cass whispered fiercely. "I've seen what's left of the stores. I see what the travelers bring. I know that all the easy raids are long gone. And…"

She didn't say the last: that there were fewer travelers and more Beaters all the time. People blamed it on all kinds of things: people were waiting out winter before they ventured out; or they had heard that the Convent had locked down; or they were afraid of Rebuilder parties; or they had gone in the other direction, to the bigger cities. The blueleaf, which had appeared to be on the wane, had merely been hibernating, and those not trained to look for the subtly shaded leaves could too easily mistake it for its benign cousin.

The words slipped out before she could stop herself: "How could you let Smoke go out into that?"

Dor shocked her by laughing, a short, bitter sound. "Woman, do you think I control what your man does? You think I control what *any* man does? Far as I know, it's still free will around here."

Cass recoiled, wrenching her arm free. "He does what you ask him."

"I never asked him to go after anyone. And definitely not

that crew. I'm not in the vengeance business, sister. Only business I'm in is my own."

"But you could ask him to *stay*—"

"It's not my place." Just like that the laughter was gone, his expression stony. "*Not* my place, or anyone else's. He's a grown man who set his way, and paid his accounts through already."

"You could—influence him. That's all I'm asking."

"*No,*" he said emphatically. "You think that's what you want, Cass, but you don't. Not really. You start trying to change someone, you lose them. Smoke's doing what he has to do. What he needs to do. You get in the way of that, he'll just resent you, until the day it builds up in him so strong he goes anyway and with a bitter taste in his mouth. He'll blame you. You don't need that."

Cass forced herself to breathe, blinked away the threat of tears. "Ruthie needs him," she whispered. "*I* need him."

"No." Dor shook his head. "You don't. You've come this far without him. Survived things no one else survived. Done things most people would say are impossible."

His gaze flicked across her face, lingering on her eyes, which she knew were different since she'd survived the fever—brighter, greener. Smoke wouldn't have told him her terrible secret, that she'd been attacked and lived—would he? Dor's tone was almost admiring, which gave her pause. The man had never had any use for her…had he? From the moment they met there had been wariness between them, distrust and dislike.

"You don't need him," Dor repeated. "And believing you do is giving your strength away. I don't have to tell you that between your girl and yourself, you don't have any extra to spare."

He hesitated, then reached for her hand. He squeezed it

once, roughly, then slid his hand up her arm to let it rest on her shoulder. The gesture was awkward—she could sense that Dor meant it to be a comfort. But it was not. It was something both more and less, something needful, and he must have felt it too because he jerked his hand away as though the touch burned him.

"Stay in the Box," he muttered, turning away. "Don't worry about trade. Everything's covered. In the spring when your garden comes up you'll be producing enough to share. I'll set it all up. I'll make sure you have what you need."

"You're leaving, too," Cass said, realization dawning on her. "You're going to Colima. You're going to look for Sammi."

Of course—she should have known it from the moment Smoke told her what happened at the library. Cass herself had risked everything to find Ruthie, so why did the notion of Dor doing the same for his daughter fill her with such bleak hopelessness? And when Dor nodded, jaw set hard, it seemed as though the air got even colder.

"You won't be alone. Cass, I'll tell Faye. I'll tell Charles. They'll look after you. I'll send word if I can, and so will Smoke. We'll both be back...you need to have more faith in him. He beat them once already—there's no reason he can't do it again. He's well armed and well trained."

"*Your* training," Cass said bitterly. "*Your* guns."

As if that made Dor responsible.

A disproportionate number of the citizens who'd survived this long had done so because they had a strong desire for self-preservation along with the skills to back it up. Skills that came from time spent in law enforcement, or in the service or jail or a gang. Dor's forces were all ex-something—ex-cop, ex-Marine, ex-Norteño...all except for Smoke.

Smoke had told Cass only that he'd been an executive coach

Before, and didn't elaborate in the months they'd been together, always deflecting her questions, turning the conversation elsewhere. Cass hadn't pushed; she wasn't ready to tell
him everything about her own past, so she hardly felt entitled
to demand the same from him.

Smoke's background may have been inauspicious for survival, much less commanding Box security, but he had some
penchant for enduring—plus the legend of the rock slide,
which was enough to earn the respect of the others. He'd
been a decent shot before joining their ranks; now he was
excellent. He'd been fit; now he was hard-muscled and lean.
When Smoke slipped out of the tent before dawn to shoot at
cans or practice strikes with Joe or put his body through ever-
harder workouts, Cass tried to tell herself, *He is doing this for
us, for our little family,* and ignore the fact that he was turning
from someone she hadn't known long into someone she didn't
know well.

"Look, Cass." Dor looked as though he was going to reach
for her again and Cass shrank away from him. "He asked me
not to say anything. He's leaving tonight. He's… He didn't
want to have to say goodbye."

Cass made a sound in her throat. Smoke wouldn't do that,
wouldn't leave without telling her—would he? Smoke, who'd
grown more silent with every passing week, whose mind
drifted a thousand miles away. Who reached for her less and
less often in the night.

"He didn't want to hurt you more than he had to. I don't—
if he…he just didn't want to hurt you."

"Well, it's a little late for that, isn't it? He knew damn well
he was hurting me—*us*—he just wasn't brave enough to stick
around and watch."

She didn't bother to mask her bitterness, biting her lip hard to keep her angry tears from spilling. She expected Dor to turn away from her, that having tried to mollify her, he would consider his duty done and return his attentions to his own problems, his own imminent journey.

But Dor did not look away, and Cass, whose despair made her want to hit and kick and scream, forced herself instead to think of Ruthie. She thought of her baby and took deep breaths and dug her fingers into her palms until it hurt, until she could speak without her voice breaking.

"It's time to go back," she said.

Dor scanned the distant hills, the streets to the right and left. They both listened; there were no moans, no faint cries, no snuffling or snorting. Only the wind, dispirited and damp, made its way down the street, identified by the signpost at the corner of the sidewalk as Oleander Lane. The sign still stood, all that was left of the oleanders that had died the first time a missile containing a biological agent microencapsulated on a warhead built on specs stolen from at least three separate countries came hurtling into the airspace above California at thirteen hundred miles per hour and struck a patch of earth in the central valley, taking out every edible crop for hundreds of miles and quite a few more that were good for nothing but looking pretty.

Even though Dor had warned her that Smoke was leaving, the stillness of the tent reached into Cass's throat and stole her breath so that she had to grab the edge of the dresser to keep from collapsing. The evidence of Smoke's absence was subtle but, for one who knew this small space as well as she did, unmistakable. His pack was missing from the bedpost there. His coat—there. He kept his shoes, both the boots and the lightweight hikers, lined up under the foot of the bed, but only the hikers remained.

The photograph of the three of them—the Polaroid Smoke had bought with four cans of chili—was missing from its frame. Cass stared at the frame, an ornate gilt one from a raid—it now held only the stock image of two random dark-haired little girls, laughing as they went down a slide.

Smoke hadn't even bothered to take the old picture out. The little girls who were long gone now, dead from fever or starvation. Or perhaps they had been victims of the Beaters, their flesh flensed from their bones, left to rot in some garden or forgotten back room. Or the evil of humanity in cold times reached up and took them. Suddenly she was so angry she had to hurt something, had to break something, if only to release a little of the fury from her body. Smoke had left Cass a picture of loss, a reminder of the anonymous grief all around. She picked up the frame—heavy, expensive—and threw it on the ground. But it bounced on the soft rug and didn't break, so she seized the heavy pewter cup from the table and slammed it into the frame's glass, splintering and breaking and crushing, sending the shards flying. Cass brought the cup down again and again until she'd smashed dents in the wood and bloodied her fingers, and then she lay down with her face in the carpet and sobbed. She didn't bother to muffle the sound; people cried here every day. Crying was nothing to anyone who might hear. Her pain was nothing to them. She cried until her throat was raw and her eyes swollen and then she lay still, and when she lifted her head the tent was nearly dark and she lit a candle and spent a long time picking bits of glass from the rug before she left to collect Ruthie from Coral Anne, to fetch her baby because it was going to be just the two of them again in the world, alone for always.

★ ★ ★

But the morning awoke in her a new resolve. Without Smoke, she had to focus on Ruthie, on creating the best possible world for her daughter from the ruins she'd been given to work with. With Smoke beside her, Cass had been able to make a home of the Box, a family from its battered and motley residents. But now that he was gone, the place's shortcomings were stark and untenable. The atmosphere of desperation, the leering old men and twitchy hopped-up scavengers. The fact that the only other child here was a shadow-boy, a damaged, elusive little hustler. How much longer would they be welcome here?

Ruthie stirred against her, dream-restless. Cass lay still, reluctant to disturb Ruthie as her resolve took shape. There was no joy to it; her purpose was doleful and raw, but it was better than being empty.

She waited for Ruthie to wake up, considering her new intention, watching the sun color the sky pale blue through the tent's open window. Yesterday's bone-deep chill was a memory, practically an impossibility. She was warm under blankets, Ruthie even warmer, her sweet face pressed against the soft cotton of Cass's sleep shirt. She thought about her plan and it took shape and grew until it seemed to Cass impossible that any other would do.

Ruthie woke and smiled when she discovered that she was in her mama's bed. She had not spoken again since yesterday's dream, and Cass wondered if she might have imagined it. But no: Ruthie had said *bird*. Cass doubted she meant the sparrows that pecked for bits in the dining area. The little brown birds were unremarkable, but other species were coming back. Maybe Ruthie had spotted a redbird or a hawk—something more noteworthy, anyway, than the flock of tiny scavengers.

"Good morning, sugar-sweet," Cass whispered and covered Ruthie's forehead and nose with kisses while her daughter laughed without making a sound, her shoulders shaking.

Then it was a matter of choosing their warmest, sturdiest clothes before the two of them went to find Dor to tell him they were going with him.

"I MEAN TO GO ALONE," HE SAID. CASS HAD FOUND him in his trailer, sitting at his desk with a steaming travel mug of coffee, morning sunlight slanting off the tidy surfaces of the cramped space, staring at a spreadsheet on the monitor that was nearly always on. Dor powered his computer with the compact generator that hummed beneath the trailer, and Smoke said he kept digital inventories, as well as some sort of forecasting software and other programs Smoke could only guess at.

Dor had offered her a chair, and Cass had taken it, grateful to be off her feet, Ruthie heavy and dozing in her arms. He'd been pro forma friendly until she'd stated her intentions.

"I can help you. I can give you a reason to be there, in the Rebuilder settlement. One they won't question."

"And what's that?" Dor didn't bother to mask his skepticism.

"I'm an outlier," Cass said, pulling up her sleeves to reveal the faint scars still on her forearms. "I was bitten and taken by the Beaters. And I recovered. And the Rebuilders know it. They want me for my immunity."

After staring at her with a preternatural calm for what felt like forever, Dor spoke softly, like a man who'd just had confirmation that his lover was stepping out on him. "It was your green eyes...yours and Ruthie's. I've never seen eyes like that, so deep and bright."

Deeply pigmented irises: a distinctive mark of the recovered. In her time in the compound, Cass had caught Dor staring at her a few times, and felt her skin burn at his scrutiny, though he always looked away so quickly that she wondered if she might have imagined it.

Cass often found herself doubting so many of her own perceptions. So much was lost to her damaged memory. And the rest of her that did remember certainly didn't want to. But now she filled Dor in on the details, leaving out only the existence of Nora.

Almost four months ago, Cass had woken, disoriented and badly scarred from a Beater attack she could not remember, in a field far from any shelter. She had wandered for weeks, walking at night to avoid the cannibals, hiding during the day, her confusion slowly dissipating, until a young girl had attacked her, thinking she was a Beater. But Cass got her blade away and used her as a hostage to gain entry to the school where the girl and her mother sheltered.

The young girl was Sammi. Long before Cass ever glimpsed Dor's tall brooding form, his inky, depthless eyes, she had made a promise she never expected to have to keep: to find Sammi's father and tell him his daughter was safe. She had done at least that, and she counted on him to remember that favor now, when she needed him.

Smoke had been at the school, and he had volunteered to escort Cass to the Silva public library several miles away, the last place Cass had lived before the attack. At the time, she didn't understand how she had recovered, but her only focus was finding her daughter. Discovering that Ruthie had been sent away from the library to the Convent in San Pedro had devastated Cass, but a more immediate problem was that the library had become a Rebuilder stronghold. Its leader, Evangeline, had learned that Cass was an outlier. She said there were a few other outliers like herself, but that they didn't have enough research subjects yet; the Rebuilders were working on a vaccine and they needed Cass for research and study.

Cass suspected there was more to the story. Evangeline had planned to send Smoke to their detention center in Colima as punishment for his part in the rock slide battle. She didn't bother to mask her hatred for Smoke, and she barely bothered to conceal her antipathy for Cass despite promising her safety. When one of the men in the shelter helped Cass and Smoke escape, Cass was sure she'd escaped imprisonment in the Rebuilder headquarters, and possibly worse.

"So you know, even if no one there recognizes you from the Box, you'll be at a disadvantage," Cass argued, searching Dor's grim expression for any sign he might acquiesce. "You'll be just another recruit, with hardly any more status than the people they convert by force from the shelters. I might be able to get more privileges. More access."

For another long moment Dor said nothing. He didn't look away, and Cass felt like he was calculating odds and dangers she could only guess at, as though he ran spreadsheets through his mind even when he wasn't staring at his screens, always focusing on a bottom line that even the end of the world could not erase for him.

"It would be better if we knew exactly what your immunity is worth to them," Dor finally said, and Cass allowed herself a tiny sigh of relief. It had worked—she had given him something he could understand, a problem presented in the language he was most comfortable with: she could be bartered.

"Yes."

"And Ruthie…"

"She's an outlier, too." Cass didn't think she could bear to tell him that story—the one before the Convent—of Ruthie being bitten, of the kindness of the woman who nursed her back to health during Cass's lost months and fever days. "But Evangeline doesn't know. She doesn't know about her at all. No one told her, even when Smoke and I were locked up in the library."

"So how are you going to explain showing up in Colima with her?"

Cass had prepared an answer for that, but she found that it was harder than she anticipated to get the words out. She took a deep breath and rushed through the rest. "We have to say Ruthie's yours. That she's your daughter. We have to say that you and I are…you know. Together. All of us. That we met on the road after I left the library, and we've been together ever since."

Dor's expression barely changed. There was a darkening of his eyes, perhaps, a slight downward pull at the corners of his mouth.

"And why would you be willing to do all of this for me? The risk goes up with every lie you tell."

"You have it all wrong," Cass said quietly. "I'm not doing any of this for you. You're just our ticket to leave San Pedro. I'm not coming with you so much as leaving here.

Because there's nothing left for us here. Ruthie needs to live where there are other children, other…families. And the Box is dying—I can see that."

Dor nodded as though her answer made perfect sense. "As long as your expectations are realistic. I mean, there is going to be less for everyone, everywhere, and no matter how hard you try, you're not going to be able to outrun that fact. You're stuck here, in what's left of the West. Those lunatics trying to hold the Rockies—they shoot on sight, so that's not an option."

"I never said I wanted to go East." The blueleaf fever that spawned Beaters after the Siege had been limited to California at first, the only state to have spread the mutant seed along with the kaysev that was meant as manna to save and nourish survivors. In a panic that the Beaters would spread across the continent, an increasingly organized army had claimed a boundary along the Rockies, and no traveler who ventured there returned to tell about it. Perhaps because of the barrier, the East had come to symbolize salvation for some.

Cass was not tempted. She would take her chances here, in the ragged remains of California. Somewhere, there had to be a place for her and Ruthie.

"You sound like you've lost hope," she accused.

He narrowed his eyes. "I'm not without hope. I'm just limiting it to me and mine. There will be enough for me and for the people I care about in this lifetime, if I'm strategic about it. It's not my job to worry about everyone else or any other time."

"And who exactly do you care about?" Cass tried and failed to mask her anger. She was uncomfortably conscious of her hypocrisy, but she didn't admit that she had had the very same sort of thoughts herself: *Let there be enough for Ruthie—let everyone else starve.*

"Sammi. I care about Sammi. And I care about my people. When I'm with them, anyway." He looked away, his gaze troubled and unreadable.

"What do you mean?" Cass waited, but she could sense Dor pulling away, following the spiral of his thoughts to a bitter place. She couldn't let him. She had to keep him here, feeling what she was feeling, if there was any chance for her to convince him to take her and Ruthie with him. "Tell me... please."

For a moment Dor said nothing, straightening the stack of papers on the desk until it was perfectly uniform.

"As long as I'm with them I care, but I don't know how I'll feel when I'm away. Faye, Joe, Three-High, Feo—all of them, they...mean something to me." He glanced at her and then quickly away. "Even Gloria. You may not believe me, but I was really sorry when she died. But three years ago I had an assistant—her name was Melissa. She kept my calendar, brought me coffee. Slept with me sometimes. I know that sounds bad, and I'm not asking for your approval—but Melissa and I were good for each other. I think I might have been closer to her than I was to my wife, at the time."

Cass murmured encouragement. She was always surprised when people assumed that she'd judge them. Cass didn't feel qualified to judge anyone after the things she'd done, the straits she'd found herself in.

"I don't know where she is now, of course—but honestly, even before this year we'd lost touch. I mean, I sincerely hope she found happiness, but it never seemed like something worth pursuing. And there've been others. My ex-wife's family, I cared about them, once. Considered her brother to be like my own for a while. Couple guys I went to college with. My uncle Zed, when I was growing up and my old man wasn't around much. All these people…"

He pinched the bridge of his nose, rubbing the skin as though it hurt. "I'm not trying to be…anything, really. Not cruel or cold. But all these people, they meant something to me, and now they're gone, and I'd be lying if I said I spent time worrying about them other than the odd thought that comes along. Who can say why? What I'm trying to tell you, Cass—I'm not a person who keeps people close. Those feelings don't stick to me, not the way they do for other people. But still. I love my daughter. I love Sammi."

Cass heard the pain in Dor's voice, and believed him. She guessed that he was one of those men who had only started learning to love when his daughter was born, and was still a beginner in many ways. Was it possible that was as far as he was ever meant to get? If the Siege had never happened, Dor would have continued on indefinitely, trading and dealing, building his financial empire, people coming and going from his life with little thought or consequence.

But Cass had seen Dor in his solitary room. Seen the humble folding chair, stored carefully against the wall. The window from which he watched the world. His exile did not feel *chosen,* to Cass, but more like a cast-off coat one wears to keep from freezing to death, ill-fitting and unfamiliar.

"I want you to know that," he murmured, not meeting her eyes. "If you're really determined to come with me. You can't expect to mean anything to me. You say there's nothing for you here. Maybe, maybe not…you've made some friends. You have your work, your garden. Safety for Ruthie. I know you probably believe…that you owe something to someone. Other people helped you get Ruthie back, so now maybe you think you have to settle some sort of cosmic debt, that you have to help me get Sammi. But you don't. I don't need you. And I won't thank you. And I won't care about you. I mean it, Cass—I'll *never* care about you."

Cass nodded and turned away from him. "That's the way I want it," she said with as much conviction as she could muster, and wondered which of them was telling the greater lie.

She asked him one favor—to tell no one she and Ruthie were going. She didn't want to go through explanations and goodbyes. Cass knew this was cowardice, but she also knew she had only so much strength for the journey, and she was not about to start spending it before they even left.

They would leave in the morning. Dor was gathering his security team late in the evening to make plans for running the Box in his absence. By now they must have noticed that Smoke was gone; the Box was not a big place, and it was his habit to check in at the gate late in the afternoon and again after dinner. Cass wondered if anyone would really expect him to return. The probability that fate would turn in his favor, that he would be able to locate the band of Rebuilders who'd burned the school, that he'd take out enough of them to satisfy the blood-longing he carried and survive—these were not favorable odds, and surely they would all know it.

Dor would tell them that *he* would return soon, also. This, they might believe. People in the Box—both employees and customers—tended to consider him larger than life. In part, this was due to his elusiveness, the way you rarely saw him in the busy paths or eating areas or market stands, but often glimpsed him at the back of gatherings, at twilight or dawn, coming and going from errands he never explained. He met with them one-on-one and in small groups, and his power went unquestioned, but he stayed out of the din and hubbub of the Box for the most part, rarely partaking in the card games and never, that anyone knew, the comfort tents.

Dor was well regarded and even liked by his employees. Certainly he had their loyalty. But Cass suspected that few, other than Smoke, really *knew* him. In fact, she was pretty sure that few of them even knew he had a daughter, since he never talked about Sammi and had paid his scouts well to check in on the library occasionally and keep their reports confidential.

Dor had proved astonishingly good at procuring things. He traded shrewdly and paid close attention to the needs and desires of his clientele, and when there was a need, he went to great lengths to see it met. When his stores of liquor dipped, he hand-selected a couple of enterprising guys, friends from Before, and turned them into winemakers. He set them up with a yeast starter, knowing that the arms he traded for it were worth far less than the alcohol they'd eventually produce. In an abandoned San Pedro microbrewery he found them carboys and vinyl hose and air locks, and they were teaching themselves to make fairly palatable wine from kaysev.

He'd found marijuana seeds so that Cass could start cultivating them in her garden. Cass was happy to have the challenge and she'd brushed off Smoke's worries that a recovering alcoholic shouldn't work in the drug business: to her, the tiny seedlings were just another plant, another tiny miracle, evidence of life's return.

Dor had even found an old-fashioned four-sided leather strop somewhere, and paid Vincent to sharpen his straight razor with it twice a week so he could indulge his single vanity, a regular and close shave.

All of this added up to an unspoken belief that somehow Dor was immune to ordinary dangers and limitations, and if he announced that it was to the Rebuilders' stronghold he was trekking, people would assume he had trading in mind. No one would expect him to fail, despite the Rebuilders' reputation for brutality and one-sided negotiation techniques. Dor was crafty and he was wily, and people would assume he would trade well and come back richer.

No one would know that what he really meant to trade for was his daughter.

Cass had her doubts. Smoke had told her that the arsenal was scrupulously guarded and locked down. There were hidden, off-site stores, but he and Dor continually worried that their supply of ammunition was low, and travelers barely brought weapons to trade anymore. There was talk of trying to forge makeshift bullets, but Dor had yet to find the materials they would need.

So Dor would not be able to trade weapons for Sammi. Also, the Rebuilders were rumored to be drug- and alcohol-free, by mandate of their leaders, and though Cass knew that there would always be a black market for a high, Dor would not be able to make an open trade for his daughter. In fact, any dealing they did would have to be illicit, because no one ever left the Rebuilders once they had joined. And there was no way to visit their headquarters other than by pledging loyalty. It was dangerous, circular logic that the Rebuilders employed in defense of their recruiting practices—once a citizen experienced the security they offered, there would be no reason to leave. And if anyone tried? Well, that was proof that they were imbalanced and guilty of threatening the cohesion of the new society. Guilty of sedition, to be precise. And that was a crime the Rebuilders would not brook.

All of this, Cass suspected, added up to be sufficient reason for Dor to accept her offer to accompany him. That—and Cass was not entirely convinced he meant to return to the Box. She knew that he and Smoke had been discussing the possibility that life in Aftertime was about to get several orders worse. Beaters, driven into town by hunger and cold, were growing more desperate and aggressive—and more cunning—so dispiriting losses would continue to mount. Stores were getting thin, raids deadlier, the weather inhospitable. The Box's bounty would be depleted before spring as trades became scarcer and meaner. Smoke had confided his fears that frequent fights would break out, that the loose system of justice would have to become more rigid, that the chain-link drunk tank in the corner of the Box might have to be upgraded into a true jail. Danger and fear would grow inside the Box's borders until eventually the dangers within would just be of a different kind than the ones outside.

Cass had been Dor's observer as long and as attentively as anyone save Smoke. Their unspoken animosity was a thorn that always stung, whether she glimpsed him watching her, hands in pockets, as she tended her garden or whether he stopped by their tent in the evening after dinner and asked with exaggerated courtesy if he might borrow Smoke for a few minutes, minutes that inevitably turned into hours of discussion to which she was not privy. Cass told herself that she resented Dor for taking Smoke's time away from her, but she knew that Smoke went willingly and that he needed the intense focus of his job. She just didn't know why, and it was convenient and easy to blame Dor…but now that she was entering into her own bargain with the man, it was time for truth only, even—especially—with herself.

Dor was leaving the Box for Sammi. He would likely go elsewhere once he found her, because staying here under deteriorating conditions ran counter to continuing to survive, and survival was something of a religion to Dor, something he did with perhaps more conviction than anyone else Cass knew. When she came here with Smoke, nearly three months back, the Box was perhaps the safest place in all of the Sierras, maybe even all of California. But now was different. Maybe the North would be better, as the Beaters migrated South. Maybe somewhere rural was safer, a farmhouse or a barn set far from the road. Maybe, for all Cass knew, Dor was considering attempting to cross the Rockies, despite his talk.

But Dor wouldn't tell his employees anything. If there were plans forming and breaking in his mind, he would keep them to himself as he sketched his possible futures and packed for the trip.

Cass would have liked to say goodbye to Faye, and maybe Coral Anne, but she didn't trust herself not to break down. Friends: it was ironic that it was only now, when the world she'd known had suffered horror upon horror, only weeks from her thirty-first birthday, that she finally had any to call her own. Faye, with her acerbic wit and moments of surprising compassion. Coral Anne, whose generosity ran as deep as her Texas drawl. Only now did Cass realize how much she would miss them. If she got word that Smoke had returned—if by some miracle he managed to outlast his mission of vengeance—maybe she and Ruthie would come back here and resume their life, if the Box were still viable.

Cass paused in her packing for a moment and considered the possibility, giving herself a few seconds, a miserly ration of hope. She could return with Sammi and Dor, and Smoke would be ready to settle down for good, his thirst for blood finally sated. He would set about insulating their tent; she would make stews from the rutabaga and onions she grew in the garden, and rabbits and muskrats trapped and traded. They would play cards with Coral Anne and that couple who had arrived from Livermore, the ones who hung their tent with colorful flags they'd brought with them all this way. Maybe other families with children would come—and she would convince Dor to let them stay. Sammi would help watch Ruthie; she would teach her to play cat's cradle and in the spring they would plant zinnias and coneflowers together.

When her seconds were past, Cass took the dream and crumpled it, tossed it from her mind like it was nothing, a senseless fancy. Her pack was prepared: a couple of changes for Ruthie, extra socks and underwear for her. A tube of lanolin and one of Neosporin, taken from the safe, among their dearest possessions.

Also in the safe was a letter Smoke had given her last month. It was written on fine stationery that bore the name Whittier P. Marsstin engraved in block letters. Smoke had carefully crossed off the name on each page—all three of them—and written in the careful script of someone mindful of economy, someone who chose each word with care. They were words of love and yet he never used the word *love,* promises made without ever using the word *promise.*

Cass had practically memorized the letter, but she left it in the safe and locked it before snuffing out her candle. As she got into the bed, shivering, and enclosed Ruthie's warm body in the safety of her arms, she imagined the words of the letter already fading from her mind, and soon the sentences and paragraphs and finally Smoke's entire meaning would be as lost to her as the man himself.

SAMMI RODE IN THE BACK OF THE TRUCK WITH the others, pretending to sleep, too afraid to speak. The men who rode back there with them—when did they sleep? Because every time Sammi opened her eyes, their eyes were there, too, dark and unreadable as they waited and watched while the rest of them huddled together for warmth.

Her mother was dead. Jed was dead. Everyone who resisted—even a little—dead, dead, dead. The only reason Sammi was alive was because her mother's last words were *Go with them, Sammi*—her name was still on her lips when she'd gone down, blood pouring from the slice in her neck.

Jed had earned a bullet. He'd pretended to go along, helping his brothers support their parents as they were herded up into the truck, holding them up by their arms so they wouldn't stumble. Stumbling got you killed—at least, that was what had happened to Mrs. Levenson, who didn't have time to get her cane when the Rebuilders burst into the burning school. She tried to keep up but she kept twisting her hip and falling, making little "oof" sounds when she landed on the ground, and the third time one of the Rebuilders had hit her on the head with his black stick and she twitched and lay still, making no sound at all. Sammi had seen the Rebuilder—a woman, how could a *woman* do such a thing?—wind up for the swing, and Sammi had played softball, so she knew, from the way the woman brought the stick back and around and down with a crack everyone could hear, that the force must have crushed poor Mrs. Levenson's skull.

And that was before they were even loaded on the truck.

There had been sixteen of them, in the end. Sixteen alive and thirty-four dead or dying in the burning school. Sammi was numb with horror as the truck ground out of the parking lot and onto Highway 161. Two of the Rebuilders, both men, both young, rode in the back with them. The one with his back to the cab and another who sat on a box, flipping a blade and catching it. It was the same blade he had used on Sammi's mom and on the others, too, the ones who tried to keep the Rebuilders out of the common room.

An older man drove, and then there was the woman—the woman who had killed Mrs. Levenson. The guard who stared at her, the one with a tiny triangle of beard and a cap with a cartoon picture of a dog embroidered on it—he had made her sit near him and Sammi wondered with a sickening feeling if it was so he could look at her. Because he just kept looking at her. Jed and his family had been made to sit on the other side of the truck bed, and Jed mouthed words at her whenever the guy on the box wasn't looking, he said *I love you* and other things Sammi could not understand, and after a while her vision blurred with tears and she couldn't see his mouth forming words. In between were the rest of the survivors.

Arthur. Mr. Jayaraman. Terry and her kids. The ones who were too old, too young, or too cowardly to fight or who, like Jed's brothers, had someone to protect.

Her mother had died trying to protect Sammi. They hadn't even wasted a bullet on her death; they'd dropped her to the ground like a sack of garbage and stepped around the pooling blood as though it was distasteful. Her mother's body was left behind in the burning building; Sammi hoped it burned all the way, to the bones—and that the bones burned, too. She didn't want the birds to get to her mother's body; she'd seen what the birds could do, the big black ones that had showed up a week ago and feasted on the carcass of a fat raccoon the raiders had caught and left out in the courtyard for skinning. Better that her mother disappear from earth as Sammi wished she herself could disappear.

Through the long night in the truck, Sammi shivered and wished she'd been killed, too. But she kept hearing her mother's last words. *Go with them.* Well, she had, and she regretted it. Even in the dark she sensed the man staring at her. She knew what he wanted to do. She wished she'd done it with Jed first, because at least then Jed would have always been her first. They had talked about it, and Sammi had finally decided she wanted to and Jed had got some condoms. They just hadn't gotten around to it. They were waiting for a night when they could be alone.

Sammi cried and felt the cold seep deeper inside her and stared at the stars. Sometimes she thought the stars were the most beautiful thing left, maybe the only beautiful thing left in the world. There were so many, it was almost like a thick and sparkling sauce had been spilled across the sky, and Sammi wondered if somewhere out there was a planet whose inhabitants hadn't messed it up, hadn't created their own monsters and poisons to kill themselves off.

She found her dad's star, and almost didn't say the words. She'd gotten used to the idea that he was dead; her mother said that it was better that way, that wishing for him to be alive was just pretending, and they didn't have the luxury of pretending anymore; but until this night she had kept her promise. Every night she found her dad's star and touched her nose with her fingers the way he taught her as far back as she could remember. "Who do I love best?" he used to ask and she would touch her nose with her finger because that meant *Me! You love me!*—but that wasn't even the real part of it.

The real part was the star and the thing they said together. Before he left, even though Sammi was fourteen and too old for it, he would always take a break from his study and come find her, and it didn't matter if she was watching TV, he would wait for a commercial; or if she was texting or painting her nails, whatever it was, he would wait and then they would go out on the deck and he would find the star and they would say it together. Just another way of saying *I love you;* she knew that now, but when she was little she had decided it had to be the same every time and so it was.

The night her dad left, his SUV packed with his stuff in the driveway, he hugged her hard and pointed to the sky and said the thing. "Never forget," he said and kissed her nose, her forehead, and then he added, "Okay?" in a way that sounded so sad and tentative that Sammi promised after all even though she was so angry she had been planning to refuse.

Tonight she almost broke her promise because he'd left her and died, and now her mom had died and she was alone, and if that wasn't his fault, well, she didn't exactly know who else to blame. So she wasn't going to say it.

But there the star was, as bright and yellow as it had ever been, and the man stared and she couldn't see Jed and she wished she was dead…but she whispered the words:

"Star bright, you and me always."

A few minutes later they stopped the truck so everyone could pee and the man with the beard, the one who stared, jumped to the ground and took them to the side of the road one at a time while the knife man watched everyone else, and when it was Jed's turn, all three brothers jumped up and attacked the guard who'd killed her mother and broke his neck before the old man and the woman shot them. The Rebuilders wrapped the body of the dead guard in a tarp and lashed it to the top of the cab. They left Jed and his brothers lying facedown on the ground. And the rest of the way Jed's mother screamed and Sammi was silent and knew she'd never keep any promise again.

DOR SCALED THE FENCE ONE LAST TIME, HIS movements quick and practiced, the calluses on his hands almost numb to the wire cutting his flesh. It was important that no one see him go. People would read things into his departure, and that could lead to trouble—looting and fighting, the kinds of things that happened when too many people shared too small a space with no one in charge. If all went well, there would be a general announcement, tomorrow, when Faye and Three-High and Joe and Sam and the rest could control the message, when they could reassure everyone that nothing was wrong, that Dor would soon be back.

He dropped to the ground and melted into the darkness quickly and quietly, and if anyone had been nearby watching they would have had a hard time guessing who had slipped past them in the moonlight.

The meeting had gone well enough. Lying to his team had become both easier and harder as the weeks had turned into months and this thing he started in the spring had grown into the community it was now, in the middle of November, two seasons and thousands of trades later.

The way Dor figured, every trade changed the Box in some small and fundamental way, shifting people's personal equations of need and loss and rebalancing the entire community's measures of hope and satiety. He believed that he was doing good, perhaps the most good it was possible to do in these times. But he had also never felt more alone. The more he was respected, the more he was admired, the further away—the more incomprehensible—other people seemed. And being in their midst didn't help. Paradoxically, the only thing that helped was utter solitude.

He had never shared these thoughts. No, they had formed and refined in private, up in the quiet of the apartment building, as he watched the sun set over the Sierras, the one view that—in the moments when the blazing red light at the horizon obscured the silhouette of the naked dead trees—still looked like Before. He loved to let the burning last rays of daylight blind him, loved the warmth on his face, and most of all he loved forgetting—even for a moment—that he was responsible for so much. He had never meant to let people rely on him, to look up to him the way they had.

At first it was the old instinct that drove him, to buy cheap and sell dear, to work the deal—and yes, perhaps, on occasion the sleight of hand, the scam—to chase the excitement of being the fastest, shrewdest, richest. Before, his clients were never the point—the deal itself was all he cared about. In the columns of numbers were wide-open spaces, races to be run, scrimmages to be played out. His investments quivered and bobbed like skittish ponies, and so what if it was all artificial, he loved the game. Dor played his clients' money like a conductor coaxing a tremulous crescendo from a woodwind section, relying on instinct as much as skill, chasing the high that came from nailing the trade, so much sweeter when he'd gambled big.

But the currency of the Box had somehow gotten away from him, so that in between the small comforts and cheap highs he dealt favors and forgiveness and loans and compassion. All of it anonymously, with only his most trusted employees acting as his agents, and it came at a cost: Dor had to be ever vigilant, aware of everything going on in every corner. He couldn't afford to slip; he had to stay strong and resolute to lead and shape the Box because, aside from him, there was no steadying standard for society. There was no system, as there had been Before, to self-regulate.

Dor had a final errand to run, but it wasn't to the apartment. He'd said goodbye to that place earlier, and if his thoughts had been truncated by Cass's unexpected arrival, that was all right. An unaccustomed lapse in vigilance, the cause of which did not bear considering—worry for Sammi, no doubt, when he could afford no worry.

When he returned—*if* he returned—there would be time to mark any deterioration of his little community and repair what he could. He supposed that it would take some time to mend things with Sammi, as well. Teenagers were moody— hell, even before the Siege Sammi'd shown signs of pushing him away, and she'd been acting up at school. Last year she was passed over for varsity softball and suspended over something she supposedly wrote in the margins of an Algebra test.

Was he to blame? Jessica would have had him think so; but she blamed him for everything. Never mind that she kept the beautiful home in the mountains, the cars and clothes and club memberships. It wasn't enough. The dissatisfied look he'd seen on her face since before Sammi was born—it was there, etched deeper than ever. He hadn't made her happy. If he was honest, it had been years since he'd even tried.

Ever since the divorce, Dor was the absent parent, the weekend visitor, the bringer of gifts and the merchant of affections, bargaining for his daughter's attentions. He wasn't the first man to make that bitter trade, and he accepted it as his due, for leaving them. He'd tried to appease Jessica by padding her support checks, paying the lawn service ahead, covering her insurance for the year. He'd learned to manage his ex-wife and daughter as well as could be expected, and now that Jessica was gone he would learn to manage Sammi again, once they were safe. Maybe the Box wouldn't be such a bad place for them to get their footing...for a few days she would be a novelty, but his staff were loyal, and they would pick up on his cues and accept her and...hell, maybe she and Cass would form a friendship, maybe Sammi could help her in the garden. Maybe Cass could tutor her, if they could round up some textbooks. It wouldn't have to be Cass, of course; Coral Anne had taught third grade, or James—he'd coached girls' softball in high school. Well. Those were details. And Dor knew better than to start focusing on details when the job at hand was still the big picture.

Big picture: things in Colima would go one of three ways. Easily, in which case they would soon be back here. Disastrously, in which case he would die, and presumably others as well, since failure was only an option after exhausting every other one. Or—and this was, of course, the most likely possibility—with difficulty and complications, starting over somewhere new if they got to start over at all. Each deviation from the plan, each small misstep or change of direction, would spiral outward in increasing magnitude, exacting changes he could not predict. A minor glitch could change the course of the entire operation, and this was what seized at Dor's calm, what impelled him out into the night when he should be resting up for tomorrow.

He walked quickly along the dark street, arcing his flashlight beam expertly, his strides long and sure. He had no particular destination in mind; he purposefully emptied his mind of as much as he could and waited to be drawn by some small signal. Dor did not believe in the supernatural, in psychic energy or parapsychology or anything like that, but he acknowledged that there was a level at which events eluded the senses that he, a human, possessed. On top of that, he believed that God, the One who seemed to have turned away from this ravaged planet, kept an inattentive eye on His creation; He might return at any time.

Dor stayed on the sidewalks, passing landmarks he knew well. The moon was high and round and supplemented the light from his flashlight. There was the Laundromat with its hulking black shapes of washers and dryers silent and still through the broken windows. The Law Offices of Burris and Zieve, the sign curiously intact, gold letters inked on glass. The alley that led to a tiny restaurant where he had once taken a date, the finest restaurant in Silva, Spanish cuisine served on mismatched Limoges by pretty Portuguese sisters…they'd lit candles in iron holders in the alley and decorated it with pots of geraniums and ivy. His date had ordered flan; she'd also given wicked head. Dor didn't remember anything else about her. Now the alley was choked with dead leaves and roof shingles, shell casings and a crushed bicycle.

Dor looked away.

They kept the close-in streets clean—picking up trash every week or so—but the farther one got from the Box the more the streets resembled the world at large, deteriorating like the set of one of those old Westerns, a ghost town. Dor walked west on Brookside, aiming more or less toward the boat dealership at the corner of Third and Industry; once he got there he would turn right and make a wide loop back to the front of the Box, where he'd enter without bothering to scale the fence. He didn't care who knew he'd been out wandering, as long as they didn't follow. The whole walk would take about forty-five minutes and might settle him enough to sleep, if he was lucky. On another night, he might have taken one of his private stash of Nembutals, if it got especially bad. But with what lay ahead he needed to keep his thoughts clear.

A sound off to his right put him instantly on alert. His gun was in hand in seconds, his feet planted and ready to run. It was true that most people didn't stand a chance in the face of Beaters' pursuit, but Dor wasn't most people…most people didn't train with an army sniper and members of the Coast Guard, the highway patrol and the Norteños. Dor had survived more attacks than he could count on one hand, and he refused to stop his nighttime wandering even with the knowledge that nests lay hidden every few blocks. Beaters usually stayed put at night, their vision compromised by their malfunctioning irises, which let in only a tiny amount of light; they spent the dark hours piled and entwined in their nests of fetid rags, four and five of them at a time shuddering and moaning in their sleep, writhing and slapping at each other as their fevered minds dreamed their horrific dreams.

This sound, as he stood still as stone and listened, was not a Beater's sound. They whistled and snuffled and moaned and cried, but this was more shrill, almost a cawing. Dor walked toward it silently, a trick he'd mastered.

Around a corner past the old doughnut shop the sounds

grew louder and there, in the tiled entrance of an accountant's office, was a jerking mass of ink-black shapes. A Beater nest. And those were bodies, two of them—that was a foot there, and another, one naked and the other still wearing a boot. There was little flesh on a foot and sometimes a Beater would not bother picking it clean if it was sated. It would leave the body in the nest after tearing the flesh from the poor person's back and buttocks and arms, the soft skin of the stomach and thighs, until later, until it was hungry again. Then, it might return to chew the tougher and leaner bits from the wrists and the face and ankles.

That's what had happened here, Dor figured, to the pair of travelers who'd made it almost to the Box. They'd been felled in their last mile by a band of the monsters who'd dragged them to their nest and then, for reasons unknown, left them there half-ravaged while they went back out into the night.

He looked closer, squinting at the shuddering pile. There, crowding the bodies and feasting on the organs, were birds like nothing Dor had ever seen, enormous black carrion birds resembling freakish outsized crows, wings quivering and flapping in ecstasy as they feasted.

Dor watched in silence and queasy astonishment. He had seen a few varieties of birds around the Box, but nothing like this. There were people who greeted the arrival of every newly returned species with celebration. Cass was like that with her plants, and Smoke and the others took delight in bringing her seedlings and roots for her gardens, or packets of seed raided from hardware stores. Word of any animal sightings spread quickly; in the past month alone people had found small striped snakes and potato bugs and lizards, and there were even rumors of a dog who'd made a few appearances at the edge of town, skittish and scared.

But these birds had to be two feet long. Their folded black wings would be as wide as a woman's outstretched arms. And they were hungry. He watched one tug at an intestine, unspooling a grisly length as it stepped backward and then the others fell upon the strand and ate.

Dor picked up a stone from the street and threw it, his aim sure and deadly. The stone struck one of the birds' heads and it fell over, its wings and claws drawn up in death. The others squawked furiously and skittered backward, flapping and jumping, one or two flying up to the second floor windows.

In the inadequate light of the moon and stars, Dor could not see much of the scene before him. He shone his flashlight beam on the bodies and wished he hadn't.

Dor had seen even more than most. He'd trained himself never to look away, to remain dispassionate in the face of horror and ruin. He'd been a baggerman, loading bodies on trucks when there was still gas to be had; he'd joined the crew that stacked and burned the dead. By then he'd moved out of the Silva house and into a friend's vacant cabin up in Sykes, and there were no more client accounts to play with and no reliable power for his laptop, and he needed to find a way to stay busy. When they quit collecting the dead, he was among the first raiding parties, the ones who brought supplies to hospitals and nursing homes, until the hospitals and nursing homes were nothing but mausoleums themselves.

He'd waited too long. He should have gone back to Silva while he still could, but in their last phone conversation, Jessica had told him to stay away. "Sammi's already lost you once," Jessica said. "She can't lose you again. I'm telling her you'll stay there, where you're safe. Don't make a liar out of me, Doran. Please."

He'd listened to Jessica and stayed. He threw himself into

helping anyone in Sykes who asked, and when the weak and vulnerable had finally all died and there was nowhere else to volunteer, he set out for San Pedro, where he'd heard about a cult taking up residence in the Miners stadium. By then he'd already decided to become a trader. He talked a guy named Nolan from an A-frame down the road into coming with him, and they loaded down a shopping cart with loot from a dozen empty cabins, liquor and candy bars and sanitary pads and antifreeze and boxes of Band-Aids. They pushed the cart the few miles to Sykes in the middle of the night, a flashlight wired to the front of the cart, though they never switched it on, preferring to take their chances in the dark. Nolan had served in the Gulf, and he knew a few tricks for sheltering, which came in handy when they got to San Pedro and spent their first few nights in a little stucco house before they found the empty lot that would become the Box. Dor still thought of Nolan every time he passed that little house.

The house where he'd come back from the creek carrying a bucket of water one morning shortly after they'd arrived and found nothing left of Nolan but the piss stain on the side of the wall where the Beaters had found him.

That was a devastating sight, worse in some ways than the many dead he later saw during scavenging missions, desiccated skeletons lying in beds and slumped at tables and many, many who still hung where they'd rigged their own death ropes. He'd found the bodies of children in their mothers' arms with holes in their skulls, and he'd smelled every taint of rot, of bodies trapped in cars and flooded basements and burned buildings. But he'd gotten through it.

He'd seen what the Beaters did, and euthanized a dozen victims who'd been unlucky enough to live through an attack. He steeled himself, and he shot them with a steady hand and a merciful heart and still was able to eat and sleep and make love afterward.

But now he looked upon two travelers who'd made it within a few blocks of safety only to be ravaged not once but twice, the remains abandoned by the Beaters only to be fought over by a species God or Nature had been careless or indifferent enough to allow to return, and Dor wondered if the balance had finally tipped to the other side, if all their work and vigilance and will to live would mean nothing, in the end, if each day or week would bring a new horror from the skies and the water and the land, and he would die as all the others had, without his daughter, without anything, and Dor turned and vomited on the street and the birds returned to their meal of carrion.

11

CASS DRESSED RUTHIE IN RED OVERALLS MEANT
for a boy, with a truck appliquéd on the front. Underneath,
two shirts. Over them, a parka with a soft band of fake fur
edging the hood. Mittens on a cord looped through the jacket's sleeves, and her too-tight boots were pulled on over long
socks. Ruthie was too hot, but the pack was full to bursting
with clothes and supplies and there was no room to stuff
anything more inside.

Dor came for them in the first light of morning, before
Cass expected him and she was glad, because she left the tent
without having time to look around one last time. The pack
on her shoulders was heavy but she was strong, her work in
the garden turning her shoulders and arms sinewy and sun-
brown, and though it was a poor substitute for the long runs
through the foothills she'd once loved, she ran around the
perimeter of the Box in the early morning when almost no
one else was awake.

She was as fit as she had ever been—sober for nearly a year, her body free of any trace of the alcohol with which she had punished herself for so long. The kaysev diet seemed to do her good. The natural immunity that was the disease's legacy kept her eyes and sinuses clear and her digestion regular. Her hair continued to grow at an astounding rate, and her nails were strong and hard and had to be trimmed constantly. Ruthie, too, was thriving, despite her silence—she'd grown an inch according to the pencil line Cass had drawn at the start of October on the bookshelf, and her molars had come in. Despite the occasionally restless night, Ruthie ate well and played energetically and these days she smiled more than she frowned.

When the curtains over the door lifted and Dor stood in the doorway silhouetted against the pale light of dawn, Cass stood, ready to go. Ruthie stared up at Dor with her usual frank appraisal. Despite the cold, Dor was dressed only in a flannel shirt over a T-shirt, and he held his parka over his arm. He had not cut his hair since Cass had first seen him, and it had grown in streaked with gray among the black and now it grazed his shoulders, the ends ragged and wet from his shower. The half dozen silver loops piercing the cartilage of his ears glinted in the light of her Coleman lantern, the use of which—with its hoarded batteries—was a special-day indulgence.

"Show me your blade," Dor commanded in a voice rusty from sleep, regarding her with an expression that suggested he was still making his mind up about the wisdom of bringing her along.

Cass's hand went automatically to her belt, which concealed a Bowen narrow double-edged blade. It too had been a gift from Smoke, traded for in a good-natured bidding war with a few of the guards. She held it out by the silver handle, its smooth curve familiar in her hand.

Dor nodded. "That will do."

Cass replaced it. "What if it hadn't?" she asked. "What if you didn't like it?"

Dor bent on one knee, and she couldn't read his expression. He held out a hand to Ruthie, and to Cass's surprise, her daughter slipped her hand into his and followed him from the tent.

"I would have given you mine."

Joaquin, the early-shift guard, mumbled a sleepy greeting and opened the gate for Dor, looking at Cass and Ruthie curiously but asking no questions. They'd encountered no one else on the walk from Cass's tent, though she knew that outside the Box two more guards patrolled, on the lookout for Beaters roused by the dawn's light. Somewhere in the cheap cots that lined the front wall, someone moaned in their sleep, visited by some terror or regret as the buzz from the night before wore off. Elsewhere someone coughed. These were sounds one grew used to, living in quarters as close as these.

Cass had not spent a night outside the Box since escaping from the Convent with Ruthie. She stared up at the darkened stadium across the street, a string of Christmas lights drooping from the upper tier the only illumination other than a faint glow from within. Somewhere inside, in the skyboxes where the highest members of the Order lived, Mother Cora slept the sound sleep of the devout, of someone confident that there was not only a higher power but a plan in which she played a vital role. Even her disastrous mistakes could not shake her convictions: Mother Cora had been wrong about the Beaters. She had been convinced they could be healed by prayer, a theological misjudgment that came with a very high price.

Convent trade with the Box had been sharply curtailed since Cass left, with only a few furtive exchanges for cigarettes and the occasional cheap bottle of home brew. No new acolytes had been accepted; hopeful travelers were turned away at the heavily guarded and shuttered entrance—and no one had left—or been allowed to leave. Dor seemed indifferent; he had no special contempt for the Order, but he didn't seem inclined to worry about their future, either, and his employees took their cues from him in this as in so many other things.

Cass turned away from the stadium; there was nothing there to mourn or miss. The flame of zealotry had burned out, and presumably their only prayer now was survival, as it was everywhere.

"How far?"

"Corner of Third and Dubost. Think she'll let me carry her?"

Cass had been about to pick Ruthie up herself when Dor swung her daughter up and over his head, resting her over his shoulders as though she weighed nothing. Ruthie's eyes widened with surprise and she dug her fingers into Dor's hair, holding on tightly. Dor winced but didn't complain, even as she pulled tighter.

Ruthie looked for a moment as though she might cry, but she set her mouth in a tight line and no sound escaped her. Dor walked slowly, taking care not to bounce her and after a moment she relaxed. She watched the scenery go by, her head turning this way and that, and Cass remembered that Ruthie had seen very little of the world outside. Once she relaxed and stopped gripping his hair so tightly, Dor closed his big hands around her chubby calves and moved a little faster.

Cass tried not to stare at them. Smoke, who had no children of his own, no nieces or nephews, who had lived a businessman's life of motels and airports and restaurant meals, had been finding his way slowly around Ruthie. Cass knew that he cared about her daughter, but he treated Ruthie with great care as though she was fragile, as though he would inadvertently, permanently damage her. He never carried her, though he would wait patiently for her when they walked through the Box. He played with her, setting up elaborate stage sets with the many toys the raiders brought back for her, but he never roughhoused. There was something about Ruthie's silence that made him treat her with exaggerated care, as though muteness was evidence of delicacy or a tendency to injury, and when they played together he chose her Playmobil characters or crayons or board books. Ruthie never seemed to mind. She had become a serious child who did not seem to miss running and tumbling and climbing trees.

But Dor handled her differently. Dor did not treat her as if she were breakable; he was easy with her. Of course, he had experience. Sammi had been little once.

Cass tried to imagine Dor with Sammi, long ago. She guessed he was far from a perfect father, given his brooding intensity, the long hours he now spent locked in his trailer and his need for seclusion. But he was more than she had ever been able to provide for Ruthie, who could never know her father because Cass had no idea who he was. Just one of the many drunk-blurred strangers from one of the stumble-home nights of those dark days. Not father material—certainly not father material; he wasn't even real to Cass, who knew intellectually that he probably wasn't even alive anymore, and couldn't bring herself to care.

She wondered what Dor had been like back then, when

Sammi was little. The tattoos, the earrings, the hardcore training regimen that left him hard-muscled and lean—these were all things acquired Aftertime, as was his facility with weapons and combat. That much she knew from Smoke. But from watching him she had learned more: he adapted to his surroundings with ease, if not passion. He was sensitive to the smallest changes in supply, in demand. He applied this to the commerce of human temperament as well as to goods and services. Running the Box required nimble reflexes, unflinching readiness, cruel precision. Shows of strength and, occasionally, violence.

Before, Dor had made his living on the internet and Cass wondered if Dor had once looked like every other Silicon Valley bean shuffler, soft in the middle and pale from too many indoor hours. It wasn't an image easily reconciled with the man she walked beside now.

After a couple of blocks Cass saw a light ahead, a flashlight casting a cone of dirty yellow onto the pavement. When they drew closer she saw that it was Joe, Smoke's sparring partner, and that behind him was a Jeep Wrangler, canvas missing, roll bars rusty. It was far from new and it was not clean, and it had a long dent creasing the driver's side, but it had not been there the last time Cass passed this street corner and she knew it was to be their ride to Colima.

A car. She drew a little closer to Dor, her boots crushing gravel. When was the last time she'd ridden in a car? Smoke and she had taken a motorcycle the forty miles from Silva to San Pedro, but before that it had been since the Siege. Even before the holiday biostrikes, riots had broken out in cities all across America; driving anywhere close to the center of towns, or past utilities or government buildings had been a calculated risk. The last of the long-haul truckers to attempt their routes found themselves hijacked by the desperate, organized highway pirates and sometimes just by bands of suburban dads made bold by their numbers and their children's complaints of hunger. So the long-haul truckers became hoarders. Schools had mostly closed before then anyway; there were no soccer games for the soccer moms to drive to. Store shelves were sparse; bands stopped touring; movie theaters had nothing new to show and mall parking lots were empty.

Once buildings started burning, and the bodies of unlucky elected officials were found nailed to city halls and hung from highway overpasses, the network of roads and highways was stricken with the kind of chaos it was impossible to recover from. Some tried to flee the cities; others packed everything they could into their cars and tried to get to urban centers, where they figured the food stores would be distributed by... *someone.* The result was gridlock, accidents, blocked roads; gas stations ran out of fuel; drivers shot each other; cars were jacked by roving bands of teenagers. Things stopped moving.

"No car seat," Dor said, swinging Ruthie to the ground. "Sorry." He took off his pack, opened the passenger door and set it on the floor under the backseat, then held out his hand for Cass's. She handed it over and circled the Jeep, peering into the cargo area.

There was a cardboard box, labeled Dole Certified Organic Bananas, butting up against six one-gallon jugs filled with water and three two-gallon drums. Probably gasoline. Inside the box were plastic bags of food: roasted kaysev beans and hard cakes, cold fried rabbit, fringe-topped celery root from her own garden, harvested before its time and nestled in rags. She felt her face grow warm; Dor must have picked it in the predawn hours; it was undisturbed the day before when she made a last check on the garden.

She crouched low to speak to Ruthie. "We're going to ride with Dor in this car." She smoothed a curl of hair off Ruthie's forehead. "I don't know if you remember about riding in cars."

Ruthie nodded, her expression careful. Cass had owned a small white Toyota so old that the finish had gone dull, but she had made sure that Ruthie's car seat was settled and strapped firmly into place everywhere they went. Mim and Byrn favored heavy American sedans in dark colors. These were the cars that Ruthie had ridden in Before.

"This is a Jeep," Cass said. "It's a little different. The roof is off so you can...so we can feel the wind as we drive. But it's very safe. Dor is going to drive us very safely."

Ruthie put a hand on the handle of the door.

"You're ready to go?"

Ruthie nodded solemnly and when Cass opened the door for her, she scrambled up into the backseat. She found the seat belt and tugged at it, holding out the buckle for Cass, who stretched it across her tiny body and fastened it.

"Don't worry," Dor said, as they got into the front. Cass buckled her own seat belt, the motion so familiar and yet so strange now. The interior of the Jeep was stark, the cover ripped off the glove box, the steering wheel wrapped in duct tape. The radio was missing, too, leaving a gaping hole in the console. The Jeep had undoubtedly been chosen because it was rugged and would perform well off road, but it was short on comforts.

Joe, who had been standing nearby and watching with arms crossed over his chest, raised his hand in a small salute. "See you in a couple of days."

"Right." Dor turned the key and the Jeep coughed into life, the acrid smell of doctored gas wafting through the air.

Almost since the moment kaysev appeared, people had been making ethanol out of it, and it had become common for those who had any gasoline at all to cut it with the home-brewed stuff. It smelled noxious and didn't often work, but after a few hiccups the Jeep started moving, slowly at first as they left the Box and the stadium and then all of Silva behind and then it was almost like driving Before.

Cass twisted in her seat to make sure that Ruthie was secure in her seat belt and saw the ghost of a smile on her lips as she played with a Top Dog sticker stuck inside a rear window. Then, leaning back in the passenger seat and closing her eyes, she felt the road rumble under their wheels and the air rush past her face and after a while she let herself pretend she was sixteen again, riding in her friend Taylor's car with the top down. And they were headed back from a concert in Stockton late at night, pleasantly high and sleepy and still believing that there was no way every year ahead wouldn't be better than the one before.

12

THEY'D DRIVEN ONLY HALF AN HOUR OR SO, Dor taking it slow, when he cursed softly under his breath. Cass's eyes flew open and she saw the dawn was breaking, a pale pink crack in the sky.

"What—"

"Shhh. Ruthie's sleeping," Dor murmured. Cass looked and Ruthie had indeed drifted off, slumped forward against the seat belt, her hair falling in her face. "It's just that there's a block up ahead."

Cass looked and sure enough, far ahead on the road, the car's headlights illuminated an SUV turned sideways and jammed up against a pair of smaller cars that had collided. On one side of the road the skeletons of pines shot up jagged against the murky sky; on the other side a cabin was set far back from the road down a dirt drive, the only building Cass could see in either direction.

"What road are we on?"

"Jack Born. It's the old canyon road from before they built the highway. Wanted to stay far clear of 161 and Matts Valley Road. The Rebuilders watch the bigger routes into Colima. I'd like to come into town with as little fanfare as possible."

"How do you know they aren't out here, too?"

Dor shook his head. "No. I send Joe down to Colima once a week or so to check. He's like the Box ambassador. He loads up on enough shit to keep them happy, takes 'em a crate or two of whatever we have too much of, call it a land tax. Nothing formal, just a handshake deal to keep them from coming knocking at our doors."

"What, like a bribe?"

Dor looked grim. "I don't know. You want to call it that, I guess that works. Price of doing business. It was also my way to keep from ever having to go face-to-face with them. Ever since I started the Box I figured I ought to keep a low profile, let someone else be the public face. Now I'm glad I did, because no one down there has any idea what I look like."

"So Joe drives this route?"

"No, never this far, anyway. He goes straight down 161, but while he's down there he takes a drive around the area a bit, checks out where they have people stationed. Joe's good, Cass…he won't tell me what he was in Santa Rita for, and I don't want to know, but he's smart and he's loyal. In fact, this is his Jeep."

Cass thought about Joe, a quiet, soft-spoken man with dark eyes and dark skin whose racial makeup was difficult to fathom. Joe had been teaching Smoke obscure Chinese martial art techniques, and though he was not a large or powerful-looking man, Smoke swore Joe could take him down any day of the week. Mostly, the man kept to himself. Cass saw him drinking at Rocket's sometimes, and once in a while he sat with Smoke for a round or two, rarely with anyone else.

"I didn't know."

Dor laughed without humor. "That's the point, sweetheart. Got to pick someone discreet. I mean, he finds an issue, we get it taken care of. No one's the wiser. We keep the roads into San Pedro cleared, we keep the Beaters relatively under control in the neighborhood, patrol it tight. And rumor gets around, the Box is the place to go for the good stuff. Joe makes sure it stays that way—get it?"

"So if there's, I don't know, a problem, a nest you overlooked…"

"Yeah, but it's more than that. Joe looks out for anything that tells a story," Dor said. "For instance. Lance and Nina? Came up here on that three-wheeler a while back?"

"What about them?" Cass tried to remember the few conversations they'd had, came up with nothing memorable. They'd traded the three-wheeler and the contents of Lance's father's gun cabinet and moved in.

"Told me about a bridge out a few miles out of San Pedro on the road into Tailorville. So I have Joe go and take a look. The bridge is out, yeah, just like they said. Now, that could be a problem for us. A perception problem, anyway."

It took Cass a moment and then she got it. "Because that's the only way into town. Anyone past there—"

"Sure as hell no one's driving in or out, and haven't for months. Place is dead. So Tailorville doesn't exist anymore," Dor confirmed. "Not in a way anyone wants to think about, anyway. So we have a little talk with Lance and Nina. Make it worth their while to keep quiet. And no one has to go to bed at night worried about a ghost town full of Beaters a couple miles up the road."

Spin control, Cass thought, amazed that such a concept could reroot so quickly after the cataclysms. She looked back at Ruthie. Maybe spin was the enduring human trait, allowing survival.

"Let me go first, okay? Just give me a minute and then I'll hook up the chains and we'll get this hauled. Cheap Chinese tin cans, shouldn't take long."

Cass watched him walk away, pistol in one hand, the other on his belt. Cass had seen his blade before, a wicked curve-handled hunting knife with a gut hook that he kept in a worn leather sheath.

Ruthie, stirring in the backseat, made a soft smacking sound with her lips, a holdover from when she was a baby and used to wake hungry for her bottle. It was a habit Cass loved, to watch when Ruthie was deep asleep, her soft lips working at nothing. But then Ruthie moaned softly and Cass's heart skipped in panic. In the gray morning light Ruthie's face looked flushed and nearly translucent, her fine hair splayed against the rough fabric of the backseat. She writhed against the seat belt and moaned again and then as Cass reached for her, her eyes flew open and she looked at nothing and said, *"Hat."*

Cass licked her dry lips and settled her hand on Ruthie's hot cheek, suddenly certain that Ruthie's word was a warning, a portent of the worst and most terrifying sort. As soon as Ruthie spoke, it was over and she collapsed back against the seat and slipped immediately back into sleep, her face serene, her outburst forgotten. But now it was Cass whose skin was clammy with fear.

She had no idea what "hat" meant. But as she looked from Ruthie to Dor, twenty feet off, making his cautious way to the wreck, unafraid yet suddenly so vulnerable, Cass wanted to stop him. Something was wrong, and Ruthie knew.

She couldn't leave Ruthie, defenseless and alone in the Jeep, could she?

But whatever threatened Dor, threatened them all.

Barely thinking about what she was doing, she threw open the door and stumbled out onto the pavement, screaming Dor's name. He turned to her in surprise and seemed to freeze as a figure flashed between the smashed-up cars and careened and rolled. There was a shot, loud on the still morning air, and Dor lurched sideways and Cass was sure he was hit until he rolled on the ground and came up in a crouch and returned fire, his aim steady and sure, and the figure jerked and seemed to rise up into the air before falling down sprawled at the edge of the wreck, his flung forearm spasming and fingers quivering.

Someone was yelling her name and Cass was running to Dor but he was doing an awkward crab-walk backward and he grabbed her hand and pulled her down with him and she thought *what if he's hit what if he's going to die* and *oh God he's going to leave me and Ruthie alone* and the panic in her heart was enough to move her to action.

She stood and seized his arm and tried to drag him to his feet, but he was stronger and he pulled her down on top of him and she felt her knee connect with his gut and she heard the sound he made. And still he clutched her and rolled on top of her and pushed her to the ground while he stood and she thought in despair *oh god don't let him die now let me go I have to help Ruthie* but he was screaming in her ear and she tried to understand but he was screaming, screaming—

"Stay here! I'll get her!"

When she finally understood, she stopped resisting and he

was up and sprinting back toward the wreck in seconds. *No, no,* she thought, *that one might not be the only one, that one lying still with its skull split on the pavement.* And then she realized that's why he'd run, and she ran after him, because if he failed then there was no hope for any of them.

Cass yanked at her gun and it was stuck in its holster, why hadn't she practiced this, she'd gone with Smoke to shoot a dozen times but she never thought it would be like this, her hands slick and shaking. But she had to do better she had to do this for Ruthie and then the gun was out, it was in her hand. There were only yards between her and the broken glass the twisted metal of the wreck, and her heart pumped with adrenaline and her legs flew and even so, somehow she had time to consider the cabin, not much of a cabin but someone's shelter nonetheless because—

Look there, from the chimney, a thin wisp of smoke drifted out
—they lived here, these squatters who lay in wait and watched for travelers coming down the road, they burrowed rodentlike into the wreck and came out only to kill and take their spoils. All of this flashed through Cass's mind as she ran, but Dor was already ducking behind the smashed sedan as there rose up the second, the one Ruthie foresaw, the one with a watch cap pulled low over a knobby head, ears protruding sharp smirk smirking he was wearing a red cap a red *hat* on his hateful greedy head and he sighted down the barrel and lined up the shot he thought he had time for, the anticipation brought him pleasure that vibrated through his trigger finger you could see the way he loved the gun loved the bullet but in the end he didn't get to shoot because Cass squeezed first and the bullet glanced off his arm and his shot went wild and then Dor stepped up and finished him off.

13

CASS HUDDLED IN THE BACKSEAT TREMBLING and shaking, Ruthie unbuckled and gathered in her arms. She wished the Jeep had locks and a roof and shatterproof glass. She wished it was made of steel, of concrete. She wished they had never come. She wished they were back in the Box, in their bed, watching the sky slowly turn blue up above them through the window flaps and who fucking cared about the rest.

Ruthie rubbed her face against Cass's shirt. Her skin was hot from sleep despite the chill of the morning air, and then she looked up with a question in her eyes. And Cass realized that once again it was not her place to wish but instead to make everything as right as she could.

"We just had to stop here for a minute, sweet pea," she said, shifting Ruthie in her arms so that she could not see the wreck in the road ahead. Or the corpse with the outflung broken bloody arm, or the other body, with a hat, slumped over the hood of a car as though trying to embrace it. "Dor went inside to get something and he'll be back in a minute and then we'll get going again."

She looked carefully at the roadside, the soft rocky shoulder, the kaysev drifts and the fallen limbs and branches. The Jeep was made for off-roading; a few stones or branches shouldn't jeopardize its axles or undercarriage or gas tank. They could survive being shaken up. Now she was grateful they'd taken this worn and uncomfortable vehicle and vowed not to mind the scratchy seat, the blowing wind and noise.

Ruthie sat up in her lap and stretched to see past Cass's shoulder, searching for Dor. Cass looked, too. The cabin was silent and foreboding, its porch railing listing and shattered, one window boarded with scrap wood. A pair of kitchen chairs sat on the uneven porch floor and it was all too easy to imagine the dead men sitting there waiting, watching, perhaps with binoculars to see down the relatively unobstructed stretch of road on which they'd approached. They'd been traveling down mountain, and the pines at this elevation were thin and sparse, and even before they died they would have provided little shade.

On the porch at the foot of the chairs were empty bottles, five or six of them, and Cass wondered if they were among the spoils of the last party to be trapped here. The men must have been thrilled to see the Jeep; there were so few vehicles on the road anymore. From time to time there was a motor-cycle, a bicycle—or something more rugged, like Lance and Nina's ATV. But full-on cars must have been rare indeed.

There—beyond the cabin, partially covered with a screen of tree limbs—she saw the junkyard of cars driven off the road and abandoned. Too many would have raised suspicion, would make a driver wonder what could have happened for so many to give up hope right here. The pile extended back several hundred feet, vehicles parked haphazardly. Lazily. It wouldn't have been that hard to drive them farther into the woods, a half a mile past the cabin, even a quarter mile, find a swale or a dip in the earth and leave them to rust and molder there for mice to nest in and birds to perch on and snakes to slither under.

Wait. A sound. A crack—oh God, another—were they loud enough to be gunshots? But what else could they be? But they didn't exactly sound right, not like the shooting practice that took place a couple mornings a week down near the Box, didn't sound—*sharp* enough, somehow, they were muffled, there was no echo. But what if Dor was hit? What if someone had been waiting for him and shot him—but if they were going to kill him wouldn't they have done it right away, the minute he came in the house? They could have been watching from the window, watching him walk toward the house, waiting for him on the other side of the door…

Cass peered anxiously at Ruthie's face, but her daughter's expression showed only puzzlement, maybe boredom, or sleepiness perhaps. She yawned and rested her face against Cass's chest and Cass thought, *That's it then, I can't leave her here alone to check it out,* and she wondered if she should just get in the front seat and turn the key in the ignition and *go.* Cass's heart was pounding so hard with fear that she was amazed Ruthie didn't mind. Would Ruthie fuss if Cass buckled her in the backseat and got out, even for a second? But what if Dor wasn't hit, what if he had done the shooting, or if he'd shot someone who shot him back—maybe he was hurt, right now, lying on the floor in agony—or maybe he wasn't even hurt that badly but he needed her help to get back out. She listened, as hard as she could, but there was nothing, just the skittering of a dead leaf now and then across the pavement.

Cass waited in an agony of indecision. She should settle Ruthie in and just make a run for it, thirty seconds tops, long enough to just see what had happened, nothing more. She didn't owe Dor anything beyond that, she reminded herself—he'd said as much, and he wouldn't want her to risk their safety if he was down. If he was *dead*—she made herself think the word.

But when she finally convinced herself to go, and tried to lift Ruthie off her lap, Ruthie wrapped her arms tight around Cass's neck and held on.

"Don't go," she whispered against Cass's skin, so softly Cass almost didn't hear it.

She froze. She settled Ruthie back onto her lap—slowly, carefully. She waited, but her daughter did not speak again. They held each other, and the leaves skittered and the wispy smoke curled out of the chimney and the dead men lay in their sticky puddles of blood. And Cass wondered if she had imagined her little girl's voice.

After what seemed like a long time, a figure came out onto the porch, and terror seized Cass as she realized she could not make it to the driver's seat in time now and she wondered if her indecision would be their death. But it was only Dor. He had a duffel bag in one hand, a plastic sack in the other, and as he approached the Jeep he gave Cass the skeleton of a smile.

He set the duffel in the back with the other things and got in the driver's side and set the plastic sack on the console between the seats and then he sat for a moment without speaking, staring forward and breathing deep. Ruthie relaxed, releasing Cass from the viselike embrace. Cass readjusted

Ruthie's seat belt and kissed her soft cheek, her fingers shaking as they traced the curve of her daughter's cheek.

Cass got out of the backseat, shut the door gently and opened the passenger door, feeling almost unbearably vulnerable outside the car. She could never be fearless when Ruthie was only a few feet away—but once she was inside again, she saw how shaken Dor looked. Cass knew then that the sounds were indeed gunshots, and that he had probably killed someone, maybe two people, and she didn't know how it felt to kill and wondered if she should offer comfort, if that was her role now, as well...but surely Dor had killed many more before and took his comfort from his own, unknowable sources. Her efforts would be awkward and unwelcome. Cass was a mother and she knew everything there was to know about her daughter, but she was not easy with other people. She observed from a distance, she read their emotions and divined their stories, but it was a strange truth that the ones she wanted most to know sometimes remained mysterious and remote.

But still.

"What...?" she said, not knowing how to ask.

"They'd laid in quite a few supplies," Dor said quietly. "Look, I didn't want to bounce Ruthie around if we didn't have to, but...hang on."

He started the car and it crept forward slowly, over the edge of the road onto the dirt, bumping and lurching. Ruthie shut her eyes, her small body absorbing the turbulent ride, Cass steadying her with a hand pressing her against the seat. They passed the wreck and Cass saw how still the bodies were, a bug of some sort flitting around the one on the ground with interest.

Then there was a sound, a stirring of the air, and a large black shape flapped past her face, only inches away, clumsy and fast and tumbling in the air, and settled on the body with a fluttering of its enormous, ragged ebony wings. The sound it made was not what you would expect from such a huge creature, it was a throat-rasping high-pitched frantic cry that split the air around Cass and she threw her arms over the seat, reaching for Ruthie whose mouth was open in a silent scream but her eyes were still shut tight *thank God* she still had her eyes shut because the next thing that happened, as Cass pressed her hands to her daughter's face and told her that *everything was going to be all right it was going to be just fine,* a second bird settled with a thrashing of feathers on the body of the hat-man on the car's hood and began to tear at his flesh with its large hooked beak. Cass knew she should look away but she did not. She watched the birds' frenzy, watched the body shudder and shake as it was molested and devoured, and then there were more, two more black flapping shapes flying in from places unknown and landing on the carcasses with joy and fury and hunger.

Soon the grisly scene was out of sight behind them. Cass kept watch out the back of the Jeep until they turned a curve in the road and the wreck disappeared and for a while she stared at the scrubby pine skeletons and red-dirt shoulders and crushed run-over pinecones in the road, all receding into the distance as Dor drove. Finally she realized she was pressing too hard on Ruthie's face and immediately she turned the touch into a caress, and she said, "It's all right now, Ruthie, you can open your eyes," and it was a moment before Ruthie did, blinking in the sun. "It's all right," Cass repeated.

"Look in the bag. There's a juice box," Dor said, and Cass took the plastic bag from between the seats and there were not only juice boxes, but Fig Newtons. Opening the packages took a while, Cass inhaling the near-forgotten scent while her shaking fingers worked clumsily, and though her mouth watered she did not take anything for herself. Dor also refused. She broke the cookies one by one, giving Ruthie the sticky halves. She held the sharp-pointed straw to Ruthie's lips and watch her drink and wondered if her daughter remembered drinking from such boxes Before, long ago, the juice dribbling down her inexpert mouth. She'd nearly mastered drinking from the straw right before the Family Services people came, her chubby hands holding the plasticized boxes with such care, her eyes widening with surprise every time the wiggling straw got away from her. Now she did fine, drinking deeply with an expression of wonder on her face. For months she'd had only the tea Cass made from her herb garden, and boiled and filtered water.

After a while, the cookies were gone and Cass cleaned Ruthie up as well as she could from the front seat and put the wrapper and empty box back in the plastic bag. It was heavy and she looked through the contents: half a dozen more packages of cookies, a large pouch of turkey jerky, several more juices. Two cans of beef broth and cans of corn, mushrooms and chili; pears and fruit cocktail and crushed pineapple.

"Wow," she said quietly.

"Best stuff's in back. Medicine, all kinds, I didn't have time to look through it. Over the counter and prescriptions—probably twenty of those. They had it all in one place, made it easy for me."

He was silent for a moment. "A couple of guns, too. They're in the back. And ammo. I thought about taking the ones off those guys…"

Cass shivered. She was glad Dor had not touched the bodies again.

"What were those things?" she whispered.

"I've seen them before, just one other time. They're…I guess they're like vultures. Carrion birds. They feed on the dead."

"I've never seen any bird like that."

"No, I know. I mean a vulture's large, bigger than most people think. But those…"

Cass thought about the great flapping wings, the lurching flight. There was nothing lovely about the birds. They looked damaged, malformed, sick—but they were also quick and determined and by the time the grisly scene had disappeared around the bend, the birds had managed to pierce and tear the bodies and their crowing beaks were covered in blood, testament to the strength of their jaws and talons.

"Where did you see one before?"

Dor looked indecisive, as though he wasn't sure that telling her was a good idea. "Yesterday. In town…in a nest. Looked like a recent Beater kill."

"Just one?"

"No, three. They must travel in flocks."

"But what does it mean that they showed up now? All this time, all these months…"

Dor shrugged. "I don't know. Maybe they've been here all along but we're just in the migration path now. Maybe they've, I don't know, evolved—but that takes centuries, yeah, hell, I don't know. New species? Eat a Beater kill, get that shit in the bloodstream, there's no telling what'll happen."

"Ruthie knew," Cass said quietly. "Yesterday. When she was napping. She said—I mean she was still asleep, she was talking in her sleep and she said, 'bird.'"

"I thought she didn't talk."

"She doesn't." Cass felt exasperation but it was as much for herself as for Dor; she was talking about Ruthie as though she was not sitting a few feet away. She doubted that Ruthie could hear their conversation over the wind rushing through the car, but still, it didn't feel right. "Not on purpose. But this was while she was sleeping. It was... I don't think she has any memory of it, like a nightmare."

"And she said *bird*. And you think that means the ones back there?"

"What else would it mean?"

"I don't know...anything. A memory, a book, a toy. A plastic fucking bathtub duck—"

"It's not the only thing she's said," Cass interrupted. "When you first got out of the car to see about the wreck? She didn't wake up, but she said 'hat.'"

"*Hat?* She said— What does that mean?"

"The second guy. He was wearing that red hat, that red wool hat on his head. He came out from behind the car after you shot the first guy and there it was."

Dor was silent for a moment, considering. "I would call that a cap. Not a hat."

"She's barely three. She doesn't know a lot of words. That's not the point."

"So you're saying she has...premonitions? That it? Of danger?"

"I don't know. I think...well, you know how I'm different, since I was attacked? How I heal faster, and my hair grows like crazy, and my fingernails. It's like everything is, I don't know. Like it's magnified somehow. So why couldn't it be like that for Ruthie? Except not just the physical part, but like... the sixth sense?"

"You believe in that shit?"

Cass colored. "I'm not saying I believe in, you know, psychics and all that. But haven't you ever just...*known* something? Something that there was no way you would know, or you know before it happens."

She sensed Dor's skepticism, but he remained silent.

"Well, I have. I think it's real. As real as anything else that's happened. And with Ruthie, it just started happening, yesterday and then again just now. She's seeing things, knowing things. I don't know if it's anything that's upsetting to her, or just scary images or…what."

Cass hated the idea of these dark ciphers visiting Ruthie as she slept, robbing her of what little peace she still had. Already she was a different little girl than the one she'd known before the zealots got her, more cautious, less exuberant, so that Cass's longing to rewind the intervening time was agonizing whenever she let herself think about what had changed. Would the nightmares take more of her joy away? Was it possible she'd misunderstood, that Ruthie's words had no connection to the things that were happening, and that Cass herself was just searching for a way for her little girl to take her place in the world again?

"Tell you what, don't get ahead of yourself," Dor said. "Like you said. She's just a little girl."

They rode in silence, the needle hovering well under thirty. Occasionally Dor drove off the road to get around an obstruction. Each wrecked and abandoned car they passed provoked a new sensation of dread, a catch of the breath amid a frantic search for fleeting figures hiding in backseats and crouching behind bumpers…but they were just wrecks, sun-heated and disintegrating, staged tableaus of twisted, rusting metal and smashed glass.

At last they reached the bottom of the long descent from the mountains, the scrub pine thinning to clusters of bent and knobby oaks in the foothills, then shrub-pocked swells and finally flat fields of dormant kaysev with the occasional weedy star thistle or tocalote poking through. Ahead stretched the road, straight and shimmering in the afternoon sun. Dor pulled off in a field so they could share some jerky and dried apricots and a bottle of water, take a bathroom break and stretch. He had planned for a two-day trip; even though he went a little faster on the straightaways, there were occasional wrecks to be cleared and obstacles to drive around, and their progress was slow.

Taking Ruthie a dozen yards from the Jeep so they could pee, Cass realized she felt more exposed from Dor's proximity than from the danger of being out in the open. During her days of wandering, when her disorientation slowly sloughed off like a snake's skin as she made her way back to civilization, she had urinated in the open and on logs with practically no self-consciousness at all. She'd been filthy, smelling like an animal, her hair knotted and her nails broken; she ate wads of kaysev leaves and wiped her mouth on her arm. Cass wasn't sure what she had been then, but it was something both more and less than human. Now she turned her back toward the Jeep, felt her skin burn with embarrassment when she pulled her pants down and finished as quickly as she could.

After that, their drive resumed, as did the silence. There were no Beaters, but near a cattle ranch whose grazing land grew thick with kaysev, they saw a chilling sight: a motorcycle overturned at the side of the road, and next to it two bodies, obviously Beater victims. They'd been there for a while, long enough for scavengers—perhaps the monstrous black birds—to pick the bones nearly clean. The bodies lay face up, their pants around their ankles, their shirts and underclothes ripped and abandoned nearby.

The Beaters had probably nested in the nearby ranch house

or outbuildings. How they'd managed to waylay these travelers was anyone's guess, but that they'd feasted here, rather
than carrying the bodies back to their nest, was surprising.
Early in their evolution, when the first fever victims passed
through the skin-picking phase, after they'd pulled the hair
from their own scalps and chewed the flesh of their own arms
and moved on to craving the living flesh of other bodies, they
were largely inept. They attacked alone, fighting each other
for victims, and feasted upon the bodies where they fell, nearly
maddened by their hunger for flesh. It had been much easier,
then, for bystanders to drag the Beaters off the victims, shooting or beating them, though in nearly every case the victim
was already infected by saliva. Citizens eventually learned that
once someone was attacked the best course for all involved
was a quick and humane shot to the head.

The Beaters also learned. By early summer they were band-
ing together in small groups and dragging their prey away so
they could feast in peace. Soon after that, they started sheltering together, and it wasn't long before they learned to seek out
locations where they were hidden from passersby but could
get out quickly to attack; they favored storefronts and other
buildings where the glass had shattered, where there was a
single way in and out.

Get enough armed people together and you could over-
whelm and destroy a nest of even several dozen Beaters. But
few were willing to risk up-close contact since the disease
was saliva-borne, meaning that not only bites but spit in an
eye or wound could also infect. A simple gunshot or blow to
the head was not a reliable means of debilitating them in the
short term: though they might eventually collapse and die,
their attenuated strength and surging adrenaline meant that
rage would propel them forward for some brutal minutes yet.

And everyone feared inciting a swarm of the cracked, bloody things.

It was these memories—this new common knowledge— that flitted through Cass's mind, even as she tried to doze, her arm slung over the back of the seat so that she could hold Ruthie's warm hand. She tried concentrating on the passing scenery, but her mind kept going back to the terrible days after everything fell apart and the survivors began to realize that no one was going to come and make things right. It had been worse, then, when it was still possible to forget occasionally—when you'd wake up and, for a moment, imagine you smelled coffee or that you heard the rumble of the recycling truck and the shouts of children on the way to school.

It had been a long time since the waking nightmare gave her even a day of peace. Traveling with a man who despised her, headed away from the trouble she knew and toward the trouble she didn't—that was not likely to change.

When the sun slipped down to touch the mountains behind them, Dor finally spoke. "We're more than halfway. Somewhere short of Glover, I think, but I don't want to get too close to town. Hopefully all the local critters are already on the move."

"You mean you think they've all gone toward the towns?"

"That, or heading south…if that's really happening." He sounded doubtful. The day had been warm, and Cass herself wondered if the cold nights alone would be enough to stir the Beaters' instincts, if indeed self-preservation spurred them to find a better climate. Even the coldest days in California's central valley rarely got below freezing, hardly a threat if they managed to take even a few simple measures to stay warm. What was to prevent the Beaters from burrowing into their nests together to share body heat and deciding that was enough?

When they saw a ranch house set up on a gentle slope a half mile away, Dor turned down the drive. He drove slowly, tires crunching against the gravel, and as they got closer Cass saw the swing still suspended from the branches of an old oak in the front yard, the hand-painted sign in the shape of a tractor that read The Vosses. Dor parked on the concrete pad near the garage and told her to stay put while he checked around. Cass tensed at the thought of being alone with Ruthie, even for a moment, but there was nothing for it. She took her blade from her belt, and made Ruthie lie down in the backseat so that she would be invisible to anyone approaching the car.

But all around them were treeless fields, save for the oak and a stand of what must have been some sort of ornamental specimen—magnolia, perhaps—leafless and barren, and a pair of old fruit trees which were covered, incongruously for the season, with pale green shoots. That captured Cass's attention for a second and she had a vague thought that if they lived until morning, she would have to come outside and examine them.

They were surrounded by grazing fields. Cattle ranches dotted the Sierra foothills on the other side, west of the mountains, when she had grown up. Stock herds of cows grazed their way on a rotation of the fields, gentle skittish beasts that produced new crops of calves every summer for Cass to admire on her runs out into the country. Now there was no evidence of the animals. They'd been felled early in the bio-terror attacks—second only to pigs—so many and so quickly that troops had been diverted and later conscripted to haul and torch the carcasses. There were huge burn sites through-out California: smoke hung over the huge feedlot operations

along I-5 for weeks as the meat burned. The barking of the
dogs over the smell was never-ending. Until, eventually, it
was truckloads of dogs and deer that joined the cattle—and,
finally, the two-legged dead.

After a tense few minutes Dor was back, coming through
the garage door which he had hauled up by hand.

"Drive it in here," he called, and Cass slid awkwardly over
the console to the driver's seat. She turned the key in the ignition, a strange sensation after such a long time, and put her
foot on the gas pedal. She checked the gauge: three-quarters
full. Drove slowly up into the garage and turned it off again,
Dor already pulling the steel door back down. The garage
smelled slightly of rot, though it wasn't overwhelming. Dor
had his flashlight on, and while Cass unbuckled Ruthie from
the back, he got a few things from the cargo area.

Inside, the house was cold but surprisingly tidy. The garage opened onto a kitchen whose cabinets hung open and
empty—raiders had been here. A few Splenda packets spilled
onto the counter and there were bottles of soy sauce and
vinegar, sticky and nearly empty, but otherwise the food was
all gone. Dishes were still stacked neatly, coffee cups hung
from hooks and good crystal goblets were lined up with care
on a bed of paper toweling. The rot smell was stronger at
the refrigerator but there was nothing to be done about that;
everyone knew never to crack a refrigerator door anymore.
Someday nothing would remain inside but dried-up crumbs,
but until then the fear of refrigerators was up there with basement doors.

Dor set the supplies down on the kitchen table: a bottle
of water, a tight-wrapped square of spongy kaysev curd, a
Tupperware container of almonds. One of the cans of fruit
cocktail from the farmhouse. As he went systematically

through the drawers and lower cabinets, an unshakable habit for anyone who'd served on a raiding party, Cass and Ruthie wandered through the house.

In the den an enormous television took up most of one wall; shelves on either side held houseplants that had dried to husks long ago, as well as trophies and photos in frames. Cass turned on her own hand-crank flashlight and saw that the trophies were from an adult softball league and most of the photographs were of several towheaded children. Grand-children, Cass guessed. This didn't feel like a house where little ones had lived. There were no toys on the floor, no high chairs in the kitchen.

There was a plaid sofa with knitted afghans folded neatly over the arms, a basket on the coffee table filled with skeins of blue and white yarn. A newspaper, neatly refolded, with a coffee cup skimmed with mold on top.

The living room was comfortable and ordinary, but Cass noticed that one of the armchairs had been dragged down the hall to block the last door. A raiders's trick: when they found something too awful to abide looking, they blocked doors with furniture, a simple courtesy to those who came after. But the drag marks on the carpet were fresh—it was Dor, then, who was trying to protect her and Ruthie.

"We can use the guest bedroom tonight," Dor said. "First door on the right. Bathroom's on the left."

Cass glanced back at the chair blocking what was apparently the master bedroom door, wondering what Dor was shield-ing her from seeing. It could be any of half a dozen familiar scenarios. The couple who lived here might have overdosed in their bed, that was the favorite for anyone who'd had the foresight to stockpile medication. Or the husband might have shot the wife and then turned the gun on himself. For those with no gun or drugs, things were messier; most people did a poor job of cutting their own wrists and took forever to die, leaving their beds soaked a bright red that slowly dried to dirt brown and earthen black if you found them much later.

There were other ways, and Cass knew she hadn't seen them all. Perhaps Dor had seen more. Perhaps he'd seen enough that the horror in the bedroom didn't bother him, but she doubted it.

"DON'T GO PAST THE CHAIR," SHE SAID GENTLY
to Ruthie, and Ruthie nodded solemnly, never letting go of
Cass's hand. "We'll see what this room is like, okay?" The
guest room was blessedly unexceptional. They were not the
first to squat here; the linens had been stripped from the bed,
though a few pillows and a puffy comforter had been left
behind. The mattress was fairly clean and Cass spread out a
few towels she found in the bathroom. The closet had been
gone through, as well; anything useful, like coats and synthetic tops and pants had been taken, leaving wool skirts and
ruffled blouses and tailored jackets, the off-season wardrobe
of a churchgoing woman in her sixties. On the shelf above the
clothing were photo boxes with neat labels: Family Christmas
2010–2013. Caymans Summer '14. Jeanelle, Grades 1-5. The
lady of the house had been old-fashioned, still printing copies
of photos on reacetate; Cass hoped her memories brought the
woman some comfort at the end, long after most people had

lost all their photos with the blink of computers turning off for the last time.

They ate by the light of a candle that Dor found in one of the drawers and afterward Cass read to Ruthie from an old issue of *Redbook* she found in the den. Ruthie loved recipes with their pictures of dishes that could never again be prepared, and Cass had built a small collection of cookbooks back in their tent in the Box. She turned the pages to an article about berry desserts and read about the strawberry shortcakes and blueberry pie and raspberry-peach cobbler, and Ruthie traced her fingertip over the glossy mounds of whipped cream and the buttery crumbs in wonder.

"Do you remember Mim's pies?" Cass asked, a lump in her throat catching her off guard. The one thing Mim did better than anyone else, a thrilling exception to her indifference to housekeeping and even the general inadequacy of her mothering, was pies. Her pastry crust was the flakiest and most tender anywhere. Cass's favorite had been her key lime, and once a year on Cass's birthday Mim would grate the limes and squeeze them by hand and separate the eggs and flute the edges of the crust and set the pies out on the counter to cool and every year they were the most delicious thing Cass had ever tasted, right up until the year Byrn moved in and Mim forgot Cass's birthday entirely.

But Ruthie only nodded solemnly. It wasn't Cass's habit to ask her daughter about the time she spent with Mim and Byrn, who had convinced the state people to forcibly remove Ruthie from Cass's trailer when she relapsed. Those were days of shame and agony as she fought her way back to sobriety again, the hardest thing she had ever done.

"Did you like the apples?" Cass asked, forcing a smile, trying to cover up the tremor in her voice and hating that the old memories could still hurt so much. "With cinnamon and nutmeg?"

More nodding. After a few more recipe images, Cass gathered Ruthie into a hug and set the magazine aside and carried her to bed, tucking her under the puffy comforter. Ruthie held on to her hand tightly, but it wasn't more than a couple of minutes before she was asleep, and Cass kissed her forehead and went back out into the living room.

Dor had cleared the remains of their meal and was stretched out on the sofa reading an old issue of *Forbes,* his long legs crossed in front of him, a pair of reading glasses on his nose. The sight made her smile—this was a different man, a far more vulnerable man, from the one who brooded in the solitary apartment as the sun set on the Box. But Dor caught her looking, and yanked off his glasses and stuffed them in a pocket.

"I put water out back," he said. "Your toothbrush and stuff's there, too."

Cass took her time, skimping on the toothpaste to make it last and brushing out her hair, slathering the lanolin on her lips as well as she could and rubbing it into her hands. The smell wasn't great but the California winter was dry and her skin was thirsty. She shivered in the cold, dampening a rag with the water Dor had left for her and rubbing it all over her face, feeling the grit from the open-air journey digging into her skin. She squatted around the corner to urinate, scanning the black road for movement, even in the silence of night unable to shake the feeling that things were lurking out in the fields, on the road. Waiting. She knew this was why they'd put the Jeep in the garage and drawn the drapes before lighting the candle: anyone—Beater or citizen—who passed by here would see nothing out of the ordinary. There wasn't another

building for half a mile; the odds of Beaters or squatters anywhere near were practically nonexistent.

Inside Dor wrinkled his nose. "You smell like a sheep
shearer."

Cass smiled. "You should be so lucky—that would mean
there were sheep left, and we could make them into mutton
burgers."

"I never liked mutton."

"Bet you would now."

"I suppose I would." Dor nodded. "Nice big slab with
American cheese melted all over it, one of those sesame seed
buns, some iceberg lettuce and a big slice of tomato."

"Stop it. That's obscene," Cass said. "But maybe some
fries—"

"Fresh cut, with the skin still on 'em."

"I like the ones that get stuck in the fry basket and go
through twice—you know, extra crispy, almost burned?"

"Nice. Here, come sit where I've got it warmed up."

Cass hesitated. The sofa was a short one, almost a love seat,
and there was barely room for her to sit next to Dor without
touching. He'd unfolded the afghans and spread them over his
lap, and he held up the ends, and it looked warm and inviting.

"I was just going to go to bed with Ruthie. You don't
mind…?"

"The couch? No. I mean, I don't fit on the couch but
the floor's fine. I've slept on worse. But seriously, come sit a
minute—I'm not tired yet."

Cass went to sit beside him.

She'd seen the interior of his trailer. It was crammed full,
his desk and a couple of chairs sharing the space with file cabinets and a printer stand, power cords snaking out the window.
There was too much furniture even before Dor moved his cot

in: bookshelves and an old-fashioned wooden coat rack and a basin with a china sink that was rigged to drain through a pipe in the floor onto the gravel yard below. There was a space heater, but Cass didn't think Dor ever used it. A shaving mirror hung on a nail.

Dor also had a tent, one as large as the one she shared with Smoke, and she knew from interrogating Smoke that it was there that Dor kept his clothes and even more books and his tools and collection of sports equipment: two sets of golf clubs, lacrosse sticks, and a couple of soccer balls. He changed clothes in his tent and showered in the communal showers. But at some point during the summer, he had begun sleeping in the trailer, and Cass didn't know why. The cot wasn't even one of the nice ones; it was FEMA surplus, like the ones near the front of the Box, the ones reserved for drunks and people who had nothing left to trade.

It was a lot to leave behind—but Cass knew that possessions meant little to Dor. He might spend his days overseeing a center of commerce, but in the end it was the trading, not what was traded, that mattered to him. And with Sammi in danger, even that ceased to hold him. He'd left the Box behind with barely a thought, and deep down Cass knew he would not return there. If they survived this adventure, his restless spirit would propel him to the next new thing, another empire, another lonely world for him to oversee.

"Smoke will be back, you know," Dor said suddenly, as though reading her mind. "When he told you he'd be back, he meant it. The only thing that will stop him is if he gets killed."

"I *know* that. But what are the odds? It's just him against everyone, every Rebuilder out there from here down to Colima. It's hundreds of square miles. They're all going to be looking for him, and by the time he finds those guys they'll probably have gotten themselves killed some other way. But there will be more to take their place."

"Cass. You don't understand. I have more…information than you realize. People inside the Rebuilders who talk, for a price. About where they go. Their routes, their plans. Smoke knows all of this, and he'll be able to find the ones he's looking for. They're not just raiding randomly, you know."

"So, great, so he'll find the guys who set the school on fire—he's still outgunned."

"Not necessarily, Cass. He's got the best weapons I could give him, enough ammo to do this ten times over and the element of surprise. Things go well, he'll take 'em out clean, get home before we do. Look, I don't take sides, but on this one I'm with Smoke and I've done everything I can to get him back safe."

"And you think you can trust your spies? What's to prevent them from turning around and double-crossing him? For all you know they're just waiting for him—"

"*Yeah,* Cass, there's a risk." Dor, usually unprovokable, cut her off angrily. "But you ought to know by now that I pay well."

"Fanatics don't care about—"

"These aren't fanatics. Just opportunists. Like me. People who recognize that there's not really much difference between the people on the outside of the gate and inside."

"*Not much difference?* I can't believe you're saying that—not after they took your daughter. Killed the mother of your child and a lot of other innocent people."

"I *hate* what they did," Dor said, "and I'm going to get Sammi back, no matter what I have to do. I'm not going to sit here and pretend to be a pacifist. Or an idealist, for that matter. I'll kill them if need be. I'm not naïve enough to think that there's going to be peace in this new society or new world or whatever the fuck we have now."

"It's not idealism to— I mean there's right and there's wrong and—"

Cass was so caught up in the argument that when Dor's hand settled lightly on her shoulder she jumped. Then she was embarrassed, and tried to pretend it hadn't happened, but she was sitting on a cramped sofa in a house that had never been hers, with a man who was not her lover, talking about the violence that they might have to commit. She felt like she might cry, and hated that most of all.

"There's not enough to go around anymore, Cass," Dor said, his voice gentler. "That's the bottom line. One way or another, the population's going to come down to what the earth can support."

"That's not true," Cass protested—even though she suspected it was. "Three-quarters of the people in California are already gone, dead. With kaysev there's enough food for everyone who's left. If people would cooperate—share skills, share the rest of the resources—there would be enough for everyone. It's just when people start trying to profit from other people's misfortune that it all goes wrong."

"Is that meant to be a dig against me? Because I run a business? Let me tell you, Cass, if I wasn't bustin' my ass to coordinate supply with need, things would be a hell of a lot worse for everyone than they already are."

Cass started to argue and then she stopped herself. Because he was right, at least a little.

Most of her anger, Cass knew, was not at Dor, even though it was easy to blame him. Much easier than admitting that much of her rage had nowhere at all to settle, that it was years' worth of stored anger at people who were long gone, at herself, at circumstances that had been forced on her, at messes she'd made and hadn't had the strength to clean up. She'd earned this fury every time Byrn let his eyes linger on her body, every time his furtive hands found her in the dark; she'd stoked it with each man to pass through her doors and back out again; cherished and honed it when Ruthie had been ripped from her, when every scar was laid open at once.

This was a dangerous road to take, and one she had found was drawing her more and more in recent weeks. Until now, until the library burned and Smoke left her, things had started to feel settled. She had started to believe she might be able to have the family she'd never dreamed she could have.

It was everything she ever wanted, so why did she feel so restless? The old A.A. answers were there, right outside her consciousness, asking to be let in—but she didn't want to try, didn't want to do the hard work of *living with her discomfort* and *feeling her feelings* and all of those words that were just words. Maybe, if the whole world hadn't gone to shit, if she had time to herself to do anything beyond the daily struggle of just living, if there was even the luxury of a single A.A. meeting to go to—maybe then, she could try to work through the bewildering maze of her own head. But in the Box, there were plenty of addicts but very few people who had any desire to do anything about it; it was hardly the place for practicing the twelve steps.

Still, she was *sober*. She hadn't had a drink in almost a year. Wasn't that enough? Why didn't that calm some of the anger?

She fell silent and Dor didn't seem to mind one way or another. He gave her shoulder a final squeeze, and folded his arms across his chest. His legs were extended out in front of him and he crossed his ankles at his feet and settled himself lower in the sofa. He looked like he ought to be sitting in front of a fireplace, or a football game on TV.

He didn't have the itch. Cass had pretended she'd obliterated the itch the first time she was sober, but that had been a hard lesson…pretending it away just weakened the dam and made room for the tiny rents that allowed it to make its insidious slow way back in. The itch was sneaky; it gained strength from the most unlikely sources. Self-doubt was manna. Shame was its lifeblood.

And there was the stupid part, the part Cass hated more than anything—the part that she would tell God, if there was a God, was a flaw in His design, unfair, counterintuitive, doomed: the genetic part. She still didn't want to believe it was true, that she, her body, her family history might have been selected in the genetic lottery to betray herself. Some people just weren't addicts, didn't have the potential, couldn't become one if they tried. Cass had learned to identify them only by learning to identify who they weren't. She could spot an addict from across a room or a bus or a party, and gradually she figured out who didn't have the itch.

Like Dor.

Cass sighed. This, of all the pointless places for her thoughts to go right now, was probably just about the most pointless. But there were ways to deal with that.

Of the many insipid-sounding A.A. catchphrases and acronyms, one of the most cloying had to be HALT—Hungry, Angry, Lonely, Tired. If you were any of these, it was a signal to stop, take yourself out of circulation, get what you needed, treat yourself gently, rest. Come back strong.

And Aftertime, there couldn't be a bigger joke. Hungry? The bioterrorists had pretty much set the stage for that, and while kaysev kept you alive, it never, ever completely satisfied you. Angry? *Fucking kidding me?* Lonely…well, Cass could teach a graduate seminar on lonely, on all its shades and flavors. And tired: everyone was tired, all the time. Deep, dreamless sleep had gone the way of hot showers and electric toothbrushes.

But there were still things she could do, things she *should* do. Things she had to do, if only for Ruthie. So Cass bit back whatever she had been about to say to Dor, and focused on breathing in and breathing out, and reminded herself to be grateful. For living another day.

For having her daughter with her.

For the meal they'd eaten, the sun on her face that afternoon.

She didn't feel gratitude, but she knew that pretending was the next best thing. *Fake it till you make it.* And so she sat, trying to keep her body as still as her mind was unsettled, and faked it.

Dor seemed comfortable with the silence. He occasionally shifted, recrossing his ankles, rubbing a hand over his stubble or through his hair, but his breathing was deep and regular and he didn't even seem to have to work at it. They were warm now, sharing the knitted comforter. Dor stretched and yawned, and his thigh touched hers, and she stayed very still, distracted from her thoughts, afraid to pull away lest he notice. But he didn't seem to notice that their bodies were touching. In fact, he seemed like he might just drift off to sleep.

For a man who preferred his own company, he seemed remarkably at ease with her. He probably—no, make that definitely—would have preferred to come on this trip by himself, but he had been nothing but accommodating since they left San Pedro. Now, at the end of the day, he seemed as though he had made his peace with everything that had happened, an almost inconceivable notion.

It was like with the itch. Cass saw it, believed it, but couldn't understand it. How could he see the things they'd seen today and not be marked by it? How could he not long to numb himself after nearly dying, after seeing what transpired in this house that was so bad? After taking men's lives? How could he—and God help her, she hated the way the old sayings colored every thought she had, as though A.A. had seeped in and taken over every corner of her brain—just *let it be?*

"Back on the road today," Cass said, her words coming out in a rush. "By the wreck. When you went inside the house. What did you find?"

Dor's ink-black eyes shifted very slightly out of focus but otherwise he showed no reaction to her question. "You saw. The food, the medicine, the guns—it was all out pretty much in the open."

"That's not what I meant."

Dor shrugged slightly, but he said nothing and didn't look at her.

"I want to know about the people," Cass pressed. "How they were living, what they were *doing* in there. I heard the shots, you know."

"I don't want to tell you," Dor said slowly. "It's not that I think you can't handle it. So don't think that. It's nothing worse than you've seen before. But it won't help you in any way. Why ask me, when this is a chance for you to stay ignorant of one bad thing? Why not take that as a gift?"

Cass shook her head. "No. I—look at me, Dor, please look at me." Wrong, wrong. But she couldn't stop, couldn't keep the words in. "I need to know everything. I need to *feel* everything. It's the only way I can…"

The only way I can keep fighting the itch.

But of course, Dor didn't speak that language and so didn't know what she was talking about.

"I can handle it," she said, changing tactics. "I…insist you tell me. We're partners, and you need me, and I deserve a full accounting of everything that affects me."

After considering her words for a moment Dor finally relented, but he didn't look happy about it. "There were four of them. The two out front and another man and a woman. The men…were doing all right. The woman, not so much. I did what I had to do. I changed the balance, the way I thought was right. The worst of them are dead, and so help me, that's all you need to know."

"*No.* Everything."

His eyes bored into hers and his expression darkened and smoldered. For a long time she thought he would storm from the room, his body tensed with furious energy, his breath coming ragged and hard, but he stayed, sitting rigid and miserable until he could manage to continue.

"All right, but I still think it's a mistake. They were well supplied, not just the food but they had a lot of firewood stacked out back, and they had a little generator, too. They had gas out back in a couple big tubs. Looked like fifty gallons or more. They take it out of the cars that come by, I expect, siphoning it off after they kill everyone and drive the cars out back. You can see from the second floor windows, there's more farther back in the woods. They've been at this for a while, Cass."

Her head had started buzzing at the word *kill*. "How do you know? Maybe they let the people go, told them to head down the road, or they could have driven them farther down themselves, made them get out and—"

"No." Dor's voice was hard. "You wanted to know, so you're going to know, but I'm *not* lying to you. Ever."

Cass nodded, chastened.

"They kill them. The one inside told me."

"Just like that? He just volunteered that up to you? Because—"

"He didn't volunteer *anything*. After I shot him in the knee. I made him tell me a few things. And then after he told me, I shot him in the head."

Cass thought about that. Counted.

"There were only two shots. What about the woman?"

"The woman, she wasn't there by choice."

"What do you mean, not by choice?"

"She was shackled to the bed in one of the bedrooms. They used metal cuffs that were too small and there was, she was bruised and cut, you know, the cuffs cut into her ankles but she had, her toenails were painted. Pink, I could still see the pink nail polish. She was…they took her from one of the cars. Do you understand what I'm telling you? She was young and if they hadn't beaten her in the face I think she might have been pretty. They killed the ones she was traveling with and they kept her for themselves. They…used her."

"Oh my God…"

"I made him tell me where the key was. To unlock her. It was the last thing he told me before I shot him in the head. I told him if he told me, I would let him go free. They kept the key on a hook by the front door, just like where you'd keep your car keys."

The buzzing in Cass's head grew louder, like flies, dozens

of flies. The place behind her eyes hurt. Her mouth felt too dry to talk, but she had to ask.

"Wait—where is she? Was she hurt? Could she walk?"

"She'd only been with them a couple of weeks. She'd lost track of the days so I don't know how long, really, but she still looked reasonably healthy, physically. Cass, I left her plenty of food and medicine and a gun and bullets."

"You could have brought her. We could have taken her with us."

Dor was already shaking his head angrily. "Damn it, Cass, I knew you'd say that. I knew that's straight where you would go. What would we do with her? She'd slow us down. She wasn't right in the head—not anymore. There's no way we could bring her to the Rebuilders. They wouldn't want her. They'd be suspicious. That house is sealed tight and she's armed and she has provisions for months, if she's careful. Most people have a lot less. A *hell* of a lot less."

Cass knew he was right. Knew it was the only way. And she had a chance. If she was careful, like Dor said, she had a chance.

Anyone who had survived this far had already proved they were tough. The weak died, it was as simple as that; if they didn't starve or catch the fever, they simply lost the will to keep trying, and grew careless. They killed themselves and took ridiculous chances and went out of their minds entirely, until everyone who was left was crafty and wily and determined to live.

Of course they couldn't take her along. Cass could only guess what shape the woman was in, and it was inconceivable that she would force Ruthie to look upon her brokenness. Cass knew firsthand that another person's suffering could seep into the vulnerable places in you, and Ruthie had suffered too recently and too much. She still didn't know exactly what had gone on in the Convent, and while she believed most of it was simply brainwashing and rigorous "educating" in the children's dorm, the deacons had forbidden the children to speak. Whatever the consequences of disobeying, they were stark enough or painful enough that the lesson had stuck, even now. There had been no marks on Ruthie when Cass rescued her, no injuries; she did not flinch the way Cass suspected a beaten child would. But she was just so silent, and without words how could she tell her mother what she was feeling? Until she was better, until she was all the way back, Cass would take no risks nor bring any more unnecessary fear into her life.

"All right," she finally said. "You're right. What else aren't you telling me?"

Dor blinked and Cass knew he had held something back. She knew it anyway, knew it from the way he refused to meet her gaze. And she had to know. Not because she needed the full catalog of horrors that had been committed in the plain cabin, but so that she could keep Dor from thinking of her as weak, so that she could keep him from wanting to protect her. She had to keep their relationship clean; she couldn't give in to the urge to let him take up even the smallest part of her burden. She had made that mistake with Smoke and she would not make it again with anyone. Smoke had protected her and she had counted on that protection and then he had left and there was nothing she could do to stop him, and because she'd given herself to him, he had taken a part of her with him and left her weaker, unwhole.

She would not allow that to happen again.

"You tell me everything," she whispered fiercely. Her hands had closed around his wrists without her realizing she'd moved, and she was squeezing hard. "Everything. *I'll* decide when the telling is done."

"It doesn't need to be this way," Dor protested. "I'm not trying to keep you in the dark or, you know, prove I'm in charge or whatever. Any kind of power I had, I left it back in the Box. Here we're equals and you don't have to fight me to prove it. Okay?"

"Don't you think I know that?" Cass could feel her face flaming with fury and embarrassment as she let go. "I could shoot you in your sleep or grab the wheel and run us off the road."

The old chorus rushed from its hidden place with greedy excitement, provoked by her momentarily loss of control: *I could fuck you or hate you or make you want me or make you despise me*...but Cass resisted. She would not give in, could not give in. Today was hard but she was strong. The future was hard but she would be stronger.

"What do you want, Cass?" Dor asked gently, surprising her. Tenderness was the one thing she had not expected of him. "I get the feeling there's nothing I could give you, nothing I could do for you that would mean anything to you. If you'd just stayed in the Box, I could have made it someone's full-time job to keep you and Ruthie safe for as long as possible. Why are you with me? Really?"

But Cass knew that danger well. The way they asked questions and got inside you and made you start to care. And she would have none of it. "Just tell me the rest."

Silence stretched between them, but Cass did not look away. A branch scratched against the kitchen window, and somewhere in the house was a sound Cass had not heard in a very long time, the tick of a battery-operated clock. She was warm under the afghan, and she could feel Dor's heat, even greater than her own, and smell the soap on his skin. The candle had burned down to the last few inches and it sputtered and flickered, light dancing around the wood-paneled walls.

When Dor finally spoke, there was no emotion in his voice. "They pile the dead fifty yards beyond the house. They don't even dig trenches. The birds showed up a month ago. They can pick a corpse clean in a matter of minutes. Sometimes there's as many as half a dozen of them and she's seen them flying from the south—she thinks that might be where they nest."

"The girl told you that."

"Yes. She would stare at the mound at night."

Cass's heart felt sick, but she couldn't stop until it was all out. "And?"

"There's a pottery bowl on the kitchen table, with a separation down the middle, like you might serve two different dips in it or something. One half, they use as an ashtray. In the other half are all the wedding rings they took off people."

Cass's vision swam. "Is there anything else?"

"Yes. The girl's name is Anna. She said when they took her there was already a girl in the room, one who'd been there a few months. One of her arms was broken and she had an infection and she smelled like she was rotting from the inside. She started screaming when she saw Anna and she didn't stop until they took her out into the backyard and shot her. Then they locked Anna up to the same bed."

15

MONTHS AGO, WHEN THE CITIES WERE BURNING
and bodies lay bloated in trenches, Cass had thought she'd seen
the worst. She remembered saying those words to herself: *at
least now I have seen the worst.* But every time some other horror came along, something she had not imagined or prepared
herself for, and she would think she could not survive it. And
then she did. And Dor's story was the worst yet.

Cass suspected that this was what determined, more than
anything else, who survived and who did not. The ability to
live through the moment when you found out you had been
wrong once again—that things really *could* get worse, that
suffering came in yet more designs, that survivors' capacity for
ruthlessness or Beaters' hunger and cunning exceeded what
you thought you knew. You could still be surprised, and you
could take it.

People died a thousand different ways—suicide, attacks,
poisoning, riots, dehydration, starvation—but Cass came to

believe that the real cause of most deaths was giving up. Lose your will and you were likely to leave a shelter door open, or forget to check for blueleaf, or cross paths with marauders—even carelessly cut yourself and die an ignominious death of infection or tetanus. Your body would bloat and rot like any other, and you would never have a gravestone or even a cross to mark the place you fell, but your silent requiem would be a song of despair, of wretchedness.

What made some people keep fighting while others succumbed? Cass didn't know. At first, she'd fought for Ruthie. But when she woke in a haze so profound that she barely remembered who she was, there was some other source of determination so fundamental that it might as well have been her very bones, her DNA. She was a fighter and she would not stop being a fighter, even if the one she'd fought hardest against most of her life was herself.

If anything could make her give up, it would have been losing Smoke—because she had slowly invested him with herself, allowed the protective layer of distrust and anger to crumble until there was a hole wide enough to let him in. She had allowed that to happen, she had slowly accumulated the hundred habits of love, and she had done so foolishly, like a teenager with her first crush.

Well. She'd never been such a girl, so there was her excuse—by the time she was old enough to have a boyfriend, her stepfather had already taken from her that possibility. His hands on her body had done more than destroy some medieval notion of her innocence, they had erased her ability to believe that someone could love her, to trust herself to be part of a couple, to believe that she could be worthy only for herself, for what was true and essential.

But then Smoke had come and everything else was so broken that she'd loved him almost by accident. When every minute felt like a prelude to death and disaster, she'd allowed herself to steal moments of comfort with him. They were to be only that—stolen moments, meaningless moments, episodes she would pretend to forget in the daylight. Only that hadn't happened. He had loved her at noon as much as he did at midnight, and having Ruthie back was so joyous and overwhelming that she forgot to keep resisting. She forgot to keep protecting herself, and she'd allowed him to take up the yoke—to care for her, to nurture her, to hold her. Sometimes their lovemaking felt transcendent, as though climax transported her outside herself for splintered moments of divinity. And sometimes, when Smoke held her afterward, it was confusingly like being held by a parent, or by God Himself, someone who would love her forever.

But Smoke did *not* love her forever. Not enough to stay, anyway. He chose vengeance—ugly, dark, violent—over her. And that was that. Her one failure, her one fall. She'd built that wall back up in record time, and it was twice-strong, twice-high.

Dor watched her carefully, and she knew he was waiting for her to crack. But she wouldn't give him the satisfaction. She was stronger than that, stronger than he knew.

"Nothing I haven't heard before," she lied.

Dor blinked, looked uncertain. "Still…"

"Still nothing. You were right to leave her the gun, but you know she's just going to use it on herself." Her voice sounded tinny, a cheap and insubstantial version. She made herself face Dor, but she couldn't stand to look in his eyes. They were cinnamon-flecked in the light, a deep, deep brown; but at night, with only the candle for illumination, they were depthless black, and she didn't dare risk being absorbed by that unknowable gaze. Instead she focused on his jaw; on the stubble that had appeared before the morning was done, on the hard lines of his bones.

"Cass…"

"It's all right." She shrugged. "It's better, really. Hopefully she'll do it outside, and that way if some freewalker comes through they won't have to deal with the mess."

Dor reached, hesitantly, to put his hand on her shoulder again. It seemed to be his entire repertoire of comforting gestures, and his touch was awkward, heavy. "You don't have to do this."

"Do *what?*"

"Act like…like it doesn't affect you. Like it doesn't hurt."

Hot, acid tears instantly welled up in her eyes, and Cass knew that if she blinked they would spill. So she would not blink. She bit down on her lip, hard enough to distract herself. "It *doesn't* affect me. How could it affect me? I don't know her. She's just some other woman. The difference between her and me is that she got caught. I didn't. I mean, yeah, it was probably thanks to you…do I need to thank you? Is that what this is about? Do I need to give you credit for the save? Okay, Dor, if it wasn't for you, I'd be tied to that bed too and she and I would be getting fucked together, fucked until we were used up and I wasn't anything at all. So, thank you. Seriously."

Cass was breathing hard, and she suddenly couldn't stand his touch, his tentativeness. She shoved his hand off her arm but she didn't move away from him on the couch; she could see his scar, the one that had slowly faded and disappeared under the hair he no longer cut, tracing across his forehead.

"Look, Cass…" Dor sounded almost alarmed, and that pleased Cass. The ravenous angry part of her trembled with excitement; she'd gotten to him. She'd provoked him. "I know you're upset about Smoke, that you're feeling—"

She hit him before she realized she was going to, flat hand across his cheek, a resounding slap that took him off guard and probably stung like hell. "You have no idea what I'm feeling," she snarled, and then she pulled back to hit him again, astonishing herself. The sprite that was her anger danced in ecstasy, sending her heartbeat wild with excitement. She felt the spittle at the corners of her mouth and the blood rushing to her face and the tingle of the slap in her palm.

He caught her wrist, hurting her, his strength a ridiculous overmatch to hers. He held her arm in the air, glaring at her, and she wondered for a moment if he would throw her to the ground. The sprite chortled within her, urging her on. *Make him,* it cried—*make him do it.*

"You don't know who I am—what I have *really* been," she said. Spittle landed on him and she didn't care.

"I know you've been through a lot," Dor said, the flash of anger quickly receding, his features rigid and careful. "I know you're tired and possibly in a state of post-traumatic stress, and what you need is to—"

"*Fuck* what I need," Cass said. "Fuck *you,* you have no idea what I need—" *You were there,* she wanted to scream. *You shot him in the head. You saw that poor wreck of a woman. You saw the rings.*

Oh, God…the rings.

They'd taken the rings, slipped them from fingers shrunk from hunger, tokens of times unimaginably long ago, of celebrations and promises. They shot the husbands and the wives in the backyard. They put the rings in a bowl. The bowl sat on the table. They smoked and ashed in that bowl. Down the hall the women cried and wished they were dead.

He was close, so close to her, his silver-streaked dark hair falling in his eyes, his expression shocked and hard, angry. Had she made him hate her? The sprite crowed with satisfaction and victory as Cass struggled to free herself from his grasp and he only held on tighter, hurting her, his fingers tight on her wrist, squeezing. With her free hand she pushed him, put her palm to his face and ground against his mouth, his teeth, and he grabbed that hand too and held it just as hard so they were locked in a silent battle. If he let go, she would claw his eyes out, she would tear his skin. She would draw blood and then he would know that he did not know what she felt, that he could *never* know what she felt.

She climbed on top of him, hooking one leg over his lap so she was straddling him, making him twist her arms painfully.

"What are you doing," he muttered, but she ignored him, she dug her knees into the sofa on either side of him, she pressed her body against him, ground herself into his lap. "What the hell are you trying to do, Cass—"

She saw the confusion in his eyes and it excited her. She knew that she had provoked him and that meant that she was the stronger one now. She had won. It had been touch-and-go, she had let it go too far—but she'd found his weakness and not given too much of herself.

"Get off of me," Dor ordered her in a strained voice, trying to hold her wrists back as she ground against him. "This isn't right. You know this isn't right."

But instead she bent down to his face and kissed him hard, her fury hot in her throat, her hair falling in his face, getting caught up in their mouths. He twisted his face away and tried to buck her off; she chewed her hair and it tasted of salt, of sweat, of dirt.

He was stronger than she was, stronger by far but she had

the advantage, an advantage formed in devastation and honed
by the knowledge that she'd never give herself away again.
She'd piled everything on the wall, the detritus of every past
hurt, every betrayal, until she had made a barrier of thorns and
broken glass and funhouse mirrors, and then she'd mortared it
with the few good things she'd ever cared about, because they
had to go, too; they had to be burned away. Her few friend-
ships, her moments of tenuous faith, a handful of pretty things
she'd collected, all crushed and tossed on the pile. She'd made
of herself a spiked and impenetrable thing, and then—in only
the last three months, oh God, how had she been so careless,
how had it come over her so fast—the wall had fallen away
like the knotted rags of a desert wanderer, leaving her naked
and vulnerable to the sun that could burn her, could kill her.

Smoke had been that sun and she'd lain under his shine,
turned her face to it and drunk it in greedily even as his heat
and light beat down on the last of her defenses, the ones that
guarded her very soul, leaving them withered and sere. She'd
made love to him a hundred times and every time she'd given
him everything, from the very first time to their last morning together, the morning of the day he betrayed her. She'd
opened every cell of her being and sealed herself to him with
her body, with her cries and her garbled love words, made him
part of her, and now she had to shed him and it was going to
be hard, hard, hard.

But she would start now.

She spat out the strands of her hair and drove her body
against Dor, feeling him grow stiff underneath her. His fingers
weakened around her wrists and she yanked them away, too
fast for him, too devious. She put her hands on his shoulders
and dug in with her fingers, knowing she was hurting him
and not caring.

He cursed and swore low in his throat, the sound of an animal, ferocious in its need, insatiable, reverberating through her body into her spine.

His hands closed on her ass and pulled her hard against him, pushing himself up against her. He dug his fingers into her waistband and yanked, the tight-woven fabric unyielding, the zipper scratching against the tender skin of her belly. "Get these off," he ordered her. "Do it now."

The anger in his voice was a spark to the tinder of her crazed greed for him. She rolled off, clumsy, knees knocking, not caring. Zipper down with fingers slick with sweat. Panties already sodden as she peeled them away. Dor kicking off his pants, pulling his T-shirt over his head, throwing it to the floor. In the flicker of the candle Cass saw his body reflected in burnished night-glow and for a half a second the sight almost stopped her—he was that beautiful, his chest muscular and smooth and dark, his sternum rent from chest to navel by a pair of scars, pebbled pocked fissures in his smooth skin, and her fingers fluttered with the need to touch him there, and then the flicker-thought was gone as he leaned naked and uncaring and grabbed her wrists again, pulling her back to him. He seized the placket of her shirt and yanked and the buttons spun through the air and the fabric tore and his hands on her back were rough as rocks, hot as embers.

He pulled her against him and his mouth on her neck was hard and his teeth grazed her skin as he lifted her like she was nothing. He found her nipple and bit. She cried out in pain even as sensation rocked her, from his hot wet mouth along her nerves to her core and out to the edges of her, the place where she ended and the rest of the universe began, that place that was lost because she was just the spiral of fury and hurt and need that Smoke had made of her when he left.

Dor lifted her hips, his hands holding her and moving her against him. She felt his cock brush against her, slick and sliding against her furrow and she threw her head back and grabbed his shoulders again and thrust against him but he held her away. God, he was just so strong, he held her as though she was a sack of feathers, a sack of dried and crumbling leaves. As though she were nothing at all.

"This is *wrong*," he said through gritted teeth, the quivering head of him hot against her, and she dug her fingers in to brace herself and struggled against him, bucking and begging with her body, and still he held her off, his fingers bruising-hard in the soft flesh of her ass. Cass's breath turned into a cry, a wail, a pleading keening and finally, finally oh *God* finally he relented and jammed her down on him with a cutoff cry of his own.

She was ready, so ready, liquid in her need and still he split her as an adze splits bark already taken from a felled tree. She felt herself cleave clean around him, he was so hard so demanding and still she wanted more of him, she wrenched and englutted and he grunted and forced his way ever deeper until there was nowhere else to go. Her keening wail turned into something else, an excited, hungry clamor that matched him thrust for thrust, urging him on, making him go faster, harder.

Dor's eyes were shut tight and he grimaced as though he were in excruciating pain, sweat beading along his brow, slicking his chest hot even as the night grew deeper and the room grew ever colder, this abandoned remote place of death and devastation, forgotten by everyone.

Cass saw how he fought himself and it excited her and she kissed him with her mouth open and tasted bitter, knew she would hate herself for it later but she drank the bitter deep, slammed herself against him and seized the energy that ebbed from him. The bitter taste was triumph, and she couldn't get enough, could never get enough.

"I didn't—want—this," he managed to get out with difficulty. Cass found his nipples with her fingers and twisted; she grazed her teeth along his jaw, nipped his flesh and laved him with her tongue. "I don't—want *you*."

Her hair had fallen between them again and she mashed her face against it, the strands gritty against her skin. And she laughed. It started deep inside her, a rumbling, unstoppable reaction to the bitterness she'd swallowed, and Dor pushed her off of him only to prop her ungently with her face against the back of the couch, her hands finding purchase on the scratchy synthetic fabric, as he took her that way, his hands on her thighs as though he would hold on through a storm, a hurricane, the wrath of God Himself—and her laughter grew and rang through the room until it finally turned into something else and there was no way to know whose cries burned the cursed and frigid air.

IN THE MORNING HIS EYES FELT LIKE THEY WERE full of fine grit, and he lay on the hard carpeted floor under the twisted blankets and thought of the shale cliffs along the Iowa riverbanks of the summers of his youth. He spent them with his Neary cousins from his father's side of the family—the Irish side—skinny redheaded farm boys reckless and restless, throwing themselves off the cliffs in banshee-screaming cannonballs into the brackish pools below. Afterward they lay on the sandbars steaming in the sun, good-naturedly insulting each other and speculating about every girl within thirty miles. Dor, younger by three years than the youngest Neary, listened while he baked deep brown, having inherited his Afghani mother's complexion. Dor couldn't keep up with any of them and so of course hadn't yet realized that in time he would be able to beat the shit out of any of them without breaking a sweat. They raced each other through the fields late in the afternoons, kicking up dust, getting it in their eyes.

Dor didn't know what had happened to any of his cousins, his good-natured doughy aunts, or his portly stoic uncles. A couple of them had sent Christmas cards last year. Dor kept them in a file folder, pushed far back in a cabinet at the office he would never return to.

Of course, they were on the other side of the Rockies. Maybe they had a chance.

Dor rubbed at his eyes, pushed himself up and leaned back against the sofa. The same sofa where, deep in the night, he'd...Jesus. No. The memories came back sharp and whole, and he gave up struggling against them. How the hell had it happened? She'd fought him hard, all lean strong limbs and teeth and that hair of hers, wild like a pale discordant halo around her face.

He remembered the way Cass looked when she first came to the Box. She'd been timid then, beat-down. He hadn't known about Ruthie at first, hadn't known what drove her, what haunted her, but they were all like that, every traveler who found their way to the Box. Loss and hunger, a mix he'd come to know well, a calculation he had a particular genius for; he could take its measure and instantly know what a person needed, and what it was worth to them. But not with Cass. Even then, there had been something elusive about her. She was scared and she was a thin line away from frantic, but you could also see her checking around for escape routes, even if she didn't know she was doing it—she was a hedger of bets, a hoarder of backup plans pinched in her fingers like a cornered fox.

Her hair had been short then, soft and brown like a boy's... ragged...as if it was torn. Her first day in the Box she'd had the barber do something to it, bleached the ends, made it stick straight up and askew. It should have been ugly. Since she'd moved in with Smoke she hadn't cut it, but she'd kept it dyed a blond so pale it was nearly white, and it had grown fast, jagged pieces down past her chin already, down to her shoulder blades, one of the strange things that made her seem so otherworldly at times. Probably another outlier trait. He saw her working in the gardens on steel-cloud fall days, her pale head unmistakable among the glossy leaves of her citrus seedlings, the carefully pruned branches of her prized fig. She wasn't a talker. He didn't know if she had ever been.

When he first did talk to Cass, she gazed straight into his eyes, a challenge, a dare, a provocation. He felt himself shut down, and he sent her away as soon as he could, unsettled and not in the mood to be. He didn't expect her to last. Later, after she and Smoke settled in, they kept their distance from each other. He knew Cass resented him for recruiting Smoke to head his security team. How to explain his choice? It was no more or less than instinct—but he owed her no explanation. He owed her nothing. She didn't work for him. She worked for no one but herself, and she gave away her herbs and roots and flowers just as often as she traded for them. Sometimes it almost seemed as though she did this to provoke him, giving away the things of most value and cherishing bits of worthless trash: broken bottles in pretty colors, soiled silk scarves and books with missing covers. Of course, it was easy to be generous when you had more than enough—Smoke earned more than they could use up. Dor rewarded Smoke well and with care because he had been right about him and did not wish to lose him: Smoke was that rarest of men, a born leader who did not want to lead. And Dor's security force—renegades, thieves, adrenaline junkies and soldiers all—could only be led by such a man. Even now Dor marveled that he was the only one who ever understood that dynamic, but he supposed that had always been his gift, understanding people's natures better than they understood themselves.

Except for Cass. It should have been easy: recovering addict, driven by loss and guilt—they were a dime a dozen, a currency so devalued they practically flooded the Box these days. A huge number ended up killing themselves one way or another. But this one had a couple of additional facets. Fiercely protective mother. Passionate lover. Survivor. Cass had become a wild card.

Dor winced. He'd seen Cass and Smoke together; it sometimes seemed as though the more he tried to avoid them, the more frequently he ran into them. After they'd put Ruthie down to sleep for the evening, it was their habit to walk the aisles and corridors of the camp, holding hands, exchanging greetings with nearly everyone, but declining offers to share a meal or play cards. Sometimes they'd be in the back of a crowd gathered to listen to someone playing the guitar or reading—Cass encircled in Smoke's arms, leaning against him with her eyes closed and a dreamy half smile on her face. They pitched in together; when they helped put up tents or mend the fence or serve meals they shared a wordless efficiency, passing each other objects with secret, intimate smiles. *Later,* their expressions often seemed to promise, *later we'll be alone.*

And it had irritated him. Dor, who was alone even when he was with others. Who chose solitude because he had never learned anything else. Whose marriages had both ended when his wives finally despaired of ever reaching him—and God knows they'd tried, the good women who'd loved him. Even his daughter, even Sammi—he'd loved her so much he had to leave her behind, because she got to him, got too close, made him feel too much.

Feeling too much was dangerous. It drained him, took away his focus, his power.

But what of Cass and Smoke? When he looked at them it was like looking through a cursed glass at his inverse. Neither was especially gregarious, but when they were together, they were unguarded, two people who seemed to be completely open to each other. Who made expression of emotion seem effortless. Who shared themselves without hesitation. How did they do it?

Still, Dor knew a secret about Smoke. He thought the two of them had shared everything, but now he realized that Smoke hadn't told Cass his one great mistake, his shame, the thing that made him leave and would always now compel him toward the abyss.

It was this secret that weighed on Dor's mind as he got painfully to his feet and folded the blankets, replacing them with care on the couch that might never again be used by anyone. Cass thought she knew everything about her lover, but there was one thing that would shock her to the core. If she knew that one thing, she would understand why her man had left. If she knew it, she might not have come to him last night, might not have thrown herself at him like her life depended on having him.

He was disgusted with himself for letting her. He should have told her Smoke's secret instead. But now it was all fucked up. One of them owed the other something—but he wasn't sure who and he wasn't sure what it was. He had a feeling that they were a combination that could never be stable, that as long as they were together they would just keep cutting and devastating each other. He should never have let her come. She hadn't given him any choice. He ought to part ways with her as soon as Colima was in view. Give her the car, the guns, the stores, everything, and tell her to take Ruthie back where they would be safe. He'd started over with nothing more times than he could count—and didn't he always come back stronger?

Only this time he wasn't sure. This time, he had the unsettling feeling that he had lost control of what came next.

17

CASS WOKE WITH RUTHIE SNUGGLED INTO HER arms, her daughter's sweet, even breaths tickling her bare shoulder.

She lay still for a moment and took stock. She'd managed to get her clothes back on last night, grabbing them up off the floor and bolting from the room, leaving Dor standing awkwardly to the side with his own clothes bunched in his big hands in front of him. It might have been funny, the way he was almost shielding his nakedness from her, after what they'd just done—except she couldn't actually see that humor in the moment.

And it didn't seem any better this morning after a restless night. Her shirt had no buttons; they'd tumbled to the floor when Dor tore it open. Cass shuddered, remembering his fury. At the time it had provoked her, stirred that part of her that couldn't back down, the hurt and angry part that had split off from the rest of her when her stepfather whispered his lies and threats. She had carried this other self with her for years, and while sobriety helped and having Ruthie helped and running helped, it never truly disappeared. It had receded, with Smoke, until it was only a distant shadow, a presence that tempered her best moments and deepened the worst.

The very few times she and Smoke argued—when she begged him to stay instead of going to train with Joe or taking an extra shift or visiting Dor's trailer—the shadow came closer, close enough to remind her of its dormant power. She coped by shutting down, by refusing to engage, by letting Smoke win every time. She pressed her lips together and didn't speak. She walked the well-worn path around the Box, lap after lap, until she was able to convince herself that it didn't really matter. So she awoke alone more mornings than not—wasn't it better to let it go than to risk her anger coming back and rupturing the peace they'd built together?

She and Dor had no peace. From the first time they met, the day she and Smoke arrived in the Box, he had seemed hard and distant. Of course, she'd begun their relationship by asking something from him. Dor did not part with things easily. As she came to learn, he exacted a fair price for everything he traded, plus his cut. No exceptions. He'd helped her get into the stadium to find Ruthie, but only after Smoke traded their most valuable possessions for the privilege. Dor paid Smoke handsomely, but she had noticed that he never traded with her, never asked for anything from her garden. It was as though he would not allow himself to, though she didn't understand why—the herbs and vegetables she grew were the only ones that most people had had for months; people had already offered fantastic trades for the tiny green oranges on her trees, once they matured.

But Dor acted as though he didn't see the garden, didn't see her. It was as though he reviled not just her but everything she touched.

Ruthie shifted in her arms, sighing and snuggling closer. Cass stroked her soft cheek and kissed her shiny hair, but she felt her face color with shame, remembering the way Dor had fought her last night. And the way she had fought harder.

He could have stopped her at any moment. He was powerful. Strong. He'd battled himself more than he'd battled her, Cass understood that. She even understood why he'd done… what they'd done; she had given him little choice. There had been some hard volatile kernel there, some imbalance between attraction and repulsion, an unstable compound which she'd deliberately ignited.

Her mortification deepened and she pulled gently away from Ruthie, tucking the blankets carefully around her daughter's small shoulders, adjusting the pillow, before sitting on the edge of the bed doubled over, her arms wrapped around her knees, her nails digging into the soft skin of her thighs, trying to make it hurt enough.

She'd seduced Dor and she'd fucked him. He may have thought he'd been culpable, that he was willing when he turned her over, took her hard, slammed home all his disgust and resentment, but he'd only done it because she gave him no choice. There was a point past which anyone could be made to lose control, and Cass was an expert at that fine line, a stellar student of lust and urgency. She had seen a thousand variations—some rolled their eyes back and others' breath came short and still others muttered and hummed—but in the end it was the same, a place where the conscious mind gave itself over to instinct. That's all it had been—not just last night but on hundreds of nights before, starting at the age of sixteen, when she'd merely been looking for an escape from

Byrn's midnight advances, for a substitute for her real father who'd left them to seek his fortunes as a guitarist in a band up and down the California coast. She'd gone looking hungrily. She'd worked her way through all the boys and then moved on to men—five years, ten years, twenty years older than her, in so many bars and parking lots and cheap apartments as she taught herself a few more tricks for forgetting.

Dor didn't know that. Even Smoke didn't know all of it, though she'd told him plenty—another mistake, another thing she'd given away. *No more giving away.* Anger colored Cass's thoughts, clouding her remorse, giving her a strained and bitter kind of strength. She forced herself to relax her grip, to stop hurting herself; she slowly sat up, breathing deep and ragged breaths.

Okay. All right. She had lost control last night, but at least she hadn't given anything away. She hadn't given any more pieces of herself away. She had been the strong one. She'd made Dor do what she wanted him to do, and so she'd won. She had to win, every time, because now it was just her and Ruthie again. Smoke was gone, and that was that, and it was up to her to make sure no one took anything from them. She would be smart, and she would be careful. And as long as she stayed strong, it would be all right. This world demanded strength.

By the time Cass went outside with Ruthie in her arms, Dor had built a fire in the back patio barbecue pit. There was split wood stacked against the shed in the backyard, and he'd laid it out neatly, a tidy flame flickering from an economical arrangement of tinder and wood. A kitchen pot simmered on top of the grate. He didn't hear her coming, and for a moment she and Ruthie watched him warm his hands high above the

orange flames, turning them one way and then the other. He
was wearing a shirt she didn't recognize—a plaid overshirt
lined with fleece, black and gray with bits of blue—and she
wondered if he'd found it in the house somewhere. If so, it
had come from the blocked-off room, the room of unknown
horrors that he had taken pains to shield her from.

Cass thought about that, watching Dor. He was turned
away from her, his gaze fixed at some distant point down valley—the direction of the Rebuilder headquarters, maybe. He
had shaved; the rough shadow of a beard that had abraded her
skin last night was gone. His hair was damp, the ends curving against his collar. His expression was hard to read, but he
wasn't happy.

Cass kicked a stone, and as it skittered across the brick patio
and disappeared into a flower bed choked with dead kaysev,
Dor turned toward her. She saw him take in her own shirt—
something she'd found in the closet of the room where she
and Ruthie slept, an older woman's shirt, cotton broadcloth in
begonia pink with embroidery on the yoke—and knew that
he too was remembering the night before, the ripping of her
buttons.

And everything else. Everything.

She shifted Ruthie in her arms and stared at the ground.
Kaysev had rooted in the cracks between the brick pavers.
Even a month ago the plant would have been lush and green.
Cass had the stray thought that now, while it was dormant,
would be the time to weed it from between the pavers so
that the roots wouldn't work their way underneath and un-
seat them. It had been a nice patio, with outdoor furniture
still covered in plastic except for a couple chairs whose covers had blown off in some storm. It could be a nice space
again, especially in the spring when the kaysev came back,

and the fields would be a deep emerald-green as far as the eye could see.

When the kaysev leaves had started to brown a few weeks ago, when they withered and shrank at the ends of the stems, when the stalks themselves turned brown and woody, some people panicked. They thought it had died. Some thought it an act of God, or a second apocalypse caused by some unknowable malevolent force. Cass reassured anyone who would listen that the plant was merely dormant. She snapped off roots to show that beneath their tough brown exterior they were still creamy yellow, dense with retained moisture, even fatter than usual. She explained that they could take ninety percent of the root for food and still leave a viable plant. But it was only after she put a dormant plant into her makeshift greenhouse, a small tent Smoke rigged from scrap canvas and plastic and poles for that purpose, and tricked it into rebirth that people believed her.

They believed. But then quickly they all wanted to know exactly when the plants would spring back to life, something Cass couldn't tell them. She was keeping a detailed, daily diary of the plants' habits, and a year from now she would be able to tell them all sorts of things. Assuming she was still alive then. Assuming anyone was around to listen.

"There's water," Dor muttered, interrupting her thoughts. "Enough to wash. And I made coffee and oatmeal." He pointed to the picnic table where a flowered mug was covered with a saucer, and a bowl was steaming in the cold air. Next to it was a smaller, second bowl and a plastic tumbler.

"I found some Crystal Light inside. Think she'll drink it? I mean, if you don't mind her having it."

"That's fine."

"Then...I'll be inside. When you're ready."

He walked back into the house without looking at her. Cass
set Ruthie down gently in front of the oatmeal and tested it
with the knuckle of her little finger. "Wait a minute. It's still
too hot."

Ruthie picked up her teaspoon and stirred the oatmeal. Cass
had traded for oatmeal for Ruthie a few times before as a treat,
the individual-serving kind that was flavored with apples or
cinnamon. This was the real stuff, the slow-cooked steel-cut
kind, and Cass's stomach growled in anticipation. "I wish we
had some sugar."

Ruthie put her finger to her own puckered mouth, touching her lips as though hushing herself. Then she scrambled
down from the table and ran for the house. Cass started to
go after her but Dor was standing at the sliding glass doors.
He opened them for Ruthie and she slipped inside and he
crouched down next to her, as she pointed and gestured. If
Cass went now it would look as though she didn't trust him.
Not that she *did*. But…not that she didn't.

Dor had been gentle with Ruthie, but he was such a tall
man, several inches over six feet, and strong and solid—Cass
worried he would frighten Ruthie. There were the tattoos,
the earrings, the fact that he never smiled—all of that. But
Ruthie followed him into the house, out of view, never looking back—and Cass sat down on the bench and tried not to
look concerned. She stirred her oatmeal. She took a sip of
coffee. It was instant, not very good, but not terrible.

After a while the door opened again and Ruthie came back,
holding a china bowl with both hands, taking tiny steps, concentrating on not spilling. She held it up to show Cass and she
saw that it was a sugar bowl, a plump white china one with a
bee painted on the side and nearly full of sugar.

"Ruthie! How did you—" Cass took the bowl from her

daughter and was rewarded with a smile. And not just her usual tentative, uncertain smile but something closer to a grin, her loose front tooth giving her a rakish look. "Did you see the sugar bowl inside before?"

Ruthie nodded and pulled herself back up onto the bench. Cass hadn't noticed the bowl. She hadn't thought that Ruthie had noticed much of anything; she'd been so sleepy. And she was surprised her daughter would even know what such a bowl was—except, of *course*—this bowl was similar to Mim's, and Ruthie had been with Mim and Byrn during those terrible months when Cass was struggling her way back to sobriety. Long enough for her to see Mim put sugar in her coffee dozens of times, two carefully measured spoonfuls stirred precisely three clockwise turns. It was a habit Cass had once loved to watch when she herself was a little girl.

"Well...aren't you clever," Cass said. She spooned sugar into each of their bowls, swirling it in and testing the temperature of the back of the spoon before handing it back to Ruthie. "Mmm, that looks so *good*. Aren't we lucky today?"

Ruthie took a bite and smiled. "Mmm."

Cass froze. It wasn't a word—not really. Just a sound. Ruthie hadn't even opened her mouth to make it. But it was a sound nevertheless. Progress. Change. She wanted to throw her arms around Ruthie, pick her up and swing her in a circle. She wanted to celebrate, to kiss her and tickle her and make her laugh. But that was too much.

She had to let Ruthie come back at her own pace, and not make her self-conscious. Self-consciousness—that thing that kills the real self. At first she had clung tightly to Cass whenever she was awake, but gradually she'd become bolder. In recent weeks she'd been happy to stay with Coral Anne and occasionally played with Feo when the older boy was willing to entertain her for a few hours. Cass's instinct was to let it lie. But as Ruthie ate her oatmeal, Cass's spirits lifted.

When she gathered the dishes and they headed back inside, there, watching them through the kitchen window, was Dor.

18

THE MORNING SKY WAS THICK WITH CLOUDS,
but there was no moisture in the air. The wind buffeted the
Jeep on the two-lane road. Dor kept his speed to thirty, even
though the road was clear as far as she could see.

Ruthie twisted in her seat as they drove away, watching
the little house recede into the distance. She'd remained mute
while Cass washed her with the warm water, brushed her
teeth and combed her hair and dressed her in clean underwear and yesterday's clothes. Cass washed herself as well as
she could, carrying the hot water around the corner of the
house and stripping naked on the dead lawn, trying to wipe
away every trace of what they'd done the night before while
she held her blade in her free hand. Outdoors, away from the
Box, she was never without a weapon, and she felt almost
unbearably exposed as the cold morning air reached her body.
She used deodorant, a rare indulgence, since she owned only
one tube and tried to make it last. After she dressed, she went

through the dresser in the room in which she and Ruthie slept, taking turtlenecks and too-big nylon underwear, as well as three pairs of neatly rolled knee socks.

"After we cross Leverett Canyon Road, Colima's only another twenty miles," Dor said after a while. "That last stretch might be tough. It's an old road, mostly just local traffic since they built the highway. Not sure what we're gonna find." He'd been drinking from a plastic bottle of water, and he offered it to her. Cass looked at his hand holding the bottle, the black lines of his tattoo curling down onto the broad flat plane below his wrist.

She didn't want to take from him, didn't want to accept any kindness from him.

They passed the occasional ranch or farmhouse, but none appeared to be inhabited. Even a couple of months ago, a few squatters were still trying to tough it out alone in their homes, boarding themselves inside and venturing out only to raid at night, trying to avoid the Beaters. For most, it was a losing proposition. Nearly all the easy pickings had been scoured from those houses and stores that weren't infested with Beaters. Water, canned food, medicine; shoes and warm clothes; toiletries and gasoline and propane—all of these were nearly impossible to find. Kaysev alone couldn't make a subsistence life out here sustainable. Waste had to be disposed of. Water still needed to be boiled. Some squatters eventually gave up and made the journey to the nearest shelter, but there were recent rumors that some shelters were beginning to turn travelers away in an effort to conserve resources. Those who spent too many days on the road were guaranteed to be attacked; there were simply too many Beaters and they were increasingly desperate and hungry. The lucky ones made it to the Box or to a shelter that would still accept them; others grew despondent and chose a quick death—drowning, hanging, a leap from a bridge or building.

Or else they joined the Rebuilders.

"What the fuck," Dor murmured softly, interrupting Cass's thoughts.

Far up the road, casting stubby shadows on the blacktop under the late-morning sun, two women stood in the road. They stood close together, one of them pointing—at them, at the land beyond the road, it was hard to tell. The other had a rifle. Cass's heart sank—if this was a Rebuilder checkpoint then all their attempts to arrive unannounced had been wasted. They'd wanted to hide the car to avoid suspicion.

Dor took his foot off the gas and coasted. When they were a hundred feet away, he braked to a stop. The women turned toward the Jeep and Cass got a better look at them, one middle-aged, the other a bit younger. Both wore their thick hair cut blunt at their shoulders; their jeans and coats were mannish and utilitarian. Sisters? Cass thought she saw a similarity in their soft jaw lines, in their slack mouths. They didn't wear the military surplus favored by the Rebuilders, didn't have the rigid, coiled stance of their leaders.

"Wonder what they're up to," Dor said softly. He had his gun in his hand—Cass hadn't even seen him draw it. "Stay here. I'll check this out."

"We could just try to drive around them," Cass said. The earth at the edge of the field was flat and unbroken; it would be easy enough to go off the road. Besides, Dor's caution gave her a bad feeling.

The whole situation felt strange. There was a good-size farmhouse set back a few hundred yards from the road, its paint flaking and some of the windows broken. The front door was open, the interior of the house a black cavern. None of the outbuildings—a large steel shed, a leaning barn, a separate garage—were large or secure enough to make for good shelter, and none had the sort of large opening favored by Beaters.

"The Jeep can handle the field, can't it?" Cass pressed.

"Terrain's not the problem."

"What," she whispered.

"I don't know. Ambush, maybe. I'm leaving the keys. I probably don't have to tell you this, but anything happens to me, you just floor it—head back to the Box. Straight back."

Cass felt the familiar anxiety flood her. After yesterday, she wasn't ready for this, for him to walk away from her again. "There's not—"

But he opened the door and stepped out before she could complete her thought, slamming it shut without a backward glance. Cass watched him walk toward the women, the gun loose at his side, stopping ten, then a couple of yards short of them. One of the women took a faltering step toward him, scratching at her forearm. The other followed, stumbling and reaching toward him, dropping the rifle to the ground, not even looking down as it bounced and a shard of plastic or wood broke off its stock.

Dor started backing away. Then he turned and bolted back toward the Jeep.

He made it in seconds and threw himself into the driver's seat, nearly flooding the engine, tires screeching on the payment as he floored the gas. The pair hesitated only a moment before following, their tentative steps increasing speed.

"What were they—"

"Hang on!" he yelled. Cass clutched the console, her heart hammering. As the Jeep swerved abreast of the two women, she saw that their clothes were soiled and their hair was knotted. They looked as though they'd been beaten, their faces bruised and torn.

"Lean back!"

Dor reached across Cass with his gun hand, firing twice before she could react, and the women spun and crumpled to the ground. He accelerated and the car stopped fishtailing and the road rumbled beneath them. Ruthie sniffled in the stunned silence.

"What did you do that for?" Cass demanded.

"They'd turned," Dor said, reholstering his gun awkwardly. "They were infected."

"*What?*"

It had been a long time, months even, since Cass had seen someone in the early stages of the fever. But yes, it had been there—the eerie flat eyes, the scabbed flesh, the scratching at the arms.

"You're sure?"

"Come on, Cass. Middle of the day? Out there in the road? They had bite marks up and down their arms. They were talking nonsense."

"You…got them both."

Like a movie—the Jeep careening, Dor's finger on the trigger inches from her face, taking the second shot before the first fully registered.

"If they'd been any further along, one bullet wouldn't have been enough to take them down like that."

Cass turned to check on Ruthie. Her eyes were wide and frightened, and Cass caressed her face, making soothing sounds and calling her "darling," promising her it would be all right.

"Why did you bother?" she finally asked. They could have just driven past, saved the two bullets.

"We might come back this way and I didn't want to deal with them twice. And there could have been uninfected in one of those buildings. Not likely, but you never know…and also I liked it. It felt good."

His words chilled her. Cass had never killed, not even a Beater.

"You're just saying that."

"No." Dor kept his eyes on the road, but he put his hand on her thigh. The touch was a fresh shock, his fingers strong and insistent through the fabric of her pants. He moved his hand slowly upward, trailing heat along her skin. Then, just as abruptly, he took it back. "I don't just say things to hear myself talk, Cass. That's a lesson right there, one you might want to take to heart. I also don't do things I didn't set out to do and I don't appreciate…"

He didn't finish his sentence but he didn't have to. Cass knew what she was being accused of and she felt the blood rush to her face.

"I *liked* it," he finally said, his voice harsh, and for a moment she thought he meant the night before. "Know what I like best, Cass? That fraction of a second between when I pull the trigger and that little bit of metal slamming into their flesh. All that—rot and disease and evil. I like knowing I'm gonna put a fucking hole in it. It's satisfying as shit when they drop, don't get me wrong, and really I'm doing them a favor. I've killed fifty of 'em at least and I hope I kill a hell of a lot more before I'm dead. But I get off on the anticipation. Okay?"

Cass clung tightly to the frame of the door she couldn't open until he told her it was time. She was at Dor's mercy and she had put herself there on purpose, her and Ruthie. She had no choice but to listen to him, to hear the words that twisted inside her.

"Okay," she whispered.

"You still want to believe you can come out of this whole. You want to believe you're the same person you were the day the first missile hit. You're not. You're *not*. You can pretend every fucking second until you're dead and you will have wasted all those seconds and all those days because there's no God for you to demand a refund from. There's nothing except this dried-up fucking husk of a planet and the poor bastards still left on it. You want me to be sorry, but I didn't make the world this way and I'm not going to apologize for scratching out a life, any way I can."

His anger and his bitterness felt like they might consume her. She knew he was hopped up on adrenaline and fury, but there was more to his rage, a fundamental belief that everything was lost except the next hardscrabble moment and the next. But he was wrong. Dor was wrong, wrong in his hate and his ferocity. Not everything was wasted, not everything was doomed.

Ruthie was proof. The birds. The clouds, too. But also the tiny kaysev seedlings—they were proof. She'd watered them one last time yesterday, in her little greenhouse, cupping a hand around them to keep the precious water drops from blowing adrift in the wind. They were the bright, pale, leaf-green of spring itself, and she imagined them thirsting for the sun, plunging their roots into the soil that Dor had given up on and finding sustenance deep down.

But Cass was no poster child for hope and Dor was right about that, at least; nearly all of it had been beaten out of her long ago. But not by the Siege. Not by the Beaters and the famine and the demolished earth and the endless river of death. No, Cass had already survived worse and that worse thing had marked her before she was even grown, and she'd reached adulthood stunted and damaged but like a tree that grows around a lightning scar, she had surrounded the hurt with the hardest part of herself and pressed on.

"No," she whispered. "There's more than you see. More than you know."

That was all either of them said until Colima loomed in the distance, a medieval desert-shadow town whose flags and turrets drifted and swam in the dusty heat.

19

THERE WERE NO TURRETS AND THERE WERE NO flags, of course. Those were an illusion of the heat rising from the blacktop and of the sun slanting in her eyes. Colima was composed not of castles and moats, but of 1980s era concrete-and-glass architecture—but near the entrance was its one nod to traditional architecture, a graceful stone building with crenellations and towers, and it was that building that stood out against the sky. The Rebuilders were in the midst of encircling the campus with a brick wall. Along the unfinished side, workers pushed wheelbarrows and scaled platforms.

Cass handed Dor's binoculars back to him, a lightweight matte-black pair that must have cost him dearly. They were crouched next to a billboard that had fallen from its supports and lay resting against the poles, propped up in a way that suggested someone had used it as a temporary shelter. With the Jeep parked behind it, the sign made an effective place to stop and rest unseen.

"There's so many of them."

Dor wiped the lenses of the binoculars with the hem of his shirt. "Recruiting's probably a lot easier these days. Guy comes to your door and points a gun at you and tells you come with him and you'll get fed and he'll give you a safe place to sleep at night, you probably don't mind the gun so much. Freedom's a luxury most folks can't afford anymore."

What about the Box? Cass wanted to ask, but knew that what Dor offered wasn't truly freedom. Once travelers traded away their goods for a high or a bender or sex, there was little in the way of value or sustenance to be had.

But at least they were free to leave, and Dor didn't advertise by gunpoint.

"Want a look?" Dor said softly. Ruthie had left off playing with her little plastic figurines and crept silently next to him. The day had grown unusually warm and Cass had taken off Ruthie's heavy coat. She reached for the glasses, but Dor picked her up and set her on his knee, then held the glasses carefully to her face.

"What do you see?" he asked, his face close to her ear. She didn't answer, but her lips were parted eagerly, and she didn't flinch when Dor gently fiddled with the focus.

"Oh!" Ruthie suddenly exclaimed when the far-off town came into view. She pointed, not taking her face away from the glasses—and Dor smiled, a broad, unselfconscious smile Cass had never seen before. He held the binoculars patiently for her; after a while she put her small hand over his and left it there. When she finally pushed away and scrambled off his knee, she was smiling, too.

She raised her hands to be picked up and Cass held her and spun her in a hip-swinging slow circle. "I love you, Babygirl," she whispered.

"I think we should get going now," Dor said uneasily. He was checking their packs, all traces of his momentary tenderness gone. "That's another mile and a half, easy, and I want to get there in the afternoon. People get sloppy before dinner—maybe we can use that."

"Use it how?"

"Think about it. Afternoons, back in the Box, Charles and them, they're looking ahead to quitting time. Travelers come along and Faye's more likely to give 'em a few extra chits just to get 'em through the door rather than haggling. Now we show up in Colima, we have a story that *almost* sounds likely... well, they're less likely to ask a lot of questions we can't answer."

"We can answer anything they ask." Cass felt her face go hot. "We just have to keep it simple. We're together, the three of us."

Dor narrowed his eyes. "That's not much of a story. What if they ask for details? We don't really know each other." His voice grew even colder. "We're strangers."

"You didn't ask for this." Cass cut him off before he could say anything else. "I *know*. You don't have to say it again."

Dor handed her the smaller of the two packs. She slipped it on, feeling her muscles flex and respond to the extra weight. It had been a long time since she'd freewalked, but her work in the gardens kept her limber and strong. She dug rich dirt from the creek banks a few blocks from the Box; she turned her flower beds with a sturdy shovel Three-High had brought back; she carried creek water in heavy buckets. When she had settled her pack, she bent to pick up Ruthie.

But Ruthie skipped out of her way, smiling mischievously.

"Come on, Babygirl," Cass said, trying to be patient as Ruthie ran to Dor and lifted her arms in the air.

Dor picked Ruthie up without hesitation and set her on his shoulders.

"You don't have to do that."

"It's no big deal. She doesn't weigh anything."

Ruthie grinned down at her triumphantly.

"Why don't you wait," she said. "Ruthie can walk for a while anyway. We can take turns—"

"It's nothing," he said.

They walked the straight road and though the late-afternoon breeze was sharp and chill, they quickly settled into a steady pace that warmed Cass. As they went, she thought about what Dor had said—that the burden of carrying her daughter was nothing—and about the way she'd taught herself to choose among the things she knew to be true, to keep only those that would allow her to go on and then banish the rest to a place of forgetting; to consider all the ways she could lie to herself, and choose among those as well; to cherish her carefully chosen lies, to nurture them so they could flourish in the arid landscape of her mind.

Dor carried Ruthie with a straight back and confident stride, but after a while there was perspiration at his brow. From time to time he hitched her up straight when she grew tired and flagged forward. Her little hands seized his hair, pulling hard, but he didn't complain. Cass found herself falling back a few steps so she could watch them, marveling at the easy way her daughter wrapped her arms around Dor's head—a *stranger's* head—and wondered why she trusted him so easily.

When they were close enough to make out the figures of the guards at the gate, he hitched Ruthie up and turned, waiting for Cass to catch up with him. "So the story—"

"What?" Cass snapped, embarrassed to be caught watching him.

Dor glanced at her curiously, turning his whole body to ensure that Ruthie kept her balance on his shoulders, and Cass almost ran into him. She kept her eyes fixed on the road. Up ahead, the uniformed men stood on either side of an opening in the finished part of the wall, their weapons loose across their chests, the sort of guns soldiers carried in videos Before in ground conflicts everywhere: black and smooth enough to be toys, powerful and deadly enough to bring down entire crowds at a time.

"I thought we should go over the story one more time."

"It's not that complicated," Cass said in exasperation. "I'm an outlier. I ask for Evangeline, I tell them I met her before. That Evangeline invited me to come. That Ruthie and you…"

But it wasn't that easy. *That Ruthie is yours.* She had to say it, not just now but again when it counted. Evangeline did not know that Cass had a child; she and Smoke had come to the library empty-handed and left with only what the resistance gave them. Now she had to pretend that she was a childless woman traveling with her lover and his daughter. She'd deny Ruthie, and there was no way to make her daughter understand what she had to do, the weight of betrayal heavier because Cass had betrayed her daughter before.

"You can still back out," Dor said, reading her thoughts. But Cass knew that it wasn't true. An hour ago—yes. She could have taken the Jeep that they had left behind the downed billboard, secured Ruthie in the backseat and pulled back onto the road and driven back to the Box. She could have passed the corpses of the fresh Beaters lying in the middle of the road, the house where they'd sheltered the night before, the house where the ruined girl had been chained to the bed. She could have stayed strong through all of that, all the way back to the Box and back to their bed and their tent, for Ruthie.

Now it was too late. They'd be seen and she could not turn around; the Rebuilders would never let her go.

"That Ruthie is yours," Cass said, ignoring him and making her voice hard. "Your child. You lost your wife and we're together now. We want to work. I used to be a florist, Before. You served in the reserves."

"That's right," Dor said, and he didn't give her anything more, he refused to acknowledge how hard it was to say the words. And that was as it had to be. It didn't matter that it was hard. Cass repeated that to herself as they covered the last of the distance to the wall: *it doesn't matter. It doesn't matter.*

Up close the men waiting for them were nothing like Faye and Charles and Three-High…nothing like Smoke. They wore various unmatched shades and patterns of khaki and camo, and their hair was cropped short and they wore sunglasses that made their expressions unreadable.

"Put the little boy down," the first soldier said, cradling his rifle with assurance. His partner took a single step forward. He wore a cap embroidered with the initials FDNY, a retro item that had become popular since the twentieth anniversary of the Manhattan tragedy. "Take off your packs and drop them on the ground. Then hold your open hands out to your sides, thumbs down."

Of course they thought Ruthie was a boy, with her clothes and her short haircut, but somehow the mistake disrupted Cass's fragile composure and she froze. When she saw that the soldiers were growing impatient, she snapped to and let her pack slip from her shoulders to the ground.

Dor set Ruthie down gently next to her, and Cass reached

for her hand automatically. Ruthie pressed her face against Cass's leg, wrapping her arms around her knee. She was frightened, and Cass wanted to sweep her up and hold her close. But she could not, and she held her breath and squeezed her daughter's hand more tightly.

"I'll search the child first." The second soldier knelt down in front of Ruthie and held out his hands. "Hey, buddy."

Ruthie clung more tightly to Cass. "She's a girl," Cass said. "She's scared. Isn't there any way you could—"

"Only take a minute." The guard pried Ruthie away from her and Cass waited for flailing, maybe even screaming, but Ruthie went limp and allowed herself to be led. Which was almost more upsetting to Cass, who wondered for the thousandth time what had happened in the Convent to make Ruthie so compliant, to drain her fighting spirit.

"Hello, princess, what's your name," the guard asked in a bored voice as he unzipped Ruthie's jacket and patted her down. He didn't seem to care that Ruthie didn't answer. He pulled her boots off one at a time and checked them, shaking them upside down, then patted Ruthie's feet through her socks before finally nodding at Cass. "You can get her back in her clothes."

Cass dressed her with trembling fingers, whispering that it would be okay and hating that she'd betrayed her daughter yet again, forced her to submit to a stranger, maybe to relive some unknown horror. How many times would she drag her daughter into fresh, unknown dangers?

As often as it took. The words echoed in her mind and Cass bit her lip just enough to taste the blood, sealing her own deal with herself. As often as it took, and now that the Box was growing more unstable every day, her job was to find somewhere new, for Ruthie and for herself, and that wouldn't be easy, or safe. Dor was their ticket. This place was their next hope. That was just how it had to be.

Their own pat-downs were brisk and professional and Cass barely registered the soldier's hands on her. Their weapons went into a plastic box, which one of the soldiers loaded onto a small cart, along with their packs, before wheeling it into the interior of the compound and out of sight. He came back a few moments later with a short young woman in a close-fitting ski-jacket and shearling boots.

"This is Nell," the soldier said, already turning back to his post. "She'll conduct your intake interview."

Cass swept Ruthie up in her arms and followed the woman, Dor close behind. Nell gave them a distracted smile and walked briskly down the wide walkway that led straight into the heart of the campus. Other than the fact that few people were outside the classroom buildings and dorms, it looked remarkably like it had Before.

Cass had been to Colima one time that she hadn't told Dor about—hadn't told Smoke or anyone. It was when she had begun her hopeful, short-lived savings account, when she thought she might really attend college. She'd come down, taken the tour, picked up the applications, but by the end of the day the voices in her head—cowed by the stacks of paperwork, the trim navy suits and polished heels worn by the administrative staff, the laughing knots of students who raced between classes—joined in a chorus of derision, reminding her she was too old, too stupid, too damaged to ever come here, and she'd gone to a bar on her way out of town instead.

The news had been full of images of the campus after the first strike. Students swarmed the green to protest the dean's decision to cut the semester short and send them home. They jeered as he solemnly announced the unanimous decision of the trustees that adequate security could not be promised. It hadn't been the first time UC-Colima had been in the news in recent years. Well before the bioterror attacks, students organized regular protests of the genetic engineering research that was rumored to be going on there. There had been footage of students ringing the biotech building holding hands and chanting—there, *that* one, that squat flat-roofed building with the curved entrance. They ran footage of minor scuffles, bricks thrown through windows, campus administrators hung in effigy. And again, later, while students were being escorted from their dorms by the National Guard, hadn't protesters set fire to a couple of buildings? There, possibly—a stubbled field across the green, empty except for tall piles of bricks, some of them singed black at the edges—could they have carted off the rest of the rubble? Or were they using the remains of the building to build the section of the wall out front?

Cass squinted against the setting sun. The wall-in-progress extended past her line of vision, around behind the campus buildings. A man wearing coveralls stood at a window nearby doing something painstaking. Puttying perhaps, or fixing hardware.

Elsewhere, a crew worked at a copse of dead sycamores, sawing off branches high in the trees, throwing them on a growing pile. Cass thought of the little crape myrtle seedling she'd been nurturing back in the Box. It was too early to know yet what color the blossoms would be—it would take at least another growing season before it bloomed—but it had the stout countenance and silvery bark of a lavender Muskogee, rare among the pink-flowering varieties. A row of them—they grew to a tidy twenty feet, rarely taller—would fit beautifully in the rectangular bed where the men were working, shading the tall windows of the classroom building and the pair of limestone benches.

Stop, she thought. She was not here to create a garden.

Halfway up the side of what she assumed was a dormitory, perhaps six or eight floors off the ground, clothesline was strung from one window to the next. A few shirts and pillowcases fluttered in the wind, and Cass thought she could make out the silhouettes of people in some of the windows.

Nell led them through the campus, skirting the deserted green, thick with dormant kaysev and, here and there, dandelions and weedy peppergrass. Cass spotted a couple of mugwort, which, if they were left alone, would grow a few feet tall and attract bees. She wondered if anyone here knew what they were doing, and scanning the flower beds, she imagined them planted with ornamental olives and weeping cherry and baby's tears between the paving stones.

She could make something of this place. The hardscape had been well-planned, the earth amended and fertilized. Things would grow here, beautiful things, and Cass could do the work she had always imagined, planning and creating gardens that would sustain people. So she would live among those whose beliefs about Aftertime were different from her own...would that be so bad? Would that be so different from living alongside some of the Box's residents?

Cass forced herself to put the gardens out of her mind as they entered the lobby of an unremarkable single-story building. Inside it smelled of something she could not identify, something fruit-chemical with a faint undertone of decay.

"You two sit there," Nell said, pointing to a pair of chairs pulled up in front of a plain desk with a three-ring binder and two pens neatly lined up next to it. "And here. For the kid."

She dragged a third chair from the corner of the room, then

sat across the desk from them. Her own chair was improbably luxurious, soft leather upholstery on a swivel base that looked like it had been looted from a law office somewhere. Who knew—it probably had.

Ruthie scrambled up onto her chair. The room was considerably warmer than it was outdoors. Late-afternoon sunlight splayed gold patches on the floor. Cass remembered the solar panels fixed to many of the red-composite roofs on the campus, providing free heat, without any mechanical investment. Before, she had always considered them ugly. Aftertime, there were a lot of "if-only" thinkers who pointed out that the seeds of a more energy-independent society had been there for decades, only to be quashed and obstructed by big-money industry and special interests. California had even been at the forefront, introducing and enforcing the Reid-Kohlm energy acts of the teens—and yet even a year ago the state was only drawing a tenth of its energy from wind and sun and other renewable sources. Every new politician made it their soapbox, until they won.

Cass helped Ruthie off with her parka and hung their coats on the back of the chairs as though they were seated in a restaurant. The moment struck Cass like so many of them did—quaint, pointless in a way; deeply sad in another; loss the faint undercurrent that ran through the simplest interactions that were now acted out, rather than simply done.

"What was this room?" Cass asked.

Nell barely looked up from her notebook. Cass spotted tiny sapphire earrings, a thin chain with a silver heart pendant, a delicate scar at the corner of her mouth, the kind of thing a little bit of concealer would have made quick work of. "It was the development office. They sat in here all day, calling up the rich alumni and asking them for money."

Cass tried to imagine the room buzzing with activity, desks where people worked and talked and laughed. Perhaps there had been pots of Boston ferns and spider plants. Children's drawings. Mugs with funny sayings and framed family photos. Paper decorations for the holidays and bakery cakes to celebrate birthdays.

"Did you ever see the campus, you know, Before?"

"I lived in Colima my whole life." Nell sighed and wrote on a sheet of paper in the binder, her fingers tight around the pen. "My sister used to work in the Engineering school as a departmental assistant. And I had a cousin who went here a while back."

Finally Nell looked up from the pad, on which she had been writing, and made eye contact. Her eyes were rimmed in red. "'Course, I'm the only one left, now."

"Look," Cass said, refusing to let herself think about Nell's story, about her losses. "I think maybe I can save you some time, maybe even cut your paperwork in half. I was, uh, kind of invited to come here? By Evangeline? I'm an outlier."

The change in Nell was immediate. She pushed the tears impatiently from her eyes and laid down her pen. When she focused her gaze on Cass it was ice cold.

"And I'm the princess in the Rose Parade."

"No, really, I—"

"Shut up, just save it, okay? I'm tired of people like you, thinking you can come in here and—I mean, do I look stupid to you? Do I? No one gets *invited* to come here. You come on your own or they haul you in, one or the other."

"But we were—"

"I said, shut *up*." Something about the woman's tone con-

vinced Cass to be silent. She wasn't going to listen, no matter
what Cass said.

And the truth was that if she was in her shoes, Cass
wouldn't either.

20

A SEARCH—A MORE INVASIVE ONE THAN THE pat-down they'd just received—would offer more convincing proof: the deeper, more pronounced scars on Cass's back, where the Beaters had torn off strips of her flesh with their teeth.

Even peeling back her sleeves might help her make her case. But her scars were so faint that they could have been anything, the mottling from a long-ago sunburn maybe, or the shadow of recent bruises. They would prove nothing, even though they were reminders of the Beater attack that Cass could barely remember.

"Look…we're not trying to make any trouble for you." Cass hesitated, not wanting to risk pushing Nell too far. Next to her, Ruthie looked frightened, sitting on the edge of her seat with her feet far off the floor, fingers curling and uncurling around the armrests. *Pick her up,* Cass willed Dor, but he didn't notice the girl's anxiety…and why should he? Ruthie wasn't his, no matter how hard they pretended.

"Just ask Evangeline to come see us," he said evenly.

Nell leaned back in her chair and stared at him. "You want me to just walk away and leave you guys here, alone, while I fetch her? Give you the run of the place? Do you know what happens to me if I lose you before we finish the documentation?"

Cass exchanged a glance with Dor. His expression was impassive; he was playing this all wrong. Nell needed to be in control. She was frightened, too, of the leaders, of her position in the Rebuilders, and her only defense was to be in command of situations like this one. Wielding power where she could. Give her that, Cass figured, and she would be more inclined to help them. "We're not asking for any special treatment—"

"You got anything valuable, like for collateral? Something to guarantee you're not going to try to run?"

"Your people took all our stuff outside the wall."

"I could take your little girl with me, I guess," Nell said, ignoring Dor's comment. "That might keep you out of trouble."

"Don't," Cass said, alarmed.

"What're you, like her new mama or something?" Nell glared at her. "All you convenient little families running around—just add water, right?"

"Do you have children?" Dor asked. Cass could have killed him.

"No. Never. But that doesn't mean I do my job any different."

"What did you do, Before?" Cass asked, trying to change the tone of the conversation.

For a moment Nell looked like she was going to answer, and Cass instinctively leaned a little closer. Nell was only a few years older than her, the sort of woman who might have been her friend…if she had friends. It was like at the bath; she felt the stirring of something, a long-buried need for community, for friendship. For a girlfriend.

But then Nell's eyes narrowed. "That's probably enough questions for now. Here's what's going to happen. I'm going to take all your basic information down. You can lie or tell me the truth. I don't much care. Hell, you can say you're Tinkerbell and Captain Hook if you want to. But I'd recommend telling the truth because it just gets harder from here. Smarter people than you have ended up sorry they tried to game the system."

"I'm not trying to game anything," Cass protested, but Nell ignored her.

She read a series of questions from her binder, taking notes as she went, and Cass answered them by rote. Her weight, the last time she knew it. Height. Family history for heart disease, stroke, high blood pressure, a dozen other things. Sexually transmitted diseases? Abortions? Cass felt her face burn as she answered the questions, her shameful past on display, though in this regard at least she had nothing damning to reveal. Even on days when she couldn't remember coming home the night before, she remembered to take her pill, and she made guys use condoms, no matter how drunk she was.

Her diligence had worked. She didn't catch anything, she checked out clean when she dragged herself in for the occasional guilt-driven checkup. So when she found out she was pregnant she was stunned. She had already scheduled an appointment for an abortion when it occurred to her that maybe she was meant to have this child, that there might be something more at work here than a birth control failure; that someone or something—some small part of the Universe that still cared about her—actually *wanted* her to do better. Not just for herself but for someone else.

"Medications?"

"What, do you mean *now?*"

"Recreational drug use?"

"No." Cass felt herself color, thinking of the times she'd readily indulge in a little of whatever was offered by whatever man she was with. Never very much, she didn't like the places it took her, not like—

"Alcohol?"

"No," Cass said much too quickly. "I mean, some, just. Ah. Social drinking, you know?"

No answer as Nell scrawled at her forms, not even bothering to look up.

"Why did you come here?"

Cass blinked. Nell looked at her expectantly.

"I told you. Evangeline invited me."

"Yeah, but you didn't come when she first asked you to, even if I'm to believe your story. Plus I have to ask. It's the last question on the form. So why did you come here?"

Cass had come here because the Box was no longer a place she could raise Ruthie...but also because Smoke had betrayed her and she couldn't bear to stay in the Box, where she had started to feel like someone she recognized again, only to have that ripped away from her.

She'd told herself it didn't matter where she and Ruthie went, as long as it was away from the Box. But that wasn't true. In all the world, at least all the world west of the Rockies, Colima was the only place that she knew still existed in a way that made any sense for raising a child. Yes, the Rebuilders were the enemy: they ruled through intimidation and fear, stole without remorse, murdered innocent people. But after the last twenty-four hours, after encountering the killers in the farmhouse and the fresh-turned Beaters, it might be the only place left outside the Box where Cass could keep Ruthie safe.

"I wanted a better life," she whispered, neither the whole truth nor entirely a lie.

The security headquarters were housed in the main floor of the castlelike building near the entrance to the campus. Nell explained that its upper floors also served as housing for all the highest-level members of the Rebuilders, the officers.

Nothing here resembled security in the Box, which comprised the open area inside the gates with their picnic tables and camp chairs and citronella candles and sputtering propane torches. There was nothing like the metal shed that acted as supply depot, arsenal and liquor cabinet; and there were no card games or dice or Frisbees or disintegrating copies of *Penthouse* or *Hustler* passing hands.

Smoke had made few changes when he took over security for Dor, deciding that the freewheeling, hard-drinking, gutter-talking brotherhood—and sisterhood, with respect to Faye alone—wasn't broke and didn't need fixing. Once in a while someone was too hungover to work and had to trade shifts. Very occasionally there was a fight that resulted in a shiner or a split lip that they got from each other rather than from their peacekeeping efforts.

The front desk here was manned by a young man in a pale khaki button-down shirt who looked like a recruiting poster for the Marines. He had an old-fashioned wire rack full of papers, and he was writing in a spiral notebook. On the desk in front of him were a pager and a coffee mug.

Here, as elsewhere, the doors and windows were propped

open to allow air to circulate. This room did not receive as much sun as the old preschool and the man at the desk looked cold, despite the fleece vest he was wearing, the gloves with the fingers cut off.

"Is Pace in?" Nell asked without preamble.

"Hi, yourself, Nell. Good to see you. How am I? Oh, not too bad," the man said, ignoring Cass and Dor. Behind him, tacked to a wall, were a large map of California and a hand-lettered sign reading HOURS: 9:00-12:00, 13:00-17:00. "Nice of you to ask, since you didn't show up to Clearings Tuesday. What's that, twice in a row?"

"Hey, I got a different assignment," Nell said defensively.

"Everyone's supposed to have Clearings. No exceptions."

"Not if you volunteer for Sanitary."

The young man's eyes widened. "You *volunteered?*"

Nell shrugged. "It beats Clearings. At least you know what you're going to be dealing with. And it never changes."

"You couldn't pay me enough—"

"So like I said, is Pace around?" Nell cut him off. "You may have noticed I'm not alone, right? These are a couple of joiners. David MacAlister and Cassandra Dollar. David's daughter, Ruth."

Ruthie, Cass wanted to correct her, but the desk jockey barely glanced at them. If this was what passed for security, maybe they could relax a little.

"Yeah, he's back there."

"Watch these guys for me?"

He regarded them impassively. "Yeah, whatever. I guess."

Nell disappeared down a hallway, leaving Cass and Dor standing. There were no other chairs in the reception area.

"May I use the bathroom?" Cass asked.

"Not without an escort. Not until you're in, anyway."

"In," Dor repeated. "How much more in can we be?"

The man lifted his wrist: there, tattooed in black, was the symbol Cass had seen once before—on Evangeline's wrist. The koru, a spiral resembling a snail shell, the Maori symbol of renewal. The symbol of the Rebuilders, deceptively appealing in its simplicity.

The sight increased Cass's sense of anxiety, but Dor only smirked. "What, you got some sort of assembly line? Everyone gets one of those stamped on their ass on the way to the welcome cocktail party?"

"Not everyone," the guard retorted. "You have to earn it."

"Yeah, what'd you do to earn it, buddy? Rack up a dozen merit badges? Learn to tie your kerchief in a pretty knot?"

Cass shot him a look. She didn't doubt that Dor was baiting the man on purpose, trying to draw him into a dick-measuring contest so he would be less likely to question their story that they were together. A family. Cass was pretty sure they'd fail any kind of rigorous questioning; Dor sure as hell wouldn't be able to prove that Ruthie was his. He barely knew her. It helped that she didn't talk, but he wouldn't be able to answer the simplest questions like whether all her teeth had come in or when her birthday was or what time she went down for a nap.

It was a successful performance, Cass had to give Dor that. The man looked like he wanted to take a swing at Dor, but Nell returned, followed by a tall, thin man with rimless glasses and a salt-and-pepper beard.

"I'm Bruce Pace," he said, extending a hand as he pushed past Nell, who managed to look both irritable and chastened. "So sorry that you weren't brought here directly. We'll get you in with Evangeline right away—she's most anxious to see you."

"All of us," Cass clarified.

"Yes, of course. You're, uh, traveling with David and his daughter?"

"We're together," she said, and ran through the list of words she could add: *lovers, a family, he's my boyfriend, we're married.* But "together" was the catchall term nowadays.

Pace's skepticism could be forgiven. Except Cass had to make him believe, had to make all of them believe so they could stay together and she could be with Ruthie.

She forced a smile and slipped her hand into Dor's. He hesitated for only a second before giving it a squeeze. "Ruthie's become very attached to me," Cass said. "She's been traumatized, and she doesn't talk much—but I think I'm getting in to her."

"Okay, right. Well, let's get you all back to see her, then."

He led them up the stairs. Windows had been cut in the stairwells, foot-wide square openings leaking insulation and wallboard, a crude but effective way to get light into the interior of the building. Two flights up, they exited into a large room that was divided into cubicles by chest-high walls. Most were empty, though there was evidence that someone was using them—jackets slung over chairs, cups and papers littering the desks. In a large open area, a couple of guys wearing old-fashioned headphones leaned on their elbows, staring at radio equipment that looked like it had been cobbled together from used parts. One made a note on a piece of paper. They barely nodded at Pace.

Beyond the open area was a glass-enclosed office whose tall windows overlooked the quad. On the polished black desk lay a notebook flipped to a blank page, a cup of water sitting on a folded paper napkin. Pace herded them inside, but there was only a single chair besides the one behind the desk, and none of them sat. Cass stared out the window, Ruthie leaning against her, until a cold, hard, familiar voice at the door made her jump.

"This must be our lucky day."

Evangeline strode around the desk, barely sparing Pace a glance; he backed out of the office as though he was happy to be gone.

The woman had changed very little since the last time Cass saw her. Her hair was still short and pale—shorter than Cass's, a butter-yellow blond versus Cass's bleach-white. She was still elegant, still beautiful; her brows tapered in a high arch that made her appear both curious and cool, and her mouth was set in a thin line. Her high cheekbones were perhaps a bit more prominent than before, and she was even thinner, her khaki shirt too large on her, her belt notched tight. But she looked more dangerous, somehow.

She stood behind her desk and regarded Cass coolly, extending her hand but ignoring Dor. "At last. I must say, I wondered if we would ever see you again, after your little disappearing act with Smoke."

"I never meant to go with him." Cass hastily launched into the story she'd prepared. "After you told me I could live here, you know, that you'd protect me, I wanted to come. But Smoke said he'd killed someone and that if I didn't come with him people would think I was part of it. Later...well, eventually he told me it wasn't true."

"But not until after you escaped with him. A...disappointment, from our perspective. And a greater disappointment that one of our own helped the two of you leave."

Cass knew Evangeline had hoped to send Smoke to Colima to be sentenced. His "tribunal" had been rushed, he was to have been taken away the next morning. The tall, bulky man who came to Cass's cell in the middle of the night made it clear he was only helping her to pay a debt to Smoke. Cass felt a twinge of guilt—Smoke had insisted on her freedom, and she'd never been sure if the Rebuilders were more angry about losing an outlier in her, or in missing a chance to make an example of Smoke. Had that big man suffered for her? Smoke could easily have left her behind, not just then but a dozen other times. He'd brought her to the Box; he'd waited for her when she entered the Convent to search for Ruthie. He'd been standing in the street in front of the stadium when Cass escaped with Ruthie in her arms, wearing the blood of the innocent.

But he had also made her love him. And then he'd left her.

"I never saw anyone helping Smoke," Cass lied. "I don't know what happened before he came for me, but he was alone when he came to my cell."

Evangeline raised one perfect brow. "Gallant of him. We went to considerable trouble to find out who the traitor was that day."

"Okay…and?"

"We established a man's guilt beyond reasonable doubt." Evangeline let a moment pass, a ghost of a smile on her lips. "He was punished. That chapter is closed."

Cass could guess what that meant—someone had been executed. She wondered if they had accused the right man. Either way, the rebellion was quelled.

It was cold justice, a ruthless order where anyone who found themselves in the crosshairs was destroyed. Cass had no illusions that it was fair. But this still might be the only place where someone like her—not an idealist, not a trouble-seeker, just an ordinary citizen looking for an ordinary life—could find a measure of safety, a routine to live by.

Even thinking that way felt like a betrayal of Smoke, of his passion and his ideals, of his willingness to avenge innocents. But in giving himself away for the people from his past, he had turned away from her. From Ruthie. And now he was likely dead, just like the man who'd helped them escape. What did that make them? Wrong, Cass thought—and soon forgotten, just a couple more decaying corpses in a land already littered and layered with them.

Life was for the survivors. And she would do what she needed so Ruthie could survive.

"So, David." Evangeline turned her chilly pale eyes on him. "What are you looking for? In our community?"

He held her gaze. "Same as Cass. Same as anyone. I have Ruthie to think about. We're trying to make a go of it. You can keep my family safe, I figure I can show you I'll earn my place."

"Mmm. Sure. It's just..." A thin smile, insincere, quickly gone. "It's just strange, though."

Ruthie whimpered and hugged Cass's waist, hiding her face in her shirt.

"I just would never have guessed," Evangeline continued, turning away from Dor and leaning in close to Cass, as though they were girlfriends exchanging confidences. "Leaving Smoke for someone so...different. Smoke's an idealist—a mistaken one, I must say, but someone who'd fall on his sword for his principles. While David...well, to put it nicely, I mean don't take this the wrong way, but he reads kind of...well, dependable. Salt of the earth. Hard worker, family man, all of that, but you've got a taste for the wild side, right, Cass? I mean, whatever caused you to fall for David? Just between us girls."

Her smile widened, and here she leaned forward, hands on

the desk as if Cass's fate hung in the balance. Evangeline truly was a beautiful woman, but cruelty made her seem brittle.

"I didn't *leave* Smoke," Cass said, knowing she shouldn't rise to the bait and trying to keep her voice steady. "I was never really with him. I only left the library with him because I didn't have any other options. Besides, as soon as we got to shelter, it was only a couple of weeks before he was gone again. He went out on an overnight raid and didn't come back. And by then I'd met David, anyway."

She turned to Dor and gave him the adoring smile that she'd practiced, an expression she hoped would convince Evangeline of her ardor—but when their eyes met her smile faltered. He was watching her with some dark emotion she couldn't identify. Anger, most likely; she couldn't blame him.

If she'd hoped that helping Dor would balance the scales between them, she realized now that was not going to happen. He'd already said he didn't need her to get inside the Rebuilder compound, and now she had burdened him with Evangeline's suspicion.

"So you fell in love with David because he was *there*," Evangeline said in a faintly mocking tone. "That makes sense, for you. Convenient. A nice guy. Maybe he gave you an extra biscuit at dinner. Is that it?"

"It was…just one of those things," Cass said, struggling to find a way to convince her. "I was…"

"Cass started a garden," Dor said, swinging Ruthie abruptly up on his hip. Ruthie looked surprised, but after a moment she snuggled against his chest. "My daughter loves plants and flowers. Can't keep her out of the dirt. She started spending a lot of time with Cass and…you know how it goes, one thing led to another."

The ease with which he lied surprised Cass. It wasn't just a fiction, made up on the spot; it was as though Dor slipped on an invisible skin and became someone else, if only for a moment. The change was subtle, hard to break down into parts. Maybe there was a bit more swagger, as though he meant to prove that he was confident with women. He held his head a little higher so that he had to look slightly down at Evangeline, as if trying to establish dominance.

The Dor Cass knew was not prone to self-importance. He was a watcher, a contemplative man who kept his own counsel.

If he could be changeable, so could she. Cass realized Dor's skill was less in the words he chose and more in the delivery, and she thought about what kind of woman would find Dor attractive, what kind of woman would be drawn to his power.

She ducked her chin coquettishly. "I needed a man," she said coyly. "David's a good one. And Ruthie gives me a reason to get up in the morning."

For a long moment the two women stared at each other, neither blinking. Finally, Evangeline laughed, a surprisingly delicate, feminine sound. "Well, let's see if we can give you another. Reason to get up in the morning, that is. As I'm sure you've already figured out, outliers are of great value to us, to our little society here."

"Because of the research," Cass said. "Yes, I remember you telling me that. How is that coming? Are you any closer to making a vaccine?"

There was the faintest flicker in Evangeline's eyes—a fraction of a second when her focus shifted, barely enough to signal that she wasn't telling the truth. "So close. The team is all very excited, of course. You're not just immune—you've used that immunity against a full infection. Let's see if we can expedite your welcome. David will need to be tested, of course. And Ruthie."

"You're testing everyone?"

"It's just a simple blood test." Evangeline pushed back her chair and they all rose, Dor picking up Ruthie effortlessly. "A finger poke, that's all they need. And I think you'll be impressed with our research facilities. It's the one area where we've retained power almost from the start."

"Electricity?" Dor asked as they followed Evangeline out of the office. She led them down the hall toward the rear of the building.

"Generators, for now. We draw a little solar power but a lot of the panels were damaged during the riots. We're working on that, but for now the team thinks we can get turbines operational by spring."

"Wind turbines?"

"Yes. The university already drew some power from them. It's just a matter of repairing the ones that were damaged and diverting the output. And we've been lucky to recruit people who know how to do that."

There was no irony in her tone, but Cass suspected that the experts they "recruited" were given little choice in the matter. Still, electric power from a renewable resource—the possibilities were boundless.

There had been talk in the Box of rigging up a crude wheel in the creek to generate some power, but so far no one had figured out how to do that. Three men who spent a couple of nights in the Box a few weeks earlier had plans to travel to the oil fields in Coalinga and find a way to siphon out the fuel—if anyone did that, car travel could be a possibility again, at least until it ran out for the second time.

And of course there was the ongoing quest to make ethanol

from kaysev. Some people believed that eventually kaysev would provide the clean, sustainable fuel that had eluded the world for centuries; for now most attempts were far from an unqualified success, difficult to refine and yielding a lot of malodorous black smoke.

Cass and Dor followed Evangeline out the back door, along a winding walkway that paralleled the new wall at the edge of campus. Between the walk and the wall was a lone building, three stories tall, plain and blocky and built of homely brown brick—a small dorm, from the looks of it. Many of the windows on the higher floors were obscured by narrow blinds, but here and there they had been raised.

Cass saw a face, round and pale, pressed to the glass of a window on the fourth floor, near the end of the building. It appeared to be a girl, perhaps a young teen. For the briefest second it seemed to Cass that the girl behind the window was staring directly at her, and her expression was one of the saddest Cass had ever seen. Then, abruptly, she disappeared.

21

"TAPP CLINIC" HAD BEEN PAINTED ON THE WALL next to the entrance to what had been a physicians' office building. Someone had carefully detailed each letter and outlined it with black.

"We aren't using the main hospital facilities at this time," Evangeline said, pointing out the large modern facility next door. The sign reading Emergency remained, but the doors were sealed with wood and more steel bars.

But the office buildings arrayed around the facility looked neat and tidy. As they approached, a guard stepped out from an overhang.

"Lieutenant Oxnard," he said briskly.

"Pace let you know we were coming?"

"Yes, ma'am."

Evangeline didn't spare him any further conversation. Inside, the familiar sound of a generator ground in the background. The second thing that hit Cass was the smell—the same industrial cleaner they'd used in every hospital she'd ever visited. The sliding glass doors didn't slide, and as they made their way through the lobby and up the stairs, they passed plenty of technology that, without power, was little more than junk taking up space—digital displays, elevators, door alarms, bays of equipment at nursing stations, telephones.

They walked down halls lit with a very occasional bulb. A woman wearing hospital scrubs pushed out of a set of doors in a hurry, pulling off a pair of gloves. She wore a turban and a fabric mask over her nose and mouth. Cass peered past her and saw—thought she saw—a woman on a hospital bed with her feet in stirrups, surrounded by more people in masks and scrubs. But the doors closed quickly and Cass wondered if she'd seen something else in the blur of people and activity.

Evangeline continued on as though nothing had interrupted the silence of the hallways.

"In here," Evangeline announced at last, and ushered them through a door to a small waiting room. The upholstered chairs and coffee table were from every waiting room Cass had ever been in—all that was missing were the magazines. A bored-looking soldier in fatigues and ankle-high boots watched with his arms folded across his chest as four wasted, thin, exhausted-looking adults in dirty clothes slumped in chairs.

The smell of unwashed bodies filled Cass's nostrils and she coughed and struggled not to gag, and then felt ashamed of herself: she herself had smelled worse not long ago, waking in a field with no memory. These people had struggled as she had; more, in fact, since they lacked the supercharged immunity the Beater attack had left her with. They'd been freewalking, on the run from Beaters and maybe from Rebuilders, as well. Whatever the case, they didn't look like they had it in them to go much farther.

Evangeline led them past the refugees without sparing them a glance. Beyond the waiting room was a warren of tiny offices. Through open doors Cass saw medical equipment, examination tables and cabinets of supplies. In several rooms, ravaged-looking patients were having their blood drawn by men and women in scrubs and masks.

"Don't worry, you're getting star treatment," Evangeline said sarcastically. Cass could tell it galled her to have to extend any special privileges to her. The woman still despised her, even more than before. "Pilar keeps her room clean. We only use it for those who, shall we say, do not pose a risk of contamination from the most common complaints."

The last office was larger than the rest. A middle-aged woman sat behind a desk reviewing a stack of hand-drawn graphs and charts, reading glasses low on her nose. When she saw Evangeline she removed the glasses and let them hang from a silver chain and smiled tightly.

"So this is our newest outlier. How delightful. I understand that Mary's cleared her schedule."

"No doubt slaughtering the fatted calf," Evangeline said with barely concealed contempt. "This is Dr. Pilar Grelo."

"Well, let's do you first then," Pilar said, reaching in her drawer for a pair of latex gloves. Evangeline raised her eyebrows. "Yes, yes, I'm still using them. I didn't get this far just to contract hepatitis or HIV. I consider gloves a perk of seniority."

Cass got into the chair as directed and laid her arm out on the platform.

"Finger, please."

She swabbed Cass's finger, and the strong scent of alcohol

filled the room. Ruthie, still in Dor's arms, wrinkled her nose and frowned.

The sharp lancet poke was quick and sure. Pilar squeezed Cass's finger and a bright, large drop of red blood appeared. She held a glass pipette to it and it was sucked away into the tube; then she tapped it onto a slide.

"Old-school," she said apologetically, as she centered a tiny square of glass on top. "It's the ultimate recycle and reuse around here—you're getting the finest in 1960s technology."

The blood bloomed under the glass into a red splotch, and in Dor's arms, Ruthie began to tremble. She turned her face against Dor's chest and held on to his shirt with her little fists. It was the blood, Cass realized.

"How fast can—" Dor started to ask.

"Results tomorrow." Pilar gave her a brief, chilly smile. "Pulling out all the stops for you."

Cass pinched her finger under the wisp of gauze Pilar had given her, the cotton pristine, unmarred by even a tiny amount of blood. She wished Ruthie would look at her now, that she could see the healing, that it would comfort her to see that the bleeding had stopped. The skin smarted, but she could sense her body responding already, healing the tiny cut. In seconds the wound would be invisible.

The Beater attack should have killed her, but instead it had strengthened her. The strips of flesh torn and gnawed from her back, the blood she'd lost, the exposure—she should have died an agonizingly slow death. Instead, her body had recovered and morphed into something stronger. Cass didn't know if it was an urban legend or not, but she'd definitely heard that the human body regenerates itself every seven years; in her case she felt as though she had been reborn in the time she was out of her mind, the days she could not remember before she woke, lying in the field. The ragged tears on her back had skimmed over, her body generating new flesh to cover the wounds. Her hair, pulled from its roots and shorn, had come back glossier and stronger. Her fingernails grew so fast Cass had to trim them every couple of days. The enamel on her teeth seemed stronger, her eyelashes thicker, her muscles more supple and flexible.

Pilar watched her squeeze the gauze to her fingertip, peering over her glasses. "So what have you been doing for birth control?" She spoke loudly, snapping Cass's attention from her daughter.

Cass reddened. Back in the Box, she and Smoke had used condoms whenever they were available. Raiders had brought back birth control pills from time to time, and Cass had considered the idea of stockpiling them, but she didn't want to mix brands or risk running out and in the end, she abandoned the idea. They'd taken chances sometimes when their stock was running low or her cycle lined up, or they were trying to be quiet and not wake Ruthie.

Near the end, when the tent in the Box was starting to feel more like a home than anywhere Cass had lived before, the chances Smoke and she took together hadn't felt so much like chances…and the idea of a baby with him hadn't seemed like the worst idea she'd ever had, back then.

"Different things," she said stiffly. She was aware of Dor watching her. Certainly there had been no discussion of precautions last night. She'd forced herself on him without considering the fact that she might conceive. But it felt impossible that the cursed and rageful thing they had done could result in anything more than release and regret.

"Conception does seem to be the one thing outliers are not very good at," Pilar murmured, tapping a finger thoughtfully against the bridge of her nose. "We're studying that, of course. There is some discussion of the elevated temperature of the body…but you aren't here to talk about that. We will supply you with prophylactics until we find out the results of your test. Now, if you would…"

This last she directed at Dor, who pulled Ruthie off his chest with reluctance and handed her to Cass. He reached across the desk, offering his finger to be stuck as Pilar selected a new lancet from a plastic box. Cass snuggled Ruthie into her lap and murmured softly against her hair, feeling her daughter's heartbeat through her warm scalp.

Dor barely seemed to notice the lancet piercing his finger, and swiped at the beaded blood as though it were an annoying gnat. Cass thought of his scars, the one on his forehead and the deep and fissured ones on his chest, which she'd seen in the light of last night's flickering candle. Dor had been wounded grievously, and Cass wondered at the tolerance to pain he must have built up—and what it would take to hurt him.

"The child," Pilar said, preparing a third slide.

"Do you have to test her?" Cass asked, as Ruthie wound her arms tightly around her neck and began to tremble again. Ruthie was stoic in the face of pain; a scraped knee or bumped shin never made her cry. But the sight of the blood had defi-nitely spooked her.

"It's a simple test," Pilar said calmly. "You yourself know it barely hurts at all. Hold her tightly please. It's better if she doesn't watch."

Better if she doesn't watch. The words echoed bitterly in Cass's mind. What would truly have been better would have been for Ruthie never to have been indoctrinated at the Convent, for her head never to have been shaved, her voice silenced with those of all the other little girls. For her never to have been forced to drink the blood of the Beaters in that sadistic ritual. Cass held Ruthie with her face against her neck and murmured softly to her, nonsense words, trying not to react when Ruthie's small body jerked and fought. Dor wrapped his hands around Ruthie's legs and held them still. When Pilar jabbed the lancet, Ruthie flailed with surprising strength, and she missed.

"Damn it," Pilar muttered.

Evangeline stepped away from the wall, where she had been watching the proceedings. "*Hold* her," she growled, "or I will."

Ruthie began to make a sound that chilled Cass. It was a scream, compressed and flattened into a thin, chilling wail, worse than if her daughter had yelled at the top of her lungs. Her face reddened and her eyes squeezed shut, her lashes dotted with unspilled tears, and she fought as though her life depended on it. Cass held on, her heart breaking, but as Pilar took aim again she knew that it would go worse for Ruthie if she continued to resist, and she held her as tight as she could.

Pilar jabbed the sharp point into Ruthie's skin with force, and blood beaded and spilled. Ruthie's eyes flew open and when she saw the blood her wail bloomed into a terrified, otherworldly shriek. She stopped only to get her breath and then she screamed again and again, an eerie banshee rupture, as Pilar fumbled with the glass slide and the tube of blood, muttering all the while. When it was done, Cass wiped Ruthie's finger on her own shirt, then wrapped her fingers around it tightly.

"All done," she crooned, whispering and rocking Ruthie. "All better. All better. All better."

Pilar busied herself at her desk, turning her back on them, arranging the samples on a tray, making notes on a lined pad.

Dor's and Cass's eyes met and he shook his head worriedly. All remained in this diorama of the aftermath of the screaming for a minute before Ruthie flailed one last time and went limp in Cass's arms, her wails winding down into snuffles.

"That's it, then, until we get the results," Pilar said, turning back to them with a tight smile. "Let's finish checking you out so we can get you over to Ellis. There's not much more we can do until we get the results back."

When Evangeline opened the office door, Cass heard crying coming from one of the other offices. Passing by the open door, joggling Ruthie to comfort her, she saw a haggard woman weeping while a man in scrubs stood over her and snipped away her hair, down to a quarter of an inch.

"Lice," Evangeline explained, grimacing with disgust. "We check everyone for parasites but these people...they're in rough shape. Hell, they've probably got worms and scabies and crabs, too. No sense tracking *that* all over the place."

After taking them to an adjoining office, Evangeline took her leave, promising to see them later. Her discomfort in the place was evident. The woman who checked them over was far more gentle than what they had witnessed with the other newcomers. She parted their hair with a fine metal comb, working under a window where the afternoon light was strongest, and looked in their mouths and under their arms. She kept up a steady stream of conversation, asking them questions about the trip, about Ruthie, chatting about the cafeteria and what was for dinner. "My girlfriend works over there and she told me they got some of that government cheese," she shared as she finished checking Cass. "How that stuff can survive a summer in a warehouse, I have no idea, but they're making some sort of kaysev mac and cheese. Do you like spaghetti, Ruthie, honey?"

Ruthie had calmed down and even seemed to have forgotten her anxiety about the blood. She almost seemed to be considering answering the woman, smiling shyly and peeking out from under her long, luxurious lashes. Cass gave the woman a grateful look. She had been ready to hate everyone, but aside from Evangeline with her frightening eyes and angry rhetoric, the people here seemed not much worse than people anywhere. Again the troubling thought floated through her mind that this might not be the worst place in the world to make a home.

"You *do* like spaghetti, don't you, noodle-girl?" Cass said, wiggling her fingers, and Ruthie laughed, her shoulders shaking soundlessly.

"Okay, your turn, noodle," the woman said, dropping her comb in a tall bottle of antiseptic. "Looks like someone's already given you a pretty haircut."

She reached for Ruthie's pale blond hair, finally long enough that it no longer stuck up like an overgrown crew cut—but when she touched the strands Ruthie ducked and made a tiny mewling sound. It took Cass a second to react—she'd been lulled by the warmth of her momentary happiness but gathered Ruthie in a tight hug as the little girl wrapped her arms around her neck and held on tight. The woman held up her hands defensively.

"I'm sorry," Cass said. "She, um, she had a…something happened."

The woman nodded and her irritation softened. *Something happened*—the catchall explanation Aftertime. Who was left who hadn't been wounded, who hadn't suffered some kind of trauma? Children's feelings were so close to the surface; they had fewer memories of Before, fewer years to learn to hide their feelings.

Only, Cass didn't know what exactly had happened to Ruthie to make her so skittish about her hair. Since she was rescued from the Convent, Ruthie was as affectionate as ever with Cass, wanting to be held more than ever before, crawling up on her lap, lifting her arms to be picked up. At night she often stumble-crawled from her small bed to theirs, making her way up and under the covers without ever waking. She liked to be hugged and tickled and snuggled, but she hated to have her hair combed, and once in a while she covered her head with her hands and shut her eyes and looked so sorrowful that it broke Cass's heart.

She knew they had shaved Ruthie's head in the Convent, but she didn't know why. Punishment? Religious ritual? While she kept up a one-way conversation with her daughter all day long, pretending that it didn't bother her at all when Ruthie didn't answer, she never talked about the Convent other than to kneel down in front of Ruthie at least once a week and remind her that she could tell her mama anything, anytime, that she would never ever be in trouble for the things she told. It was a lesson from a book she had once owned, something pressed in her hands by a well-meaning woman in A.A. the week after Cass had finally talked about what her stepfather had done to her. The book was called *It's Okay To Tell* and it was supposed to teach you how to deal with children who had been victims of abuse.

Offering the book was breaking the rules—in A.A. you were never supposed to give advice and Cass was pretty sure that the book was just another form of advice. Cass thought the advice rule was stupid—after all, what was the point of coming to meetings if no one was allowed to tell you what you were doing wrong? The woman was a fortyish, bloated blonde who seemed entirely without color, from her bloodless lips to her pale, cloudy eyes to her mud-colored clothing. She had pressed the book in Cass's hands and then held her gaze a moment too long, and Cass started to get uneasy. The woman wanted something from Cass, something Cass didn't know how to give—to be understood, to have someone acknowledge how she'd been hurt, to offload even a little of her pain. They stood that way for a second, each of them holding one end of the book, until Cass mumbled her thanks and yanked it from the woman's hands and bolted from the building.

She'd driven to a grocery store that was open all night and parked under the streetlights and read the first chapter. She couldn't put the woman's hungry expression out of her mind. When she couldn't stand to read any more, she opened the door of her car and leaned out, her hair brushing the ground, and slid the book behind the front tire. She closed her door and backed over the book, then drove ahead and back over it a second time, before driving home with her hands shaking on the wheel, not understanding what had happened. She never went back to that meeting.

But she remembered that first chapter. "Silence is toxic," was the title. It talked about shame and "interrupting the message," and so all this time later she knelt before Ruthie and said it was okay to tell, that her mother would always listen and never judge, that she was the most beautiful and loved little girl in the world, perfect in her mother's and—she felt only a little self-conscious about saying it—in God's eyes, as well.

"Well, you're all done here," the woman said now, bringing Cass back to the moment. "I don't need to check her. I don't want to upset her, poor thing. I can see you're clean as whistles, all three of you."

She summoned Pace, who led them back outside. More

hallways, more doors, out in the air again; it took a moment for Cass to get oriented. The wall was visible here and there between the buildings; from a distance it looked pretty, even quaint, as though ivy might grow up its sides, as though kids might lose softballs over the top.

Some people said the Beaters were getting smarter all the time. What would happen if they found a way to get over the wall? There had been evidence of cooperation among them over the summer—hunting in groups, for instance. A single Beater could be overwhelmed, beaten, even killed with a relatively low risk of infection, but three or four were another matter entirely. They had been smart enough to figure that out. What if their next leap forward was to drag things—pallets, wheelbarrows, crates—over to the edge of the wall until they could scale it?

Except that this wall wasn't meant simply to keep the Beaters out. It also kept the people inside.

Past the old bookstore—there were still pennants and T-shirts and plastic mugs in the display windows, though sun-bleached—toward a pair of low-slung, pebble-walled buildings, among the older ones on campus, built fifty years earlier when they favored odd angles and small windows. Wheelchair ramps led up to the door of each building. Someone had spray painted words on each building, an inexpert job with paint drips along the bottom of the blocky letters. Infirmary was written on the side of the building on the left. Pace led the way up the ramp of the other building, which was labeled Ellis.

"I suppose it's a little sentimental," he said. "Ellis Island and all that. Mary can be...what's the word. Grandiose? Well, you'll see. She'll probably come by tonight or tomorrow."

"Who?"

"Mary Vane. You know. She's in charge."

Cass had heard about her back at the library; Smoke and the other guards passed along rumors about her, bits picked up from travelers, from the few who'd encountered the Rebuilders and not been recruited. She was supposed to be some sort of brilliant scientist, a visionary. People said she had worked for the government, or a drug company, or that she taught at the university. A few said she'd been serving time. Really, no one knew for sure.

"What's she like?" Cass couldn't resist asking.

Pace hesitated, his posture stiff. "Extraordinary, of course. A natural leader. Gifted...passionate."

Euphemisms, Cass figured, trying to guess what he was really saying. It was no surprise that he was giving her the party line.

"Who's in the infirmary?" Dor asked.

"When people arrive here with conditions that cannot be treated quickly, or if they are contagious, they stay there while their case is considered."

"So it really is like Ellis Island," Dor said. "What happens to the ones who don't pass the test—you throw them overboard? Send them back where they came from, like they used to at the real Ellis?"

"We have a clinic," Pace said, ignoring his tone. "You'll be amazed. I mean, of course our hope is that you never need it but they do amazing things there. Full triage and emergency facilities, and they can do certain types of surgeries. They've done an appendectomy, a cesarean birth. Set lots of broken bones. If people can be cured, they cure them."

He opened the door with a key and ushered them in.

Little natural light made its way through the high transom windows, and in the large open room a single floor lamp was lit. Two men sat at a dinette table in the semi gloom. They got to their feet, one nearly knocking over a plastic tumbler, and Cass saw that they were armed, guns and Tasers on their belts.

"Hey, Pace," the taller one said. "Heard you'd be coming by. We're ready for 'em."

"These gentlemen will take good care of you," Pace said. "Kaufman and Lester, this is Cass Dollar and David MacAlister. They'll be with you overnight. The young lady's name is Ruthie."

"Nice to meet you," Lester said, giving Ruthie a slight bow and a crooked smile. Cass liked him immediately, then chastised herself for it.

"I'll be going, then. I'm sure I'll see you tomorrow."

The door shut with a resounding click, followed by the sound of a dead bolt sliding home. Pace, locking them in. Cass automatically looked for another door; there it was, through a narrow kitchenette, the bold-lettered Exit sign still in place above. No doubt locked, as well.

"We're glad to have you folks," Lester said. "Kind of dull around here today. Sometimes we're full up and sometimes it's like this. Ain't a whole lot going on, and we get sick of each other's company, mmm-hmm."

"Thanks, man." Dor shook hands with both men. Cass watched the way he stepped closer than most men would, the way the quieter Kaufman hesitated, the way Dor pretended not to notice. His grip was hearty, overly so, and Cass knew she was the only one who could tell this was another variation of himself, slipped on for reasons known only to him. "Appreciate it. Nice, the way you have it rigged. Got to say I'm looking forward to a decent night's sleep. Been a while."

"'At's a shame, ain't it." Lester shook his head, making a

gentle tsking sound. For some reason Cass thought of the skycaps lined up at the airport with their scanners and auto-taggers. The ones like Lester who had that old-fashioned way about them, a retro courtliness, really cleaned up in tips. "'Specially when you got the little ones. I think we have something for her round here. Got some games and puzzles. Let me look, now. Little lady, you want to see what we have back here?"

Ruthie nodded without making any move to let go of Cass. Lester chuckled.

"Well now, maybe in a minute. I think you'll like what we got, though. This used to be a preschool for kids 'bout your size."

"A preschool? On campus?"

"Yes, ma'am," Kaufman said. "Little kids here. The in-firmary next door was K through three. Student teachers from the School of Education did their practice teaching here. Worked out good for us, since the other one's got the separate classrooms, which is better for the, uh, communicable type people.

"And we got the one big room," Lester added. "Not much privacy but most folks are only with us a few nights before they get their more permanent-type arrangements."

A dozen narrow beds lined the wall, neatly made up and far more uniform than the accommodations in the Box, which were cobbled together from raids on houses and an army surplus store.

"Got those from the FEMA warehouse outside town," Kaufman said, noticing where they were looking. "Back during the fires in '14 when they set up a Central Valley supply depot. They never used them all and they've been sitting there ever since. Tip-top shape. New as can be. Gotta love the federal government, right?"

Across from the beds, forming small conversation areas between the windows, were easy chairs and love seats clustered around coffee tables to form several conversation areas. Books and games were stacked on the tables; a half-finished jigsaw puzzle was laid out on one of them. In the pool of light cast by the lamp, two people sat silently. A pale, thin young man lay back in a recliner, a blanket pulled up to his chin and tucked all around his slight body. He appeared to be sleeping. Next to him a middle-aged woman sat with her feet tucked under her in the corner of a love seat closest to the young man, a ball of green yarn spinning slowly on the cushions next to her. She didn't look down at the flashing needles, at her fingers working the yarn, but watched Cass and Dor and Ruthie carefully, as though she were forming an unfavorable opinion of them based on criteria knowable only to her.

"Just the five of you tonight," Lester said with manufactured cheer. "David, Cass, this is Malena and her son, Devin. Guys, this little one is Ruthie."

Malena nodded; Devin didn't stir. Lester turned away from them and spoke quietly: "You might want to just keep to yourselves. I'd say she's got a fair number of, you know, anger issues. I know you've been on the road—no need for you to have to deal with that right now. Why don't you just relax. Dinner'll come around in—" he checked his watch, an expensive old gold one, the sort that wound itself "—another half hour or so. There's towels in the bathroom if you want to clean up. If you need to go to the bathroom, just let one of us know and we'll escort you. It's right in back so at least it's not far."

After another moment's settling in, Cass took Ruthie to the

bathroom and cleaned as much of the grit from the journey as she could, Lester waiting patiently outside in the darkening evening of a tiny courtyard, as though he was her prom date, and she was feeling a little more comfortable. A night in a bed with clean sheets, secure in the knowledge that nothing bad would happen at least until morning, *would* be nice, especially since the presence of the others meant she wouldn't have to interact much with Dor. Discussions about their next move would have to wait. Cass felt a little guilty about that, knowing he must be even more anxious about Sammi now that they were so close, but there was nothing to be done about it. As nice as Lester was she had no doubt which side he was on.

Dinner had arrived when they got back. Malena was trying to coax her son to eat, holding a fork near his lips and murmuring as though he was a toddler. There had to be something really wrong with him, Cass decided, and she turned away from the unfortunates the way she—the way *everyone*—had learned to do. Tragedy wasn't contagious, but the emotions that went along with it were, and if you wanted to be able to handle your own burden you had to resist picking up even a fraction of anyone else's.

Places were laid for them at the dinette table along with Dor and Kaufman and Lester. Cass cut Ruthie's kaysev curd into bite-size pieces and helped her spoon up her peas—canned, with a sprinkling of fresh mint that made Cass suspect the Rebuilders had an extensive greenhouse of their own—so that none would fall from her spoon and go to waste. She was about to start on her own dinner when a loud, piercing tone filled the large room.

Ruthie jammed her hands over her ears and her mouth wobbled, and Cass wrapped her in her arms. Thankfully, it was quickly over. A man's voice came on: "Details two and five report to the Tapp Clinic. Repeat, all members of details two and five, please report."

22

"SHIT," LESTER EXCLAIMED, PUSHING AWAY THE dinner he'd barely touched. "Can't believe we got another one. Seems like I was just up."

"Somebody in five keeps drawing the short straw, I guess," his partner replied.

"No, it's not that. I'm just sorry to leave you with the rest of the shift." He looked genuinely sorry, Cass thought. She wondered if the two men were close. "You know how they drag it out."

"It's okay, go. I'm fine."

"Yeah, it's just—" He inclined his head in the direction of Malena and Devin and frowned.

"Nothing's going to happen in the next hour," Kaufman said quietly. "Nothing I can't handle. And you know if you don't go—"

"We're damned if we do and damned if we don't," Lester

said, pushing back his chair. "Okay, okay, but I'll get back as fast as I can. It's probably just another ragbag."

"Hate that. For your sake I hope it's just one this time."

"Yeah. Anyway, have fun. Ladies." Lester bowed his lanky form deeply, waggling his thick eyebrows, which caused Ruthie to giggle silently. He made a less elaborate bow in Malena's direction but received no response for his trouble other than a frosty glare. After he let himself out the building's front door, Kaufman checked the lock before returning to the table.

"Sorry about that, folks." He stared at his food, frowning.

Cass noticed that Dor had slid his dinner slightly closer to Kaufman's, his long forearms resting casually on the sides of the tray, a posture that emphasized his size and bulk. He'd made quick work of the curd and vegetables and mopped up the last of the sauce with a piece of bread, a hard-crusted, dense slice that was the characteristic taupe color of kaysev flour and studded with unfamiliar grain. Not wheat. Millet, perhaps.

Cass wondered when she'd be able to see the Rebuilders' gardens, to discover what they had cultivated here, if there were many plants she had not been able to grow in the Box herself. She'd had little luck with grains so far.

She was surprised by the intensity of her longing to see what else they had managed, to beg or steal cuttings and take them back to her own garden. To the soil she'd amended with compost cultivated in the narrow strip of land between apartment buildings across the street from the Box's entrance. Smoke and some of his guys had installed chain-link at either end of the plot for safety, and she loved to let her mind wander while she worked, enjoying the sun on her neck, the good earthy smells of the black earth. Even the rotting, decomposing garbage and leftovers did not bother her; when she turned a shovelful of earth and came up with a wriggling clot of worms, she was filled with the kind of intense joy and pride she hadn't felt in a very long time.

Despite the pleasant memories of her garden and her determination to wait until morning to focus on their next steps, Cass had trouble getting through her meal. She was tired from the trip, worn-out from the adrenaline spikes and crashes. Numbed by terror and faintly nauseous from all the blood that had been shed in the past twenty-four hours. She tried to force herself not to think about the car-crash decoy and the bodies picked clean by the birds, the terrible things that had happened in the house, the Beaters in the road—but she couldn't shake the aftereffects, the anxiety and fear. She helped Ruthie eat instead, and listened to the men's small talk, and stole glances at the tired woman across the room, who was doing the same thing she was, trying to coax food into her sickly child. Each time Malena caught her eye, Cass looked quickly away; it was too hard to see the desperation on the woman's face. Her eye sockets were sunken and purple, her hair lay in lank tangles, and her hands shook faintly. Cass could only imagine the prayers she had said for her son's recovery. Evidently God had not yet come through, and it looked like Malena had stopped eating and sleeping.

Dor made idle conversation and Cass also watched Dor watching Kaufman. She thought she saw something—a flicker, a moment of change when his keen black eyes seemed to focus like the sights on a laser. Cass knew Dor was mapping this man out. She supposed he had a plan—if not yet, he would soon. She was certain Dor was drawing conclusions about Kaufman, about Lester and Malena and even the sick boy in the chair. It was what he did—he observed people so intensely that he picked up on many things they didn't even know about themselves.

It was only one of many reasons she had avoided encounters with Dor, and he was not hard to avoid. But it would be a lie to pretend that she didn't watch him. Yes. When he wasn't looking, she watched him watching others, and it was like this, always. The laser focus. The absorbing of details. The filtering of distractions. The considering and calculating. And then—yes, just like now. The moment when Dor came to some conclusion, and his features relaxed and re-formed, chameleon-like, into a new public character he would play to achieve some unnamed end.

In the Box, these changes were subtle. Sometimes Cass convinced herself that Dor wasn't even aware he was doing it. Often he retreated to his most frequent mask, the one she thought of as his default but not necessarily true self: friendly but aloof, terse but rarely angry. A myth. He was the benevolent but unattainable man behind the curtain, the merchant, the moneychanger, the keeper of scales and coin. The guarantor.

Now, however, he put on a different face, one Cass hadn't seen before. She paused in surprise, a spoon lifted halfway to her lips, as Dor eased down in the chair, extended his legs under the table, and crossed his hands on his belly in an attitude of self-satisfaction.

"Man, I could sure use a frosty cold one right now," he said. "Raiders game on TV, halftime with those girls? You know, those little black skirts? Sorry, hon," he added automatically, shooting her an easy grin that didn't reach his eyes.

Kaufman chuckled. "Don't be saying that around here. I hear you, but in case you haven't heard, this place is dry. No booze, no smoking, no fun."

"No shit." Dor looked crestfallen. "Damn. So I guess I won't be getting my bottle of Jack back that I've been carrying around for emergencies."

"No, I'd say that's a negative. Though you can bet someone's gonna be enjoying it on the sly tonight. There's a little... creative warehousing going on, know what I mean?"

"Yeah, I hear you. Like any military."

They sat in companionable silence for a moment. Dor let it ride out, shaking his head sorrowfully. Then he said, "Yeah, so the—what did you call it? Ragbag?"

"Oh, that." Kaufman glanced surreptitiously at Malena and her son, then at Cass—she made sure she was looking away, as disinterested as she could manage to appear—and lowered his voice a notch or two. "We're not supposed to talk about that while you're in here—but, man, you gotta understand about some of this shit before you see it, y'know? I mean, you don't want to get taken unawares."

"Uh-huh, sure."

"Well—it's one of Mary's things."

"Mary—what is it, Mary Vane?"

"Yeah, she's been in charge since the start. Anyway, she's okay. I guess. I mean, some of her ideas are a little out there. They say she was some sort of government scientist or something, I don't know. But this, see, sometimes someone comes in and it's obvious they're infected. It's happening more lately. People eat any shit they can get their hands on, out on the road. Get hungry enough and they're not careful and they end up eating blueleaf roots, especially now it's going dormant and it's hard to tell which is which."

Dor's eyes flickered again, the tiny opening and shutting of the mask. Or maybe the flicker was the fleeting dimming of his true self, ceding to the intense demands of maintaining this other, dampened self. Either way, he didn't look at Cass.

So the Rebuilders had managed to make great strides ahead, again. Just as with the outlier immunity, they knew things here in Colima that people elsewhere—even in the Box where there was plenty of everything, plenty of smart people—took much longer to figure out. The Rebuilders understood the threat inherent in the dormant kaysev. People on the outside should have understood the danger, should have been wise, allowed fear to lead them. Cass had learned to detect those dormant plants that were dangerous and she had taken pains to teach all of the gatherers how to tell the difference between the edible kind and the blueleaf. She had actually only seen blueleaf twice since moving into the Box, and both times it was raiding parties who brought it to show her, specimens they'd found in drifts far out on the perimeter of their patrols. Anywhere people sheltered, summer vigilance seemed to have ensured that the poison strain had been obliterated.

"That's bad, man," Dor muttered, shaking his head.

"Tell me. We got a whole group here don't do anything but work on that shit. Everything we eat, they grow, even our kaysev. We don't eat anything from outside. They got them this whole greenhouse they're building. It's cool. Just wait until you see it. But anyway, that same test, you know the blood test for outliers?—they can use it to tell if you're infected, too. But, well…you know how it is. You don't really need it."

He looked down at the table, and Cass imagined they were all thinking the same thing. The infected went feverish within hours of ingestion. At first, nearly a year ago when the kaysev first appeared, you might think you had a bad case of flu, that your light-headedness came from the fever's onset, or something like that—hell, it had been thought a drug like acid at one point—but now everyone knew the set of symptoms that arrived all together: the luminous, jaundice-darkened skin; the fever that could go as high as 106 degrees in an adult, higher in a child; the odd bright luminosity of the eyes as the pigment intensified and the pupils shrank.

"Mary, she won't take any chances. If they're infected she won't put 'em in the infirmary long enough to get the tests back. Too dangerous, you know?"

Dor nodded. The disease was transmitted through saliva, not blood. You could touch the blood, even drink it, as some of the Order had done, and there was no chance of infection. But a bite—even a graze—led to the appearance of symptoms within a few hours. And for everyone but outliers, the disease was irreversible.

"What if they're immune, though?"

Kaufman shook his head. "It's too risky. I mean, it's only one in a couple hundred. The odds of finding one who's already starting to turn—well, it's just not worth the risk."

Cass felt her face go hot. So Kaufman didn't know about her, didn't know she was an outlier, or that she'd been one of the ones who turned.

"So what exactly do they do?" Dor asked, interrupting her thoughts. "To the infected?"

Kaufman winced, his mouth tugging down at the corners. "Ah, hell. I guess it's the most fair thing for everyone, given the circumstances, but...well, they rotate it among the security details. Anyone with firearms training. It's a firing squad. Out in the PAC courtyard. You know, the old Performing Arts Center...they use it for assemblies and... Things."

Firing squad. The words buzzed in her mind, forming an image of a blindfolded prisoner shackled to a post. Cass had seen so much, but it was the horrors that "decent" humans inflicted on each other that never failed to shock.

"Yeah, they just bring a dozen or so rifles from the armory, enough for whoever shows up. Only two are ever loaded. They tie the, you know, the infected person up and get it done."

"Jesus," Dor said. "So it's what, voluntary…?"

"Hell, no, I wouldn't exactly say that. You don't show up, you damn well better have a good excuse. I mean, there's a few things that qualify, like if you're on security, if you're in the clinic, something like that. But a situation like what we have here—hell, we don't really need two on staff here at Ellis. It's mostly so one of us can be in the john or whatever—yeah, it wouldn't look good."

Dor thought for a moment, wiping one big hand across his face. "What would happen? Something like that, you don't show up for your shift?"

"Man, I would *not* want to be that guy," Kaufman said. "In theory, there's this whole review system in place, a whole escalating scale of consequences, but way things are right now— how you have to, like, *shortcut* the *theoretical*—let's just say they don't hardly ever get to the finer points of justice, know what I'm saying? Most times you fuck up, you're gonna end up in the detention camp. I mean, something like this, you'd get work detail. I don't know, maybe you'd get a couple shifts with the diggers or something. But if you screw up too often and end up being tagged a problem—and they start forgetting to check on you? Leave you in there for too long, maybe with the general population? Let's just say it's not a place I'd want to be."

After that, Kaufman turned the conversation to other, easier topics: TV shows they missed, a memorable Giants game from the last season anyone played. Cass tuned out the words and just let the conversation flow around her, savoring the tone, normal in a way nothing was normal anymore. She got Ruthie settled in one of the beds, the sheets stiff but clean, smelling vaguely of lye or some other harsh chemical.

Before, when the power started to flicker differently from the way rolling brownouts normally did, sputtering for a moment or two before going out entirely, Cass sensed a terrifying loss coming, a return of the fear she'd been keeping at bay. It wasn't unfamiliar, and Cass knew that the way to handle it was to keep breathing, in, out, in…out…until it passed.

Humans had a visceral fear of the dark—all of them, from the smallest toddler to the frailest senior citizen. If Cass had ever doubted that the fear was inherent, those first hours without electricity—literally among the darkest of her life, as the power failed for the last time in the predawn hours back in March—made the point. Electricity and power had been weakening for days, and there had been an uptick in the riots, a surge in the senseless destruction wreaked by the roving bands of angry and restless citizens.

But when the lights went out forever, there was a brief and reverent silence when Cass felt as though the soul of the city had been sucked out. It had literally felt as though everyone who was still alive stopped breathing for a moment—and then the first cry carried out on the wind, grief-struck meaningless keening that was more intense than anything she'd heard. It was joined by another and another and another, until the street outside her trailer echoed with a terrible symphony of devastation.

Moment for moment, there was nothing more horrific than the Beaters, of course. And perhaps nothing more poignant than fever death, watching someone you loved slip into a luminous delirium, clutching and babbling, hot-skinned and gorgeous in their last hours, before death saved them from the ignominy of turning. But of all the abominations, the loss of power felt most like the loss of civilization.

There had been little pockets of power since then. Those who owned generators—if they were able to protect them from marauders and looters who would kill for as little as a case of bottled water or a tank of propane—consumed their foul-smelling noisy power in furtive bursts. And of course there were batteries, for a while. Some people jealously hoarded their batteries for emergencies, for flashlights and radios they were convinced would start broadcasting safety instructions again someday, somehow—and others used them up quickly, bingelike, playing music and games and movies on their big or tiny screens. Devices that turned human energy into power—shake flashlights and bicycle generators and the like—were suddenly coveted above nearly everything else.

But here in Colima it was almost as though the power had never gone all the way out. A grid was up and running. Its source was still the temporal and noisy generators, but the idea that Evangeline had planted—turbine and solar power, unlimited! Freely available even in the punished and thwarted new atmosphere!—was intoxicating. Cass wondered how long the novelty would last; people here seemed to have quickly readjusted to the idea of power, to an expectation of its availability. Society absorbed what was available with something approaching indifference. The same people who thought they would never again hear a song on the radio likely now barely registered the loudspeaker system, the space heater in the corner of the room.

It was a little like sobriety. That was the notion that had come to Cass as she'd pretended not to watch and listen to the men talking, fussing with Ruthie and trying to get her to finish eating. The first days of sobriety were a novelty. Hard, but oddly thrilling. You flirted with the idea, telling yourself that it didn't matter, that you didn't really need to be there, lumped in with the others, the *real* addicts. And yet you heard the voices, *one day at a time one day at a time onedayatatime,* whispering in your mind. You got through the day outside yourself, surprised. Is that me, seriously? Not going to the fridge? Not getting out the bottle? Is that me putting on my pajamas as though I were anyone else, as though I am really not going to have anything before bed? Is this me lying here in this room in the dark, my heart beating so fast I can't keep up listening to it, as though I could fall asleep and dream like anybody else?

Is this me in this same bed in the morning? Did I really not drink last night? The sheer wonder of that realization is enough to get you through the strange and terrifying morning, when you do not stir whiskey into your coffee, when you do not pretend you left your purse in the car so you can have a quick nip.

And that evening. And the next night. And so on until it's not new anymore, until sobriety isn't a surprise but an obligation, a dreary habit. Until you don't so much congratulate yourself as wonder if this is really any better.

So it must have been for the new Rebuilder recruits. Power. Light, heat. Not like Before, of course—those times had faded like a distant dream—but more or less predictably, and more or less on demand. A thrill, a luxury—safety! Yes, it must feel like safety, that first day.

And the next day, it's barely diminished. The day after that, if you are a believer, perhaps you are still thanking your god... but maybe the next day you reach for the switch and bathe

the room in light and you forget to be quite as grateful. And before long it's just another habit of your new life. Switch, the light comes on…switch, it goes off. You grow complacent.

But for tonight, at least, Cass let herself feel grateful. The temperature was still chilly enough that Ruthie's nose was ice-cold when Cass bent to kiss it, though she was warm under the stack of blankets, sleeping deeply. Cass accepted the maroon parka Kaufman offered her from a stash in a closet, and she would have drawn her chair near the space heater in the center of the room, under the single light fixture, if Kaufman hadn't gotten there first, settling into a folding chair with an old Vince Flynn thriller. Cass didn't feel like making conversation, so she sat on the edge of Ruthie's bed, absently rubbing her back through all the blankets. Malena hadn't left her son's side. It appeared that he would spend the night in the chair, rather than one of the beds; Cass could hear her murmuring to him softly from time to time.

Dor seemed restless, pacing the room, picking up objects and putting them down, looking out the windows into the darkness. When Lester returned, he was in the kitchen alcove, drinking a glass of water that he poured from a large plastic pitcher. He set down the glass and Cass watched him tense. Without a weapon, he seemed at a loss. His hand went to his hip where he carried his gun and, finding it missing, he made a fist and thumped it lightly against the counter.

"Back so soon," Kaufman said in a playful falsetto, putting down his book. "How was your evening, darling?"

"Ah, fuck you, dear," Lester retorted. Both of them seemed to be making an effort at cheer. Lester closed and locked the door carefully behind him, and then stood for a moment blinking in the pool of light and scanning the room. "Everybody accounted for?"

"Yeah, we're all happy campers here. Got the hatches battened down and so forth. Fact I was just trying to decide between the Macallan 12 and the 15," Kaufman added sarcastically.

"Yeah? I'd take the 12 any day. Anyone pays more for three more years in the cask's just throwing money away, you ask me."

"Hey," Kaufman said, "you think they're still making that shit over there? I mean that's some pretty primitive work, you know? Burning peat and all? I seen this picture of this scotch factory or distillery or whatever they call it, they got like these scythe things? Old dudes wearing waders and tromping around the countryside. Hell, it's a perfect industry for Aftertime. Got nothing but time to let that shit ferment over a peat fire. Nothing but time, Aftertime. What do they make it out of, anyway? Do you know, MacAlister?"

Dor pushed himself off the counter and wandered closer to the other men. Lester helped himself to a chair, his posture ramrod straight and his eyes roving restlessly over the floor. Kaufman looked worried. Cass guessed he was trying to take his friend's mind off the things he'd just seen and done. The execution…the rifles, no one knowing which carried bullets and which blanks. The body slumping forward in death.

The unlucky ones who had to haul it away, a bag over its head to guard against exposure to any post-mortem fluids. Would there be graves here in Colima? Trenches? Pyres? Some other method?

"Barley, I think," Dor said.

"You Scottish? Ain't that your people make that stuff?"

"My mother was Afghani. My dad was Irish. Came here in '88. Only drink my mom knew how to make was Nestlé Quik, and my Dad was a Bud man."

That got an appreciative chuckle from Kaufman, but Lester barely reacted.

"Well," Kaufman said, stretching out in his chair with his hands clasped behind his head. "I got first shift. Lester, you might as well see if you can catch a little sleep, since you actually worked tonight. Nothing much happens around here, folks, and the morning alarm comes early, so you might want to go ahead and get some rest yourselves. Besides, they turn the lights off at ten."

Dor cast a questioning look Cass's way. It was the moment she had been dreading. They were pretending to be a couple. Dor had laid their things at the foot of one of the double beds next to Ruthie. And now he slipped an arm around her waist. Cass stiffened at his touch, but there was nothing to do but yield to the pressure of his hand at her waist and let him lead her to the bed. When he sat on the mattress and removed his shoes, she hesitated only a moment and then did the same.

He pulled the sheets and blankets back for her, an elaborate show of courtesy that reminded her of this 1940s movie, this comedy with Barbara Stanwyck in Connecticut. All that was missing were a pair of pinstriped pajamas for him and a sheer peignoir for her, a thought so ludicrous that it almost made Cass smile. Dor, with his black eyes and corded muscle and twining tattoos, would look absurd in Brooks Brothers; he was at home in his ancient jeans frayed at the seams.

After she clambered awkwardly under the covers, he followed with exaggerated care, staying on his side. For a large man he was remarkably deliberate in his movements, and she could sense him making himself compact, crossing his arms across his chest and his legs at the ankles. In moments his breathing grew regular and deep. She doubted he was sleeping, but she wouldn't be surprised if he had gone to some disciplined corner of his mind, practicing breathing exercises maybe, a ritual emptying of the mind. Maybe something he'd learned from Faye or Three-High—or, just as likely, from Joe, who was rumored to have spent five years in maximum security at the Santa Rita jail.

Cass's own breath was shallow and jagged, reflecting the turmoil barely below the surface. Cass had never been good at containing her emotions, her wild bursts of fear and despair and fury and loneliness. As a child she had no means to displace the hot emotion that coursed through her, that controlled her mind and body. Alcohol had taken care of that, for a while, with its gift of numbness, of release.

Now, she had a few skills and a lot of practice under her belt. She had all the A.A. sayings and practices and slogans, a secret cache of tricks that had gotten her through many despairing nights. She tried them now, remembering the soothing words with her face turned away from Dor.

It wasn't enough. Cass lay awake, eyes as unblinking and wide as though they'd been propped open with toothpicks, heart racing and fears dancing in the corners of her mind, waiting for her vigilance to flag. The fears meant to rule her, to own her.

But Ruthie's soft sleep sounds were a comfort, an anchor. Ruthie shifted and sighed, and Cass reached between the beds and touched her daughter's downy hair and her soft cheek and that gave her the strength to beat the fears back a while longer.

Before long the lights blinked out, and not long after that Kaufman left his post in the dark at the table and Cass could hear him settling himself on one of the beds near the door, not far from Lester, who was snoring gently. After a while she heard snuffling coming from that side of the room. It took her a few moments to understand that what she was hearing were muffled sobs, the sound of a grown man crying into his pillow, hating his tears but unable to hold them back. When the sobs turned to soft, regular grunting a little later, when the man found release in a whispered throat-catching moan, Cass was even more certain it was Lester. That was the last release left, in the end, wasn't it? A way to know that you were still human, that you still had a heart, the release that bathed your pain in beautiful colors, if only for a moment, before bringing you gently back to yourself, emptied and ready to rest.

She blessed the poor man and wished him peace, even though she didn't know the words herself.

After that, though, she was able to doze in fits and starts, her mind slipping back and forth between reality and the shadowed landscape of dreams. Deep in the night, she woke to a murmuring voice; it took her a moment to realize it was Malena, crooning to her boy. Even though the darkness was complete Cass knew that the woman would be holding her son close, cradling his failing body like an infant in her arms, that she was singing the songs she'd sung him when he was a baby and was offering her soul for a moment's comfort for him, the only gift she had left to give. Cass squeezed her eyes shut against the sound. It was too much for her to bear, another woman's anguish.

Let Ruthie live, she prayed, and then she felt her face go hot with mortification because she knew she'd trade the boy's life twice over—a dozen times, a thousand times, countless lives she would trade, children loved by mothers just like her—she would trade all of that if Ruthie could live.

God, please don't hate me.

Or hate me, if You must, but let her live.

Cass knew that God understood her well, because He had crafted the crevices in her soul that picked up stain and edges as it fell. He knew the terrible thoughts she had and He knew she deserved nothing, that she was the unworthiest of souls. And yet He had brought her this far. She had traveled to the edge over and over again, and each time He had picked her up and carried her back.

Deep in the night, Cass felt both the greatest clarity and the greatest confusion about God. During the day she doubted His existence. Aftertime was inhospitable to faith, with its mixed signals of decay and renewal, its cruel hardships and paltry rewards.

But alone, at night, Cass caught glimpses of Him. She felt sure He existed and He made all this, everything and everyone. Only His purpose remained unknowable. Did He let Cass live because He hated her? Or because He loved her?

23

CASS EVENTUALLY DRIFTED INTO SLEEP AGAIN with this question on her mind and dreamed of a tree with no leaves that bore bitter hard-shelled nuts. The nuts fell to the ground and broke open, revealing withered and blackened meats. In the dream Cass fed them to Ruthie, one after another, growing more and more frantic as her daughter weakened and starved.

Dor's hand was on her hip when she woke from this dream, sweating and anguished. "Hush," he whispered, but he did not take his hand away.

"Was I...?"

"Crying. I didn't want you to wake the others."

She waited for him to say something comforting, that it would *be all right,* that she could *go back to sleep now.* He didn't. His hand covered the roundest part of her hip, his thumb resting lightly on the hip bone. He was no longer at the edge of the bed. He was too close. Inches away. She could feel his heat. She could smell his smell.

After what felt like a long while it occurred to Cass that she could move his hand. She'd just been too disoriented from the dream, that was all, but now she pushed his hand away, only he held it there, his fingers digging into her soft flesh, thumb deep in the hollow below the bone. He had a strong grip on her, and as she struggled against him he pushed back. He would leave bruises, if he wasn't careful.

"Let go of me."

"No."

Their words were whispered, greedily consumed by the silence of the night. Cass sensed the others' sleep was at its deepest; it must be the hours before dawn, when the soul repaired itself and the unconscious mind decided whether it would fight another day. It was the hour when the innocent dreamed elaborate, fantastical stories and the ravaged slipped gratefully to their deaths—perhaps Malena's son was dying now in his mother's arms. There was little risk of waking anyone, but Cass felt a stirring of something like fear.

"I said let go."

Dor hooked a leg across her and then he was on top of her, pinning her. He rested his weight on his elbows, he wasn't hurting her—but she could feel his arousal and it made her catch her breath.

"You had no right," he whispered softly, his breath soft on her face. "Everything you do, everything you've ever done, it was someone else who paid your way. You take things, Cass. You came in the Box, you came in *my* home and you started taking. Smoke paid for you then and he kept paying."

No, Cass wanted to say, *you're wrong,* but his weight on her chest kept her silent. He didn't sound angry. But he was wrong. She wasn't like that. What about all the years when things were taken from *her?* What about the things she gave away, over and over and over again? Her body, her hopes, her pride?

"Maybe this is the perfect place for you," Dor continued. His voice was soft, controlled, emotionless. "Rebuilders are big on taking what's not theirs. Just like they took Sammi. They took my daughter and they'll regret it, I'll make sure of that. But you, you'll fit right in here, Cass."

She struggled under him, pushing at his chest with the flat of her hand. But he just seized her hands and pinned them to the mattress above her head. She pushed against his calves with her feet, grunting with effort, and he hushed her again.

"You want me off of you?"

"Yes."

"Right now?"

"Ye—"

But he lowered himself against her, very lightly, his physical control exquisite. He brushed against her and her legs opened automatically, treacherously, and Cass realized she didn't want him gone at all. She—her body, her willful unrestrainable body—wanted him pressed against her, smothering her, taking the breath from her. Entering, stroking, seizing, pummeling, pounding, crushing, drilling, defiling, befouling her. She wanted him and he knew it.

"See?" he said sharply, his anger showing at last and now it was her turn to shush him, because no one could see, no one could know what she had wrought between them. It didn't matter that they were pretending to be a couple, that everyone expected them to be together—no, no one could know about her detestable hungers, her faithless betraying core. "How could you do this to him?" he continued, his body rigid above

her, unmoving; he had pulled away from her so that the only contact between them was his hands on her hands, his thighs on her thighs, he kept himself apart from her, he'd captured her but he would go no further. "How could you do this to *Smoke?*"

Now it was Dor who had no right. No right to say that name, no right to call him up from her bitter heart. Smoke was gone because Smoke had left her and Smoke had put aside her carefully built and given love as though it was nothing. It was for Cass to know and no other; it was for Cass to grieve, and no other.

"How dare you judge me," Cass snapped, and for a flashing brief second Dor looked contrite.

"I didn't mean—"

"You don't get to judge me," Cass repeated, but she knew what he saw when he looked at her—he saw the girl whose bed didn't get cold between men, the girl who'd do it in the back of a truck or up against a propane tank or in a gas station bathroom, the girl who didn't say no to the things nice girls didn't do, the girl who gave it up and spread it wide and swallowed. The girl who'd find her own cab home and didn't mind if you passed out after or came over with a six-pack and a hard-on.

She knew what he saw when he looked at her: he saw *her*. The real Cass Dollar, the one who'd been gone for a while, banished by the long hard climb to—and through—sobriety, dealt a devastating blow by her love for Smoke. Cass had dared to hope that old self was dead. But no. Dor saw it, he knew it, and now she couldn't deny it, not even to herself.

"Fine," he said, breathing with difficulty. He was impossibly hard when he brushed against her, he had to be using all his strength not to take her. Say what you will but Cass Dollar was magic with a man, the old Cass Dollar, they might regret it later, they might kick her out before they got their pants back on but in the moment they never said no.

They *never* said no.

And that was Cass Dollar's only power.

She bared her teeth and lunged for him, managing to graze his jaw before he jerked away. "So get off me," she taunted. "If you're so concerned about Smoke, get off me and neither of us'll tell him. Our little *secret*."

She spat the word out—and Dor did pull back. How he managed to lift himself off her, propped above her on the strength of his arms, his abs, sweating with the strain of it—only touching her hands, the outside of her legs where his knees were pressed to the mattress. She laughed—the demon from last night; this was how it had ended then, with her laughing maniacally and how it had spurred him, how he had driven himself into her.

"Go ahead," she said, "get angry, only it's not me keeping you here, is it? You're free to get off me, only..."

Only no man ever did, and her genius lay in that bitter drink she used to go back for, again and again. She took them to her and in the moment of her triumph, when they crashed into her and lost themselves, was that tiny second where she was suspended between this life and what might have been, and she felt—

—something. She *felt* something, wanted perhaps, or loved, or even just connected. Who knew? It was not a thing you could judge because you only understood it when you were in it and then it was over, lost except for the longing, a dream that slips away while you come awake.

"You can't," she panted. "You think you're so noble treating me like a slut but who's on top of me now? You're like a dog, no better than an animal."

She lifted her hips and ground them against him and he moaned, deep in his throat, as though he was in pain, as though she was ripping his entrails from him. Her legs were strong, and she pushed against him so hard he had to release her hands to avoid losing his balance, and she seized his ass and pulled him greedily against her. "Kiss me," she muttered, and when he wasn't fast enough she grabbed the back of his head and pulled her to him, pulled his hair and bit his lips and knocked her teeth against his and he let go then, didn't he, a torrent unleashed, a flood bursting its bounds. His mouth was on hers and he was inside her, his arms around her everywhere. All over her body as he drove deep and shuddering. She wrapped her legs around him tight, she met every thrust with her own. She urged him faster she took him harder. His hands found their way into her hair and they pulled hard they yanked her head back and his mouth was on her throat, for a moment she thought he'd tear it open, bleed her out while he fucked her and that was the thought that triggered her laughter one last time but he slammed his hand over her mouth and kept it there while he emptied himself into her and she realized she wasn't laughing at all but losing herself in a chasm wider than any she'd ever known and she shut her eyes and bit down hard and tasted salt and blood and later, when the last wave rocked her like a rag doll she wondered if this time maybe maybe maybe she wouldn't have to wake up at all.

24

CASS WOKE IN RUTHIE'S BED, WHERE SHE'D
retreated as soon as the thing of the night before was over.

She opened her eyes without moving and saw that Dor
was at the table with Lester, dressed, his hair wet, reading a
paperback book. How had she slept through everything—the
sounds of people waking, dressing, making coffee?

Dor turned a page. He lifted his mug to his lips. Set it
down.

Ruthie nestled close against Cass's chest and Cass tried to
put everything out of her mind but her daughter. *I am here I
am here I am here for you.* But only hours ago, there had been
nothing in her mind but crazy rage as she bit down on Dor's
hand and silently screamed, not five yards away.

She had to go to the bathroom. She wanted to clean herself
and she had to pee. She grated her teeth against each other
and got out of bed as carefully as she could, pulling the covers
back in place and smoothing them down.

"Good morning," she mumbled, not looking at anyone.

When she returned a little while later with Lester, feeling a little calmer after a shower of lukewarm water in a public stall, Kaufman was there as well and food trays had arrived. Cass checked on Ruthie, who was still sleeping. Over on the other side of the room, Malena and her son slept, too. The woman had to be exhausted from her round-the-clock vigil. Well—almost around the clock, anyway, Cass thought. No one had been awake besides her and Dor, at least for a little while.

Malena was going to wake up sore. She had pulled a straight-backed chair close to the recliner where her son lay, and leaned against his shoulder, her head at an uncomfortable angle, her hands clasped in her lap. As Cass watched, the woman shifted in her chair, her eyelids fluttering and her mouth forming silent words. She woke with a start, a muffled exhalation, and her hands went straight to her son's face and her fingers danced under his jaw, searching for a pulse and then, when she found it, clasping his face gently. She caressed his hair as he slept on, unmoving. In the morning light Cass could see that his skin was sallow and waxy. He looked desperately ill, and if Cass had to guess she wouldn't expect him to live many more days, and the thought was too much and so she busied herself with making the bed.

When someone touched her shoulder, Cass startled and backed away, but it was only Malena. "You'll stay with him," she said urgently. Up close Cass could see the deep grooves in her skin, the bruise-purple smudges beneath her eyes, the sagging of the pale crepey skin under her chin. Her coarse hair was salted with gray, loose strands clinging to the fabric of her coat. She smelled of many days without washing, and her breath made Cass turn away.

"Stay with Devin. Please. I'll be just a minute," she repeated.

"Come on, Malena," Lester called from across the room. He sounded indifferent, even irritated, but Cass remembered the night before, his muffled sobs. Cass knew that equation well. He didn't have enough left over to care about Malena. "Come with me now, you can have a nice shower."

"I'll stay with him." Dor set down his coffee mug and book. "I'm glad to. I'll watch him, your boy. I'll make sure he's okay."

The woman's eyes darted back and forth between Dor and Cass. "But it has to be…"

Cass knew what she meant: a woman. It has to be a woman, a mother.

"No. You go with Cass. Take a little time for yourself. I'll watch him."

Dor said it with finality, firmly. It was his way, to take charge, to feel responsible. Cass realized she'd never seen it that way before; she'd always thought of the Box as his trophy, a symbol of his striving and his wealth. But it was also his sanctuary, one he shared with anyone who came along… unselfishly. Bravely. She had wanted to think his controlling and calculating was exclusively for his own gain. But maybe it really was for other people.

"Come on," she said, linking her arm with Malena's, finding it thin and bony. "Let's go. We need to go for a few minutes. It's going to be fine. Dor will take good care of your son."

Malena allowed herself to be led, like a child, looking over her shoulder at the sleeping young man the whole way. Lester walked in front of them and Malena leaned practically weightless on Cass's arm. "Devin will be nineteen next March," she said, and Cass knew that the boy would never see another March.

"He's a handsome boy," she said softly.

"He needs Beclosterone. Only twenty milligrams twice a day, that's not so much. And they have it here. You know they have it here, the Rebuilders? You know that?"

Cass nodded, though she had never heard of Beclosterone and while she was sure that the Rebuilders stockpiled medicine as well as everything else, she also knew that they would not spare medication for a boy who was this sick. After all, he couldn't work, and even though he looked like he was starving he was still a drain on resources.

"We find out today if we're outliers. We get the results today."

"Do you think...you are?" Even as Cass asked the question she knew it couldn't be true, that the woman's desperate hopes would be dashed.

"Yes," Malena said too quickly. "Yes, I'm sure of it. Devin, anyway. He's always been special, ever since he was born." Her eyes flickered and burned, and the skin at the corner of her mouth twitched with a manic tic. Cass wondered if she was losing touch with reality after her long journey, little food, little sleep. "Did you see him?"

"Yes, I did," Cass said softly.

"All he needs is just twenty milligrams of Beclosterone. Every day. But even every other day would help. It would be something. Do you know that when he was born he had a full head of hair? A fair child like him—do you know how rare that is?"

Cass murmured sympathetically, but Malena didn't seem to hear; she went right on talking.

"He took his first steps before he was eleven months old.

Never crawled. Just that determined, he was. When they diagnosed his asthma, they said I'd always have to limit his activities. But I said no. I said, Devin will never allow that. He needs to be up and around, with all the other boys. He played varsity soccer his sophomore year. And that's on a team that went to State three of the five years he was in high school. And he never sat out a game. With his meds he does perfectly well."

They had arrived at the bathroom, Lester nodding at them to go in. Cass led Malena inside and she looked around as though surprised to find herself there. "I'll just be a moment," she said, with a trace of dignity, and Cass saw a shadow of the woman she must have once been—a suburban mother who had a weekly manicure and sat in the stands at every one of her son's games, cheering every time he even came close to making a goal.

But when Malena emerged from the stall, she began talking again, not even looking in the mirror as she made a half-hearted effort to wash her hands.

"They say if Devin's an outlier he can have his medication. Then he'll be just fine again. They do so much for the outliers."

"Like what?"

"They get all the best things. Everything they need. Medicine. Food. Everything. And they don't have to work, not hard labor anyway." She flapped her damp hands. "Devin's not cut out for manual labor."

"He's... You take good care of him."

"In Tapp," Malena continued, not listening. "We had the whole day in Tapp, all those tests, there was a lady who talked to us. She liked Devin. She could tell he was special. I think she could tell he was an outlier."

She was clearly teetering on the line between reality and wild hope. Maybe someone in the clinic really had talked to Malena, given her a false sense of promise. Felt sorry for her, no doubt—one look at her son's poor ravaged body would pull anyone's heartstrings. Cass wondered if it was worth trying to tease out the facts from the fantasy. "What about families? Do they break them up? I mean, if one of them's an outlier?"

Malena's face, which had been bright with possibility, lost some of its energy. She stared down at the basin of water, the thin film of grime on top, and frowned. "Well. I don't know. I mean. I think I would go with him, as his caretaker. I've been there for Devin his whole life. It wouldn't make sense for me not to."

Cass sighed, and decided she'd pushed Malena as far as she could without sending her into an anxious spin. She thought about the first time she met Evangeline, how excited she had been that Cass was an outlier, the promises she'd made for a privileged future. Was it so hard to believe that the Rebuilders would cherish their outliers, treat them with a measure of respect? Was that why Evangeline had come to despise her, knowing Cass had turned away from the privileges the Rebuilders promised? Privileges maybe even she didn't get?

They were still half a dozen paces from Ellis's front door when Malena suddenly stopped and clutched Cass's arm.

"Mr. Pace is back," she whispered, "There he is."

And indeed, Pace stood in the doorway, sipping from a bottle of water, looking well rested in a fresh, ironed camo shirt, his hair damp and combed back from his forehead. Cass could feel her hands tremble as Malena tugged her closer.

"This means he's in. Mr. Pace must be here to get him. Oh my God, I knew it, this mean's Devin's in!"

She broke away and ran the rest of the way, Cass close behind. Her anxiety swelled into full-scale dread. If Pace really was here to greet outliers… Suddenly she wished she'd been honest with Malena from the start, if only to have prevented this moment, this false gift of hope which now seemed like the greatest cruelty.

Malena rushed up to Pace as though she might embrace him, and then stood awkwardly with her arms hanging at her sides. Suddenly she seemed uncertain of herself.

Pace extended a hand. "Malena Fowler, isn't it? Welcome to Colima."

"Yes, yes, thank you." Hastily Malena shook the offered hand. Two other people stepped from behind Pace—Lester and Kaufman. Malena craned her head around the group, looking into the room. Cass could see through the open door: it was empty, except for Ruthie sitting on a chair at the dinette table, with a bowl in front of her. When Ruthie saw her she slipped off the chair and ran to her, darting around Pace and the guards. Cass picked her up and Ruthie held on tight.

"You've already taken him?" Malena demanded, her voice going high and shrill. "You've already taken my Devin? Can I go see him?"

Pace exchanged a pointed look with Kaufman. "You told them about the modification?"

"No—" he replied hastily "—I didn't say a word to them, I swear."

"Lester? What about you?"

"No, we were together the whole time. He didn't say anything."

"What are you talking about?" Malena demanded. "What *modification?* What are you doing with my Devin?"

"Relax," Pace commanded, his face pinched with irritation. "The procedure is standard for the entire general population.

Please don't worry. Your son is in good hands. I understand that he is ill, and he will be given his medication while he is recovering. He'll receive a standard dose for the next three days. And I'm sorry that we cannot provide medication after that, but your work evaluation will take into account his condition. We'll try to find a position that allows you to spend as much time with him as possible until his determination."

"But this is all wrong!" Malena cried. In Cass's arms, Ruthie whimpered softly and pressed her face against her neck, and Cass rubbed her back, trying to soothe her. "My boy is an outlier. Devin is an *outlier!* He's supposed to get his medication! You have to take *care* of him!"

Kaufman stepped forward and took a gentle but firm hold of Malena's arm. She tried to shake him off, but he held fast; she was no match for his strength. Pace stepped out of the way, trying to conceal the look of distaste on his face.

"We'll do everything we can for him," he said stiffly. "But medication for chronic conditions is available only for outliers."

"But Devin is an outlier!"

"No. No, he's not. His test came back negative."

"You're lying! Why are you lying? You wouldn't be here if he wasn't an outlier, you can't—"

"I'm here for *them.*" Pace nodded in the direction of Cass and Ruthie.

It took a moment for comprehension to dawn on Malena's outraged face, but it was quickly replaced by fury. She wrestled her arm free and threw herself at Cass. "*You?* You can't be an outlier. You tricked them. You made them believe your lies! What did you tell them, you whore? What did you do?"

Kaufman moved quickly, pinning Malena's arms behind her and dragging her backward.

"Where did you take him?" she screamed, spittle flying. "Where have you taken Devin?"

"The same place every man goes who fails the test," Pace said impatiently. "To be neutered. Now, if you'll come with me."

"*Neutered?* What—"

"He'll be given a vasectomy under sterile conditions. He'll be made as comfortable as possible."

"Trust me, it's hardly the worst thing anyone's been through around here," Kaufman said. Malena stopped resisting and slumped against him.

"Only thing you need is a bag of frozen peas," Lester said, not unkindly. "I mean, if we had ice."

"Or peas." Kaufman winked at Cass, but she could only stare back, stunned. Was he trying to joke with her? Cheer *her* up?

"They run old movies off the generator," Kaufman said, leading Malena toward the table, but she went limp, her knees buckling. Cass rushed to help and together she and Kaufman lowered Malena into one of the chairs. "Get a bunch of guys lined up on the couch—they're all in it together, it's not so bad. And you miss a couple days off work. You know, not the worst thing ever to happen, hear what I'm saying?"

"But my son is a *boy!* He's not even a man yet!" Malena looked wildly from one of them to another, pleading, tears welling in her eyes. She jerked away from Kaufman but he held her wrists tightly. "Don't let them do this. You have to tell them. They made a mistake. Devin is an outlier. Tell them to do the test again."

"Ma'am…" Kaufman started. His face was carefully flat, not without sympathy. He exchanged a look with Pace. Cass knew what they were thinking: the boy would be lucky to survive a week, much less all the way into manhood.

And what of Dor? She knew she shouldn't care—after all, who wanted to bring children into this world? And she supposed the procedure he'd receive was probably no more dangerous than the drive down here. It might take him out of commission for a couple of days—but she could use that time to learn, to explore, to see if she could find out where Sammi had been taken.

She found herself unexpectedly thinking of Dor's tawny skin, smooth and hot under her hands in the cramped den of the house two nights ago. With only the single candle for light, she hadn't been able to see anything but shapes, shadows—but his skin was surprisingly silky under her fingertips, his chest muscular and practically hairless. Somehow she'd expected the tattoos on his arms and neck to have a texture, a surface that would abrade or pulse. But no…

Of course last night she'd seen nothing in the dark. With her hands pinned above her head she'd felt—well, of course she'd felt him in other ways. When he brushed against her, gritting his teeth and making a strangled sound in his throat. When he'd entered her in one pitiless thrust—

Cass felt her face flame and tried to look away, but Malena was staring at her beseechingly. "Make them understand!" she implored.

"Malena…"

"Make them stop!" Her voice escalated to a scream as she tore one arm free and reached for Cass, her hand thin and grasping, her nails bitten and ragged. Cass lurched away from her, bumping into Ruthie, who had silently followed her back into the room. Cass saw that Ruthie's face was pale and anxious, her eyes wide with fear.

"Don't worry," she said hastily, picking Ruthie up and turning her, away from the sight of Malena, red-faced and desperate.

Her little girl whimpered against her neck. At the sound of her faint mewling Cass tried not to react, but she hadn't heard that sound since getting Ruthie back, save a few times while she slept. Slowly, cautiously, she pulled Ruthie away and examined her face. Tears streaked her cheeks and her hair was damp, a few strands stuck to her skin.

"Help him," Ruthie whispered.

Help him.

Help the boy who Cass thought Ruthie had never noticed, who had neither spoken nor moved since they arrived, the boy who was little more than a ghost lingering between life and death.

Cass swallowed the lump in her throat and pressed her cheek to Ruthie's. Of all the things she'd longed to hear her daughter say...her first conscious sentence was this, a plea for something Cass could not promise—for all she knew the boy was already gone.

What was she supposed to say?

She had vowed, the day she stole Ruthie back from her own stepfather that she would shield her daughter from all the ugliness in the world. No man would ever do to Ruthie what Byrn Orr had done to Cass—he had put his clammy hands on her and told her that she wanted it, that she was a dirty slut who needed a man to drive the sinfulness from her. That she was born unclean and his touch would redeem her. That had been the third-worst of his lies, after "I have to do this because I care about you" and "You made this happen."

Lying on her side, face turned to the wall, while Byrn pushed her nightgown up over her buttocks, Cass had promised herself once she got away, she would never let anything like this happen again. Instead she'd won her freedom only to squander it on one drunken, faceless encounter after another. But when Ruthie was born she realized that she could protect her daughter from the ugliness of the world, even after she'd failed to protect herself.

"Help him, Mama," Ruthie whispered a second time, and Cass felt rent in two. How to protect her now from the most basic ugly truth of the world? How did she tell her daughter that they could not save everyone? That they had to let some people die, Aftertime, because there just wasn't enough to go around? Not enough resources, enough time, enough energy—enough of anything?

"Oh, sugar," she heard herself say, and she held Ruthie close, rocking her against her body. "Sugar."

She could not make this impossible promise. She'd just make everything worse. She couldn't help Devin, and soon he would die, and she would be in the position of having to tell Ruthie that she hadn't been able to help him after all. Ruthie would know that Cass had lied. Cracks would form in Ruthie's trust. And trust was the only gift Cass had to give Ruthie besides her love. Didn't her daughter deserve to know there was one person on the earth who she could always count on? Even Devin had that—as unstable as Malena was, upbraiding Kaufman and Lester and even Pace, screaming about her son—she had never flagged in her dedication to him.

Cass had made one other promise, in a moment of weakness. Several months ago, when she'd first awoken after the Beater attack, she'd met a girl in the library that had been her shelter. Sammi—Dor's daughter. Sammi was lively and brave, and when she asked Cass for a promise, she could not say no. Sammi had asked Cass to find her father. And Cass, tired and lonely and unmoored, had said yes. It had simply been easier than saying no.

Cass never believed it would happen—but it had. The odds of finding one man in what was left of the little mountain towns dotting the Sierras...well, the odds were small. And yet she had ended up in the Box, with Dor, and she'd passed on Sammi's message of love and hope and longing for the father she never forgot.

Cass knew better than to ever imagine that she was blessed, that there was a lucky star over her or a divine shepherd looking out for her. Her own father was little more than a distant memory, a hazy dream that she'd relegated to the other memories of childhood, in a far corner of her mind. And yet, the thing she had promised had come to pass—she had found Dor. If it had happened once, wasn't it possible that it could happen again?

But try as she might, Cass could not embrace faith, not this time.

"It will be all right," she said to Malena, who'd sunk back into the chair. Cass chose her half-truths with care. "But we can't do anything now. I'm sure they'll let you see him soon—right?"

"Uh...yeah, soon," Kaufman said, hedging. "I mean, maybe not today, what with the...procedure and all. But tomorrow. For sure tomorrow."

"I have to wait here until tomorrow?" Malena wailed. "I don't get to see him?"

Pace picked up a sheet of paper. It was printed with a grid, handwritten words lined up in the squares. "Actually we got your work assignments. Devin...well, given his special status and all, they're going to do a special determination."

"What's that? What the hell is a determination?"

"All it means is special circumstances." Kaufman looked increasingly uncomfortable. "Look, I'm sure he'll get some sort of desk job. Or something."

"Yes, I can't make any promises but they're looking for a few people in the records department," Pace said, but he wouldn't meet Malena's eyes and Cass figured he was lying. "And you're not going to be too far off. You're in the receiving depot. Trust me, that's a good assignment. You should be happy."

"Shit, I started in demolition," Kaufman said. "Breathed mortar for two weeks. I would have loved to get receiving."

"What about me?" Cass asked. "And David?"

"You're an outlier," Lester said, with a trace of envy that he didn't bother to mask. "That's way different."

"I'll have an assignment for you soon, but it's only temporary," Pace said crisply, giving Lester a disapproving glance. "For one thing, you'll be spending a lot of time in research. As for David, he'll be considered for an assignment from the regular population pool. That may change when you move to permanent outlier quarters. But no moves will be feasible until spring, at the earliest. There's a great deal to do. Now, let's get everyone moving. There's a new group that should be here any minute."

As he and Kaufman talked in low voices about how best to move Malena, Lester touched Cass's arm, his expression wistful.

"Those outlier quarters? When they get them done, it'll be the closest thing anyone's going to come to Before ever again."

25

DOR WAS WAITING WHEN LESTER ESCORTED CASS
and Ruthie to their room in the temporary quarters reserved
for those waiting on their permanent assignments, a nearly
empty floor of an unremarkable brick dormitory. The door
of their room was propped open and he was sitting on the
edge of one of two narrow beds, his jaw set in a hard line. He
jumped to his feet and stood glowering, large hands hanging
at his sides.

"Where have you been?"

"What are you doing here?" Cass couldn't help staring at
his crotch, which looked like it had the last time she'd seen
him—if he'd had a vasectomy, he'd also had a remarkable
recovery. He was wearing the same jeans he had on yesterday
and a shirt she didn't recognize. He'd shaved, but it wasn't
the precise, close shave he preferred, and she supposed no one
had returned his pack to him yet. Dor's one indulgence was
his razor, which he paid the Box barber to sharpen twice a

week. Entrepreneurs themselves, raiding parties often brought shaving cream or new straight blades to barter with Dor.

"I've already been snipped," he growled, "like I told you all before. We could have saved a little time if you'd listened to me." He directed this at Lester, who shrugged and turned to go, hand on the door frame.

"Just following orders. Besides, it's not like you had to go through hell to prove it. See you around."

His steps echoed down the hall. They were on the second floor of a boxy brick dorm. It was eerily quiet; Cass supposed most people were working at whatever jobs they'd been assigned.

"How did you prove it?" Cass kept her voice casual, unwilling to let out any of her emotions, especially not the embarrassment and shame that came to the surface the minute she saw him.

Dor shrugged. "Jacked off into a Dixie cup. With a copy of Penthouse from 2012. You'd think they'd be able to find a few copies from last year, given all the raiding they do."

Cass felt her blush deepen, but she was determined to keep things light between them. "Who was on the cover?"

"I didn't notice. I just looked at her tits."

"Ha." Cass didn't believe him. Something in her wanted to think he probably didn't look at anything at all, that he closed his eyes, that his mind was somewhere far away and unknowable to anyone but him.

And if she imagined for a fraction of a second that it was *her* he saw when he closed his eyes, then she was the biggest idiot of all, pathetic Cassandra Dollar, wondering, as she had a thousand mornings after, if the man she brought home was thinking of her as he drove back to his own house or apartment or trailer or wife, wearing the clothes he'd had on in the bar or party or parking lot or wherever they'd met. No man ever did, of course, she knew that now. They thought only of making a clean getaway, of washing all traces of her down the drain.

But Dor couldn't get away. Dor was stuck with her. Well, they were both adults—they would just have to find a way to deal with it.

"How did they know…you know?" Cass asked, aiming for nonchalance. "I mean, are you really, um…"

"Shooting blanks? Yeah, I had a vasectomy after Sammi. I think they just put some on a slide and check it out under the microscope. Hell, you could probably do it with one of those cheap scopes they use in middle school. The little fuckers are swimming around in there or they aren't, you know?"

Cass wrinkled her nose. "Um."

"Look, Cass, long as we're on the subject…" His brief attempt at levity, rare enough for Dor on the best of days, was clearly over. He turned away from her, made a show of lining up the items on one of the two student desks—a pen, a pad of paper, a plastic cup—in perfect symmetry. "Just in case you're wondering, I have no issues." He cleared his throat. "Health issues."

For a moment Cass didn't understand—and then she did. There had been a recent outbreak of crabs in the Box; one of the most popular items being traded lately was RID shampoo. There had also been a couple of HIV-positive people in the box—once-hardy people who, deprived of their medication, were now getting sicker and sicker. Safe sex, once as easy as a trip to the drugstore, was a lost luxury—though most people were willing to take the chance, given the life expectancy Aftertime. Smoke had told Cass one day, shaking his head in amazement, that in the comfort tents sex with a condom brought the seller almost no premium over sex without—no one believed they'd live long enough to suffer the consequences. As one old-timer put it, a phrase he repeated every time he scraped up enough to afford a night's entertainment, "I'd rather die with a smile on my face and a withered dick than with all my parts working and nowhere to use them."

"Oh," Cass said in a small voice. She focused on Ruthie, who had slipped over to Dor's side and was looking longingly at the neat row of objects. Cass knew Ruthie had her eye on the pen and paper, her favorite entertainment in all the world.

"And you? You…and Smoke—everything…healthy?"

Anger rose like sap in Cass's veins. *None of your business,* she wanted to say. The last time she and Smoke had made love, the morning before he betrayed her, she lay in his arms afterward—foolishly, obliviously—thinking that they would never be separated in this lifetime. That he was the last lover she would ever have.

But she'd been wrong, and now it *was* Dor's business. Because she had made it his business.

This is wrong, he'd said.

I don't want you.

But she had forced him.

And then last night he had punished her, and she'd fought him for it, demanding more.

She hung her head. "Yes. I, uh…before Smoke, before everything, I had a checkup, must have been a year and a half ago. Clean bill of health."

"You haven't—?" Dor said in surprise, then stopped abruptly, holding up a conciliatory hand. "I'm sorry. Not my business."

Cass knew the source of his surprise—that she hadn't been with anyone besides Smoke. She supposed she'd earned it. You didn't sleep with two-hundred-plus men between the age of sixteen and twenty-eight—stopping only because you had a baby, because you believed God had given you one last chance by entrusting you with another life—without earning some sort of taint, some sort of permanent patina of promiscuity. When Cass had returned to A.A. for the second time, after her disastrous relapse, she took to dressing like a matron for a while, desperate to obliterate her past. She had been convinced that there had to be something she could put on—the rosewater cologne that reminded her of her grandmother, an unflattering skirt that hit her midcalf, a hair band that made her look like a soccer mom—that would disguise her. But no. The men still looked at her the way they looked at her. And Smoke had told her a hundred times that she was sexy, that she was hot, even now when she dressed only for survival. He whispered it when he came up on her watering her seedlings or rubbing dust off her ankles with the towel they kept by the front of the tent. But Cass knew what he was really saying: that she was marked, that she could never shake it, never make it go away. She could never know if he really saw her, the real her, past this other, the mark.

But this was Aftertime. She couldn't let her lifelong shame, her old scars, stop her from doing what needed to be done. So she faced Dor squarely, forced herself to look into his flinty eyes. "I haven't been with anyone besides Smoke for almost two years," she said. In fact, it would have been since the moment she discovered she was pregnant, the moment everything changed, except for her one relapse, when she'd traded thirty-one months of sobriety for the bender that got Ruthie taken away from her by the people from Children and Family Services.

"All right then." Dor gave the cup a final nudge and then,

without comment, picked Ruthie up and settled her into the desk chair, smoothing down one of her shirtsleeves that had gotten twisted around her arm. He slid the pen and notebook into her reach. "We've got an hour before someone's coming by. I'm going to lie down. I didn't sleep much last night."

He stretched his long, lanky form out on the bed closest to the windows, crossed his arms over his chest and closed his eyes. Cass watched him with envy. He seemed to be able to turn off all the thoughts churning in his head, to make himself oblivious to everything around him. Obviously he preferred solitude—his self-imposed exile in his trailer was evidence of that—but he fell asleep almost immediately, as though he was alone in comfortable and familiar surroundings.

"Are you doing okay, sweetie?" she whispered to Ruthie, crouching down to look at the picture she was making. Like all her drawings, it was a series of scribbles, roughly round bubbles crosshatched with bold swipes of the pen. The day would probably come when Ruthie could draw a recognizable figure, but it was far-off. Still, she concentrated with the focus of a draftsman doing painstaking precise work and her every mark was deliberate.

Deliberate—it was the perfect word to describe Ruthie, or more precisely, to describe the little girl she had become since her time in the Convent. Cautious, careful, painstaking. Cass missed the old carefree Ruthie so much it hurt—missed her laughter, missed the way she ran shrieking when they played tag, missed the way she collapsed into giggles during tickle fights.

Ruthie looked up from her drawing and smiled. That would have to be enough.

"Okay, then Mommy's going to try to take a little nap, too. All right? I'm going to close the door, and I don't want you to open it. Not for anyone. If someone comes, if someone knocks, I want you to wake me right up. Understand? Me or Dor."

Despite her doubts about her ability to sleep, when Cass lay down she felt anxiety lessen a little. She was exhausted, and the mattress was soft and surprisingly comfortable, and the sun through the windows warmed the room. She began to drift, and the feeling was unexpectedly pleasant. Soon visions of her garden back in the Box swirled through her mind, the gaillardia plants sprouting buds and the ivy sending out pretty twining trailers. She dreamed of her garden until a sound interrupted her dream and she sat bolt up and discovered that she and Dor were alone, that the sun had crept higher in the sky and Ruthie had disappeared.

Cass rolled off the bed and hit the floor unsteadily, her legs heavy with sleep, her breath caught in her lungs. She steadied herself by clutching the bed frame and propelled herself toward the door with a surge of energy fueled by terror. Not again.

Not again.

Her panic lessened only slightly when she ran into the hall and saw a doughy woman with unusually careful posture walking slowly down the corridor toward the stairs, carrying Ruthie. When Ruthie saw Cass, she began to struggle.

"Mama!"

It was the loudest sound Ruthie had ever made. Cass ran down the hallway as the woman rocked Ruthie in a lazy slow dance as though she wasn't screaming, wasn't struggling. By the time Cass reached the pair, the woman clutched Ruthie more tightly in her arms, locking them around her small back so she was trapped. Ruthie pushed against the woman's body as hard as she could, her pale skin damp and red with exertion.

"It's all right, baby," Cass said shakily, stopping short in case the woman had anything even crazier planned. "It's all right. Listen, she's frightened. If you could just set her down—"

"She's fine," the woman retorted, a little testily. "I have nieces, two of them. I know my way around kids."

Was the woman as deranged as Malena? Cass turned over options wildly in her mind: make a grab for Ruthie, wrestle her away, run. But she saw that the woman had a blade at her belt, and Cass was unarmed. She would have to reason with her.

"Such a nice little girl," the woman crooned, swaying back and forth. She was a dark-haired woman of medium height, slightly overweight, with her hair cut short and large eyeglasses with frames that overpowered her face. She was wearing a plaid skirt and plain, black high-heeled pumps, an unusual outfit in these times when everyone dressed for practicality. "Such a good girl. Being so good for Auntie Mary."

Mary—Mary Vane? Could it be? Cass edged slowly closer.

"She's heavy," she said, willing her voice to be calm. "Ever since she turned three, I can barely lift her myself. Here, let me help you."

"Well…all right. We can have another playdate later, can't we, little Ruthie?" the woman said, setting Ruthie down on the floor and wincing when she straightened again, rubbing the small of her back. Ruthie rushed into Cass's arms and Cass lifted her and felt the tension leave her small body, absorbed her relief as she went limp.

"She's just so *lovely*," Mary said, as though nothing were amiss. "There's nothing in the world like a child to give you hope, is there?"

Cass gaped at Mary. Despite her beatific smile, the effect fell far short of kindliness. She had the crafty look of someone with an unspoken agenda.

"I didn't mean to worry you," Mary added. "You and David looked like you needed your rest, and Ruthie didn't seem to mind when I picked her up, so we were just walking up and down the hall together. I'm Mary Vane, of course," she added, offering her hand for Cass to shake.

Dor stumbled into the hall, rubbing his hair with one hand. "Everything okay?"

"Certainly. Why wouldn't it be?" Mary turned her wide smile on him. A tenuous grasp on reality, a zealot's single-mindedness: these words came to mind. She wasn't so different from Evangeline—but in her way, she was more frightening. Evangeline's anger made her predictable; you knew she would seize every opportunity for cruelties small and large. But Mary's changeable veneer could be concealing anything.

The mask Dor had assumed last night with Kaufman slipped back in place. "Nice joint you're running here."

"Thank you. I'm here with good news. What are the odds," Mary said, drawing out her words, savoring them. "Your daughter—and Cass—*both* outliers. It's statistically so unlikely as to be—well, not impossible, of course. Very little is impossible in nature, a fact that my colleagues are prone to forget, to their peril. To all of our peril. One has only to look at the centuries of human history that brought us to this juncture to arrive at that realization. But people don't often learn from history, do they?"

The look on Mary's face was calculating and intelligent, crafty and more than a little manic. Dor stepped subtly closer, putting his body between the two women.

"They told me Ruthie had a…strong reaction to the tests,"

she continued. "I'm devastated, just utterly devastated, to think that we caused her any anxiety. But of course I wanted to see her for myself. She's our youngest yet, you know—our youngest outlier." She looked at Ruthie with something like hunger, and Cass edged closer to Dor, holding Ruthie tightly.

Mary's gaze traveled over Cass: her face, her arms, lingering on the faint traces of the scars left over from bite wounds along her forearms. Cass felt her skin prickle and tingle under Mary's scrutiny.

"Evangeline told me something very interesting," she continued. "She says you were attacked by Beaters. Last summer. That you actually survived. I can't tell you what this means, to our research, to our development program...."

Cass sucked in her breath. There was only one way Evangeline could have found out—by bribing or torturing the information from Cass's only friend at the library. Elaine had helped her, had promised to keep her secrets. But how long would she have been able to keep them once Evangeline started pressuring her to tell?

Mary reached out a thin and bony hand, the nails chewed to red-rimmed scabs, and touched Cass's skin so gently that the hairs tickled. It was all she could do not to jerk her arm away as she told a partial truth. "I don't remember what happened to me."

"Mmmm," Mary hummed, and her hand slowly closed around Cass's arm, tightening her grip until her knuckles went white. She lifted Cass's wrist and stared at the pale soft underside, her nostrils flaring as though she was trying to *smell* the flesh. Then, abruptly, she released her and turned to Dor.

"I understand you were asking about the medical facility, David."

Dor's only reaction was a slight twitch of one eyebrow.

"Were you employed in a medical field, before? A physician perhaps?"

"No, sorry. I...sold computers, though. Had a few hospitals for clients."

"Oh, I see. Well, as you might imagine, we do not have a great need for technical computer workers. Construction, yes. I don't suppose you know masonry? Glazing?"

Dor shrugged. "I'm handy. I'm sure I can learn."

"Mmmm." She gave him a long look before turning her attention to Cass. "You, on the other hand, will be spending lots of time in the Tapp Clinic."

Cass kept her expression neutral. "Whatever I can do to help."

"That's what we like to hear." Mary's smile widened. "Tell you what. How about you and I take a quick trip over there right now—just us girls. We can leave Ruthie here with her daddy, get you back in time for dinner. I'd love to show you around the facility myself—I hope you'll forgive me a little bragging, but I'm just so darn proud of what we've accomplished so far."

"We've already seen some of it, when we had the blood test yesterday."

"Oh." Was it Cass's imagination, or did Mary's smile slip a little? "Okay. Yes. The blood test. It's too bad that..." She sighed, and for a second she looked petulant, like a spoiled child denied an audience. "They didn't show you the operating arena yet, did they? The patient rooms?"

"Uh...no..."

"Good! Because I want to show you those myself." Mary's good humor was instantly restored. "It was my idea, you know, using that building for the clinic. I modeled it after some of the World War I hospitals. It was really amazing, you'd have soldiers laid out in hotel lobbies and—oh, but we can talk about it on the way."

"Sure…great."

Cass avoided Mary's eyes. She was picking up on things she didn't like, things that set off her internal alarms. Cass, who had learned to read her mother's expressions and her stepfather's moods as a survival skill, who had listened to a hundred tortured souls baring their deepest secrets in church basements, was far more sensitive than most people to the subtleties of human exchanges. She was picking up something disturbing about Mary, a need for attention bordering on narcissism, a near-manic changeability of her energy. Occasionally, there was someone like this in a meeting, though they never lasted long. Their need for attention was never sated in the anonymous gatherings, which focused on the steps rather than the individuals.

She gave Ruthie a quick kiss and—since Mary was watching—kissed Dor, as well. Her lips brushed his cheek, warm and rough with stubble. The kiss caught him off guard; she had already moved away from him when he caught her arm and pulled her back.

For a moment she thought he was going to chastise her, question her—but instead he kissed her again, a real kiss, his mouth hot on hers, claiming her, tasting her. Before she could think she was kissing him back, a rush of sensation and need that ended too quickly when he broke from her and murmured against her ear. "Be careful," he whispered, and then he released her.

Cass put her hand to her mouth, breathless. It had been a physical response—nothing more; synapses conditioned to fire in response to stimuli, and yet as they left the room Cass couldn't help turning to watch the man she barely knew cradling her daughter and staring at her with an expression as indecipherable as it was intense.

26

THIS TIME, THERE WAS NO ONE LYING ON THE
table in the operating room. There was no one there at all,
except for a young ponytailed man who was setting out instruments in neat rows on a table.

"We use kaysev-based alcohol to sterilize our instruments,"
Mary said conversationally. Any traces of her earlier moodi-
ness, of the manic scrutiny, had disappeared when they began
the tour. Mary pointed out each feature of the clinic as though
she alone had been responsible for creating it. "And we use
it as an antiseptic, too. It's remarkably effective. We have a
whole team looking into new ways of preparing and using
kaysev. They're working next door—know what I named that
building?"

"Um, no…"

"The Carver Lab, after George Washington Carver. You
know, the peanut guy? He invented more than a hundred
different products—all from peanuts."

"Really?" Cass remembered Carver from a grade school song they'd had to sing about him, but she feigned ignorance. Mary craved recognition, and letting her be the expert seemed like it couldn't hurt. "Like what?"

"Well, a lot of food products of course, and cosmetics and medicinal applications. But what you don't hear much about is that he was able to use peanuts to manufacture gasoline and explosives."

"Gas from peanuts?"

"Sure. Just like any other plant-based ethanol—like kaysev ethanol, if you want a good example. Winter's set us back, but I'm confident we'll be manufacturing clean-burning ethanol by summer. But anyway, if you look at the way history's been depicted in our country, there's this relentlessly pacifist bent to it that isn't helpful. I mean, peanut butter's great for cheap nutrition and all—in a way it's kind of a parallel for kaysev, I guess—but real societal change doesn't come without firepower, without fuel and weapons and engagement. And casualties. Lots of casualties."

Cass focused on keeping her expression neutral while the woman talked about her theory of progress. All the while, it was becoming increasingly clear to her that Mary was danger-ously out of touch, maybe even crazy, speaking as casually of rebellion and violence as if she was discussing her grocery list. How had such a woman become a leader of the Rebuilders? How did she command their loyalty?

They had reached the end of a tour of the second-floor operating rooms, and though they had run into half a dozen staff and one groggy-looking patient being treated for a bro-ken arm, Cass had seen no recovery rooms, no evidence of the ill or injured. The casualties she was talking about could well include the survivors of the attack on the library—including Sammi, if she'd been injured.

"What's on the third floor? I mean, you were saying they're doing the vaccine research here. Is that upstairs?"

Mary's expression shifted, a hint of darkness settling around her eyes. "We're just using it for storage at the moment. We'll be expanding to fill up everything around here soon. But there's something else I'd like to show you now."

She led the way down the stairs, past the first floor, down to the cement-slab basement. In the stairwell there were no openings to let in natural light, and a single bulb, inadequate for the job, lit the space just enough to prevent them from stumbling. There was a smell here, something earthy and unpleasant and hard to place. The paint was stained and peeling, and someone had used a marker on the wall to sketch grossly exaggerated anatomical rendering of genitalia with an indecipherable caption.

"You know, Cass, that I am very hopeful about the role you can play here in Colima," Mary said, ignoring both the images and the smell. "But Evangeline has some…concerns, I suppose you might say, that I would like to put to rest. She has nothing to do with research, but I have found that it's best to address this sort of thing quickly. And decisively. You know, without a lot of fussing around and double-talking. What do you think of Evangeline, by the way?"

"I—uh, well, I don't really know her," Cass hedged. Was Mary questioning one of her top lieutenants? Or was it possible that Evangeline wasn't as powerful as she wanted people to think? "I met her at the library, and—"

"Evangeline tells me you were traveling with Edward Schaffer, whom I believe is also known as Smoke."

The uneasiness Cass had been carrying throughout the day

tightened in her stomach. "I mean, yes, I was traveling with him but we had just met that day, at the, uh, school where he was sheltering. He was just, he offered to escort me to the library and I was glad to have him along."

"You know that he is an enemy to our work, our vision. That he murdered some of our people who were on a peaceful mission."

"I…had heard, later."

She forced herself to stay completely still, giving away nothing, as Mary watched her, frowning. At last, the deep-etched lines on her forehead relaxed, and she sighed.

"I suppose you couldn't have known that when you met him. I have to say, it's a real shame that the people at that school engaged my team and made bloodshed unavoidable. Of course we would have liked to accommodate all of them. But more to the point, the school was a more than serviceable shelter, and they had laid in enough stores to last through the winter."

Cass's uneasiness intensified; she had little doubt that those stores had been taken and brought to Colima along with Sammi and the few other survivors of the battle. And she was equally sure that the bloodshed there could have been avoided if the Rebuilders hadn't unilaterally attacked the shelter and brutalized the people living there. But she forced herself to remain quiet.

"Anyway, perhaps I should just show you what I brought you here to see, instead of talking on and on and on. Ha!"

And with that odd punctuation, they had reached the bottom of the stairs.

Mary took a key from her pocket and unlocked the scarred metal door before them. She pushed it open and stepped out of Cass's way, giving her an unobstructed view of a large,

open, murky corridor lined with half a dozen hospital cots
and a couple of straight-backed chairs. Men in Rebuilder uni-
forms rose from the chairs. People lay in several of the cots,
motionless and covered with blankets, their forms but lumpy
masses in the dark. Doors leading off the corridor opened into
a mechanical room, where the building's HVAC equipment
sat silent and still.

"We reserve this little area for our special cases—our patients who are headed for detention, assuming they survive."

Cass took a closer look at the beds. A large man lay on his
side at an awkward angle; it took Cass a moment to realize he
was handcuffed to the bed frame. His eyes were closed and
his lips were dry and rimed with crusted spittle, and a soiled
white bandage wound around the top of his skull. His chest
rose and fell with quick, shallow breaths, but otherwise he
didn't stir. It seemed likely that he needed more care than he
was getting.

Neither of the uniformed men made any move to join Mary
and Cass. One stood with his feet planted a few feet apart,
hands clasped behind his back; the other slouched against the
wall, eyes roving back and forth over the beds as though he
expected their occupants to make a run for it at any moment.

"Are these guys doctors?" Cass asked, already knowing the
answer.

Mary barked a short laugh. "Hardly, but they're Detail
One, the highest security rank. Alvin, come here a moment,
if you'd be so kind."

The slouching guard ambled over with the clumsy gait of
the extremely muscular. His neck was so thick he couldn't
button his khaki shirt all the way, and his sleeves were tight
over his biceps.

"This is Cassandra Dollar. She's an outlier."

Alvin nodded. "Ma'am."

"I believe she will have a particular interest in the patient in bed number two. He's still out, I take it?"

"Yes, Doc dosed him again 'bout an hour ago. They're keeping them all quiet for us."

"Can't question the wisdom of that decision," Mary said dryly, but the irony seemed lost on the guard. "If you'll be so kind, I think we'd like to see the patient for ourselves."

She led the way to the end of the row, Cass staring at the cots as they passed. One of them held a woman with greasy black hair that fell past what was left of an eye, now little more than a sunken socket. Both her arms were casted, so there seemed no need for shackles, but as they passed Cass saw that her ankles were circled by metal cuffs. A thin trail of red-tinged drool leaked from the corner of her mouth and a fly buzzed around her motionless head.

Cass wondered if she was dead.

When they reached the last cot, Alvin carefully folded down the blanket and sheet covering the man lying there. A weak moan escaped his lips and a tremor racked his body.

One arm was bent at an unnatural angle across his chest, the hand splayed against a torn and filthy shirt. The fabric was ripped in several places, and a long gash of his exposed arm was crusted with grit and seamed with yellow pus, the wound extending under the fabric of what remained of the shirt. As Cass's gaze traveled down the wounded arm, she saw that the hand had been badly mangled, the little finger and part of the next one missing, the stumps ragged and oozing, black with dried blood.

Cass drew in her breath. "Why…?"

"This is a special case," Mary said, and there was something odd and breathy about her voice, a sense of anticipation, of

excitement. "One of the ones who was injured in the skir-
mish yesterday up north, brought in on the truck: I'm a little
surprised he's still with us, to be frank. In our charter it's
written that we do not provide aid or succor to perpetrators
of war crimes on either side of an engagement, and you can
witness that we haven't. He has received no pain medication,
no antibiotics, no dressing for his wounds. He was tried in
absentia at the time of his crimes, and he would already be in
detention except that the nature of his crime calls for solitary
confinement and we didn't quite have that ready for him—
he'll be our first such prisoner and there's a bit of urgency to
get this one right."

A feeling of terrible inevitability was uncoiling inside Cass,
a horror that was building and drowning out the sound of
Mary's voice. Tried in absentia…crime calls for solitary…first
such prisoner…

"Who…?" she whispered, licking her dry lips, suddenly
unable to speak.

"Of course, they patched him up a little, because no one
wanted him to die on the trip down here," Mary continued,
and Cass could feel her unblinking gaze on her. "He and
these other two, they were lashed to the back of a flatbed
we use for supply transport. Didn't want them soiling any of
our passenger vehicles. Tell me, Cass, are you familiar with
Clausewitz's 'Principles of War'?"

Cass forced herself to meet Mary's relentless gaze. *Answer
her,* she commanded herself desperately, because to do otherwise would bring suspicion down on her, suspicion she could
not afford.

"No, I'm…afraid I'm not."

"Well, that will make for a fascinating discussion one day
soon. If you'll indulge me. Clausewitz was a nineteenth-

century Prussian soldier and a brilliant strategist. He said everything in war is simple, but the simple is difficult."

"Oh…I see." But she didn't see, didn't have any idea what Mary was trying to say.

"So many of my staff, they've lost any appreciation for history they might once have had. But I like to think I'm a true student of history, one who searches for meaning in the shape of what has come before and—well." She chuckled modestly. "Cass, may I speak frankly with you? I feel like we have a special affinity, me with my—well, what some people call my crackpot theories about society, and you with your genetic anomaly.…"

Mary droned on as Cass willed Alvin to get out of the way so she could see the broken man's face. Finally, having adjusted the linens to his satisfaction, he stepped deferentially out of the way.

And Cass got a look.

But what was left of his face was smashed, mangled, crushed. The skin was swollen and blackened. The lips were split and bloodied. The eyes were purple and swelled shut, and a gash across his cheek revealed the muscle below, a glint of white tooth. His hair was matted with red-black blood, and it was impossible to tell what color it had been, but Cass didn't need that clue, because around his neck the man wore a simple leather cord from which, unbelievably, a small token still dangled.

Under a layer of blood and grime, the facets of the tiny crystal teardrop barely sparkled.

Cass had stolen the crystal from a man who had shown her great kindness. A squatter who lived with his memories and a dwindling cache of weed in the middle of Silva, not far from the library where she'd once lived with Ruthie. Cass had accepted his offer of shelter for the night, and in the morning she stole the pretty little suncatcher, slipping it into her pocket without ever knowing why.

The next day someone else had stolen it from her. Pretty things had no place Aftertime; it seemed almost fitting that it should slip through her fingers before she ever had a chance to cherish it.

But one other person had been with her when she'd first pocketed it, had been there when the thief took it from her.

That person was Smoke.

Cass felt the cry building deep deep inside, gathering speed and urgency as it traveled along the tendons and nerves and veins of her body, ready to burst from her lips in a desperate anguished keening. It was *Smoke* who lay before her, beaten and unconscious.

Smoke. Her lover. Her betrayer. Here, on the edge of death.

He was the first and only man she loved and in this moment Cass realized that she hadn't even begun grieving his loss, that she didn't know the first thing about grief. She felt she could lie down next to him and welcome the blade to the throat, the steel barrel to the temple. That she could die right here next to him. Her fingers twitched with the urge to clasp his savaged hand; his blood would flow on her skin, and she would press herself to him, cradling the ruins of his body, and she would breathe in the presence of Death hovering, and she would say, *Take me, too.*

Cass was frozen—she was made of ice and of glass and of marble. Mary was watching her. Mary was observing and calculating and judging. Cass no longer cared. Let the woman have what she wanted. Let the crazy woman with her history and her plans and her schemes—let her have the death of Smoke and Cass and every other innocent on her hands. In death they would all be free.

Except

Except for the thing that always brought her back, every single time.

Ruthie, whose voice had been bound and locked, had spoken her name today. *Mama.* Ruthie clung to her, Ruthie trusted her. She could not let Ruthie down. She could not die now—*I'm sorry but I must decline your generous offer, oh, Death,* she could not lie down here and could not breathe out for the last time and mingle her blood with Smoke's.

She had to deny him. Even as she accepted the terrible truth, she was steeling herself, composing her features; her eyelids lowered in a virtuoso approximation of indifference and her lips curved in a bored frown. She turned away from him and looked deep into Mary's eyes, and traded one heartbreak for another.

"I feel the same way," she lied, and her lie was deft and convincing because it had to be. "I've always loved history. But if this...man did the things you say he did... I'm sorry, I guess I just can't handle it with calm the way you do. The pain he caused..."

She stutter-stepped backward, faking a stumble, letting her voice go frail and shaky. Mary's hand shot out to steady her and Cass forced herself not to react to the woman's clammy grip.

"I'm sorry," she repeated, deliberately turning away from her broken, wounded lover. She could not look at him, not now, not while she told her lies. "Only, right now, I think I need to get back to David. He'll be wondering where I am. It's been a long day."

Mary studied her for a long moment and then nodded.

Alvin didn't have to be told twice; he was already adjusting the blankets around Smoke, straightening the pillow. Mary walked back down the corridor toward the stairs, ignoring the other prisoners. The other guard had remained standing the entire time; he nodded fractionally when they passed by.

"What will his punishment be, anyway?" Cass asked as casually as she could.

"Considering that he murdered two people who were traveling on a mission of peace, and attacked one of our teams this morning, while they were on their way to rescue a group of endangered shelterers—I'd say there's little chance of leniency."

So he'd found them, Cass thought. The ones who'd burned the library. "Oh," she said as neutrally as she could, hiding her disgust at Mary's casual use of the word *peace*.

"We're still tracing the intelligence breach, trying to figure out where he got his information," she added. "Earlier, when I told you I'd been talking to Evangeline…she thought you and he might have been close."

"Me and *him?*" Cass feigned confusion. "But I don't know anyone here. I mean I just got here, how would I…?"

And there it was, the moment when she had to pretend the hardest thing. To stave off the pain of what she was about to do, she let herself spin back into a memory.

A spring morning two decades earlier, following a long winter of heavy rains. An El Niño winter. Her mother had been irritated that the rains had washed out the gravel from the flower beds; weeds had begun poking through the matted layer of sodden leaves that had collected there. Mim had never been much of a gardener, even before her dad began taking longer and longer trips up and down the coast with his band.

And now, trying to juggle her job and Cass, she didn't even pretend to make an effort.

Under a clump of sycamore leaves, Cass found tender green shoots that were unlike any others. She was waiting for Mrs. Cross, who drove her and Shelby Cross to school on Tuesdays and Thursdays. When it was Mim's turn to drive, Mrs. Cross always waited in the driveway with Shelby, wearing her ratty old terry cloth robe and sneakers. Mim dressed in a satiny gown and matching slippers but there was no way she'd ever come outside to wait, and so Cass had been poking around at the edges of the garden, saying the names of the plants she knew from the books she checked out of the library. Foxglove, anemone, hyacinth. And there: palest green, stems twined together.

She'd knelt down, trying to keep her knees off the soggy ground—her mother would throw a fit if Cass went to school dirty—and gently pushed the leaves out of the way, exposing rich black dirt, a couple of roly-polies, the mound of new growth. The pale green shaded to pure white at the base of the stems, and in the center of the mound was the beginning of a cluster of tiny flowers. Each fragile white blossom was encased in the thinnest possible corona of leaves, and as Cass wove her fingers into the stems, loving the way they felt against her fingers—dewy and full of potential—they trembled and quivered. Cass gently twisted and braided the shoots, thinking that the plant would grow that way, its stems twined and inseparable as they grew tall and strong, and everyone who passed by would wonder how they came to be that way.

Cass remembered exactly how the plant had felt in her hands all those years ago, even if she didn't know where the memory had been hidden or why she'd kept it for so long. But this was what she thought of in the second that the strings of her heart were gathered and knotted and tied so the lifeblood would no longer flow through them, when she betrayed the only man to ever take her heart.

The day after the rains, Cass had come home from school with a plan to make a circle of pretty, smooth stones around the plant, to protect it from neighborhood pets and kids on bikes—and found it mown down by the gardener, who'd blown the leaves and the topsoil out and left the flower bed shorn and empty and that was how it stayed all the long season until all that remained was the dead and dried skeletons of a few abandoned plants and the weeds that nothing would stop.

"Oh," she said, faking sudden realization. "Do you mean *Smoke?* That guy who came to the library with me? That's him? We didn't exactly get to know each other very well...."

"I see," Mary said, as the door shut behind them with a solid click. "Well, Evangeline wanted to be sure you had the chance to see him. See if there was any, you know, unfinished business between the two of you."

"Unfinished or otherwise—there never was anything to begin with."

As they walked across the campus that had once been home to tens of thousands of students with bright futures and now housed only schemers and the desperate, Cass wondered if she'd settled her debts, now that she'd betrayed the man who'd betrayed her first.

27

SAMMI LAY IN THE NARROW BED AND WONDERED if she hated Jed's killer enough to give her a reason to live. She had never killed anyone, not even a rabbit, but she thought she could kill the man who drove the truck. She imagined her blade slicing through his flesh. She thought about how his blood would spurt and how she would feel when the blood finally slowed and the man was dead.

She glanced across the gulf between the two beds. Roan had stayed up late with her, whispering and whispering. They brought Sammi and one other here last night after it was dark.

Sammi had finally fallen into a dreamless sleep and when she woke up the sky was pink and orange and the truck was parked behind a big, ugly concrete building that smelled like garbage, and the guards were yelling at everyone to get up.

She knew where they were: Colima, which used to be the university but now was where the Rebuilders built their new town. All the adults in the school hated the Rebuilders, but

Sammi hadn't given them much thought until last night. They weren't real until they set the school on fire. Until they started killing everyone. Now as they yelled and pushed, Sammi felt like she herself was only halfway real, like part of her was somewhere else entirely. Not with her mother, and not with Jed, though she would have liked to be; she wished she was dead with them but instead she was here, and as she stood shivering with her back against the truck, having to pee, her hair stuck to her face with snot, she felt the first tiny pocket of rage split open in her gut, because the Rebuilders had kept her alive after they took the only people she cared about.

Sammi was nearly fifteen, and in her life she'd been angry and she'd been pissed off and she'd been irritated, bored and upset and every variation on mad—and scared, definitely scared—but she had never felt quite like this. She wrapped her arms around herself as the guards took her and the others— only eleven of them now, since Jed's parents had been taken somewhere else when his mother wouldn't stop screaming— for a walk through campus, noticing the way this new kind of fury was the color red and blinding, which was interesting because she couldn't really see it. It started with that one little pocket but then it turned out there was more of it, way, way more stored up inside her and as they walked it sort of expanded and reached its hot tiny bursts out into the rest of her body, up into her chest and her throat, out along her arms to her fingertips, which she flexed and clenched experimentally. They were still her hands, her fingers…but they were the hands of someone different now, too. Someone who had no one, who was alone in the world.

The guards took them to some sort of medical building where they had checkups. Nurses, or doctors, Sammi didn't know, combed through her hair and her pubic hair and examined her all over and drew her blood. A rude woman with an accent gave her an exam—on the inside—and told Sammi that she wasn't pregnant and Sammi barely listened. She was taken to an outdoor shower and the water was freezing cold and the soap was handmade and scratchy. She was given new clothes—the old ones were filthy, covered with ash and the dirt of the truck and the journey—and they were soft and worn in and because they weren't the khaki and camo that everyone else seemed to be wearing, Sammi supposed she was not yet a Rebuilder.

Kathy and Mr. Jayaraman from the library tried to talk to her. A few of the others tried, too. But Sammi didn't answer and after a while they stopped and then everyone was quiet. In this way the day passed by, the library shelterers being taken away one by one and returning with their new clothes. Sammi dozed, lying on the carpeted floor. It did not occur to her to wonder what sort of building they were in until the room grew dark with the approach of night. Then she looked around at the others, some crying, some staring, and realized that none of them cared.

It was almost dark when a tall, thick-limbed older woman and a young man in soldier clothes came for her. Sammi had followed them out of the room, down stairs she didn't remember climbing, into a parking lot before she realized she hadn't said goodbye to anyone. Something told her she was not going to see them again and she wondered why she didn't feel worse about that. But then the soldier opened the passenger door of a compact car and Sammi got in the backseat, and the soldier and the woman got in the front seat, and it was the cleanest car Sammi had seen since everything happened Before, it even smelled kind of new—and that was something she didn't expect to ever smell again—and the soldier drove slowly out of the parking lot and onto a road that wound through campus, the headlights illuminating pavement ahead that was free of wrecks and skeletons and downed trees. It looked seriously like Before, which was kind of interesting—it was almost like watching a movie, like none of this was happening to her—when she realized there was someone else in the backseat with her.

"Uh," she said, surprised, and instantly regretted it, because she didn't feel like making conversation, not even with this girl who looked like she was only a couple years older than Sammi. In the library—as happy as she was to have Jed, as nice as his older brothers were to her, as cool as it was to be in charge of the child care—she had often wished there was a girl near her age. Just to hang out, just to talk about the things that you didn't talk to your boyfriend about, and you *really* didn't talk to your mom about. But that was then. And this was now.

"Do you know where they're taking us?" the girl whispered. In the dim light inside the car, she looked pale, with a long face and small features. Badly cut hair ended just below her earlobes. She smelled like mothballs and medicine and sweat. "No one will tell me."

"No." Sammi knew she should say more, but couldn't think of anything worth the effort.

"How long have you been here?"

Sammi sighed, and on the exhale said, "I got here this morning." She hoped there would be no more questions.

"I've been here four days. They treated us—me and my uncle—for scabies. I didn't have scabies, I kept telling them that. I don't know…maybe mosquitoes. Or probably a spider bite. I don't know where they took my uncle."

Sammi felt mildly disgusted and moved farther away from

the girl, jamming herself into the car door. She didn't know what scabies were, but they sounded nasty. Maybe they were an STD. Probably.

"I didn't eat dinner," the girl continued. "I haven't been eating much lately. We were living over in Brill—do you know Brill?—it used to be a resort." She didn't wait for Sammi to answer. It was like she was just talking to hear a voice. Sammi thought that if she could just get back into herself she would feel sorry for the girl, but she felt outside, and above, anchored to her body only by the unfurling thread of red energy that leaked out from inside it.

"We were sheltering in the office of the main hotel. There was a room there with no windows, my uncle said that was best. The other people got the regular rooms. No one wanted the cabanas. I mean, you're in your own building, no one can help you, you know? The Beaters got Jillian—she was this woman my uncle was kind of with, sort of—anyway, they got her last week. When the Rebuilders came everyone thought it was the Beaters again. I mean, not the people on duty, I guess they knew what was happening because they saw the truck, but it was before dawn and there was a lot of screaming and *that's* why people thought Beaters."

"Oh," Sammi said. How bad would it be to ask the girl to be quiet, she wondered.

"Don't worry about them," the girl said, misunderstanding her shortness, pointing at the front seat, where the man and woman were staring straight ahead, not speaking, not paying attention to anything but the road. "They haven't said anything to me at all since they came to get me."

Sammi knew she was supposed to talk next, to ask a question or say where she had come from. They passed playing fields on the left, and to the right was a woods. They were driving in a circle, weren't they? But wait, there was the wall, the one she'd seen that they were building around the whole place. To keep out Beaters. To keep people like her locked in.

She and Jed used to watch Beaters out the windows of the middle school's little fake lookout tower, their favorite place to hide out after their day care shift; they weren't the only people who used it for privacy, so they couldn't make out or anything, but they held hands and watched the little groups of Beaters bashing themselves against the walls surrounding the school, trying to get in. They always eventually wandered off.

Sammi and Jed amused themselves by trying to spot the repeaters. It was hard to do because of the way the Beaters deteriorated. The new ones—of which there were few these days, though there was a rumor that a new wave was beginning since people had started eating the blueleaf roots again—didn't look too bad, mostly messy and scratched. The worst were the ones who'd been around since the beginning; whole big patches of skin would have fallen off, with the muscles and guts and bone showing through. They were missing teeth and even their lips, since they usually ended up chewing them off, and their arms and fingers were bony, red gooey messes, their hair pulled out and their scalps crusted and bruised. The old ones, you couldn't even tell half the time if they'd been men or women.

Sometimes Sammi and Jed could make it out by the clothes. It was pretty rare for a Beater to put on new clothes, although they could always surprise you. They spent ninety percent of their time doing the same things over and over, picking and gnawing at themselves and each other and wandering around in their lurching, drunken little gangs, picking up anything shiny that caught their eyes. But once in a while they would do something, well, *human,* which was actually really freaky. Like last week, Jed had pointed out a short, heavy one—a man, they decided—who was trying to shove something into the heavy locked metal box that held the sprinkler system's controls, out beyond the decorative benches on the parking lot side of the school. There was a narrow slot above the lock, and the Beater worked for a long time, pushing and jamming the object, and when it finally gave up and wandered off, they saw that it had been trying to push a magazine through the slot that was too small for it. Jed thought the Beater was trying to return a book, that it thought the school was a library. Sammi thought it was trying to mail a letter. The magazine flapped in the wind for a while, sodden and damp, and the next time they were up in the watchtower it was gone.

They never told anyone what they saw; they kept it to themselves. Somehow, when it was just the two of them, it could be funny, sometimes. If Sammi tried to tell her mom, she was likely to get started on one of her crying jags that ended with her pulling Sammi into her arms as though she wanted to just hold her forever. Sammi hated that; she always wanted her mom to let go, but that seemed rude, and she would just stare over her mother's shoulder, smelling her body odor and feeling her tears falling on Sammi's shoulder and wetting her shirt, waiting until her mother finally released her. It wasn't like that with Jed.

But Jed was gone.

Sammi felt a sob fighting its way up from deep inside her and she didn't want that, couldn't deal with whatever this girl and the people in the front seat would do. She didn't want their pity, and she sure as hell didn't want anyone interrogating her. So she squeezed her teeth together and forced the sadness back down. There would be time—eventually—for that.

But just then the driver pulled into the parking lot in front of a C-shaped, concrete-sided building three or four stories tall. The car coasted to a stop in the entrance in the middle of the C. Sammi tried the door handle, but they had the child locks on.

Inside this building it was just a repeat of the morning. Rebuilders in army-type clothes with weapons, lots of paperwork everywhere—it was still a shock to see everyone with actual clipboards rather than ePads and smartphones. The man who'd driven them disappeared, but there were others. The older woman from the car ushered them here and there and then disappeared with the other girl, and Sammi didn't see either of them again.

A plaque mounted near the front entrance said Genevieve Sanders College of Nursing. So it was a school for nurses. And come to think of it, the lobby reminded Sammi of the home where her mother's mom, her grandma Beth, had lived until Sammi was eleven, when she'd died at the end of a long summer. Sammi and her mother visited a couple times near the end, when Grandma Beth was confined to her bed and not talking anymore, and Sammi always held tight to her mother's hand as they went through the hushed lobby with its shuttered snack stand and the pretend beauty salon where volunteers did manicures during the day.

After the other girl was led off to some other part of the building, Sammi was taken up to the third floor by a woman who introduced herself as Mrs. Henderson. She was old enough to be her mom, but she seemed so tired and disinterested that Sammi wondered if she'd been woken from a deep sleep to tend to her. Only a few bulbs burned on the floor, but the floor was polished and clean, and the furniture in the sitting area was arranged neatly.

"Keep your voice down," Mrs. Henderson said, not bothering to mask her irritation. "Everyone's asleep. I'll take you to your room but we'll wait until morning to show you around." Sammi followed silently, trying to tread softly so her footsteps didn't echo in the hall. When they passed a bathroom they heard the sound of someone throwing up, moaning in between bouts of retching.

"Wait," Sammi said, finally stirred to a reaction. "Shouldn't we, like, check if she's okay?"

"She's fine," Mrs. Henderson said impatiently, but Sammi remained rooted to the spot. All day she'd just stood by and done nothing as every person she'd ever known was taken from her, as she was finally taken herself. She'd thought she was done caring. But hearing someone's misery like that... she couldn't walk away.

"I could just check real quick," she offered.

"It's just morning sickness. Half the girls here have it, it's nothing."

Understanding dawned slowly on Sammi, chilling her to the core. This wasn't just a dorm for girls—it was for *pregnant* girls.

"There's been a mistake," she said, her voice sounding strange and thin. "I'm not—I'm not pregnant. I shouldn't be here."

The woman finally looked at her, really looked at her, for the first time. In her expression Sammi saw a combination of pity and contempt. "Not right now," she muttered, "but a month or two from now, you'll be in there with her tossing your cookies like all the rest of them."

It was only when Mrs. Henderson opened the door to Sammi's new room that she noticed what she'd missed before: that spiral tattoo on the woman's wrist, the same one the guards had who'd attacked the library, the ones who'd burned the place down and killed everyone.

What the hell kind of place was this? Sammi had started to shake right after Mrs. Henderson said the thing about getting pregnant, but she'd tried to hide it. Every time she thought things couldn't get any worse, it somehow got worse. She wanted answers, but she wouldn't get them from this woman. Maybe, in the morning, she could ask her roommate.

Mrs. Henderson gave her a tiny flashlight, the kind you'd get on a key chain at the dollar store. Sammi swept it across the objects in the room: two twin beds, a single dresser, drapes drawn tight. A pair of flip-flops tucked neatly under the other bed, where a sleeping figure lay facing the wall. Mrs. Henderson pointed to the towels folded neatly on a chair, to the plastic bucket that she called a "potty," and told her not to sleep through the breakfast bell because there wouldn't be a second one.

Then she told Sammi not to wake her new roommate, whose name was Roan.

R-O-A-N—she spelled it before she left.

Sammi went to her new bed, suddenly more exhausted than she ever remembered being, and ran a hand over the blanket. Cotton, rough-knit—like the cheap ones they had back at the Grosbeck Academy in the nurse's office, where Sammi had gone only once, when she got her first period in the middle of Spanish and she had to wait for her mom to come with a change of clothes and a sanitary pad. Her mom had surprised her by taking her out of class for the rest of the day, and they'd gone to the best restaurant in town and her mother had ordered Sammi one Shirley Temple after another and a glass of pinot blanc for herself, twisting it by the stem rather wistfully.

Go with them, Sammi.

Sammi shut down the thought as fast as she could but it hadn't been fast enough. A little had gotten in, the memory that could only lead to others and, inevitably, make her face the loss that was bigger than her whole life. Her mother in the nice restaurant that day, after the lunch crowd had come and gone, bars of sunlight making their slow way across the white tablecloth. Her mother smelled of Kenzo Flower, her favorite perfume, and she'd worn a soft green jacket and one of the silver necklaces that her friend Dulcette was always making after her husband ran off. She had carefully lined her eyes with a deep shade of purple—on another woman it might have been garish but on her beautiful auburn-haired mother it was just right, exotic without being too out-there. Men noticed her mother. Even her father—Sammi had memories from when she was really little, back when they were still getting along, her father catching her mother reaching into the tall cabinets for a platter or a cookbook, up on her toes, and he would run his big hands over her waist, her hips and pull her to him like he couldn't believe his luck.

But that had been a lot of years ago. They hadn't been in love for a long time. Her dad was in the office most nights, and he left before she got up in the morning. Honestly, when he moved away, it wasn't like she saw him much less. Those weekends at his place—the giant charred burgers he made for her, "Sammi style" he called them, dripping with provolone and crisscrossed with bacon, even though she hadn't eaten anything like that since she got to high school and had to force herself to eat even half...the awful pink satin comforter he'd bought for her even though pink hadn't been her favorite color since she kindergarten—those had been awkward, for sure.

But what she wouldn't give for one more.

28

CASS RUBBED AT HER EYES. IN THE DARK NO ONE could see the way her face got blotchy when she cried. No one would be able to tell that her fine pale hair was matted to her forehead with sweat, or that she scratched long furrows in the tender skin of her wrists, a nervous habit that summoned just enough pain to keep her mind from spinning out of control.

Ruthie had wedged herself in the crook of Cass's arm. The bed was narrow, but usually she could sleep easily with Ruthie next to her. Tonight was different. Tonight, Ruthie was restless and couldn't seem to get close enough. As Cass lay awake trying not to cry, Ruthie burrowed and flailed and sighed and whispered half words, caught between sleep and waking.

Just as Cass had decided that she might as well get up, maybe sit in the straight-backed desk chair pulled up to the window and stare out at the moon for a while, she felt Ruthie's eyelashes flutter against her neck.

"Shh, shh," she whispered automatically, wrapping Ruthie in her arms and rubbing her back. She'd always been able to soothe Ruthie back to sleep, but now her daughter fought her, wiggling and pushing her away.

"Mama."

Cass froze, then leaned up on her elbow so she could look at her daughter's face in the moonlight. Ruthie's voice, even though she'd heard it now half a dozen times, even though she rejoiced at its return, still seemed fraught with dark enchantment. Ruthie's eyes were open but unfocused, and she reached for Cass's arm and held on, her little fingers digging in tight. Cass stroked her cheek, and found it hot and damp.

"What is it, Babygirl?"

"Help Smoke." Ruthie's eyelids fluttered shut and she rolled over and pushed her fist against her mouth, but when Cass grabbed her hands she came willingly, burrowing back into Cass's arms.

Cass barely dared speak, her heart thudding and her mouth suddenly dry. "What did you say, Ruthie?"

"Help him, Mama."

Then she seemed to relax, her body going limp. After a moment she yawned, a long, luxurious yawn, and in seconds she was asleep again, tucked up against Cass. It was almost as though the words had fought their way out and, now that Ruthie had finally spoken them, she was able to rest.

Cass lay very still for a long time, her mind racing. Once before, Ruthie had insisted she help, but she hadn't been able to, that time. Devin was dying, Devin might well be dead already, and there was nothing Cass could do about it, nothing she had done about it, besides give his mother false hope, besides leaving them behind and being relieved by that.

Now Ruthie was insisting again. Ruthie knew something

was wrong. Ruthie knew Smoke needed help. Call it a sixth
sense, or intuition, a gift or a curse—it didn't matter. Ruthie
knew things and she saw things, and there was no way for her
to un-know or un-see them.

Moments ticked by, Cass barely remembering to breathe,
as Ruthie's command took on the shape of a plan, risky and
costly and inevitable.

Finally, Cass slipped out of the bed. The nightgown they'd
given her was too small. The fabric was stretchy and thin, and
molded itself to her ass and thighs as she tucked the covers
back around Ruthie, shivering in the cold night air. It would
be far more practical to change back into the clothes she had
been wearing earlier—but as she thought through her next
moves she decided to wear the nightgown.

She knelt on the cold synthetic tile floor and trailed her
fingertips through Ruthie's soft hair and hummed very softly,
decorating the edges of her daughter's dreams with her voice,
a faint soundtrack that would linger and soothe her fears if she
woke up before Cass returned.

Dor slept a few feet away, his arm up over his head, his
hands fisted. He did not snore. He barely appeared to breathe,
but Cass saw his chest rise and fall very slowly in the light
from a glowing digital clock on the nightstand.

She rested her hand on Ruthie's back and gave herself one
last chance to change her mind. Going out into the cold night
meant leaving Ruthie here alone with Dor. Ruthie was so
small and defenseless and solemn, her childhood like a wilted
petal that lay rumpled at her feet—but she was also an outlier.
Her small teeth were sharp and white and perfectly formed.
Her eyes were clear and bright. Under her soft skin her bones
and muscles were strong and getting stronger. Ruthie could
run faster, jump farther, climb higher than other children,

and if it came down to it, she would survive other hurts better, too—the kind that came from being abandoned over and over by a mother who just couldn't keep her safe *and* fulfill her promises to this world.

On the other side of the equation was Smoke. Her lover, the one person on this earth who she had given everything to, the only man besides her father who she had ever trusted—he lay broken and abandoned in the basement of a building far from anything that had ever been home to him. Maybe he was already dead.

Smoke had betrayed her, and his betrayal was a weakness, but perhaps Cass was even weaker than he was because she could not forget him. She could not force herself to rip out the part of her that had been changed by him, could not toughen up the part that had gone soft for him, could not ignore the longing for him that had become as much a part of her as her own name.

She thought she could outrun Smoke by coming to Colima. Now she knew that was never going to be true, not even if he had died that day, if he'd never been brought here, not even if he'd never come back and had forgotten her and gone to live another life. Smoke was imprinted on her and would be a part of her until her own death, whether it was the next hour or whether she lived many more years.

Now Cass had to go to him, knowing she might not return. Danger waited in a dozen, a hundred different forms. She wasn't afraid of dying—she would die for Ruthie, in agony if that's what God demanded—but dying for Smoke seemed like an indulgence.

Other mothers would never leave their children's side. But Cass was not other mothers. She was the one who had traded her baby for a bottle of jack, a jug of pinot grigio, a whiskey

and Diet Coke in a plastic cup. She had left her daughter crying in her crib while a stranger tore off her sweater in the next
room. The very night that Ruthie had been taken from her,
she had sobbed motherly anguish with her face in the carpet
only until she found the strength to crawl to the refrigerator
and drink every beer she had left.

The shame and regret reached up from the depths and
grabbed greedily, ready to call Cass a bad mother, undeserv-
ing. But Cass resisted. She had atoned and would keep atoning.
Ruthie had spoken Smoke's name. Ruthie said she must go.

And Ruthie would be safe here. In the other bed was a man
who had raised his own daughter, a man who was good with
children. You could see it in the way he was with Ruthie—
anyone would know that Dor was a natural. When he touched
Ruthie she beamed. When he teased her she sparkled with
mirth; when he complimented her she swelled with pride.

Cass knew that Dor would lay down his life for Ruthie,
likely would for any child. If Cass were to die, Ruthie would
learn to love others. She would grow up protected and cherished and if any sane person had to choose between Cass
and someone like Dor, the decision would be easy. Nothing
personal. Nothing against Cass, who had *tried*.

So far, trying had not been good enough. Cass had failed
the people she loved over and over. But she was about to try
harder.

Cass bent to her daughter's cheek and kissed the damp skin,
her lips trembling—but she would not cry.

She gave Dor a long, hard look in the dim light and slipped
out of the room.

She heard voices the minute she opened the door of the stairwell, men's voices, low and punctuated with laughter. Her

heart was already pounding, and she paused in the hallway, guiding the door gently shut so that it would make no sound.

Two men sat at a small table, the kind that might have held a drink next to a sofa, back when living rooms were full of things like cocktail parties and hors d'oeuvres and casual conversation and flirting. They had dragged the improbable table between them and set some sort of small, high-tech tripod light on top, illuminating a wooden tray filled with tiny glass pebbles, a game Cass had never seen before.

She slid the heavy overcoat she was wearing off her shoulders, revealing the scoop neckline of her thin nightgown. Her nipples hard from the cold, she had to resist the urge to cover her breasts. Instead she faked a yawn and allowed the coat to slide farther until it covered little more than her forearms and rested, drooping around her waist.

In the past she would never have gone out like this. The nightgown, though snug, wasn't truly sexy; it squeezed all of her flesh, flattening her roundness, doing nothing for her curves. Also, she was wearing heavy socks and her boots, leaving only the pale flesh of her shins exposed beneath the gown.

Still, this was enough to pass for provocation now. She'd seen it in the library, how small glimpses of flesh—less than graced the naughty stereographs of the 1940s, even—could make a man stutter and swallow hard. If a woman emerged from the bathroom stalls wiping her bare damp forearms on her pants, eyebrows would rise. A woman who brushed her hair in the conference room at night, revealing a triangle of her neck in the light of a candle, this could stop a man.

Cass stood in the circle of light cast by the lamp and pretended to scratch an itch on the top of her thigh. "Excuse me," she said in a bored voice.

Cass felt that chameleon self coming on. She'd studied hard, and the stakes had been high; life was harder before she learned to interpret and predict the interplay of emotions between her mother and her many lovers, especially once Byrn had taken up residence. She'd built a nearly encyclopedic understanding of what a man's moods could signal—and from there it had been a simple enough step to copy them herself.

"I'm new," she continued. "And I'm sorry to bother y'all but I get headaches? And they said something about maybe I could have something for it. Just a Tylenol, one's all I need."

She waited, knowing the timing was important; the men glanced at each other skeptically but were barely able to tear their eyes from her body. One of the men was tall and stocky, red-haired with a sharp cleft to his chin, his face all harsh planes. The other had a thick, gray-peppered moustache and a ring of longish hair around his bald spot. While Cass watched, he shoved his hand through his hair in a vain attempt to force the hair across his head, and Cass felt a wave of revulsion. Mim once had a boyfriend who spent fifteen minutes at the mirror every morning arranging and spraying his thin strands of hair on top of his head. He was an unusually strong perspirer, and within an hour the fabric of his shirt would be ringed with sweat under the armpits and his bald head would shine.

He was hardly the worst of Mim's boyfriends, though.

When her gaze fell on the red-haired man's wrist and she saw the koru mark there, she relaxed a little. So it would be him. That would be better. There would be no painful memories complicating what was already an odious task.

"Girly, ain't you heard, the drugstore's *closed*," the mustached man said, drawing the last syllable out and staring unabashedly at her chest.

"Oh, I'm sorry, I thought it was different for outliers," Cass said, flipping her hair over her shoulder. "That's what they told me, anyway."

"Hang on." The red-haired man's voice was sharp, inflected with some sort of northern accent, Canadian or Wisconsin or something. "You're an outlier?"

Cass nodded, giving him a slow, smug smile.

"C'mere."

She hesitated for a moment and then approached him. The heavy coat tugged the fabric of the nightgown even lower.

He pulled a small penlight from his pocket and shined it on her face.

"What's your name?"

"Cassandra."

He played the light over her hair, her face, down her neck, then let it linger on her breasts. "Well, *Cassandra*. You got some way of proving that?"

Cass stared him directly in the eye and ran her tongue slowly along her lower lip, letting it linger in the corner.

There was an art to the pause; Cass had not always been a master. You had to wait longer than you thought you should, longer than was credible. So long you were sure they would find you ridiculous. But they never did, not when you let your eyelids drift down and breathed a little deeper, lips parted as though in anticipation. As though you could *taste* their gaze, as though you wanted more.

When it had been long enough, when his eyes had widened so fractionally she almost missed it, she spoke again, husky and low. "I might."

"Hell, I probably got something," the balding man said. "Back in my—"

"I'll take her," the red-haired man interrupted. "I could

use a walk anyway. About to die of boredom, stuck here with the likes of you all night."

"Ah, suck it, Ralston. What, you're going to just take off? What if there's a code?"

Ralston shrugged. "I can answer it from Tapp as easy as I can from here, can't I?"

"That what you're gonna tell Chen? That you figured—"

"Chen's not interested in how I spend my time," Ralston snapped. His voice had gone hard. For a moment there was silence between the two men, and then the guard with the mustache nodded once and fixed his gaze on the abandoned game pieces.

The koru. The hierarchy. The Rebuilders relied on a rigid structure and that meant those below had little to say about the doings of those above.

Ralston gave her a fake little bow. "After you. Cassandra."

He took her not out the front entrance but down a corridor to a side door, which was fitted with the same sort of low-tech hardware that the Rebuilders had used to replace all the electronic locks. When he took his key chain from his belt, Cass caught a glimpse of a gun and her heartbeat quickened.

All she was hoping for tonight was to get close to Smoke, to see for herself if he was dead—or whether he had a chance.

Would she be able to tell? Would it be obvious? Cass thought it probably would—everyone had become connoisseurs of death since the Siege. At first it was just the fever; one learned that when the sheen evaporated and the flush deepened, when the skin went from rosy to grayish-crimson, that the coughing was close behind and the final hours of demented mumbling were imminent.

Later, when the streets were empty except for Beaters, when there were no hospitals and doctors had no tools or medications to practice with, they learned about other kinds of death. In the library, Cass had watched a man die in anguish from a burst appendix; his writhing grew so terrible that Bobby had finally put the man over his strong shoulders and taken him outside the gates; when he returned alone no one asked questions. Later a pregnant woman arrived, carried by two men; her labor had begun in the house where they'd been squatting, and when she failed to deliver in the first twenty-four hours they brought her to the shelter; she was almost unconscious when she arrived; the men's coats were slick with her blood, and she died after only a few weak cries, sodden with more blood than Cass had ever seen, even after all this time.

During the riots people were trampled and beaten, and Cass saw blood on the streets whenever she went out. A human body, crushed and dragged, could leave a stain far greater than you'd ever imagine. Was that what had happened to Smoke? Had his blood been spread across the cracked concrete of a road, or the dried thatch of kaysev in a field?

Her need to see him spurred her along and she followed Ralston outside into the cold air. He wrapped an arm around her before they'd gone three steps, and she caught the odor of his breath, stale and faintly tinged with chewing tobacco.

"You must be cold."

Cass laughed. "Not really, not now."

"What are you really after? I can get you some pop bottle crank. Maybe hollies. I can't get you into the medical supplies, though, honey, not even with this." He held up his wrist; even in the moonlight, augmented by the occasional spotlight at the entrances to campus buildings, she could make out the black smudge.

"I'm not...that's not what I want," she said.

"Yeah? Don't tell me you really do have a headache, darlin', cause that's gonna cut into our fun." He laughed at his own attempt at humor. "That's what you had in mind, right? A little fun? Listen, I can get us into a party, a few people I know. Real discreet. They know how to—"

"I need to get in the basement of the Tapp Clinic," Cass interrupted, slipping her hand into his waistband. "Where the prisoners are. I need to see one of them. That's what I really want. I'm willing to…show my appreciation."

"Hold *on* a minute." Ralston stopped, gripped her arm hard above the elbow. They were behind the building, in between a couple of aluminum storage sheds sided by sharp-branched dead bushes. Above, the moon emerged from blowing wisps of clouds and glinted off his hungry eyes. "Are you out of your fucking mind? If there's a detail summons while we're over there, how'm I gonna know? I can't miss again—"

"Your friend can come get you," Cass said silkily. "He could be there in two minutes. He'll do it, if you tell him to. Nothing's going to happen in two minutes."

"But the basement's guarded."

"Where we just *were* is guarded." Cass knew she needed to play this just right, and she made her voice go lower. This was the trick—blow out most of your breath, speak on the dregs. A whisper with a promise. "Look, I just need to see my friend for a minute. Nothing illegal, I promise. Just to make sure it's really him in there, okay? You can make that happen for me, right?"

"Not unless I cash in every chip I've got. Do you know how many—"

Cass stepped in closer and reached down, her fingers finding him and squeezing before he knew what was happening. A vulnerability they never thought of until too late.

He was hard already, harder instantly beneath her hand.

Good. She traced a fingernail along the taut fabric of his pants, and leaned in to whisper in his ear. She darted her tongue out as she spoke so that it just brushed lightly against the inside of his ear, and he moaned before she got the first three words out. "I know what I'm doing."

He seized her hips and ground against her, backing her up against the shed. The metal was shockingly cold even through her coat.

"Show me."

"I can do things you'll remember," she said, for the moment letting him crouch and buck against her. Distaste eddied in her mind, but she focused on Smoke, on the reason she was here, and made herself go outside herself, let herself drift up until she was outside of her body, looking down. From that vantage point, somewhere in the thin winter night, drifting above the unlovely blocky sheds, the dead landscaping, she saw Ralston hump and heave, and considered something that she hadn't thought about in a long time:

Sex was ridiculous, nothing more than homely rutting. The expression of the basest of instincts, twitching and spasming, hormones unleashed and sloshing through the body's systems. A cock, a cunt—God's joke, a jigsaw puzzle simple enough that even the dumbest beasts could figure it out. The lengths that people went to to organize and ornament it… Every species, the males mounting and holding fast with claws and paws and flippers and, when those failed, with teeth—blood and pain and yowling and violence were just part of the process. The system was gamed against the females, who fought and cried out as they were fucked and impregnated and then left to stagger off to dens and warrens and shitty apartments, bruised and savaged, reminded of the terrible imbalance of nature's arrangement.

That other, that lovely, that desperately beautiful thing, it had been a lie, a fantasy. A trick of her imagination, a leftover illusion from some fairy-tale place she'd gone to escape the horrors of her adolescence. No matter that it had seemed real with Smoke.

"Slow down, cowboy," she whispered against his neck. "You're going to get there too quick. Let me take you there nice and slow."

"Aw, shit," he moaned, but he did what she commanded, going still, shuddering against her. "Are you a pro?"

The words didn't carry the sting they might once have. Hell, maybe she had been, sort of, though it wasn't money that changed hands back then. Cass had traded in desperation and forgetting. And she had given good value, at least on those occasions when she didn't pass out.

No danger of passing out tonight.

"I'm just really good at what I do," she whispered. Then she lifted one foot to the other shed, pressed her boot against the side—then the other. The sheds were far enough apart that she had to arch her back to wrap her legs around his waist, but she knew that the move had its appeal, for some, anyway. She held the position, undulating slowly against him, her muscles straining and her arms quivering with the effort. Long enough. Just long enough. "Let me give you a taste now. Then take me where I want to go, and we'll come back and finish."

Ralston could barely contain his excitement. He seized her ass and squeezed, and she knew it was an effort for him not to plunge against her again. "Go down on me now," he panted. "Then later I take you however I want."

"Yeah," Cass moaned, feigning anticipation. "I want to suck you now. I want to swallow your cock—"

"Up the ass," he interrupted, and she knew he wasn't even hearing her; she was indifferent, it made no difference to her. "If I want. Whatever I want. You got to do whatever I want."

"You take me to see him and I will." Cass cupped him in her hand and squeezed, hard enough to get his attention. "If you don't, I'll never give you a second look. I'll go back and do your friend and *he'll* tell you all about it. You hear me?"

"God, no," Ralston moaned, planting his face in her shoulder and raising his hands in supplication. "I'll get you there. I'll get you in, I swear. Whatever you want. I just need to tell King where we're going."

That was all she needed to hear. Cass lowered her feet to the floor and slid down to her knees, the metal cold against her back.

29

A DIFFERENT GUARD IN THE BASEMENT NOW, just one for the overnight shift—a muscular, short fiftyish man with a tight build and a hole where his front teeth used to be, a scar twisting his lip. He either wasn't afraid to fight or had been in one that had been stacked against him. Either way, it was something to worry about.

He was reading a magazine—on the cover was a celebrity chef Cass remembered from the magazines she stocked in the QuikGo, had a restaurant in New York or New Orleans or somewhere that pretty people used to go. Cass hung back in the shadows as Ralston said a few quiet words to the man. He called him Jimbo and grabbed his own crotch, and motioned for her to step forward. Jimbo looked her over, up and down, not even trying to hide his interest. Cass wondered if she'd have to do him, too.

It didn't much matter. Ten minutes on the ground didn't mean much to her right now other than a few scrapes on her knee, a crick in her back. The way her lips got numb and swollen from her teeth. Nothing. Less than nothing.

She was about to see Smoke. She craned her neck, looking down the hall, which darkened to inky black at the end. The guards had a single lamp between them, a bulb in a socket tied to a pipe, the way that was so common nowadays. No shade, so you could get away with low wattage. The CFL bulbs were probably good for a few more years, anyway, and that was a longer horizon than anyone was worried about these days.

"Who is he to you, anyway?" Jimbo demanded, taking a toothpick from a shirt pocket and going to work on his yellowed teeth. "Boyfriend?"

"None of your business," Cass muttered. But the notion seemed to occur to Ralston for the first time, and he hitched himself up a little taller. Great. Perfect time for dick-measuring.

"Well, come on, let's see if he's croaked yet."

Down between the cots, Jimbo leading, Ralston behind him. A powerful stench rose from a figure huddled on a blanket on one of the cots they passed, urine and vomit that no one had bothered to clean. Cass wondered what Jimbo had done to deserve this rotation.

When they were close to the end of the row, Cass rushed ahead, past the man she'd just pleasured and the one with the cruel eyes, unheedful of the risk, of the imbalance of power. There. The last cot, covered like all the others in a dark, rough blanket, a figure bent and flung, silent in sleep or death.

Smoke

Suddenly the thought of him burst through her like every flavor she'd ever tasted, every sunrise that ever blinded her eyes, every pain that ever touched her nerves. A memory— Smoke as he turned away, Smoke moments before he left her to seek the sort of justice she didn't believe in. His eyes were blue, October skies and buttonweed, shaded with sadness. His hands work-rough and strong, clenched at his side. His mouth...his mouth that she had kissed a thousand times, full and sensuous, tensed now with rage.

He'd been ready to die, she knew that, and she had hated him for it, for wanting revenge more than he wanted her. Only that knowledge had kept her from running after him, for sinking to her knees outside the gate and wailing for him to return to her.

Instead she had hardened herself against him. She was not an ordinary woman, she had not lived through ordinary trials and she did not have ordinary strength on which to draw. She had been hurt so often that she was more scar than flesh, and when Smoke left her Cass had carved flint-edged fury from the shards of her devastation. It was not a comfortable thing to bear, but she'd done what she had to, followed Dor in the opposite direction from where Smoke had gone. Now she understood that she would have chosen death herself if it hadn't been for Ruthie, and so she'd taken this path, a man who could keep her child safe, a chance to burn herself out bright if that was to be.

Only now she was inches away from Smoke, who she never thought she would see again, and the furious heart of hers disintegrated and the jagged pieces were made dust and everything was gone but him. And her longing for him. And she gasped from the shock of it and knelt down next to the cot.

There was no smell of death, no smell of rot, but still the air was tainted with the cold metal scent of blood. Cass tried to say his name but nothing came to her lips; her throat was dry. She lowered her hands to the mattress, crushed the cheap fabric of the blanket in her hands and pulled it gently away, and lowered her face to his chest. If he was dead—but no, through the filthy blood-matted fabric of his shirt she felt the warmth of him, and he shifted and moaned and she felt his chest vibrate with the effort to speak.

And she was crying. Just like that, hot tears streaming silently from her eyes. Behind her the two men began arguing, but she blocked them out and focused on Smoke alone. She found his face with her hands and gasped to feel the scabbed flesh, the jagged uncleaned wounds and she jerked her hands away.

"Shine the light on him," she demanded, croak-voiced, and someone put a boot to the side of the bed and gave it a vicious shove, causing Smoke to cry out in pain.

"Fucker took out Calder and Boone." Jimbo's voice was cold and hard.

"Boone's dead?" Ralston sounded shocked. "I didn't even know he was on that detail."

"Yeah, him and Calder and Zhao and Lorenzo, Lorenzo just got promoted to Detail Five, this was his first recruiting trip."

Cass remembered the name Calder—one of the guards who'd taken over the library when she and Smoke got there. He'd been a prematurely gray man who spoke little but had a habit of touching the handle of his blade every few minutes. Had he burned the school? She supposed he must have; Smoke would not have executed him otherwise.

"They say he shot Calder in both knees and elbows with his own gun," Jimbo went on, as though reading her thoughts. "Told him he was going to keep going until he'd used up every Rebuilder bullet they had. Calder choked to death on his own blood while he was begging for one to the brain to finish him off. Death in a warm bed is too good for this one."

"No shit," Ralston said, but he clicked his penlight on and shone it on the bed, no doubt curious about a man who could go up against four men and kill two of them before they got him.

Cass was not prepared for the sight of Smoke—he looked even worse than he had hours earlier, when Mary's scrutiny prevented her from looking too close. Now she could see that his nose was broken, his eyes blackened and swollen shut. His lips—his beautiful mouth—were split and bloodied, black crusted blood on his chin.

His head rolled back and he tried to raise his one arm, but it lay at a wrong angle and only twitched before falling back. Broken. The other arm, the one with the ruined fingers, was bound in dirty rags; blood had soaked through the knotted fabric and Cass saw that flies were settling and swarming around it. She realized the flies were the source of the buzzing that she'd thought was only in her head.

"Zhao got 'im," Jimbo muttered. "Pretended he was down and when this asshole was done with Boone he went to drag the body—he'd already got Calder stowed, don't know what he was fixin' to do with 'em—anyway he holstered up and Zhao shot him clean through the shoulder. Missed the bone and came out the other side. Lorenzo was trying to get off a shot but he'd been lying on his gun hand, it'd gone numb, is what he said."

Ralston made a grunt of disbelief. "Lorenzo's a douche. He just made a shitty shot, is all."

"Yeah, maybe. But he's the douche who brought Smoke back here along with Calder and Boone's bodies."

"You proud of your boy?" Ralston demanded, crouching

down next to Cass and nudging her shoulder. "Proud of him torturing an unarmed man?"

Cass said nothing, focused on Smoke. As gently as she could she pried his eye open, saw that the eyeball was rolled up in his head. Whatever sounds he made were from deep within his semiconscious state, but that didn't stop her from trying.

"I'm here," she whispered, and bent to kiss his cracked and torn mouth. She tasted his blood, felt her tears splash on his wounds.

"That's foul," Ralston said. "Don't put your mouth on that, not when you owe me the next hour. I don't want none a his nasty."

They didn't know, and Cass forgave that comment even as her fingers traced lightly on his shirt, looking for the wound, the bullet's exit. They didn't know what Smoke had been avenging. They'd heard only one account, riddled with inaccuracies and outright lies. They didn't know that the Rebuilders Smoke killed had lined up the residents of the library, shot the older men one by one before moving on to every resident who dared to object. She remembered Nora, her nervous quick movements, her badly cut hair, the way it fell around her face, making her gaunt cheekbones look somehow elegant. Her sad black-brown eyes.

And Sammi's mother, the first and only time Cass ever saw her, when she dragged Sammi in from the fields to the safety of the school shelter. The way Jessica had fallen to her knees when she saw that her daughter was safe, the wildness in her expression that spoke of frantic worry.

The two women had been ordinary. A mother, an aunt, but they had stood up to the Rebuilders and for that they had been executed, their bodies draped in a heap in the center of the school, left to burn and burn and burn.

Cass doubted the story Jimbo told, that Smoke had continued shooting a downed man, but thinking about the fire, she realized that perhaps she would have done the same if she had been there.

She found the torn place in the shirt, slipped a finger through the hole and searched for the wound in Smoke's shoulder. His skin was impossibly hot; infection must have set in. There. It was a jagged hole, but not too large.

Why couldn't it be Smoke who had her immunity? Cass supposed that if she was the one shot, her body would immediately start healing. It happened with cuts, even deep ones. There would be no infection, and the severed nerves and vessels would eventually knit back together. But not Smoke. He was nothing special at all. He had never been a soldier, never worn a uniform, had only learned to sharpshoot, to run with a heavy pack and scale obstacles and make strategy on the fly when he started working for Dor.

Had Dor taught him brutality, too? She'd seen Smoke, on the mornings she followed him, her jacket's hood pulled up all the way for warmth. She'd watched him practice the chopping fist motions that Joe taught him for hand-to-hand fighting; watched him run up and down the steps of an apartment building until he was drenched in sweat, his calves trembling and his lungs fighting for air. Smoke had worked so hard to make himself dangerous. Was it all for this? All so that he could fight against an enemy so powerful that it barely flinched before replacing its fallen?

Would Smoke's actions mean anything at all? Death was cheap; the world would not miss a few more men in the prime of their lives.

"When did he get here?" Cass asked.

"Two nights ago," Jimbo said. "The recruiting party spent

the night up at Emerson Gap, they were heading up to Sil-verton. There's a group up at the old MegaBass Pro Shops, that big one they built back in like '14 or '15, something like that…bought a wakeboard there once." He spat off into the darkness, spittle falling on Cass's exposed neck. "Don't know how this asshole knew to look for them there, but he was waiting. He was up in a tree the whole time, waited until they made camp and rushed them after dark."

Dor. Dor had told Smoke where to look. Three nights ago when Smoke left on the motorcycle Dor gave him, armed with weapons from Dor's private arsenal, Dor had told him exactly where he could find the Rebuilder party.

Was that why Dor let him go so easy? Why he tried to put Cass's fears to rest? Was it because he really believed Smoke had a chance? Or because he didn't want her running after him? Cass's anger at Dor grew; it was one man against at least four. The element of surprise was good, that was true; without it, Smoke would not have been able to take out even the two he did. But how could Dor have expected him to win? All the target practice in the world, all the jogging and weights couldn't prepare him for his first actual battle, and he'd gone in alone.

"Why?" she whispered, lowering herself as gently as she could against Smoke's body. He had slipped back into uncon-sciousness, and she felt only his weak heartbeat in response. Why had he thought he could do this? But she already knew the answer—he'd never intended to live; he only meant to take out as many of them as he could before he died.

Would he be satisfied now to know that he'd killed two? It didn't seem like much of a trade for one's own life.

She forced herself to stand, letting her hand linger on

Smoke's unhurt shoulder for a moment. She faced Jimbo and hugged herself in the cold.

"I need you to make him live," she said quietly. "Medicine, antibiotics, whatever you have. I'll do anything for you. Anything."

Ralston sputtered a protest, something about the next hour, and she placed a hand on his arm to quiet him. "I remember our bargain," she said steadily, before turning her focus back to Jimbo. He was watching her carefully, his wiry gray eyebrows knit together.

"I'm an outlier," she said, waiting to make sure he understood. "I'll have certain privileges. Freedoms. I'll be able to come and go...to come to you. As long as you keep him alive, you can have..."

She shrugged off her coat, letting it hang at her elbows, and for the second time that night she strained against the thin fabric of the nightgown, hoping the light from his small flashlight would illuminate the shape of her breasts, of her taut stomach, her hips. She cupped one breast, lifting it for his appraisal. "You can have anything you want," she finished, and then she couldn't help looking to reassure herself that Smoke was still unconscious, because even though she could give herself away, could give away every last cell of her body, every wracked corner of her soul, he could never know. This would be her gift to him: he would never know that his life was what she bought with her trade.

"You'd like that," Ralston said, and for one confusing moment Cass mistook his tone for jealousy, for anger that she was so quick to offer what she'd just given him, down on her knees on the cold ground, but when he seized her wrist and twisted it so that she had to bend double, Cass realized that she had made two important misjudgments:

First, she'd forgotten that—just like in the Box—the most important positions were given to those who'd done the security jobs Before: the cops and Marines and highway patrol, the prison guards and gangbangers. The hard men.

And second, that even a man who thrusts against you with the strangled cry of an adolescent, who shudders as he spills his seed inside you, unmindful of his momentary vulnerability, his shaft already going soft between your teeth, will forget all that when he believes he's been wronged.

"You can see your murderer boyfriend all you want in detention—if he lives that long," Ralston spat.

"I never stood against the Rebuilders," Cass protested, but already they were leading her down the hall, forcing her to go too quickly, so that she stumbled and nearly fell, her arms yanked cruelly as they pulled her along, and when they passed the staircase and continued into a little room, a closet where brooms and supplies were stored, Cass knew with horrifying certainty that they meant to deliver her their version of justice—and that she'd brought it on herself.

But she'd done worse. And she'd no doubt do worse again.

30

DOR RUBBED THE METAL BOX, RUNNING HIS thumb over the smooth silvery surface, before slipping it back in his pocket. He sat on the edge of the bed Cass had left. Ruthie, sensing his closeness in her sleep, had rolled closer to him and hooked her small hand over his leg.

Ruthie was an odd child in some ways, cautious and easily spooked, but at times Dor caught glimpses of the mischievous spirit hidden within her. Subdued, maybe, but not quashed. At times it seemed that even Cass could not detect the sly little grin that flashed across Ruthie's pretty features when she had played some tiny trick for her own amusement, some clever gesture just because she could. A mother, tasked with protecting her child from birth, exhausted from the dangers and heartaches, could easily miss such moments.

Not long ago, Dor had come across Ruthie in the Box with Feo, playing a game they'd invented that involved Feo standing on a gentle berm where Cass had planted pine seedlings.

The boy stood patiently, whistling. The object of the game seemed to be for him to pretend he was all alone and for Ruthie to try to sneak up on him. There was something desperately sweet about the boy—tough and disrespectful to most adults, his face generally wary and mistrustful—whistling with his hands in his pockets until Ruthie, over and over, came charging at him from behind the little trees, slamming her little body into him, and every time he acted as though she had taken him completely by surprise and fell to the ground. They rolled together, Feo yelling in pretend terror, Ruthie shaking with her soundless laughter, until she disentangled herself and went running off to hide again.

Dor figured Ruthie would be fine. After all, he'd been through fourteen years with Sammi; fourteen years of heart-stopping terrors and humbling corrections, the usual drill for a first-time parent. He'd overprotected, sure, but at least he'd been wise enough to let Sammi go when she needed to test herself. That was something Jessica had not been able to do. Jessica smothered—she was a great mother, at times, but now Dor could only pray that some of his lessons had taken root, that Sammi understood she had the strength inside her to face whatever was happening to her.

Tomorrow he would find her. He didn't know how, and he didn't know where. But he would find her.

Tonight he had to find Cass.

He knew something had gone wrong. Sensed it the way he observed coming changes in the weather, the moods of his people or the stores coming in for trade. Dor was so finely attuned to the energy around him that it was painful at times. That was why he lived apart, in the trailer that was little more than a tin prison; it was better than being in the midst of all those lives being lived around him. The static could be almost

unbearable on days when he was weakened by a lack of rest
or a too-strenuous workout—all those people, their tempers
and desires and jealousies on display for anyone who looked.

Well, for people like him, anyway. And he'd sensed the
change in Cass immediately. He just didn't know what it was.
Still didn't. But in the time she'd been gone in the afternoon
and come back, something had changed. Something at the
Tapp Clinic had stripped her of her fragile strength, hardened
and wounded her.

Dor scooped Ruthie up in his arms. She was so light, hardly
a burden at all. He hated bringing her. She should stay and
sleep, but it wasn't safe yet; he didn't know who to trust. That
had always been his strength, choosing those he could trust.
But now he had only himself. So Ruthie would come.

It would be awkward and it would increase the danger for
both of them. But what other option did he have? Waiting
it out, waiting for Cass to come back, might be the smartest
thing to do; after all, he was here for Sammi. Venturing out
would require him to use resources that were meant for her.
He would risk showing his hand, alerting the Rebuilders that
he wasn't who he pretended to be. In the worst case, he would
endanger his own mission, and his chances to get Sammi back.

Nothing mattered more than his daughter. He would trade
any living soul for her without hesitation—even Cass's, if it
ever came to that.

But leaving Cass to an uncertain fate was not an option,
either. He had always told Sammi that she had to stand up for
the things that mattered. And Cass, despite their awkward
relationship, despite the things they had done—or maybe because of them—mattered.

There was no other way. He put the silver box back in his
pocket, careful to make sure it was properly closed first, pro-

tecting the soft rubbery ball with its cells of gel and powder separated by the thinnest membrane. He shifted Ruthie so that he could hold her in one arm. In the other he held one of the darts he'd smuggled in the hidden pocket along with the silver box. And he set out down the darkened hall.

The way the tree had grown, struggling for purchase on the slope behind the fence that marked the far end of the park, made a perfect saddle in which Cass could sit with her legs dangling above the creek. The creek was dry in all but the few rainy months of spring, dotted with stones submerged in cracked earth, tall dead weeds, jackrabbit warrens. It wasn't much to look at, certainly not compared to the park, which the developers had situated at the end of the broad avenue that ran through the neighborhood, so that you could see it from the entrance and the mouth of every cul-de-sac. They'd made it nice, nice enough to justify the prices they charged for what were just glorified tri-level tract homes.

Mim had fallen in love with the development—granite countertops, his-and-her sinks in the bathrooms, three garage stalls, architectural columns separating the dining room from the great room—and would not be swayed, especially when a bank-reclaimed model came on the market cheap. She and Byrn spent their weekends shopping for outdoor furniture and bar stools, and Cass wandered down to the park and found this secret place where no one came.

The developers put in the usual specimens, agapanthus and gaillardia, dwarf Japanese maples and society garlic. Hedge roses lined split-wood fencing, and ornamental plums shaded banks of New Guinea impatiens and dianthus, snapdragons and alyssum. But after all the houses were sold, the association hired a cut-rate gardener who did little more than mow and blow, and within a year the plants were stunted and dying.

Hardly anyone came to the park. Kids in this neighborhood—with the exception of Cass—were overscheduled after school: lessons, sports, art classes. And there were no old people. Other than a few mothers with toddlers, it was usually just Cass.

Her special tree was really an overgrown madrone bush. Cass had been attracted to its red-brown smooth bark and gnarled branches. Along the base of the trunk where she liked to sit, the bark had peeled away, revealing a silvery-green surface underneath that she loved to run her fingertips along. It was so smooth, smoother than any other tree she'd ever seen. Cass had always been fascinated by different types of bark. On the old redwoods she'd seen on a class trip to Muir Woods, it was so light and porous that it seemed impossible it could protect a tree so massive. Sycamore bark was scaly and split. The old oaks in the foothills were rough and splintery.

In the late summer, little red berries appeared on the madrone's branches. The berry clusters had sharp thorns, and Cass broke them off and wove them into long strands, like a necklace of teeth, of claws. She peeled away the bark with a fingernail, leaving curls of it like wood shavings to fall to the dried grasses. Sometimes she gathered stones from the creek and made little cairns around wildflowers that took root in the richer soil of the creek bed. Later, much later, she would learn the names of the plants, but then she thought of them by their flowers. Fringed purple; bright yellow puff; white-going-to-pink star.

She sat in the embrace of her tree and ran her hands along the smooth bark and breathed the faint sage scent of the sun-baked weeds and listened to dogs barking several blocks away, the faraway roar of the freeway half a mile to the south. She concentrated hard on all of these things, sense-memories and wishes, and in this way she made them disappear—the two men who'd dragged her to the broom closet, the one who held her hair in his fist and the one who was unbuckling his pants—taking herself back in time to her secret garden.

She breathed the scents of that other place and time and thought of the butterflies and ladybugs and bees that landed on the leaves of the shrubs and flowers, and when there was an enraged shout and her head was jerked up hard, her eyes flew open just in time to see Jimbo teeter and fall as a second and third burst of sound echoed off the room's walls.

A man stepped into the light of the lantern Jimbo had set on the floor.

Dor

And clinging to him, her arms wrapped tightly around his neck, her face pressed to his shirt, was Ruthie.

"Take Ruthie. Go in the other room," Dor growled.

Cass reached for Ruthie, seized her out of his arms.

"Wait for me there," he said.

Cass did.

The man had gone down on his good knee, clutching the other one where blood was spurting out, basting his boot with hot red blood. The other, the one who'd been stripping off his pants—Dor's vision went black at the thought—was slumped to the ground. The dart was imbedded in his shoulder; even if only a fraction of the toxin entered his system, he would be out for many hours, and not feel very good when he woke—especially when he saw what Dor had done to him with his own blade.

Dor grabbed the unconscious man's collar and dragged him

to the side of the small room, his belt buckle banging against the floor as he went. The man was not light, but adrenaline and fury pounded in Dor's blood and it felt good to slam the man's limp form into the wall.

Dor snapped on the man's flashlight, arcing it back and forth. The room had been used for a supply closet of some sort; on one high shelf were spray bottles partially filled with pinkish liquid, but otherwise there were only cans of powder, a few crumpled pieces of paper, water stains on the walls, tiny black pellets on the floor signaling that rodents still thrived down here. A bucket in the corner had the stink of human waste; Dor guessed that the guards used it as a lavatory, emptying it only at shift change.

In the beam of the flashlight the man on the floor looked even paler, his eyes wide with fear, his lips pulled back from his teeth in a parody of a grin.

"What do you want," he said.

"What's your name?"

"Ni-Nigel Ralston."

"Where are you from?"

"What the fuck do you care? What do you want?"

Dor delivered a rake-fist jab to Ralston's sternum, a baji quan move he'd practiced a thousand times. Ralston coughed and cried at the same time, doubling over. That seemed to make his knee hurt even worse, and Dor waited until he stopped writhing.

"I want to know something very specific from you," Dor continued, crouching down so he could look the man more or less eye to eye. "I want you to answer right the first time. I don't want to hear 'I don't know.' It will go badly for you if I hear 'I don't know,' which I can appreciate is not what you wanted me to say right now, seeing as there's a good chance that you won't be able to help me."

Dor waited for the man to nod that he understood.

"If you can't help me, and you tell me that, I'm going to kill you."

The man made a frightened little gasp.

"I know, I know, it's not fair, is it? Just like it's not fair that you were about to rape a defenseless woman a few minutes ago."

He leaned in closer. Inches from Ralston's face, he could see that tears leaked from the outer corners of his eyes, and a thin line of drool trailed down his chin. The stench grew stronger; the man had soiled himself. Well, a shattered kneecap probably hurt like hell.

"A girl was brought here in the last few days. Fourteen years old. Dark hair, light brown eyes, five feet four inches tall. She was with a group sheltering in a school half a mile southwest of Silva."

"I wasn't there when they came in, I didn't see them, I don't—"

Dor jabbed the barrel of his stolen gun into the soft flesh along the man's jaw. "Don't say you don't know," he said softly. "Shut the fuck up for a minute and listen, and think about the fact that I already killed one man tonight." He waited until Ralston nodded, choking back a trembling whimper.

"I'm going to let your buddy on the floor there live. You saw what I did to him—he's gonna have a hell of a time pissing for a while, but he might live, if he practices good hygiene."

Ralston squeezed his eyes shut and nodded harder.

"Okay. I don't care about any of the people that were

brought in except that one girl. I need to know exactly where they would have taken such a girl and how I can get there. Tell me everything you know about security, who and what I'll need to bypass in order to get to her. Think hard and convince me you're not leaving anything out, because you know what happens if I'm not convinced—I kill you."

Ralston told. He cried while he did it, ropy threads of mucus running from his nose, and his voice cracked and broke, but he told. When he was done it took everything Dor had not to kill him then, not to take his boot and crush the man's skull against the floor.

Instead he choked down his own bile and fury and made Ralston tell him where and how to get a car.

And then Dor killed him. A single bullet to the temple.

He'd broken his word, and he felt a faint compunction about it. But lies were going to be the least of his sins tonight.

31

CASS SANK INTO THE STRAIGHT-BACKED CHAIR where Jimbo had been sitting when she arrived, settling Ruthie into her lap. She cupped Ruthie's face in her hands, willing them not to tremble, and channeled everything she had into a mother's lie.

"Everything's going to be fine, Babygirl," she murmured and kissed Ruthie's cool cheeks over and over. "Dor brought you for an adventure, didn't he? I know you were sleeping, and now it's time to go to sleep again. We'll do a magic trick—you'll fall asleep right here, with me, and when you wake up again..."

Cass stopped herself. She had been about to make a promise to Ruthie that she could not keep: she was about to say that Ruthie would wake up in a nice bed, with Cass, everything snug and warm around them.

But after what had happened...

How could she have been so stupid?

Ruthie yawned and her eyes blinked heavily, and Cass smoothed her hands down her pajama-clad back and tucked Ruthie under her chin, and in seconds her daughter was sleeping again, soothed and unafraid.

Cass stared into the gloom, down the row of cots. At the end, in the silence and dark, was Smoke. There were no sounds, no movement from that direction; in the other direction, around the corner in the anteroom, Cass heard a sharp exhalation and the sounds of retching. Please don't let it have been Dor, she thought. She needed Dor to live. To prevail. Whatever he'd done, whatever magic he'd summoned to get past the guards at the dorm, at the doors of the Tapp Clinic, past anyone he met along the way—she needed him to keep doing it.

Cass was past the point of wondering how Dor had managed anything. She'd seen him do the impossible too many times before; it was his particular alchemy, procurer of the unimaginable, keeper of the peace in times of anarchy. He was larger than life in his person, taller and broader, with his glowering good looks—he was like the animated heroes in the old video games and the newer holographs.

The vomiting turned to pleading, and Cass turned away from the sounds. Dor could kill Jimbo, he could kill Ralston, and Cass would not care. But that still left the problem of their next move.

If Smoke was dead, Cass could leave him here. She was not sentimental about his body after death; she'd seen enough bodies in enough states of damage and decomposition that she had no romantic illusions about what remained behind. Beaters. The dead. Human tissues were fragile, unlovely things; they grew cold and waxy and then they began to turn to rot and pus and slime. If Smoke was dead, the place inside her where she carried his loss would be scoured and cauterized and she would stumble out of here a broken woman, but she would be able to do what she had said she would do, to follow Dor to the end of his quest, however it turned out.

If Smoke was alive…

She had to know. If Smoke was alive she could not leave him here. She did not know what would happen, how she would care for Ruthie, if she could barter herself for Ruthie's safety. But for now she only had to know about Smoke.

She cradled Ruthie in her arms, adjusting her shifting and sighing sleeping body to fit in the crook of her arm, and she stole down the corridor in the darkness. How long had it been since Ralston and Jimbo had dragged her to the closet—an hour? Less? More?—long enough for things to happen, for the angel of death to come and take his own.

The puddle of light coming from the closet did not reach this far. Cass used her free hand to feel around like a blind woman as she navigated the last of the cots. Under her hand a figure moaned but it was not Smoke. An empty cot…another…and then a wall.

A wall. Empty cots.

Panic ignited inside Cass—where was he? Where had he gone? She stumbled back to the last cot, felt frantically along its lumpy surface, the sheets and blankets that were still damp and hot. Still holding Ruthie, her back in agony from the strain of crouching down with the extra weight, Cass knelt and began feeling around on the ground.

A few feet away, a movement, a rustling, a faint cough.

Cass crawled toward the sounds, touched something, fabric, patted, a limb, a leg—

"I dreamed you came."

It was Smoke's voice. Weak, thin, broken—but it was

Smoke. Cass gasped and barely caught herself from falling on him, she could crush him, she could hurt him, she scrambled for his hands, found one and held on.

And then suddenly they were cast in light.

Dor stood above them with a flashlight, his pants covered in blood. On the floor Cass got a good look at Smoke. He'd been trying to crawl down the corridor toward the exit. His head lolled against the floor, his eyelids lowered and quivering, his mouth slack.

Had she imagined his voice? She pressed his cold hand to her face, felt his fingertips brush her eyelashes. Dor's face grew stony.

"Cass," he sighed. "At least now I know why you left the room. Is he dead?"

"Not yet," Cass whispered.

"Stand up," Dor said. "Can you carry Ruthie?"

Dor bent and gathered up Smoke's body. It sagged lifelessly as Dor slung him over his shoulders and prepared to carry him back out of the subterranean basement.

"Where are we going?"

"Someplace safe. I had thought it would be just you and Ruthie…but. Well. As soon as you're safe, I'm going after Sammi."

"How—where—?"

"I made him tell me."

"Who?"

"The tall one."

Ralston.

"I'm…sorry, Dor." Cass felt her face flood with shame. She hated that he'd found her that way, burned with the memory of not just her near rape but also what she'd done earlier in the evening. Everything she'd done was for Smoke, to save him, but Dor had seen her on her knees with two men standing over her, and she hated that he had seen her defenseless, had seen her with the fight gone out, that he might believe she had given up. Jimbo had seemed to enjoy her fear; he'd only gotten more excited when she resisted—so she'd stopped resisting.

"You have nothing to apologize for."

She searched his face, his hard-set jaw and flinty eyes, and found compassion there, even stronger than his anger. And she breathed.

"How did you know where to look for me?"

"I talked to the other guy. Back at the dorm."

"And he just told you?"

Dor scowled. "After a bit. Look, Cass, I didn't come here to kill innocent people, but anyone who's made it up to being a guard in the Rebuilders—they're not exactly innocent. It's not like in the Box."

Cass didn't doubt it. "But how...they took everything from us when we got here. Where did you get a weapon?"

"No, not everything. My shoes...my jacket, I had them made specially. There were places to hide things."

He slipped a thin, double-sided blade from his pocket. "Japanese ceramic. Harder than steel."

"But how did that help you get past the guard?"

"It didn't. I have Joe to thank for that."

Cass remembered all the times that Smoke disappeared early in the morning to practice with Joe, the obscure martial art involving rigid fist strikes that could break a branch, a plate. "That guard, he trained in the Marines. You can always tell a guy who learned to fight in the Marines—they all train to the same standards. I learned that from Three-High."

So it had been the Marines. Three-High sometimes talked

about the Three Borders War, the last one anyone was left to
report back from, when the U.S. won a decisive ground battle
over enemies who'd already exacted their revenge in advance
with their avian poisons. He was one of the few people Cass
had seen Dor spend much time with, besides Smoke. It was a
sign of Dor's determination that he had learned enough in the
months since he started the Box to take down a professional
fighter.

"Anyway, Joe's trick shut the guy up long enough for me
to get him restrained." Dor frowned at his blade and slipped
it back into his pocket. "I had to use that a little to convince
him that I really wanted to hear what he had to say. Turns out
he didn't care all that much about revealing where his friend
was, after I…showed him I was serious."

Dor dug in his pack and came up with two more guns. The
ones from Ralston and Jimbo. "And now we have these, too.
Which one do you want?"

She chose the smaller one, a small black semiauto. It wasn't
so different from the one Smoke had insisted she practice with
on several occasions. "I don't know how much good I'll be.
With, you know, carrying her."

"Hopefully you won't have to carry her for long. Are you…
all right to walk?"

For a moment Cass didn't understand the question, and
then she realized that Dor was carefully not looking at her,
at her body; he focused on a place over her shoulder, but his
face was lined and sorrowful, a dozen years older than he'd
looked even that morning.

He'd spoken to the guard. He knew what she'd traded.

Cass's face flamed. "I'm fine."

"I'd just leave you here, it should be relatively safe now that
they're down…but I don't know when shift change is, and it's

already nearly dawn. And besides, the other guy's going to be waking up in an hour or two."

"He's not dead?"

"No. Like I said, it was never my intention to kill when I came down here. I brought some darts, the blade. I had hoped it might be enough…that was probably naïve."

"How many darts do you have left?"

"Three." He grimaced. "And there's a problem with them, you have to be close enough to jam them in by hand, because I couldn't figure out a way to bring a tranq gun in here. I nailed the guy in there because I was practically on top of him when I came around the corner. And I had it in my hand. Otherwise…"

"So you just left him there?"

"Not…without a souvenir. Something to make sure he doesn't do this again, to some other woman."

"What…"

Dor made a slicing motion. "Assuming he doesn't bleed out, or die of infection, he's gonna be pretty damn tender for a while."

Cass felt no pity. Despite the fact that she had given herself away to get here, down to Smoke's prison, there was still a difference between what she had given Ralston in trade and what Jimbo meant to take from her without compunction.

"What did you find out about Sammi?"

Dor's face went dangerously blank. "She's in a dorm, where all the girls her age live. It's not too far from here, maybe half a mile."

"What aren't you telling me?"

"Nothing. They just…the girls live together, the young women. There's about forty of them and four guards on duty at night. I made him tell me. Two more come on at six in the morning, so we need to move fast."

"How are we going to find out which room she's in?"

"Leave that part to me," Dor said. "But listen, here's the problem. I can't carry Smoke that far. He'll slow us down too much."

"I'm not leaving him," Cass said quickly. "I can't leave him."

"Cass…" Dor's face was shadowed with anxiety and something else, some dark thing. "Look at him. He's lost a lot of blood from his shoulder. He's been beaten, probably tortured. There's a good chance he's bleeding internally. There's no guarantee he's going to make it. Is it worth the risk…?"

"You can go without me," Cass said. "I know you need to go to Sammi. I understand. But I can't. If they find me and Ruthie…I can convince them I'm innocent. I'll tell them you shot them when you found us together, that you went back to, I don't know…"

It was all tangled in her mind, the men who had been killed tonight, the trail of violence and cruelty that had brought them here. "I don't know, I'll figure out something. I'm an outlier, Dor, they need me. I have something valuable to trade with them."

His eyes narrowed with anger. "*No*. You can't stay here. You don't know what they mean to do with you."

"I know they mean to keep me hostage, okay? And I know there's no guarantee they'll ever find the vaccine, and I could spend the rest of my life being poked and studied for nothing—but is that so bad? I'll be with Ruthie, and we'll be safe, and—"

"*Cass!*"

There was something so dangerous and fierce in his voice that Cass shut up and listened.

"They're not making a vaccine. They're not studying outliers. They're using them...*harvesting* them. For breeding."

For a moment Cass didn't understand.

Harvesting...

And then she put it together.

The young girls, in the dorm.

The woman, with her legs in stirrups.

"They've made a baby farm," she whispered.

"They mean to populate this entire place with outliers," Dor said. "They're using outliers to make embryos, and sterilizing everyone else."

"They can't—I don't know, make a vaccine, like Evangeline said?"

Dor shrugged. "Sure, maybe—if they had all the time in the world, equipment, the best scientists. But selective breeding—that's easy to do—hell, look at history."

"But who would—I mean, there aren't enough outliers..."

"All they need is donor eggs and sperm—it doesn't take all that many outliers to produce those. They create the embryos, then use the youngest, healthiest girls to incubate them. The babies get taken away to be raised by the Rebuilder leaders, and the girls keep on breed—"

"Oh, God..."

"And they took Sammi there. Cass...she's only fourteen."

In her arms, Ruthie stirred, her body soft and warm against hers. Her baby, her life. She would never have brought Ruthie into this world if she knew what it was going to become. And now the Rebuilders had made it worse. They meant to doctor up embryos in a lab and grow them inside little girls—prisoners—only to rip them away before they could even hold the babies they'd given life to.

A memory flashed of the day Ruthie was born. It had been an easy labor, made all the easier because Ruthie had been early and small. In the midst of her labor pains Cass had sobbed because she believed that if only she hadn't been drinking before she knew she was pregnant, in those early weeks, she could have carried Ruthie to term. In her third trimester she had begun dreaming that her baby was born dead, a shriveled and wounded thing, doomed by her demons.

The doctor on duty had been kind enough; one of the nurses wiped the tears from her face with a cool cloth. But it wasn't until Ruthie had been placed, pink and wriggling and healthy, on her chest that Cass finally believed. And in that moment everything changed.

She'd been thinking of giving her baby up for adoption, had met with the social workers already and begun the paperwork. She knew she wasn't ready, or worthy. But when Ruthie lay in her arms and Cass heard her cry for the first time, she knew that everything good and worthy in her life would, until the day she died, revolve around this tiny person. That redemption was possible. That she could be someone who mattered. And that God had given her this chance and she must not squander it.

Her first words to Ruthie, whispered so softly that the doctors and nurses did not hear, that no one save her baby girl would ever hear, were, "You're mine, and I am yours."

Here in Colima, they were taking newborns from girls' bodies, leave them hurting and bereft, only to impregnate them again and again. She thought of Sammi, that beautiful girl, the dusting of freckles on her nose, her glossy ponytail. Cass would offer her own body, give away her own eggs, if it would save even a single one of the girls from such a fate—but as long as the Rebuilders survived, all would be in danger.

Dor cupped her chin with his free hand. "Cass. Look at me."

So she did. She looked at him as though for the very first time, into his black eyes, the hard planes of his face. This was a man she'd used and who had used her. She'd blamed him for things that were not his fault and sought from him things that were not his to give. She'd clung to him and run with him, and tonight she'd nearly ended his journey before he got Sammi back.

"I'm sorry," she whispered, tears pooling in her eyes. She wanted to say she should never have come, but that too would be a lie; she had to be with Smoke, and Smoke was here.

It was Smoke who should never have left, but she finally understood that without seeking vengeance Smoke would have withered and died from within. He had been willing to trade his life for those that burned the library, and he had succeeded.

Perhaps he was ready to die. Perhaps, in his brief lucid moments, he even *planned* to die.

I dreamed you were here.

It might have been his dying dream, but Cass intended to prove him wrong.

"We'll all get out," she said to Dor, but this promise was meant for Smoke.

32

CASS DOUBTED DOR KNEW THAT THE PLACE HE'D
left them had once been a wisteria arbor.

Now the vines were little more than sticks. Their leaves
had fallen and their delicate branches snapped. It wasn't ideal
cover, but it had the advantage of being close to the Tapp
Clinic, down a service road at the edge of the wide campus
lawn. Dor had propped Smoke up so that his head rested on
a swell in the recently landscaped earth that somehow made
her think of Gloria's grave mound.

As Dor slipped away into the predawn, Cass sat cross-legged
and held Ruthie in her lap and took Smoke's hand, hot with
fever, into her own and thought about all the dead in the
world, how there could never be enough memorials, enough
trees planted, enough marble stones to stand for everyone.

Time passed.

Far off to the east, the first faint glow of morning appeared
at the horizon, and the stars began to dim. Cass thought about

334   SOPHIE LITTLEFIELD

the fact that these were the same stars that studded the sky over the world Before; they would continue to shine whether the world renewed itself or failed. They were the same stars that witnessed her birth and the ones that would shine on the night of her death, whether it was this day or one many years from now, and in theses thoughts she found comfort.

They were wedged in a narrow space between the wall of a classroom building and the latticed arbor twined with dead vines, sitting on a bed of landscaping bark. Few sounds reached them in their hiding spot—a machine starting up somewhere several buildings away, the crunch of gravel underfoot as people passed by across the lawn once or twice, guards doing their security detail.

Once the wall was completed, there would be little reason for guards to roam the campus. Only the highest levels of the Rebuilders were armed. The rest—the newcomers, the workers, the baby makers and children—were powerless, incapable of revolt or even posing an inconvenience. Already, as the community was still being built, it relied on order: schedules and timetables and hierarchies, weights and measures and zero tolerance in judgments. Cass didn't doubt that, for many, this was welcome. For every person who chafed under the Rebuilder rule, there were probably several more who were so grateful for the shelter, the promise of safety, that any trade-offs they made in terms of personal freedom seemed like a bargain.

Even, she thought with a shudder, the baby farm. As horrified as she was by the prospect of human eggs being systematically harvested, fertilized and implanted, she could imagine that for some women the trade-off might feel like a reasonable one. And there was no doubt that the first-generation outliers, even though they were little more than glorified breeding machines, would enjoy freedoms and benefits that others would not.

Cass brushed Smoke's hair, damp against his fevered skin, away from his face. She had adjusted his filthy dressings as well as she could, retying the torn bandages and wiping away as much grit and dried blood as she could. Now that they were outdoors he began to shiver. She took off her own jacket and covered him with it. She wore only the nightgown, her underwear ripped and abandoned back in the closet, but she was warm enough, overheated by exertion and adrenaline.

Smoke hadn't woken from his fever coma, but occasionally he muttered pieces of words and once she thought she heard him say her name.

More time passed. Ruthie fidgeted, half asleep, too.

Cass tried not to focus on how long Dor was taking. His plan had been a simple one: break into the motor pool much as he had broken into the Tapp Clinic, using the darts if possible, the guns if not. Once he'd secured a vehicle, he would come back for them and then they would go together to break Sammi out.

He had tried to talk to her about what she would do if he wasn't back by the time the campus began fully waking up. He wanted her to leave Smoke there, to take Ruthie and turn herself in. But Cass knew they were past that stage.

The first thing she heard was the grinding of gears. It sounded like a lighter version of the dump trucks that used to drive past a house her mother had once rented. Before she met Byrn and was still scraping to get by. The house was located near a quarry, and in the afternoons the trucks would drive by, loaded down with rough limestone, switching into first gear when they hit the hill at the corner of Creasy Springs Road. Before she identified the sound she felt it reverberating up through her body. Smoke must have felt it too, even in the depths of his unconsciousness, because he rolled to his side and his eyelids fluttered. So intent was Cass on making sure Smoke was all right that she didn't actually see the vehicle until it rounded the corner and approached along the service road.

It was a FedEx truck, the logo still painted on the sides, its back cargo area open, its doors missing. Only the running lights were on and Cass wasn't certain it was Dor until he parked and jumped down from the open driver's seat. And even then it took a moment, because he was wearing the fatigue pants and khaki shirt of the Rebuilders, a black baseball cap pulled low above his eyes.

"In the back," he said. "Hurry." Without waiting for a response he picked Smoke up, not gently. Cass wanted to tell him to take care, but she was too afraid. She carried Ruthie to the cargo area and clambered inside, boosting Ruthie up to the waist-high floor first. Flattened cardboard boxes lined the floor, an improvement over the hard metal on which she'd ridden two nights earlier. Bungee cords dangled from the walls, and dust and broken bricks cluttered the corners. Whatever they'd been using it to haul had left the floor and walls dented and creased, and the rope net someone had rigged across the back opening had torn free and lay in useless coils.

After settling Smoke on the floor of the truck, Dor paused before jumping down to the ground. "I'm driving straight there," he said sharply. "If I have any trouble with the guard, I'm going to have to shoot. I can't risk him warning the dorm that we're coming."

"What about the darts?"

"I only have two left. Here." Dor reached into his pocket and handed them to her. They were like small syringes with synthetic feathering at one end. "You have your gun, but use these if you can, first. Just jam them in."

"Why? Why won't you take them?"

He looked into her eyes, searching for something. "You haven't killed anyone yet," he said softly. "I have. It won't cost me nearly as much to do it again."

Dor had changed. Something was missing, some light had left him. He was no less determined to free Sammi—if anything he seemed more amped than ever. But his eyes no longer held the promise of hope.

Cass slipped the darts into her socks as the truck began to move, the only place she had to stash them. As the tires hit potholes, Smoke cried out in pain. A good thing, because it meant that he was still aware, if only dimly, of his body.

The smell of exhaust was strong in the truck, and Cass coughed; she was coughing the first few times Ruthie spoke so it took her a while to realize that her daughter's voice wasn't just in her imagination.

"Mama."

Cass looked down to see Ruthie had got up on her knees and was holding on to her arm for support, her face only inches away.

"Ruthie, what—? Ruthie," Cass said, breath caught in her throat. She didn't want to make a fuss, to draw attention; she had worked so hard to convince Ruthie that it didn't matter if she talked, that she could heal at her own pace.

"Is Smoke okay?"

Ruthie's face was tight with worry, her wide eyes sad, her rosebud lips pursed in concern.

"Oh, baby…"

It had never occurred to her to tell Ruthie what had happened to Smoke. Ruthie had been napping when he left, when

Cass said her angry last words to him. She had not been with Cass when she made her bargain with Dor. Cass had tried to make the trip to Colima sound like an adventure, and she had taken care to say that Smoke was on an adventure of his own, but at the time Ruthie hadn't seemed too worried about him.

And there had been Dor—Dor who was so good with children, who played with her and roughhoused with her, Dor who carried her on his shoulders as though she were as light as a butterfly. Smoke and Ruthie had spent many hours together, but they were quiet hours, walking slowly around the Box or reading together. With a burst of guilt Cass remembered the dozens of times she had wished Smoke had been easier around Ruthie, that he had taken more readily to a parental role. Even his kisses seemed awkward, his arms stiff when he held her.

But now, looking into her daughter's worried face, she saw how wrong she had been. Ruthie had been damaged, had lost part of herself in her time in the Convent. Smoke had come to them without any knowledge of children, without knowing how to be with her. Together, they started slowly and moved forward hesitantly. But now that she was remembering Cass realized how often she saw them together, not talking, doing little more than sitting.

Healing.

She gathered Ruthie into her lap. "Babygirl," she whispered. "We are going to do our very best to make sure that he gets better. Smoke is hurt, but we are going to help him."

Ruthie held on.

Moments later the truck ground to a stop.

He thought about checking, just checking one more time. To make sure they were all right. Cass, Ruthie...even Smoke, though there was a darkness to that thought; sure, Dor was glad Smoke had pulled through, more than glad, but things were different now in a dozen different ways.

No. He wasn't going there now, because all that mattered in this moment was finding Sammi. And it turned out to be a damn good thing he didn't go to the back of the truck. When he got out and started toward the building, the guard was waiting for him.

"Who are you?" she said, squinting in the dawn light. Her hand rested on her belt, on the holster of a weapon. "I don't know you."

"Name's Wentworth. I've come out to take a look at the generator cells."

"What? No one said anything—no one's mentioned a service call."

Please, lady, don't make this a thing. Dor had only his blade or his gun at this point, and he couldn't risk her alerting anyone else that he was there. "I was supposed to get here last night, but we had a problem at Tapp and I couldn't get away until just now."

She looked even warier as she stepped back. "Look, I don't mean to be a pain about this, but let me just get—"

She stopped abruptly, her eyes going wide, before she sank to the ground, teetering on her knees before falling forward on the drive. Dor, acting on instinct, caught her before her face hit.

Cass stepped from behind her. "I used a dart."

"What the hell are you doing out of the truck?"

"I saw her come out. I knew she wasn't going to believe you...."

"I could have taken care of her."

"Yeah, by killing her. This way there's one less."

He couldn't argue with that, though he wanted to, wanted to argue with everything Cass said. Since he'd come across her—moments from being violated, Cass who always seemed stronger than everything and everyone, vulnerable like that—he could barely contain his need to protect her, to lock her up tight and take her away from here. It was like those days back in the Box when he saw her wandering across the street to her herb garden, when he held his breath until she was safe again behind the chain-link on the other side. Well, he would protect her now, just as soon as he got Sammi; he'd get them all out of here, back where they belonged. He fingered the silver box in his pocket, his insurance: inside was one of the most volatile explosives ever created, one of the prizes in his extensive arsenal. The second the gel met the powder, it would take out half a city block. He'd been so tempted to use it on the fetid basement of the Tapp Clinic, to blow up not just the two dead men but to obliterate the entire place, every remnant and memory of what had happened. But there'd been others there, innocents, so he'd swallowed back his rage.

He understood Smoke's quest. If he hadn't needed to come for Sammi, he would have joined Smoke in hunting down the people responsible for the library raid. He would have been happy to pull the trigger.

"Go back with Smoke and Ruthie," he said roughly. "That's enough risk for tonight. I'll be back before you know it, and I'll need you to be ready to go."

She didn't go right away. She stood shivering, with her arms crossed across her chest, in her thin nightgown. "Take this," he said, pulling off his own parka.

"No, I can't," she said, but when he tossed it to her she caught it.

And because he couldn't stand to watch her put on the coat

that was still warm from his body, he stalked past her and into the building, refusing to turn around. "It'll just slow me down anyway."

33

IT WAS TAKING TOO LONG.

Cass had gone back into the truck like Dor ordered her. Smoke's chills had subsided; her coat seemed to be keeping him warm. Ruthie sat cross-legged at his side, watching him with a serious expression on her face. Cass stared out the back of the truck; the sky was lightening at the horizon, but no one had come or gone from the building. Nearby, the guard's unconscious body lay in a landscaping bed behind a hedge of dead oleanders.

For the first time in many months, Cass wished for a watch. It seemed like it had been half an hour, but what if it had only been a few minutes? Dor's plan had been simple enough; he was going to take the first guard or attendant he could find, threaten them into cooperation, and demand to be taken to Sammi. The rooms in the dorm where she and Dor had spent the night were unlocked. But would they lock the girls in here, to deter them from trying to escape?

But what if Sammi wasn't here? What if they'd already taken her for... Cass shuddered, not wanting to think about the procedure, the violation of a body, in its own way just as horrific as what had nearly been done to her earlier tonight. Sammi was still a child; Cass had not been a child for decades.

If they had taken Sammi to the Tapp Clinic, maybe she was there on the upper floors, resting, recuperating, being tested. Or maybe she was here, but Dor couldn't find her; maybe he was going from room to room, taking greater and greater risks.

Cass thought about driving away, leaving Dor here to fend for himself. It was the second time in their journey that she had considered abandoning him. The keys were in the ignition. She knew the way across campus to the incomplete section of wall, and she could easily drive out and be on the road in minutes. Sure, they might come after her; once they discovered the dead men in the clinic basement, Smoke's empty cot. There could be a bounty on her head as there had been on his. But with a head start, she could be back up to the Box by the time anyone had a chance to catch up. Suddenly all the reasons not to go back didn't seem so insurmountable. There was gas in the truck, she was armed, she wouldn't stop until she saw the welcoming lights along the chain-link fence. Even if they sent a team, a dozen Rebuilders, Dor's people would defeat them handily.

Dor's people. Dor.

She couldn't just leave him here. He would never have left her behind.

She looked at Ruthie, so serious, so concerned. "Babygirl, let's get Smoke into the front of the truck, where it's nicer," she said. "Then you can take good care of him for a few minutes while I go help Dor. You can do that for me, can't you?"

Ruthie nodded gravely and placed her hand on Smoke's arm, as though she was comforting him.

It was hard work, half carrying, half dragging Smoke off the bed of the truck, and up into the cab, Ruthie continuing to want to touch him the whole way. He woke, moaning, from the pain, and for a few moments he seemed to fight her, as though he didn't recognize her. But by the time she got him to the open passenger door he had stopped struggling and looked at her through heavy-lidded eyes. "You look... like her," he muttered, and when she gathered all her strength and tried to lift him onto the running board, up into the cab, he sighed and dragged himself inside, collapsing onto the seat.

Ruthie crawled up beside him and knelt on the floor, re-suming her vigil. Cass brushed a kiss on her cheek and had started to close the passenger door, when Ruthie gave her a small smile.

"I'll help him, Mama."

WHEN SAMMI WOKE AND SAW THE FAINTEST pink of dawn through the window, it took her a moment to remember where she was and how she came to be there.

And then it took only one more moment for Sammi to come to a decision.

Last night she'd been numb. Shocked. Too much had happened. The truth kept getting revealed a little at a time, all through the terrible day, as the Rebuilders' true nature slowly came into focus. They were evil, even the ones who didn't carry guns or set fires. Some things were even worse than just killing people. They wiped out everyone you cared about and then they led you away, and expected you to just go along with them and do their things. They pretended this place was normal, pretended this was like some big happy town—but behind closed doors all kinds of horrors were waiting. They made girls pregnant—Sammi didn't even want to think about how—and kept them in this place, and who knew what came after that? It was sure to be awful, and now that Sammi had finally gotten some rest, she suddenly knew that she wasn't going to accept this fate without a fight.

All the pieces were in place—she was a girl whose fears had been burned away by one loss after another, in a place where they counted on fear to keep people down—so she wasn't worried about how this journey would end, exactly. She would live or she would die, and she didn't much care which.

But the Rebuilders needed to know that they couldn't just throw people away like they didn't matter. That people were more than nothing. Her mother's life had ended with the soundless arc of a sharpened blade, no more than a seeping pool of blood on the earth. Jed lost his life in the blink of an eye, as did his brothers. And Mrs. Levenson, and countless others, and the Rebuilders would just go on killing and killing until people stood up to them, and Sammi figured she might as well be one of the ones who fought.

So when the faint pink appeared in the sky outside their narrow window, Sammi pushed back her blankets and put her feet on the cold floor. She waited for her eyes to adjust to the dawn and squatted over the big plastic bowl.

"It gets easier."

Roan's voice startled her and Sammi saw that she was sitting up in bed, hugging herself.

"What does?"

"Peeing like that. I refused to do it the first month I was here. I thought I could out-stubborn them, you know? But the thing is, when you're pregnant it's a lot harder to hold it. Now? I pee like three times a night."

Sammi stared at her silhouette in the darkened room. "How pregnant are you?"

Roan laughed, somehow managing to make it sound sad. "You don't ask someone how pregnant they are. You say, how far *along* are you?"

"Oh."

"They say I'm six weeks. I guess they'd know."

Sammi wasn't sure how to say what came next. "Uh…how did you, I mean, you weren't pregnant when you got here… were you?"

Roan frowned. "Didn't Mrs. Henderson tell you?"

"Tell me what? I mean, she hardly said anything to me. I got here in the middle of the night and I think she just wanted to go to bed. She acted all pissed off that she had to take care of me."

"God, what a *bitch*," Roan sighed. "Okay, so you might as well hear it from me, right? You're here to breed. They're going to impregnate you with outlier sperm so you can have an immune baby. Then when the baby comes they take it. They give it to one of the higher-up families to raise, and when they get the new outlier neighborhood finished, all the kids are going to grow up over there." Roan's voice was dull, as though the desperation of her situation had sucked the life from her.

Sammi's throat felt dry as Roan's words rang in her mind. *Breed. Impregnate. Immune baby…they take it.*

"Wait, you don't get to, you know, take care of it? Your-self?"

Roan laughed, a short, bitter sound that disappeared into silence. "We're just the baby factory," she said softly. "At least we don't have to work. I mean, they feed us pretty well, it's safe here…and they do it in vitro, you know? I mean, it's not like you have to, umm…"

When her voice trailed off, Sammi felt like she should say

something, like she should offer something in exchange for Roan's attempt to reassure her. "I'm…sorry."

"It's okay," Roan said, hugging herself and looking away, and Sammi saw the way she wrapped her arms around her stomach, and somehow that was the saddest part.

"Look—Roan, I'm leaving here, right now, before things get— I mean, I don't know anyone here, I don't have any attachments, I think I might as well try." Sammi could feel her face flush, the embarrassment of talking to someone who was practically a stranger, even if she felt like someone Sammi could be friends with. "But if you wanted, you could come too, you know?"

Roan made a sound in her throat, a skeptical dry sound. "Thanks. But I'm kind of stuck here. I mean, they've been giving me actual prenatal vitamins. They got maternity clothes and baby clothes. Where else am I going to get those? And besides, if anything goes wrong with…you know, the birth or whatever, there's doctors here to take care of the baby."

Sammi stared at her roommate, taking advantage of the darkness to shield her curiosity, realizing that Roan couldn't help loving the child growing inside her.

"Yeah," she said, trying not to think of her own mother, of Jed's mother, the way they died with their children's names on their lips.

"Look, if you're really going to go, at least let me help. You won't get farther than the elevator by yourself. All the guards are armed."

Sammi's determination faltered. "I saw the one on this floor and the one in the lobby. The one downstairs looked like we woke her up when they brought me in. I'm fast," she added—she held a pair of records, the 200 and the 400, and track wasn't even her main sport, she'd only done it as a favor to the coach, who also happened to be her government teacher, and who always said she'd never seen a girl with as much grit per square inch as Sammi. That was the kind of thing that made all the girls roll their eyes, but did she ever wish Coach Hansen was here now.

"Fast is good," Roan said, and Sammi could see the flash of her white teeth, even in the dark. "But it won't help much if they shoot you. What you need is for them to be paying attention to something else. There's one sure way to get them off their feet. Let me help, and I can make it so no one notices you, and give you a chance to get out of the building."

Sammi hesitated. "But would it get you in trouble?"

Roan waved away her concern. "No, not what I'm thinking of. In fact everyone will probably be glad for a little excitement. It's so fucking boring around here, nothing ever happens. But listen, where are you going to go when you get out?"

"Anywhere," Sammi said with conviction, "as long as I don't spend one more day here. With *them*." She felt her body shiver as she spat the word, and realized that she was made of hate now, that some of the goodness inside her had been replaced when they took everyone she loved from her, one by one. But that was okay, because the hate canceled out her old softness, too.

"You're kidding, Sammi. You'll never last out there past the wall."

"I used to go out by myself all the time," Sammi said, remembering those thrilling nights when the raiders at the school let her tag along, the silver of the moon, the smell of night mixing with the sounds of their boots on glass on the streets, the calls of the birds that were starting to return.

"You're braver than me," Roan muttered, shaking her head.

"Besides, I won't be going far. All's I need is to get to that neighborhood by the water tower." She could see it clearly from their window: on the other side of the wall, where they were still building it and the gaps were barred by nothing more than plywood barriers, past a couple of strip malls and flat-roofed commercial buildings, was a neighborhood of little run-down ranches, the kind that students probably used to live in, with couches on the porch and bikes chained to the railing. She'd find the right one, the one she could be safe in, until she figured out what to do next. And if not—well, better to die out there, than live in here.

"A couple of people have tried, before," Roan said quietly. "At least, that's the rumor."

"Yeah...? And?"

She shrugged. "Who knows? I mean, it's not like they come up here and give us reports. A lot of people think the guards found them and killed them, but maybe..."

Maybe. That was enough to hang her hopes on, such as they were—the thinnest strands, next to nothing, all she had left. Yeah. Sammi would take *maybe.*

"Okay. Tell me what to do."

Five minutes later Roan led her down the hallway, toward the guard desk at the edge of what they called the recreation room even though all they had for recreation were a few ragged copies of *What To Expect When You're Expecting* and Chinese checkers and *People* magazines read so many times that they were held together with tape. Roan's heart pounded as she forced herself not to turn around to check on Sammi, to make sure she was keeping to the shadowed spaces in front of each door, staying a few paces back. There were only a few lightbulbs for the whole hall and Roan was counting on the darkness to help keep Sammi hidden.

Mrs. Wight had been sleeping, she could tell, because there was a crease on her face where she must have been resting her head on her arm. When she saw Roan she pushed a hand through her graying hair and frowned.

"What is it, Roan?"

Roan clutched the fabric of her nightgown and did her best to look terrified, staggering the last few steps toward the desk, biting the inside of her cheek. "It's—I think I'm spotting, Mrs. Wight. I had the worst cramps, they woke me up."

Mrs. Wight blanched and staggered up from her chair. "You're sure? Did they just start?"

"It hurts, Mrs. Wight, I'm bleeding bad, I think I might pass out—"

Through slitted eyes she watched Mrs. Wight dig for her radio, backing away all the while. Just like she thought. They put Wight on overnights for a reason; she was as useless as she was lazy. Roan clutched the arm of a sofa and did what she thought was a pretty good job of swaying on her feet as though she was about to faint, while Wight barked orders into the radio. Good. She'd have the doctors out of bed, and Mrs. Poehlmann, who was in charge of the whole place, and by the time they got around to figuring out that Sammi was missing, she'd be long gone.

Sure, Roan would be in trouble, even though she'd dumped the plastic potty on her mattress and planned to pretend that she'd only peed the bed when cramps woke her. They might buy that—and she'd say she had no idea that Sammi meant to bolt, even though she was already slipping into the stairwell, one pale hand raised in a goodbye wave, and then she was gone, Wight never having noticed her at all.

Roan figured she'd probably have to go over to Tapp and spend the day being examined, but at least they were all so concerned about her baby that they'd treat her okay. By night she'd be back here, and some poor citizen would have changed her linens and cleaned up her room, and she could go back to waiting, waiting, waiting for the day she both longed for and dreaded, when her baby would be born into this stupid place.

All that waiting. Well, at least she'd caused a little excitement for once.

Roan slid down onto the couch and let her eyes flutter shut while Wight yelled.

CASS HAD FINALLY GOTTEN RUTHIE AND SMOKE into the cab, and had been about to head into the building when lights went on in the second floor and, seconds later, the third. She heard shouting through the open lobby door.

She took a sharp breath and turned the key with shaking fingers, and was reaching to put the truck in gear, to make their escape, when she thought of Dor again inside.

She couldn't do it. She was armed, and she was able, and as long as that was the case she had to try. She pulled the truck around the corner, where it was hidden from the front of the building by the oleander hedge.

If she failed now, someone would find Smoke and Ruthie here. They would kill Smoke, but Ruthie was an outlier, and a child, and they would take care of her.

"I love you," she mouthed as she slipped out of the car, and she had almost reached the entrance when a car came around the corner so fast that the tires shrieked, and stopped a few feet from the front door. Two men jumped out, leaving their doors open, and ran inside. Now that Cass had a view into the enormous high-ceilinged lobby that formed the entire ground floor of the dorm, bare except for a few clusters of furniture on a patterned rug in the center, she saw that a dozen girls and young women were gathered at the other end, hugging each other and screaming.

Between them and her, Dor was standing with his hands over his head, a short middle-aged female guard backing him toward the wall with a rifle that looked outlandishly large in her hands. Nearby a girl with long honey-colored hair was kneeling on the floor, a second female guard holding a gun to her head and yelling something at the two men from the car.

Cass didn't think. She raised the gun Dor had given her and remembered sunlit afternoons when her father took her out in the field by the pond, setting up cans along the falling-down fence, the way he wrapped his arms around her when he taught her how to sight down the barrel.

Two dozen steps to the open doors and the woman never stopped yelling and Dor never turned around and the girl on the floor was the only one who saw her. As the guard behind her turned toward the two men crossing the lobby, the girl rolled out of the way and Cass took her shot.

The first man went down like a rock. As the other spun around and dropped, Cass fired again and again but he didn't stop, he turned in a circle and came up shooting back at her. Cass felt the pavement at her feet break and splinter and she dived through the doors into the building, sprinting to the shelter of a sofa, her heart racing, ears filled with screaming. There was another shot, and another, and more screaming, and someone ran past her, out into the night. She peeked around the sofa and saw the shooter crouched low, crawling toward her, and even as their eyes met he took another shot but it went wide.

"Outlier! I'm an outlier!" she screamed. "I'm putting down my gun and we can figure this out! Don't shoot anymore. I'm an outlier!" She had to get to Dor, had to trade herself for him and Sammi. She could make this right. The Rebuilders would understand the trade they proposed—they would know that Mary would value her life far above the others'. Dor was strong and he was good. He was Sammi's father and he was a good father, and he would make sure that Ruthie was safe. He would take Smoke and if there was a chance for him, Dor would find that chance. Everyone she loved could live, maybe even thrive, and all Cass had to do was stay here.

"Shoot me and Mary will know you killed an outlier," she yelled. The girls clustered at the back of the room stared at her, holding each other and crying. She scanned their faces, frantically searching for Sammi. "Every girl here will tell them. They're all witnesses. But if you let this man and his daughter go I'll put down my gun. I'll come without a fight."

There was silence, and Cass took a deep breath. That was it, all she had to offer.

She came out from behind the sofa, standing up. The man in front of her didn't lower his gun, but he didn't shoot, either. Behind him, the gray-haired woman stared at her with fury. At her feet, the other woman guard twitched and moaned.

A low, guttural cough echoed through the still room. Cass looked around wildly for its source.

Then her gaze fell on Dor.

He knelt on the floor, clutching his head. Blood ran through his fingers.

Cass had been willing to strike a bargain with the Rebuilders—her life for Sammi's and Dor's freedom. But they hadn't listened to her. They'd shot him. Once again they had taken what was not theirs, and this time Cass would not stand for it.

"Deal's off," she whispered to herself.

And she pulled the trigger.

The man was only a couple of yards away. Too close to miss, and he fell practically at her feet. Cass barely glanced at him. Instead, she got ready to take her next shot.

But as she tried to steady her shaking arm, tried to blink away the sudden blurriness in her vision, the female guard staggered sideways and fell, her final shot going into the ceiling, tackled by several of the women who'd been clustered in the back of the room.

One of them broke away from the others and kicked at the fallen guard, screaming, and the gun went spinning and sliding across the floor, coming to rest under a vending machine that had long since been looted of the last of its contents.

Cass surveyed the scene in stunned amazement. She longed to sink to the floor herself, adrenaline giving way to trembling terror, but now there was another girl who'd just made enemies of the Rebuilders.

Cass could shoot the two women guards. Up close, she saw that the one who lay spitting and gasping had the mark of the koru on her wrist. She was high-level Rebuilder. There was no reason to spare her.

"Where's Sammi?" she yelled at nobody in particular. "The new girl? Where is she?"

The long-haired girl who'd been kneeling on the floor crawled away from the center of the room, then stood and ran toward her.

"Where's Sammi?" she asked again. Up close, Cass saw that her wide, pretty face bore more anger than fear. A tiny diamond pierced her nose, and it flashed in the lobby lights.

"She escaped."

"Escaped—*where?*"

"Out there. Over the wall. Like, ten minutes ago. That's where she said she was going, anyway. I helped her. I'm—I was her roommate. Roan."

Cass's heart sank. All the blood, all the dead, everything they had done to get here, and now Sammi was gone, and Dor was shot. Outside, in the truck, was her own daughter, and Smoke, near dead. How had this happened, how had so many people ended up depending on her? And what was she supposed to do now, when they had reached the end of her options?

Already tonight, Cass had killed twice and given away her innocence. Very little remained. Was it enough to take care of the people she loved? Cass had no idea. But it would have to be enough for tonight.

Do the next right thing.

Cass swallowed hard, and swiped at her eyes with her free hand.

"You," she ordered to the girl who'd kicked the gun. "What's your name?"

"Leslie."

"Okay. Pick up the guns. There—and there. Get his."

After only a second's hesitation the girl did as she asked, crouching down to reach under the vending machine. She jammed it in the pocket of her flannel pajama pants and scrambled to collect the rest of the weapons.

"You can't stay here," Cass said, holding out her hands

for the guns. "You're the enemy now. You have to come with us."

Leslie nodded, handing over the weapons.

Cass took a deep breath and looked at Dor. *Please please please,* she prayed. *Let him live.*

"We need to go now," she said. The last of the girls—seven of them, she saw now—had fallen quiet and backed up, away from the scene in the center of the lobby, against the wide glass window that looked out on a courtyard that must have once been pretty, and was now filled with the skeletons of ornamental trees. "Roan and Leslie, help this man. He comes with us. All of you can, too. But you have to come *now.*"

"No," the gray-haired guard said, in a steely voice. "No one leaves. Leave this building and they'll shoot you on sight. Stay here and we'll guarantee your safety. You and your babies."

"Babies they won't let you keep," Cass snapped. "Your choice. We leave now."

Roan and Leslie crouched next to Dor and helped him to his feet. Cass could see the bloodied place on his skull, obscured by his long thick hair. He swayed, but the girls supported him, staggering under his weight, their pajamas already streaked with his blood. He stumbled, his ankle buckling, and for a second Cass anticipated him falling to the shiny waxed floor of the lobby and knew that if he fell, they would have to leave him. Already the guard in front of her was edging away, wriggling like a snake; Cass knew she had only seconds to decide whether to shoot her. Either way, she had to get out now, even if it meant leaving Dor here, injured and alone.

Her finger was tightening on the trigger, tears obscuring her vision, when Dor grunted and staggered two steps forward. In the split second after she shot the floor inches from the crawling guard's face, she took a chance and focused on him.

His face was ashen and he leaned heavily on Roan, but he was moving, the girls half dragging him along. At her feet there was screaming, and Cass tore her eyes away from Dor to see the guard scrabbling at her face with her fingers, trying to dislodge chips of tile that had embedded themselves in her skin.

Cass flipped the gun in her hands and brought it down, holding tight to the barrel, as hard as she could against the woman's skull, and she cried out and fell to the floor. Then Cass stomped with all her weight on the other guard's hand, feeling the bones shift and break, trying to ignore the screaming.

She should have killed them. *Should have killed them.* The thought ricocheted around her brain as she jammed the gun in her waistband and ran, avoiding the corpses of the men she'd killed, their blood seeping slowly onto the floor. The girls had gotten Dor out the door, into the night, and Cass could no longer see them.

"Last chance," Cass called, turning around in the wide doorway and addressing the girls in the back of the lobby. One of them ran toward her with a backward glance over her shoulder, and then a moment later, two more. The rest of them shrank against the window, some of them sobbing.

"All right," Cass said, as the three followed the others through the door. "The rest of you, make them understand you had no choice. Tell them I was armed. *We* were armed. They'll be here soon. And you—" she had to choke down bile when she addressed the two guards. "I may regret letting you live. I already do, in fact. But you're not worth the hit on my conscience. Treat these girls well."

She backed out into the night, the cold reaching for her. "You can't have the future," she added as she turned and ran, but her words were lost on the night air.

ROAN'S TEETH CHATTERED BUT SHE DIDN'T notice until she bit her tongue and tasted blood.

The truck jounced along, wheels screeching, taking turns hard so that she and the other girls slid and rocked, holding on to each other for balance.

Next to them, on the cold truck floor, was the man they'd dragged from the lobby. She'd barely caught him when he passed out, holding him so his head didn't hit the hard floor. The blood flow had slowed—she thought it had, anyway, though it was hard to tell in the dark. And his pulse still felt strong to her, strong enough, anyway, as she pressed his wrist between her hands.

In her lap was the silver box. He'd given it to her before he passed out, and told her what to do with it.

Roan had trusted men before and it usually didn't work out very well. She'd been pregnant before, but lost the baby before she got around to figuring out how to tell Darryl. Faking a miscarriage tonight hadn't been all that hard, since she'd had a real one not even a year ago. That baby, she'd wanted, wanted desperately, even if she was only twenty-two and an art student with a coffee shop job and no way to support a child. When Darryl came home the night after she miscarried, he found her puffy-eyed in a darkened room and asked her what was wrong; she'd said it was nothing and he said he guessed that was right, she had nothing to be sorry about and she was lucky to live in a place he paid for and all she did was sit on her ass drawing like a three-year-old while he worked two construction jobs to support them, which wasn't really accurate even besides the fact that she worked, too, because one of the jobs was just pickup work on weekends and the other hadn't been full-time since the economy tanked—*besides,* Darryl left her anyway a couple of weeks later, almost like he'd made it his project to find something real for her to cry over.

Roan decided she wouldn't date anyone after that so it was kind of fitting that the guy who got her pregnant this time didn't even take his clothes off, he was just a doctor with cold hands and not much to say.

But the man lying next to her in his own blood on the floor of the truck was different. He was old enough to be her dad, but when he'd spoken to her his voice was gentle. Even as she and Leslie dragged him out of the dorm he'd tried to be considerate, tried not to lean too hard, had stumbled along as best he could, biting down the pain.

And he'd pissed off the Rebuilders and maybe that was enough for her.

She released his wrist and carefully laid his arm against his chest, and then she picked up the box and opened the lid and took out the small round thing. It was cool and squishy in her

hand. They wanted her to trust them, the wounded man and
the woman driving. Roan didn't see why she should—but
then again, she didn't see why she shouldn't. They hadn't done
anything to her yet, and that was more than Roan could say
for the Rebuilders. And she was already involved, wasn't she?
The minute she decided to help Sammi, she was involved,
she supposed. She probably should have just gone with her to
begin with.

Roan rolled the cool, squishy ball in her palm for a moment. Then she crawled to the back of the truck and watched
the road disappearing under the wheels. Outside the sky was
gray. And there it was, just like he said, the building like a
castle, with all the fancy trim around the top. Near the front
there was a commotion, guards in their camo clothes yelling,
others streaming from the doors. As the truck sped past she
saw two of them raising their arms, holding weapons, trying
to fix their aim.

She watched the building go by and then she flung the
thing the man had given her, threw it as hard as she could and
watched as it struck the castle wall and burst into a flame big
enough to swallow the whole world.

37

THE SKY BEHIND HER WAS A FLOWER, YELLOW TO orange, a poppy unfurling across the night.

The explosion had rocked the truck as she drove and Cass's instincts made her grip the wheel tight, made her press the pedal down. Nothing could shake her now. Nothing could stop her now.

Dor had done it—that much she was sure of. Dor had blown up the leaders' headquarters. She didn't know how. Knowing was a luxury for later, if they survived. *When* they survived, Cass muttered to herself, pushing the truck even harder as they tore across the savaged streets. The girl said Sammi'd headed toward the water tower so it was toward the water tower Cass drove. Ruthie had twisted around to watch, her mouth dropped open in surprise, but she didn't appear frightened, which was a little miracle right there. Cass kept one hand on Smoke's neck, and though it was cool and clammy and crusted with pus and blood, she could feel his pulse faint but steady.

He was alive, and alive was all she was asking for tonight.

Outside the wall, the run-down student neighborhood butted up close. Unlike the streets surrounding the Box, these were choked with weeds and trash; junked cars lay where they'd collided.

The Rebuilders made no effort to make the world outside their walled-off compound more hospitable. Cass supposed they didn't give a damn about anything or anyone that they couldn't leverage into more power for themselves, power with which to build their twisted dream society. They were content to leave the landscape ravaged and burning behind them after they plundered.

As they neared the water tower, Cass slowed the truck, navigating the narrow streets of the humble neighborhood. No one would be pursuing them now. With any luck, most of the top leadership would have been asleep inside when the building blew—Mary, Evangeline, all of them. It was a shame that they would have died instantly, would never have the sickening realization that they had lost, that their empire was doomed.

No time to savor the thought now. Cass rolled the truck's windows down, scanning the streets and yards and houses for movement, listening for cries.

And it wasn't long before she heard them.

Them.

Her heart skipped when she heard the barking excited shrieks of Beaters who'd caught a scent. This was the sound you heard before they fed, when they *attacked,* like the baying of a pack of hounds on the hunt, a deafening chorus as though each of the things were trying to drown out the others' voices.

Sammi was still alive—but unless she was luckier than any of them had been yet, she wouldn't be for long.

"No," Cass whispered, looking frantically around the cab. No one here could help her, and she would have to leave her daughter with Smoke once again, alone, while she fought to make things right. The cries were coming from up ahead, a narrow side street made nearly impassable by the shitty cars thrown on either side. Windows were broken, shingles ripped from roofs and dead trees downed, all of it bathed in a strange soft orange glow from the fire that lit up the sky behind them. Far away behind her, she could hear the sounds of chaos, frantic yelling over a loudspeaker and the pops and crashes of secondary explosions and a building falling in on itself.

But the Beaters' hunting cries were ten times louder.

She was close.

At the end of the block a pickup lay smashed and broken across the intersection. Someone had rammed it, over and over again—maybe the SUV that was abandoned half on the lawn of a little white ranch house. She could not drive around the wreck, and as Cass jammed the truck into Park she was already throwing open the door, because she had to go the rest of the way on foot, and fast.

A hand pressed to Ruthie's soft cheek, a whispered promise, and a moment spent checking that the cab was as impenetrable as she could make it, the windows rolled up and the doors shut tight—and Cass ran to the back of the truck and squinted into the open doors. Dor lay on the floor, unmoving, but Cass had no time to examine him. Five girls huddled together against the far wall.

"Who has the guns?" she demanded. Three of the girls raised their hands in the darkness, not speaking.

"Can any of you shoot?"

Two hands lowered.

"I can." It was Leslie, the girl who'd tackled the guard. The brave one.

"Then you come with me."

But she was already jumping to the ground. "It's the new girl, isn't it? Roan said she escaped."

"Yes." Cass sucked in a breath, looking at the frightened girls who remained. "Shoot," she urged them, a hopeless prayer. "Shoot anything that comes."

Then she and Leslie were jogging toward the sound. A left at the corner, a flash of movement half a block ahead—then a stumbling clumped shape: Beaters. Three of them, lurching across a lawn. They halted, breathing hard.

"You killed Beaters before?" Cass asked the girl at her side, a girl who looked barely older than Sammi in the odd orange glow.

"Yes. I was in the Guard, was supposed to go to Yemen—I know what to do." And at that Leslie broke away, running faster than Cass, whose exhaustion felt like a layer of lead slowing her down. Cass wanted to chase after her—how could the thin, almost delicate young woman take on the things by herself?

In that second, time suspended while Leslie ran, Cass remembered the other running girl, all those months before, when she had not yet returned to herself, when she was a torn and ravaged thing walking the burnt fields. That day, Sammi had sped toward her with a blade, her hair flying behind her, heartbreaking in her fearlessness. Cass could do nothing but watch, helpless, as a child was forced to play a hero's part once again. Now it was Leslie who ran headlong and fearless into hell, and Cass could not help her, either. But she could do what she had come here to do.

"Sammi!" she yelled, praying the girl was inside the house, that she was behind stacks of furniture barricaded against a door and jamming windows shut. But even as she prayed for luck she saw a shape move on the porch of the brick house not ten yards from the Beaters—and as her feet flew faster, the last of her breath ragged in her throat, she saw the slender form of Sammi silhouetted against the brick, a wall someone had once painted a pale yellow that looked enchanted in the rosy light of the burning dawn. Sammi held something in her hands and swung it left and right—a broom, a bat, it didn't matter, it would be nothing against three of them.

Only…it wasn't three.

Around Cass, the vague roar that she thought had been coming from the scene of the explosion grew louder, the rumbling sound taking shape and dissolving into discrete voices. Beaters growling and braying, and from every direction—was that possible? Was it—Cass prayed—a trick of the wind, of acoustics and her own galloping fear….

Her frantic gaze caught on Leslie and Cass saw that the girl had heard it too. As she hesitated, arm upraised with her gun pointed at the sky, the first wave of them crested the street from the direction they'd arrived.

Four of them. No—more. Lurching and pushing at those in front of the pack, a half a dozen, ten—and then she lost count, because others were coming across the lot on the corner, slamming through shrubs without bothering to go around, tripping and clawing and screaming. The screaming.

And there were others, from every direction. The neighborhood was lost to these things. They must have nested here because of its proximity to the Rebuilders, their quarry tantalizingly close and maddeningly unreachable, and for every citizen they managed to fell, a dozen, a hundred more Beaters arrived to join the hunt. You could hear the frustration and hunger in the chorus of their cries, and even as the full horror of the situation reached Cass, one of the three who had been stalking Sammi turned back and attacked Leslie.

And then it twisted and fell and the crack of the gunshot came a split second later and Cass realized that Leslie taken her shot from only a couple of feet away, had steeled herself not to flinch and not to run and had done everything her training told her to. The head or the neck—she must have nailed the base of the skull, the luckiest or most skillful shot. Not many people could make that shot, even that close, but Leslie fired twice more before darting backward, out of the range of the nearest beasts screaming with delight and hunger and reaching for her.

And then she stumbled. Her ankle caught on a rock, a branch, a doubt, nothing at all, and down she went, bouncing on her hip and rolling, the two Beaters crowing victoriously.

Cass burst out of her momentarily paralysis, fueled by her terror and her rage, cursing herself for hesitating. She fired and one of the creatures lurched and danced, but she'd hit the torso or the arm and it wasn't enough, they would keep going to the girl until their dying breath. It was down, it seemed paralyzed on one side, but it was already crawling toward Leslie, and the other one was only a few feet away. Cass fired again but the clip was spent, and she cursed her aim, cursed the waste of that last bullet.

Sammi came flying down the steps of the little brick house and Cass started to scream for her to go back, run the other way, damning Leslie to a hideous death to give Sammi a chance, but the words had not left her lips when Sammi was on the closest Beater, slashing and slamming with what Cass now saw was a length of lumber, what had once been a porch rail, bent nails forming one end. She made contact with the thing's skull and Cass imagined she felt the impact in the ground beneath her feet, who would have guessed a girl as small as Sammi could hit like that, and she was already winding up to do it again, screaming non-words as she fought, and Leslie was scrambling to her feet and then she fired one more time and the thing's head was half gone and still it stumbled, a monster with no heart and no brain, nothing but its hunger, its desperate hunger.

Leslie grabbed Sammi and they ran, ran from the Beater that Cass had shot that was on its knees now, shuffling toward them and moaning. They caught up with Cass and all three of them turned and ran together, hands clasping and hair flying, toward the truck that sat half a block away, half a block closer to their escape from this doomed and burning place.

But their path was blocked. Three Beaters had made it to the street already—from which direction, Cass had no idea—and the swarm approaching in front of them was only half a block away now, scrambling toward the truck. The girls were in the truck, exposed, unprotected. Dor was there, unconscious on the floor, unable to help, unable to protect himself. If the Beaters reached the truck before Cass did, they would push and climb and crawl to get inside the cargo area, stepping on each other's bodies if they had to, and once they were inside, they would not even have to drag their prey away to feast because the truck offered them exactly what they wanted: a shelter with only one way in, a dark box that would serve as their butcher's table and which would run with the blood of the fallen.

And how long after that before they attacked the cab, with Smoke and Ruthie inside?

Leslie broke away, dodging left and sprinting straight for

the three Beaters, screaming one long powerful cry of determination, and Cass was moving too, because she would not
let the girl go alone. Leslie had several yards on her and she
did not slow down, she slammed into the closest Beater with
her full momentum, leading with her shoulder, and the thing
went down with Leslie on top of it but at the last moment she
rolled away, came up in a crouch and fired.

All of it so fast and breathtaking Cass wasn't sure she even
knew what had happened, and that was training like nothing
she'd seen. Leslie might not have anything on Smoke or Dor,
but in sheer bravery she was made fast and nimble and she was
already advancing on the next Beater.

In Cass's hand was her blade and how it got there she wasn't
exactly sure, and Sammi at her side went left so Cass went
straight on, and in the seconds that it took to close the gap
and slice the neck and oh God don't look don't look don't *look*
at the gawping mouth hole the leaking eye sockets the putrid
ragged hairless scalp, burst of blood and still not stopping,
Sammi disappeared from her view and all that was left was to
pray as she and Leslie ran for the truck.

The truck rocked on its wheels, slammed into by the bodies
of the Beaters. How long until they figured out how to get
inside? The floor was only waist-high, no challenge for a citizen, but the Beaters were clumsy, they flopped and thrashed.

Leslie ducked under a Beater's reaching arm and disappeared around back, and before Cass could protest Sammi
went flying past too.

This time she didn't hesitate. Last time it had nearly cost
Leslie's life. Now that life was almost certainly spent, and
Sammi's too, but if Cass didn't get in the cab and go, it would
all be for nothing. Her heart pounded with exertion and agony but she grabbed for the driver's-side door, and when it

wouldn't budge she remembered she had locked it and fished the keys from her pocket and jammed them at the lock with shaking fingers. It was impossible to see inside, her eyes were stinging with sweat and it was dark but inside that cab were her daughter and her lover and she had to live for them, she had to survive for them, and after several scrambled tries the key went in and she turned the lock and was about to yank open the door when she heard Sammi scream—

And she was halfway around the truck when she realized what a terrible mistake she had made but she couldn't let the girl be dragged off and eaten, one last terrible indignity in a life that had been much too short with far too much suffering and loss, and if she had to kill Sammi herself to save her those final moments of terror she would do it.

Around the back of the truck it was worse than she ever could have imagined, the piled crush of Beaters a hideous squirming mound of hands scrabbling for the metal truck floor and mouths making cutting bites at the air, only to be pushed away by others as they fought for purchase.

But one had made it almost all the way up onto the floor. Sammi's scream had been an attempt to deter it. She and Leslie fought the mob, Sammi with her nail-studded board and Leslie with a branch. Leslie was losing, a Beater grabbing and snatching at the weak weapon, and as Cass reached her it grasped the end and yanked and Leslie stumbled, but Cass was ready with her blade and the force of her fury slashed through the thing's neck along with the razor-sharp metal.

Cass seized Leslie's hand and pressed the keys into it. "Go!" she screamed, and Leslie didn't need to be told twice, she was gone in a flash and Cass saw the truck dip slightly a second later and knew that the girl had made it.

There was only one chance now, one single chance for her

and Sammi. She grabbed the girl's hand and Sammi met her gaze and in her shining eyes Cass saw mirrored back a spark of the hope she'd barely kept alive, and all of the molten rage that had been forged in the past days.

Cass squeezed her hand, once, and then screamed, "Now!" even as the truck rumbled to life, and they ran for it.

This time she could not squeeze her eyes shut against the horror as they ran headlong into the writhing mass of bodies. Sammi, rounding the edge of the horde, propelled herself across the far edge of the opening, kicking at a skull and stepping on the Beater's shoulder, and then she was in. Cass caught a flash of the terrified girls backed up against the wall of the cargo area, the single Beater who had made it inside crawling toward them with its mouth wide and howling. For a moment she didn't see Dor and she thought he'd been dragged out, but then she saw that the girls had pushed him behind them, that he was lying against the wall, the girls' bodies forming the last barrier in front of him.

Only one of them still held a gun and she didn't have her finger anywhere near the trigger. As Cass watched in horror the girl used it to club at the Beater's face, and its head snapped back from the impact but then it grabbed her, grabbed the gun and her hand with it and that was when Cass threw herself onto the pile of squirming bodies, hands pulling on decayed shoulders to get her higher and she sprinted up the pile, feet landing on shoulders, heads, a shifting mass below her but then she was in, her knees slamming hard on the metal floor and she grabbed the Beater's feet with all her might and pulled, feeling the shifting bones and rotting flesh beneath its filthy trousers, and the Beater screamed louder but did not let go of the girl—

—and Cass braced herself with her feet jammed against

the wall and pulled with everything she had, every ounce of energy and shred of life left in her and the Beater slid a little further, but it wasn't until the truck shot forward that the force of momentum knocked the girl to her knees, and still the Beater would not let go, so that as it slid from the truck it dragged her with it and they fell as one to the road, and as Cass and the others watched the terrible scene fade from view, the truck picking up speed as it careened away from the doomed neighborhood, they could only pray that the girl had been knocked senseless by the impact before the Beaters fell upon her.

THEY DID NOT RETURN TO THE BOX.

As Colima faded from view and the sky lightened with the dawn, Cass huddled with Sammi and the others in the back of the truck, all of them holding each other as they were jostled by every crack and rock and pothole in the road. Cass put her arms around Sammi and held on and let the girl cry, remembering the moment of their first meeting, all the things that had happened since then. She wished she could erase it all, give Sammi back everything she had lost. Instead she had only one gift for the girl—her wounded father, and as they held each other she whispered a version of the story of their journey to Colima, a gentler version, one in which truth was bent and shaded to take away its power and to let her know how much Dor had wanted his daughter back.

After a while Sammi pulled away from Cass and lay down on the cold metal floor next to her father, her lips moving with words that none of them could hear. Cass put a hand to

Dor's face, checking the wound at his scalp. It was not deep. He would live.

The other girls were named Sage and Kyra. Sage sobbed and couldn't catch her breath, and Kyra crouched in the corner with her arms wrapped tightly around herself, her eyes wide and staring. Cass had made little headway in comforting them when Leslie pulled off the road in a barren stretch of highway surrounded by kaysev-studded fields.

Everyone but Smoke and Ruthie and Dor got out of the truck and there was a reckoning in the golden dawn. The girl who'd been dragged out of the truck by the Beaters had been named Amber. None of them had known her well. They said a few nice things about her, from what they did know. Miraculously, neither Leslie nor Sammi had been bitten—Leslie insisted they strip and every inch of their skin be examined.

The guns were gone, except for one that had ended up lodged in the corner of the cargo bay. By unspoken agreement, Leslie took it before handing Cass the keys and getting in the cargo area with the others. "I'll talk to them," she said softly, indicating Kyra and Sage and Roan, who leaned together with their backs to the wall, their eyes puffy and swollen from crying.

Inside the cab, Smoke and Ruthie slept on, and Cass kept her eyes fixed on the road ahead. An hour out of Colima, Cass saw a sign for the Delta, and remembered a sand bar where she'd once spent a high school weekend at a friend's vacation trailer, jumping off a party barge into the cool waters of the farm canals, lying about their age and getting high with burnished construction workers from Sacramento. The network of waterways and redneck cul-de-sacs would provide ample cover from the Rebuilders, at least until they worked out a plan. Cass felt sure they could find shelter there; the sun was barely up, the tank was nearly full, they were decently armed.

In the back of the truck were five girls they had stolen from the Rebuilders, but they had traded fire and destruction for their plunder.

She hoped Evangeline and Mary had died in the explosion, but she hoped once again that they'd lived long enough to know what was coming, that as the beams fell on them and the flames licked their skin, they knew it was Cass Dollar who'd brought her gift of terrible rage.

She couldn't bear to return to the Box with Dor and Smoke, both injured, both vulnerable. Either could lead, either could own the place, but not like this. They would live or they would die, but she would not take them back like this, weakened and needful.

And she couldn't take a chance on leading the Rebuilders back to the Box. Those who survived the explosion would not know where she and Dor had come from, and she would not risk attracting their wrath if they were somehow followed. Not with her friends there. Not with Feo there.

Before the sun was high in the sky, Smoke had stirred next to her several times. She touched his face every few minutes, alternating with checking on Ruthie, who slept on the floor, curled in a ball. Cass drove as carefully as she could, mindful of every bump and crack in the road; in the back of the truck, she knew the girls were huddled over Dor.

She passed a marina, a motel that looked familiar. She cast about in her memories, trying to remember where the turnoff was. When the road wound along next to the canal and she looked down and saw thickets of cattails, a rowboat bobbing next to a dock on which a pair of bright red clogs still sat, it came back to her.

She had switched on her turn signal before she remembered there was no one to see it. She took a soft right and slowed to five miles per hour, remembering that long-ago day when a boy named Trace Pritcher had untied her bikini top and told her he'd loved her as she finished off her own spiked Big Gulp and then started working on his. She'd been pleasantly drunk when he'd clumsily pushed down his board shorts and lowered her to the dock, and she'd closed her eyes and imagined that he was the boy who would love her forever.

Cass knew that she would never see Trace again, that his body was moldering in a ditch or basement or parking lot somewhere, his bones baking in the sun and freezing in the night rains. So many good, beautiful people had died, but she had lived, and she did not know why. But she had her daughter, and the man who she loved and would never stop loving. She pressed her fingertips to his face for the hundredth time, found his pulse and prayed. And in the back of her truck she carried girls who teetered on the brink of womanhood, girls who she was now responsible for, who—God help all of them—needed her.

But that was not all. There was also the man she'd crashed up against, like the tide throws itself onto the shore. He had saved her and she had saved him; she had tasted the salt of his sweat and his blood on her lips, and she had known the shape of his grief and his longing and she had drunk it in and wanted more. She had seen him and she had not turned away, and he had known her and had not turned away.

Cass's vision darkened with her swirling thoughts, and so she gripped the steering wheel hard and focused on the black-top ahead, until she was back in herself. There was the chicken stand and the parking lot and the waterslides. There was the bait shop and the liquor store. There was the freezer where she'd bought bags of ice for half-assed margaritas.

A pickup was parked across the road, and from the bed a man rose up, a shotgun loose in his hand and a bandanna tied around his tangled hair. He was late twenties, maybe a little older, deeply tanned with laugh lines bracketing his mouth. A second later a pretty young woman pulled herself up next to him and rested her arms on the side of the truck, staring at the approaching truck with curiosity.

These were not Beaters. And they were not Rebuilders.

Cass took a deep breath and tried to think of what she could say, how she could introduce her ragtag group, the people she carried with her. She tapped the brakes and coasted to a stop. She put her hand on the door handle, but before she opened the door she took a deep breath, and traced a cross over her heart and whispered a cautious prayer.

You got us this far, she whispered. Now take us home.

★ ★ ★ ★ ★

ONE DATE WITH THE BOSS CAN GET COYOTE UGLY....

C.E. MURPHY

PRESENTS ANOTHER RIVETING INSTALLMENT IN THE WALKER PAPERS SERIES!

Seattle detective Joanne Walker has (mostly) mastered her shamanic abilities, and now she faces the biggest challenge of her career—attending a dance concert with her sexy boss, Captain Michael Morrison. But when the performance—billed as transformative—changes her into a coyote, she and Morrison have bigger problems to deal with. What's more, one ordinary homicide pushes Joanne to the very edge....

SPIRIT DANCES

Available now!

LUNA™

www.LUNA-Books.com

LCEM325TR

Domino Riley hates zombies.

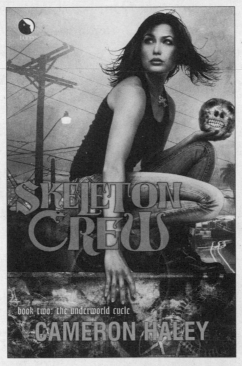

Bodies are hitting the pavement in L.A. as they always do, but this time they're getting right back up, death be damned. They may be strong, but even Domino's mobbed-up outfit of magicians isn't immune to the living dead.

If she doesn't team up with Adan Rashan, the boss's son, the pair could end up craving hearts and brains, as well as each other....

SKELETON CREW

Pick up your copy today!

LCH326TR

*Experience the magic once more with
this fantastic tale from* New York Times
and USA TODAY *bestselling author*

MERCEDES LACKEY

Now available in paperback!

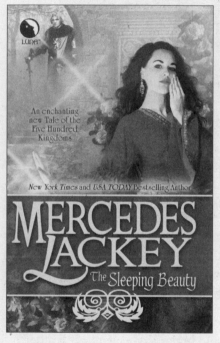

**In Rosamund's realm,
happiness hinges on a
few simple beliefs:**

For every princess
there's a prince.

The king has
ultimate power.

Stepmothers should
never be trusted.

And bad things come
to those who break
with Tradition....

**"She'll keep you up long past your bedtime."
—Stephen King**

Pick up your copy today!

LML327TR

There's more to Kaylin Neya than meets the eye....
New York Times bestselling author

MICHELLE SAGARA

is back with two classic tales from her beloved
Chronicles of Elantra series.

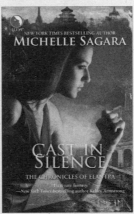

Both available in September 2011.

And look for the latest volume in this darkly magical series:

Coming in October 2011.

LUNA™

HARLEQUIN®
www.Harlequin.com

LMS337CSTR

Orphan. Crusader. Angel. Thief.

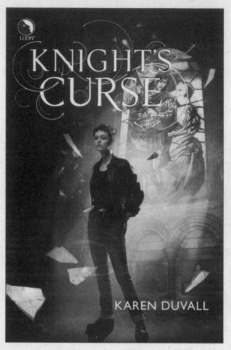

A skilled knife fighter since the age of nine, Chalice knows what it's like to live life on the edge—precariously balanced between the dark and the light. But the time has come to choose. The evil sorcerer who kidnapped her over a decade ago requires her superhuman senses to steal a precious magical artifact…or suffer the consequences.

Coming soon!

www.Harlequin.com

LKD340CSTR